MYSELF MY ENEMY

This is the story of a tragic queen told as though by herself, during what is undoubtedly the most turbulent period of English history.

Henrietta Maria's father was murdered a few months after her birth and she grew up in a court of intrigue which was constantly on the verge of conflict until the arrival of the future King of England on a romantic visit to Spain.

Eventually Henrietta Maria herself was betrothed and embarked on the stormy years of a marriage which seemed doomed to failure overshadowed as it was by the malevolent Buckingham.

But out of these tempestuous beginnings grew one of the greatest love stories of all times and Henrietta Maria fiercely loyal in love, impetuously ruthless in hatred, stood beside her husband through his tragic progress. This is an account of a most successful yet disastrous marriage between a man of honour determined to do his duty as he saw it, and a woman entirely devoted to helping him. Blindly they blundered through the years, watching the fall of Strafford and the rise of men such as Cromwell, Hampden and Pym, unaware even of the spies in their own household; and so came the inevitable march towards war, Englishman against Englishman, Cavalier against Roundhead, the sequel of which was played out on a cold January day in Whitehall.

At the centre of the disaster stand the King with his unswerving belief in the Divine Right of Kings and his Queen, warmhearted, passionate Henrietta Maria who was her own greatest enemy and that of those whom she loved best.

There is that other Charles, witty, calm, inscrutable refusing to be influenced by his mother, coming back to claim his rights; there are Mary, James, Henry and Henriette all determined to go their own way; and so Henrietta Maria must retire to the *château* of Colombes, a lonely doubting woman to brood on the past and ask herself How much was I to blame?

For a complete list of
books by Jean Plaidy
please see pages 383 and 384

JEAN PLAIDY

Myself My Enemy

BOOK CLUB ASSOCIATES
LONDON

Photoset in Palatino by
Kelly Typesetting Limited
Bradford-on-Avon, Wiltshire
Printed and bound in Great Britain by
Richard Clay Ltd., Bungay, Suffolk

Contents

The Dowager Queen

When I sit here alone in my *château* of Colombes, which I inhabit by grace of my nephew that great and glorious ruler whom they call The Sun King, I often think back over my life—one which has had more than its fair share of sorrow, humiliation, intrigue and tragedy. I am old now and my word stands for little, but though no one listens to me, I am allowed my comforts, for after all they must remember that I am the aunt of one King and the mother of another; and kings and queens never forget the deference due to royalty, for if they did not show it to others a day may come when it is not shown to them. Royalty is sacred to royalty – though not always so, alas, with the people. When I think of the manner in which the people of England treated their King – the wickedness, the cruelty, the bitter, bitter humiliation – even now my anger rises to such heights that I fear I shall do myself an injury. I should be old enough to restrain my temper now; I should remind myself that I have my silent accusers who would say that if the King had not had the misfortune to marry me, he would be alive and on his throne at this moment.

That is all in the past . . . all dead and gone. It is a new world now. There is a King on the throne of England for the Monarchy has been restored. The people love him, I am told; and indeed I was aware of this when I paid a visit to England not long ago. My dearest Henriette – the best-loved of all my children – glows when she talks of him. She always loved him dearly. He is witty, they say; he loves pleasure but he is shrewd. He is his grand-father – the father I never knew – all over again. He has charm though he is ugly. He was born ugly – the ugliest baby I ever saw. I remember when they first put him into my arms, I could not believe that this little unprepossessing thing could possibly be the child of my handsome husband and myself – for in spite of my small stature and certain defects, I was regarded in those days –

even by my enemies – as having a goodly share of physical charms.

Are the troubles over? Is this the end of the nightmare which overshadowed England for all those years? Have people learned their lesson? With flowers and sweet music they welcomed Charles when he returned and there was rejoicing throughout London and the whole of England. They had done with the hideous Puritan rule. For ever? I wonder.

So Royalty has come back into its own. But it is too late for me. I am here, grateful to be in my small but beautiful *château* during the summer days, and in the winter, if I wish to go to Paris, my nephew has put the truly splendid Hôtel de la Balinière at my disposal.

He is kind to me – my glorious nephew. I think he has been a little in love with my sweet Henriette. And my son is kind, too. He always was – in that careless way which makes me think he would do anything for peace. I pray he will hold the crown. Louis respects him for all that he seems to devote himself to pleasure, and his great preoccupation would appear to be with the next seduction.

He looked at me so wisely when I was last in England. I begged him then to come to the true Faith, and he took my face in his hands and kissed me, calling me 'Mam' as he used to when he was a little boy. 'When the time is ripe,' he said enigmatically.

I never did understand Charles. I only know that he has this power to win people to him. He has grace for all his height, and charm which outshines his ugliness. If he could but get a child all would be well for England – as well as it could be, that is, unblessed by the true Faith as it is. And that may come. It has been my hope for so many years that it will.

Charles's wife, dear Catherine, is so docile and so much in love with him. How can she be when he parades his mistresses before her and refuses – though in that charming, lighthearted way of his – to give up his profligate way of life?

I tried to talk to him when I was there – though more of religious matters, I must admit, than the need to get an heir. Catherine must be at fault. God knows he has enough bastards scattered throughout his kingdom, and he distributes titles and lands among them with a free hand. One of his courtiers said that a time will come when almost every Englishman, even from the remote corners of the country, will claim to be descended from Royal Stuart. And he cannot get one legitimate heir!

Life is strange. And I am now near to the end of mine. I think often of my dear husband Charles – of his saintly goodness, his gentleness, his loving kindness, and most of all the love which grew between us, though we had many a disagreement in the beginning, and in those early days there must have been times when he wished he had never been persuaded into the marriage, for all the good it was said it would bring to our two countries.

I dream of him now . . . going to his death on that cold January day. They told me he had said: 'Give me an extra shirt. It is cold and I could tremble from the wind, and those who have come to see me die would think I trembled in fear of death.'

Nobly he went out to die. I see him in my dreams and I say to myself: 'What did *I* do? If I had been a different woman, is it possible that this great tragedy, this murder, need never have happened?'

I want to go right back to the beginning. I want to think of everything that happened. And then I want to find the answer.

Could it have been different? Is it really possible that it need not have happened the way it did?

One cannot call the man who wielded the axe the murderer. But what of those cold-eyed men who passed the sentence?

I hate them. I hate them all.

But was I the one to blame?

The Early Days

I was born into a troubled world and when I was only five months old my father was murdered. Fortunately for me at that time I was in my nursery and knew nothing of this deed which was said to have had such a disastrous effect not only on our family but on the whole of France.

Everything I knew of him was through hearsay; but I was one to keep my ears and eyes open, and for a long time after his death, he was talked of, so that by cautious questioning and alert observation, in time I began to learn a great deal about the father who had been taken from me.

He had been a great man – Henri of Navarre, the finest King the French had ever known – but of course the dead become sanctified, and those who are murdered – particularly those in high places – become martyrs. My own dear Charles . . . but that was a long way ahead in the future. I had much to endure before I was overwhelmed by the greatest tragedy of my life.

So my father died. There he was one day in good health – well, as near good health as a man of fifty can be who has lived a life of much indulgence – and the next a corpse brought home to the Louvre and laid on his bed in his closet there while the whole country mourned and the ministers guarded the palace and us children, particularly my brother Louis, who had then become King. And all the time I was sleeping peacefully in my cradle unaware of the action of a maniac which had robbed France of her King and me of my father.

There were seven of us in the nursery at that time. The eldest was Louis, the Dauphin, who was eight when I was born. After him came Elizabeth, who was a year younger than Louis. There was a gap of four years between Elizabeth and Christine and then the family increased with rapidity. There had been the little Duc d'Orléans who had died before there was time to give him a name, and after that Gaston and then myself, Henriette Marie.

My mother may have been unsatisfactory in the eyes of many but she certainly filled the nursery and that is said to be the first and most important duty of a queen. The people disliked her as much as they loved my father. For one thing she came from Tuscany, being the daughter of Francis the Second of that land; and the French had always hated foreigners. Moreover she was fat and not very handsome and was of the Medici family. People remember that other Italian woman, wife of Henri Deux, towards whom they had shown more venom than to any other monarch, blaming her for all the misfortunes of France, including the Massacre of St Bartholomew and the deaths by poison of many people. They had made a legend of her – the Italian poisoner. It was unfortunate that my mother should bear the name of Medici.

However, while my father had been there my mother was unimportant. She had had to accept his infidelities. He was a great lover of women. The Evergreen Gallant, the people called him, and right up to his death he was involved with women. The Duc de Sully – his very able minister and friend – had deplored this characteristic; but it was no use. Great king that he was he was first of all a lover and the pursuit of women was to him the most urgent necessity of his life. He could not exist without them. While this is doubtless a great weakness in a king, it is a foible which people indulgently shrug aside and indeed often applaud. 'There is a *man*,' they say, with winks, nods and affectionate smiles.

Even at the time of his death he was involved in a romantic intrigue. I learned all about it from Mademoiselle de Montglat, who was the daughter of our governess and who, because she was so much older than I, had been set in charge of me by her mother. I called her Mamanglat as at first she was like a mother to me and later like an elder sister; and I was more fond of her than anyone I knew. Mamanglat became affectionately shortened to Mamie, and Mamie she remained to me forever.

We were all terrified of Madame de Montglat, who was always reminding us that she had the royal permission to whip us if we misbehaved, and as we were the Royal Children of France, higher standards had been set for us than for all other children.

Mamie was not a bit like her mother. Although in a way she

was a governess, she was more like one of us. She was always ready to laugh, tell us the latest scandal and to help us out of those scrapes into which children fall and which would have brought down the wrath of Madame de Montglat on our heads if they had come to her knowledge.

It was from Mamie that I began to understand what was going on around me, what it meant to be a child in a royal nursery, the pitfalls to be avoided – the advantages and the disadvantages. It seemed to me that there were more of the latter and Mamie was inclined to agree with me.

'Your father loved you children,' she told me. 'He used to say you were all beautiful and he could not understand how two such as the Queen and himself could have begotten you. I used to have to peep out at you because my mother forbade me to appear before the King.'

'Why?'

'Because I was young and not ill favoured – good looking enough to catch his eyes, she thought.'

Then Mamie would be overcome with laughter. 'The King was like that,' she finished.

Being very young and ignorant of the world I wanted to ask a great many questions, but did not always do so being afraid of exposing my ignorance.

'You were his favourite,' said Mamie. 'The baby – the child of his old age. He was proving, you see, that he could still get beautiful children – not that he need have worried. There was constantly some woman claiming that her child was his. Well, what was I saying? Oh . . . you were the favourite. He was always fond of little girls and weren't you named for him . . . well, as near as a girl could be. Henriette Marie. Henriette for him and Marie for your mother. Royal names both of them.'

From Mamie I learned the gossip of the Court – past and present – much that was necessary for me to know and more besides. I heard from her that before he had married my mother, my father had been married to La Reine Margot, daughter of Catherine de Medicis – one of the most mischievous and fascinating women France had ever known. My father had hated Margot. He had never wanted to marry her and it was rather dramatically said that their marriage had been solemnized in blood, for during the celebrations the most terrible of all massacres had taken place – that which had occurred on the Eve of St Bartholomew; and it was because so many Huguenots had been in Paris to attend the marriage of their leader's son to Catholic Margot that they had been conveniently situated for destruction.

I supposed something like that would haunt a bride and bridegroom for ever. It was a mercy that my father escaped. But all his life – until the last fatal moment – he had had a knack of escaping. He had lived his life dangerously and joyously. Often careless of his royalty he had had an easy familiarity with his men. No wonder he had been popular. He had done a great deal for France too. He cared about the people; he had said he wanted every peasant to have a chicken in his pot on Sundays; moreover he had brought about a compromise between the Catholics and Huguenots and that had seemed an impossible task. He himself had paid lip service to the Catholics with his famous quip of Paris being worth a Mass when he had realized the city would never surrender to a Protestant.

He had been a wonderful man. When I was very young I used to weep tears of rage because he had been taken from me before I could know him.

He had been a good soldier, but it was said that he never let anything – not even the need to fight an enemy – stand in the way of his love affairs.

The object of his passion at the time of his death had been the daughter of the Constable de Montmorency. She was only sixteen years old but no sooner had my father set eyes on her than he declared she must be his 'little friend'.

Mamie loved to tell these stories. She had a certain histrionic talent, which she loved to display and which often made me helpless with laughter. She could never tell anything dramatic without acting it. I remember her explaining, dropping her voice to conspiratorial confidence.

'However . . . before presenting his daughter Charlotte to Court, the Constable de Montmorency had betrothed her to François de Bassompierre who was a very magnificent gentleman of the House of Cleves – handsome, witty, and as he was also a Gentleman of the King's Bedchamber, he was much sought after. Monsieur de Montmorency thought it an excellent match.

'But when the young lady came to Court and the King saw

her, that was the end of her romance with François de Bassompierre.'

How I loved to listen to her as she threw herself into the part
she was playing for me!

'The King was determined that Bassompierre should not have
her because he was a passionate young man and deeply in love
with her and therefore could not be expected to become the kind
of accommodating husband whom the King favoured because
they were always willing to stand aside when the need arose.
One morning – so the story goes – when the King was about to
rise from his bed, he sent for Bassompierre – remember he was a
Gentleman of the Bedchamber. "Kneel Bassompierre," said the
King. Bassompierre was astonished for the King was never one to
stand on ceremony, but if you wish to present some suggestion
which may not be acceptable it is always best to reduce the person
whom you intend to deprive or displease by stressing your own
superiority.'

I nodded. I could understand that.

'The King was full of guile. He knew men well and that meant
he could usually wriggle satisfactorily out of awkward situations.' Mamie had thrown herself upon my bed and assumed an
air of royalty. ' "Bassompierre," said the King, "I have been
thinking a good deal of you and I have come to the conclusion
that it is time you were married." ' Mamie leaped from the bed
and assumed a kneeling position beside it. ' "Sire," said
Bassompierre. "I should be married now, but the Constable's
gout has been troubling him of late and for this reason the
ceremony has been postponed." ' She was back on the bed, royal
again. ' "I have just the bride for you, Bassompierre. What think
you of Madame d'Aumale? When you marry, the Duchy of
Aumale shall come to you." "Sire," said Bassompierre, "have
you a new law in France? Is a man then to have *two* wives?" ' She
was back on the bed. ' "Nay, nay, François. In Heaven's name,
one is enough for a man to manage at a time. I will tell you all. I
know of your commitment to Mademoiselle de Montmorency but
the truth is that I myself have become madly enamoured of her. If
you married her I should begin to hate you . . . especially if she
showed any affection for you. Now I am fond of you, Bassompierre, and I know you would be the last one to wish for a rift in
our friendship. Therefore I cannot see you married to this girl. I

shall give her to my nephew Condé. That will keep her near me
. . . in the family . . . and she can comfort my old age. Condé
likes hunting better than women. I shall make him an allowance
as compensation. Then he can leave the delightful creature to
me." '

Mamie looked at me and raised her eyebrows. She was a little
breathless jumping off and on the bed and having to play the two
parts in the drama.

'Poor Bassompierre!' She was herself now, the wise story
teller. 'He saw that it would be impossible to go against the King's
wishes, and when he told Mademoiselle de Montmorency what
was planned she cried: "Jesus. The King has gone mad!" But very
soon she grew accustomed to the idea and after a while she quite
liked it. The whole Court was talking about the change in bridegrooms, and very quickly Mademoiselle de Montmorency
became the Princesse de Condé.

'Now this led to other complications. The Queen accepted the
fact that the King must have many mistresses but she hated there
to be one who could influence him so much. She had never been
crowned and a monarch always feels insecure until the crown has
been placed on his – or her – head in solemn ceremony. So the
Queen cried: "I want to be crowned!" and because of the guilt he
felt about Charlotte de Montmorency the King, who had brushed
aside this matter of the Queen's coronation whenever it was
raised, had to give way to save himself from violent recrimi-
nations. Then to make matters worse, the Prince de Condé
became so enamoured of his wife that he decided that he would
no longer stand aside. She was after all *his* wife, and he secretly
left the Court with the new Princesse and took her to Picardy, and
since that might not be far enough he carried her on to Brussels.

'The King was desolate. He was mad with grief and threatened
to follow her. Now a King cannot move far without everyone's
knowing, and who would have believed that a King who had
been on most excellent terms with so many women at the same
time, should take such steps for one. People were saying that it
was a secret move to go to war. So the King found himself in the
centre of a controversy. The Duc de Sully was worried and he told
the King that his conduct over the Princesse de Condé was
destroying his reputation . . . not his reputation for being a rake
. . . that was unimportant and he already had that in any case. It

was only when his amours intruded into statecraft that there was danger.

'The affair had made the Queen more restive than ever. She was demanding her coronation, and the King, feeling he owed her some recompense, at length agreed that it should take place.

'Now at this time the King had a strange presentiment. Kings' lives are always in danger so perhaps it is natural for them to have presentiments. Well, some time before, the King had been told that he would only survive a few days after the Queen's coronation, and it was for this reason that he had never wanted her to be crowned; and if it had not been for his guilt about the Princesse de Condé, he would never have agreed to it. However, now that she was to be crowned, the feeling of disaster grew and grew and he became so certain of his imminent death that he went to see the Duc de Sully about it, which shows how strongly he felt, for the Duc was not the man even a king would go to with a story like that.

'So the King went to the Arsenal where the country's weapons were stored and where the Duc de Sully had his apartments.' She was acting again; the same role for the King, but Bassompierre had been replaced by the Duc de Sully. ' "I don't understand this, Monsieur le Duc, but I feel in my heart that the shadow of death is right over my head." "Why, Sire, you alarm me. How can this be? You are well. Nothing ails you." The Duc de Sully had had a special chair made for the King to sit in when he visited him. It was low and very regal. The King sat in it, and looking very grave, he said: "It has been prophesied that I shall die in Paris. The time is near. I can sense it." '

'Did he really say that?' I asked. 'Or are you making it up?'

'It is all true,' Mamie assured me.

'Then he must have been a very clever man to see into the future.'

'He *was* a very clever man, but this is apart from cleverness. It is the special gift of clairvoyance, and magicians and sorcerers had been saying that the King would meet his death in Paris, and if ever the Queen was crowned, then the blow would fall.'

'Then why did he allow my mother to be crowned?'

'Because she would give him no rest until he did; he felt guilty about the Princesse de Condé; and he hated to deny a woman anything – even the Queen. He thought: Once I have given the

Queen her coronation – which is what she wants more than anything – she will leave me to pursue my heart's desire.'

'But if the prophecy was coming true how could he have his heart's desire with the Princesse de Condé?'

'I can tell you no more than what happened. In fact, the Duc de Sully was so impressed that he declared he would stop the preparation for the Queen's coronation as the thought of it so filled the King with foreboding. The King said: "Yes, break if off . . . for I have been told that I shall die in a carriage, and where could it be more easily done than at such a ceremony?" The Duc de Sully gazed earnestly at the King. "This explains much," he said. "I have often seen you cowering in your carriage when you pass certain places, and yet I know that in battle, there is not a braver man in France." '

'But they did not stop the coronation,' I pointed out, 'for my mother *was* crowned Queen of France.'

Mamie continued with her narrative. 'When the Queen heard that the coronation was to be cancelled, she was furious.' Mamie did not attempt to imitate my mother. She would not dare go as far as that. But I could imagine my mother's rage.

'For three whole days the matter was disputed. There will be a coronation. There will not be a coronation. And at last the King gave way in face of the Queen's demands and the coronation was fixed for the thirteenth of May at St Denis.'

'Thirteenth,' I said with a shiver. 'That is unlucky.'

'Unlucky for some,' agreed Mamie portentously. 'So she was crowned and it was arranged that on the sixteenth she should make her entry into Paris. Now. . . .'

She paused and I watched her with rounded eyes for I had heard the story before and I knew that we were approaching the terrible climax.

'Now . . . on Friday the fourteenth the King said he would go to the Arsenal to see the Duc de Sully. He was not sure whether he wanted to go or not. He hesitated. First he would go and then he thought he would not . . . but in the end he made up his mind. It was just to be a short visit after dinner. "I shall soon be back," he said. When he was about to get into his carriage, Monsieur de Praslin, Captain of the Guard, who always attended him even on the shortest journeys, came forward. "No need," said the King. Mamie waved her hand imperiously. "I don't want any attendance today. It is just to the Arsenal for a brief visit." Well, he got into the carriage and sat down with a few of his gentlemen. There were only six of them, not counting the Marquis de Mirabeau and the equerry who sat in the front of the carriage.

'Now comes the dramatic part. As the King's carriage came into the Rue de Ferronnerie close to that of St-Honoré, a cart came into the road, and because this blocked the way a little, the King's carriage had to go near to an ironmonger's shop on the St Innocent side. As the carriage slowed down a man rushed forward and hoisted himself onto the wheel and trust a knife at the King. It entered right here. . . .' She touched her left side. 'It went between his ribs and severed an artery. The gentlemen in the carriage cried out in horror as the blood gushed forth. "It is nothing," said the King. Then he said that again so quietly that it could scarcely be heard. They took him with all speed to the Louvre. They laid him on his bed and sent for the doctors – but it was too late. To the sorrow of France, the King passed away.'

I had heard the story many times and it never failed to move me to tears. I knew how the Duc de Sully had made everyone swear allegiance to my brother and how the entire country mourned, and that the mad monk Ravaillac was caught and torn apart by four wild horses to whom his body had been attached before they were sent off in different directions.

I knew that my mother had become Regent of France because my brother was only nine years old and too young to govern.

Had my father survived the assassination everything would have been different. As it was, I, a baby in her nursery, was to live my early years in a country torn by strife.

I attended a great many ceremonies of which I was unaware. Mamie told me of these later. Sometimes I tried to delude myself that I remembered – but I could not have done so. I was far too young.

The whole of France was mourning my father and calling vengeance on the madman who had killed him. There must have been a certain relief that he was a madman and that no revolutionary coup was intended. France had been satisfied with her King while he lived and when he was murdered he became a near saint. That was good because it augured well for my brother who was such a boy at the time, and ministers are always afraid of boy kings. They mean too many people near the throne jostling for power.

I was taken in the procession with my brothers and sisters. People wept, I was told, when they saw us. It was the impression the Duc de Sully wished to create. He was one of the greatest statesmen in the country and my father had recognized him as such. Now all his allegiance was for my brother who had slipped from the rôle of Dauphin to that of King.

How maddening it is that I cannot remember anything of what pased and had to rely on Mamie's accounts. She made me see it clearly but I was never sure that she was absolutely accurate; but it is the custom for children, however young, to be present at their dead parents' obsequies and naturally I, as one of the Children of France, must have been there. 'You rode in the carriage in the arms of my mother,' Mamie told me; and I could imagine that child sitting there held firmly by a stern-faced Madame de Montglat and later being with her at the bier on which my dead father lay.

Madame de Montglat would have guided my hand while I sprinkled holy water on my dead father's face. I hoped I performed the act with dignity, which must have been rather difficult in the arms of Madame de Montglat; but presumably I made no protest which was surely all that could have been expected of me.

My next public appearance was at my brother's coronation, but as I was then only eleven months old I remember nothing of that either. The ceremony in the Cathedral of Rheims must have been very impressive. Louis was nine years old then and a boy king is always so appealing. I never really knew Louis well for he was no longer in our nursery after he became King. Even my elder sister Elizabeth was almost a stranger to me. Christine was with us for a while, but Gaston and I were closer than any of the others because we were near in age of course.

Mamie told me afterwards that on the great occasion I was carried by the Princesse de Condé who, now that the King was dead, had been allowed by her husband to return to Court.

So these great happenings took place when I was too young to know what was going on. It was a little frustrating afterwards to have known I was there and have no recollection of it.

But I was not going to remain a baby forever and I began to grow up in the nursery which I shared with Gaston and Christine, presided over by the stern Madame de Montglat and with Mamie there to bring laughter into our days.

My first real memory is of going to Bordeaux with a great cavalcade led by my mother to deliver my eldest sister Elizabeth to the King of Spain that she might marry his son and heir. At the same time she was to receive Anne of Austria, the daughter of the King of Spain, who was to marry our brother Louis. The importance of this occasion can be imagined, but at six years old this was just an exciting adventure to me. I did not know, of course, that the country was seething with discontent.

I loved ceremonies – all the pomp and glitter and the fine clothes, even though these were often uncomfortable to wear. I can remember Gaston often tore off his ruff and cried because it hurt his neck. He was severely beaten by Madame de Montglat who made him wear even stiffer ruffs to teach him a lesson. All people must be taught discipline, said Madame de Montglat, and none more so than royal children.

Poor Gaston! He was very rebellious in those days but I was even worse and gave way to my infantile furies by kicking, screaming, biting any hand that came near me, and lying on the floor and kicking.

'Disgraceful!' said Madame de Montglat. 'What would the Queen say?'

Those words could always sober us. 'I am afraid,' Madame de Montglat would warn, 'that if your behaviour does not improve I shall have to tell the Queen.'

The Queen paid visits to the nurseries very rarely and when she did it was a great occasion. She seemed enormous to me and was like a great battleship – invincible. One knew that she was the Queen as soon as one set eyes on her. When she arrived everybody changed – even Madame de Montglat – and became watchful, making quite sure they observed every trick of etiquette. They dared not forget for one instant that they were in the presence of the Queen. Not that she would let them! Gaston and I would come forth and bow low. She would incline her head, accept our homage and then take us onto her ample lap and kiss us.

Sometimes we thought she loved us dearly. She would ask what we were learning and remind us that we must never forget that we had had the good fortune to be brought up in the Holy Catholic Faith. I learned later that there was trouble in the country between the Catholics and the Huguenots and that when my father had been alive he had held that trouble in check. Now that he was dead the same leniency was not shown to Huguenots and in view of the fact that the country was less prosperous than it had been – owing to my mother's less effective rule – trouble loomed.

But what did a six-year-old girl sheltered in her royal nursery know of these matters?

Gaston and I would vie for our mother's interest while she was with us, and talk about her for days after her visit; we looked up expectantly every time a visitor came but after a while we ceased to expect her. I never did understand my mother. She was fond of us that was clear – but whether as her children or the Children of France, I was never quite sure. But I was fascinated by her – and Gaston was too. She was the Queen as well as our mother and we saw the effect she had on everyone in the nursery and we thought it must be wonderful to have people bow when you came into a room and show such respect for you.

It was always impressed on us that we must not forget that we were the children of a King and a Queen – and a King of France at that. Royal dignity must be maintained throughout our lives; and we must never forget that we were Catholics and we must uphold the true Faith wherever we found ourselves.

In our games we played Kings and Queens, and Gaston and I used to fight over which one should sit on the throne – an improvised chair – and receive the homage of the other.

'A King,' said Gaston, 'is more important than a Queen. In France a Queen cannot be Queen in her own right, because of the Salic Law.'

I was not going to allow that.

'A Queen is more important,' I said.

'No, she is not.'

My temper flared up. There were times when I hated Gaston. Madame de Montglat said I must learn to curb that temper of mine or it would destroy me one day. That made me think. I wondered what it was like to be destroyed. She made it sound terrible and sometimes when I remembered her words they did sober me a little – but not for long. I could never resist the joy of letting myself fall into a rage. It was the only way I could express my anger.

But I had an irrefutable case on this occasion and I let my rage simmer. 'What of our mother, eh? She is a Queen and the most important person in the land. She is greater than the Duc de Sully who used to be so important and is no longer so. Why? Because our mother does not like him. A Queen can be as great as a King . . . greater perhaps. What about wicked Queen Elizabeth of England who defeated the Spanish Armada?'

'You mustn't speak of her. She was a. . . .' He put his lips to my ear and whispered the terrible word: 'Heretic!'

'Queens can be as good as Kings and this is my throne so kneel to me or I shall send you to the torture chambers. But first I will tell our mother that you think Queens are of no importance.'

It would have been wiser to play at puss-in-the-corner or blind-man's-buff.

But for all our quarrels we were fond of each other.

Monsieur de Breves, who was a very learned man, came each morning to give us lessons in the nursery. These were for my elder sisters Elizabeth and Christine, but Gaston and I took part. Perhaps Monsieur de Breves was too learned to understand young children; perhaps Gaston and I were incapable of giving our minds to anything for long. (My sister Elizabeth said our minds were like butterflies flitting here and there and seemed incapable of settling anywhere long enough to absorb everything.) In any case Gaston and I were not academically inclined and while we sat listening to Monsieur de Breves and making futile attempts to grapple with the problems he set us, we were waiting impatiently for the time when we could go off to our dancing lessons.

At least our dancing master was pleased with us – and particularly with me. 'Ah, Madame Henriette,' he would cry folding his arms across his chest and raising his eyes to the ceiling, 'but that was beautiful . . . beautiful. Ah, my dear Princesse, you are going to enchant the Court.'

I was never happier than when dancing – unless it was singing.

I noticed one day when we were in the schoolroom listening – or trying to listen – to Monsieur de Breves, and I was thinking how pretty Christine's dress was and wondering whether I might ask Madame de Montglat if I could have one like it, that Elizabeth was looking rather sad and very preoccupied and was not paying any attention at all to Monsieur de Breves.

I thought: I believe she has been crying.

How strange! Elizabeth was seven years older than I. She and Christine were great friends although Christine was a good deal younger than she was. Elizabeth had always treated Gaston and me with a kindly tolerance. She had always seemed far beyond us – almost grown up. It was difficult to imagine her crying. But yes. Her eyes were red. Something had happened. I wondered what.

Monsieur de Breves was standing close to me and had picked up the paper on which I was supposed to have written something – I was not sure what and I had been so concerned with Elizabeth that I had not thought to look at Gaston's and copy his, although this was always risky for what he wrote invariably displayed as great an ignorance as mine.

'Ah, Madame la Princesse,' said Monsieur de Breves sadly, shaking his head, 'I fear we are never going to make a scholar of you.'

I smiled at him. I had for some time realized that when I smiled in a certain way I could melt the anger or disappointment of a number of people. Alas, neither my mother nor Madame de Montglat was among them.

I said: 'No, Monsieur de Breves, but my dancing master says that my dancing will delight the Court.'

He smiled faintly and patted my shoulder. That was all. No reprimand. What a smile could do! If only I could turn the magic on Madame de Montglat.

My thoughts went back to Elizabeth and later on I came upon her sitting alone.

She had gone back to the schoolroom expecting no doubt to find no one there at this hour, and she was sitting on a window seat, her hands covering her face.

I was right. There were tears.

I put my arms about her neck and kissed her.

'Elizabeth,' I said. 'Dear sister. What ails you? Tell Henriette.'

There was a brief silence during which I thought she was about to order me away angrily. I gave her my conquering smile and suddenly she put her arms about me.

'There!' I said. 'There!' I patted her back, marvelling that I, the baby, should be comforting my elder sister.

'Dear little one,' said Elizabeth, more kindly than she had ever spoken to me before – not that she had ever been unkind, only seeming to be unaware of my existence.

'You are unhappy. What is wrong?'

'Oh, you wouldn't understand.'

'I would. I would.'

Elizabeth sighed. 'I am going away . . . away from you all.'

'Away? Why? Where?'

'To Spain.'

'Why are you going to Spain?'

'To marry the King's son.'

'The son of the King of Spain! Oh, Elizabeth, when the King dies you will be the Queen of Spain!'

'Does that surprise you?'

'No,' I said. 'I know we all have to marry. What surprises me is that you are sad when you are going to be Queen of Spain.'

'And you think that is worth . . . losing everything else for?'

'It must be wonderful to be a Queen.'

'Oh, Henriette, what of your family? Suppose you had to go and leave us all . . . go to a new country. . . .'

I considered it. Giving up everything . . . Mamie, Gaston, Madame de Montglat . . . my sisters . . . my mother. . . . And all in exchange for a crown!

'You are too young to understand, Henriette,' went on Elizabeth. 'It will come to you one day. You must be prepared for it.'

'When?'

'Oh there is a long time to wait yet. How old are you? Six. I am seven years older than you. In seven years your time will come.'

Seven years! It was too far in the future to be considered. It was longer than the time I had been on Earth.

'Louis will be married too,' said Elizabeth. 'Lucky Louis, he will not have to leave his home.'

'Do you hate going so much?'

'I don't want to leave my home. To go into . . . I do not know what. It's frightening, Henriette. It will be easier for you. You will have seen my going . . . and Christine's before your time comes, so it won't be such a shock.'

She set me down and blinked away the tears.

'Don't tell anyone that you found me like this. Not even Mamie or Gaston.'

I promised.

'Our mother would be angry. She thinks it is wonderful that she has brought about this match with Spain. Some of the people are not too pleased.'

'Who isn't pleased?'

'The Huguenots.'

'Huguenots! What concern is it of theirs?'

She took my face in her hands and kissed me. It was rare affection from Elizabeth.

'You are so young,' she said. 'You don't know anything of what is going on outside.'

'Outside where?'

'In the world . . . beyond the Court. Never mind. You will in time.'

She had stood up and, straightening her dress, became the Elizabeth I knew, inclined to be disdainful of her little sister's youth.

'Run along now, dear,' she said, 'and forget what I have said.'

But of course I was not going to forget. Many times I was on the verge of telling Mamie or Gaston. I felt it very difficult to restrain myself for I should have felt very superior for once to have discovered something they did not know. But I remembered my promise.

I did not have to wait long, for a few days after my encounter with Elizabeth our mother arrived in the nursery. Gaston and I did our ceremonious bows and when she held out her hand to us we approached and stood one on either side of her. I found myself staring at her bosom, which always fascinated me. It was one of the biggest bosoms I had ever seen and very different from that of Madame de Montglat, which was almost non-existent.

'Now, my children,' she said. 'I have come to tell you some very good news. Your dear brother the King is about to be married.'

I gasped and stopped myself just in time from blurting out: 'But I thought it was Elizabeth who is going to be married.'

We saw little of our brother Louis. Now that he was the King he

was too important to be in our nursery and had to be taken away
to have special tuition.

The Queen went on: 'His dear little wife will come here to be
with you for a while . . . but only until she is old enough to go to
her husband. We are going to Bordeaux where we shall meet the
new little Queen of France, whose father is giving her into our
care. She is to be married to your brother. And now that we are
taking his daughter from the King of Spain we think he might be a
little unhappy so we are giving him our Princess Elizabeth. She is
to be the wife of the son of the King of Spain. You were both at the
proxy ceremony. You don't remember. You were too young. It
took place three years ago at the Palais Royal. You were only four
then, Gaston, and you were three, Henriette.'

'I remember,' cried Gaston. 'There was dancing and a
banquet. . . .'

'I remember too,' I put in, although I did not, but I was not
going to be outdone by my brother.

'Well, that is good,' went on our mother. 'There will be a real
marriage now. So we are all going to Bordeaux and I have decided
that it will be good for you children to come too.'

Our mother drew away to look at us closely.

I could see the questions trembling on Gaston's lips, but he was
always afraid to speak too freely in our mother's presence.

The Queen went on: 'It is a most happy occasion. It is an
alliance with Spain. The daughter of a Spanish King will be a
Queen of France and our daughter a Queen of Spain. Fair
exchange, eh? Spain will be our ally and my daughter . . . Queen
of Spain. She has married well, and what delights me as much as
her crown is that she is going into a Catholic country.'

I was afraid then that our mother was going to ask how we
were getting on with our religious instruction and I was just as
scatterbrained with that as I was with other subjects.

But, however, she did not. She was clearly too excited by the
marriages she had arranged.

'There will be many preparations to be made,' she said. 'You
will have new clothes.'

I clasped my hands in joy. I loved new clothes and I knew that
those we would have to attend a grand wedding would be very
grand indeed.

The preparations for this great occasion went on. I learned

afterwards that there were murmurings in the streets against my mother but I did not know of them then.

We seemed to spend long periods being fitted. I laughed at Gaston in his scarlet velvet coat and broad-brimmed beaver hat. He looked like a miniature cavalier. And I was like a lady of the Court in my puffed sleeves and wide cuffs, looped-up skirts and laces and ribbons. Everyone in our household came in to admire us and we loved our clothes – apart from the ever-present ruffs. 'I shall never get used to them,' I declared; and Gaston hated them even more than I did.

Elizabeth's gown was more glorious than anything we had ever seen. I heard my mother say that she must impress the Spaniards with our infinitely better taste. Poor Elizabeth, in spite of the fact that she was going to be a Queen in a Catholic country she stood with a look of cold indifference on her face while she was fitted with the most sumptuously trimmed gowns; and I could not forget the sight of her sad face above all that splendour.

In due course we left for Bordeaux. On some occasions I rode on one side of my mother, Gaston on the other.

I heard two people whispering. I think they were minor attendants. 'She thinks the people will so like those two pretty children that they will forget how much they dislike her.'

And there was no doubt that the people liked us. I smiled and lifted my hand in acknowledgement of their cheers just as I had been taught to do.

They cheered Louis too. After all he was the King, and I heard Elizabeth say to Christine that he was too young to have done anything the people did not like.

'All their blame is for our mother and the Maréchal d'Ancre,' said Elizabeth.

I wanted to know more. Why should they blame my mother, and who was the Maréchal d'Ancre, that Concino Concini about whom I had heard people whispering?

Although I hated to learn lessons I was avid to gather information about what was happening around me. The trouble is that when you are six no one considers you seriously enough to talk to you.

We stayed at castles and great houses on the way to Bordeaux and there we were entertained lavishly. Gaston and I were allowed to dance on certain occasions and I sang, for singing was

another of my accomplishments and my singing master said I had
the voice of a nightingale.

My mother was very pleased with us, and I kept wondering
whether it was because she loved us or because it was necessary
to make the people pleased with the children she had brought
into the royal nurseries so that they would forget those mysterious things she appeared to have done which annoyed them.

However neither Gaston nor I was given to introspection –
certainly not at the ages of seven and six; and we were going to
enjoy ourselves.

'This is an exciting life!' I said to Gaston; and he agreed whole-
heartedly.

In due course we reached Bordeaux.

We were not present at the important ceremony of handing
over the two Princesses, but we did dance at the celebrations
which followed; and when we left Bordeaux we had lost our sister
Elizabeth and had gained a sister-in-law who was known as
Anne of Austria and, as she was married to our brother Louis, she
was Queen of France.

When we returned to Paris the excitement increased. We had
to show Anne of Austria and her attendants how much more
cultured we were in France than they were in Spain.

As we came into the city, the narrow streets were crowded with
people who had come to see the new Queen. Nobody loves
pageantry more than the Parisians and they evidently liked the
look of Anne as she rode beside Louis at the head of the
cavalcade. She was a tall girl with a good figure and as fair as I was
dark. Moreover she was young – just about the same age as
Louis. She had beautiful hands, which she was fond of bringing
into display, and she seemed very sure of herself. I thought we
might get on well together for I had already discovered that she
was not very good at learning but enjoyed singing and dancing as
much as I did.

We rode past the new house of the Place Royale and the Place
Dauphine which my father had caused to be built. I had been
watching Anne to see if she was impressed by our grand city. My
father had believed in building and he had made great
improvements in Paris.

'Ah, Madame la Princesse,' the old ones used to say, 'you are lucky to live in such a city. In my day it was a very different place. Thanks to your great father we have now the finest city in the world.'

I had heard how he had completed the old Arsenal – that building to which he had been making his way when he was murdered – and he had built the Hôtel de Ville also. I had been taken to see them on one occasion and I had been completely overawed by the magnificent staircase, the moulded ceilings, the sculptured doors and the most wonderful fireplace in the throne room.

My father had done all that. People constantly said, when speaking of him: 'What a tragedy! Oh what a tragedy for France!'

And sometimes I felt a flash of uneasiness because I realized that criticism of the present rule was implied – and present rule was, of course, my mother, for Louis was too young to be blamed for anything.

I was so proud as we approached the Louvre. We called it the New Louvre because the ancient one had become so unhealthy and decrepit that François Premier, who had loved fine buildings, had decided to rebuild it. It was hardly begun when he died, but the next King, Henri Deux, and his wife Catherine de Medicis also loved fine buildings and they went on with it. I, too, love beautiful things and until the day I left France I was always thrilled by that glorious façade of Jean Bullant and Philibert Delorme every time I went past the New Louvre.

Now the celebrations began in real earnest. We could be so much more lavish in Paris than they could be in provincial towns, and we were going to show these Spaniards how rich and clever we were.

For a while everyone must forget his or her grievances and enjoy the occasion. I had rarely seen my mother so happy. She was so pleased with the marriages. Later she began to imbue me with a firm belief in the true Faith and the determination to preserve it wherever I was. There were two precepts which must be upheld at all cost: the true Faith and the determination to enforce it on all people for their own good; and the other was the importance of Royalty, the right to rule which had been bestowed on kings and queens by God: The Divine Right of Royalty.

But stern as she was on these two points, she did enjoy

feasting, banquets and fêtes; and she was determined to indulge these pastimes no matter what old Sully would say. Not that that mattered. He could grumble away to his heart's desire in retirement. He had been shown the door as soon as he had lost his master.

No expense was to be spared. Everyone was going to rejoice in the marriage which she – the Queen Mother now that there was a new Queen – had brought about.

For me it was a wonderful time. I forgot lessons, the dull routine, the admonitions of Madame de Montglat – they were all in the past. Here we were celebrating the marriage of our King, and I was going to enjoy every minute of it.

I danced. I sang. 'What an enchanting creature little Madame Henriette is!' I heard that more than once and I was quick to see the pleasure in my mother's face.

Such happiness! I prayed that it would go on for ever.

There was Spanish influence in quite a number of our entertainments – in honour of the Queen, of course. Some of our gentlemen performed the Galanterie Castellane and there were quadrilles and Spanish dances. Gaston and I learned a little Spanish *pas de deux* which we performed together to the delight of everyone at Court. Some of the company dressed up as gods. I sat round-eyed watching while Jupiter led in Apollo and Diana; and then came Venus, who knelt before our young King and Queen and chanted verses about La Belle Espagnole. Poor Louis hated it all and found it very hard to smile and pretend he was happy. Perhaps he had not wanted to marry and was a little worried about all it entailed . . . just as Elizabeth had been. The Queen however threw back her long fair tresses and flourishing her pretty hands quite clearly enjoyed it.

At one point my hand was taken by an old woman who made me sit beside her.

I did not know who she was at first but I was intrigued by her and considerably overawed. She had a regal air so I guessed she was of importance but I could not think what she could want with me.

Her old hands clawed mine and she studied me intently. I could not take my eyes from her. Her face was wrinkled; her eyes were deeply shadowed; but she wore so much rouge and white lead that from a distance she might have been quite young. She

had a wig of luxuriant black curls, and her clothes struck me as
belonging to an earlier age. Her gold-braided houppelande was
certainly out of date.

She said: 'So you are the little Madame Henriette.'

I agreed that I was.

'And how old are you?'

'Six years.'

'A baby,' she commented.

'Indeed not.'

She laughed and touched my cheek. 'Beautiful soft skin,' she
said. 'Mine was like that . . . once. When I was your age I was the
prettiest girl in the whole of France . . . and I was the cleverest,
too. I was old for my years, they said. Are you, little one?'

'I don't know.'

'Then you can't be, can you? Little Margot knew everything.
She was born with knowledge.'

'Are you . . . La Reine Margot?'

'Ah, so little Madame Henriette has heard of me! Yes, you
might have been my daughter – think of that. I was your father's
wife before he married Marie de Medicis.'

I was overawed. I had heard of her, of course, but never had I
thought I would meet her. She had been notorious in her youth
. . . and after.

She said: 'Your father and I hated each other. We fought like
two wild cats. Then we divorced and he married your mother. If
he had not, *you* would not be here, would you? What a calamity!
Can you imagine a world without Madame Henriette?'

I remarked that it would be rather difficult for me to do that if I
were not here.

She laughed.

"He hated me, but he hated his second wife even more, they
say. Strange is it not, that a man who loved women more than
any other man in France should have had two wives whom he
hated.'

'You should not talk about my mother like that.'

She came close to me. 'La Reine Margot always says what she
means and cares not whom it may offend. So do you think little
six-year-old Madame Henriette will stop me?'

'No,' I answered.

'I like you,' she said. 'You are very pretty. I will tell you something. You are prettier than the new Queen. I don't think our lord Louis is very impressed with her, do you?'

'My mother would not wish me. . . .'

'To give an opinion? But, little Henriette, when you grow up you are going to state your opinions whether people like it or not. Don't you agree with me?'

'Yes, I expect I shall. But I have to get a little older first.'

'You are getting older every minute while you talk to me. Oh, little one, do I look very old to you?'

'Very old.'

'Look at my beautiful skin. Look at my lovely hair. You do not know what to say, do you? Once I had beautiful luxuriant hair. Many men loved me. Oh yes, I have had many lovers . . . and still do. But not so many now. I don't remember ever having been innocent as you are, my beautiful child. When I married your father I was not innocent. It was an ill-fated marriage. The streets ran with blood. Have you ever heard of the Massacre of St Bartholomew's Eve?'

I said I had.

'Catholics and Huguenots – and your father coming very near to death then. They meant to get him. But he survived. He would. Like a country boy, he was . . . crude . . . rough . . . no mate for an elegant Princesse . . . not cultured as I was. We disliked each other from the start. Catholic and Huguenot . . . I wonder if they will ever live in harmony.'

'I hope that the Huguenots will give up heresy and come to the true Faith.'

'You are repeating what you have heard, little one. Don't do that. Think for yourself as I always did. Do I frighten you?'

I hesitated.

'I do,' she went on. 'Well, now go, little one. You are a beautiful child and I hope you will have as vivid a life as I have had.'

I said: 'I like sitting here talking to you.'

The hand pressed mine and she smiled.

'You must go. Your mother would not wish you to talk too long with me. I think she has noticed us . . . or one of her spies has. The King is her son but I have as much right as anyone to be here when there is a wedding in the family.'

A young man was approaching and I saw her interest in me fade.

He came and bowed before her.

'*Ma belle Margot!*' he said softly and she smiled and held out her hand.

I knew it was then time for me to leave.

I never forgot her and was extraordinarily moved when a year later I heard that she had died. She was sixty-three years old then and I found it hard to believe that anyone could live so long. When Mamie came to us she told me lots of stories about La Reine Margot; her life seemed to have been one long succession of lovers and wild adventures. I was surprised to hear that she and my mother had been quite friendly.

'I should have thought she would have hated my mother who took her place,' I commented to Mamie.

'Oh no,' Mamie corrected me. 'She liked her because of it. Every time she saw her she would say how lucky she was to be rid of your father. And your mother was in sympathy with her because they had both had to – as they would say – "put up with him" and knew what a troublesome matter that could be. It made a bond between them.'

So she was dead and that wild and exciting life was over for ever.

Those celebrations were certainly an important event in my life. I ceased to be a child during them. For instance it was the first time I saw the Maréchal d'Ancre about whom people were constantly talking. Christine pointed him out to me. 'Look,' she said, 'there is the Maréchal talking to our mother. I don't think our brother likes him very much.'

'Why not?' I asked.

Christine was about to speak when she looked at me and I guessed she was reminding herself that I was only a child.

'Oh, he has his reasons, I'll swear,' she said and then she left me.

I noticed my brother, the King, was sitting looking at the proceedings with a disconsolate air. His Queen was beside him, smiling, fluttering her fan and now and then putting up one of her hands to touch her mantilla – not to adjust it but to bring her pretty hands into prominence. She looked very Spanish and I wondered whether the people were going to like that. Louis spoke very little to her. He stammered quite a bit when he was in a temper or alarmed about something. I suspected he was in one of his stammering phases now.

Then he was smiling suddenly because Charles d'Albert had come to sit beside him and it was immediately clear that he enjoyed the company of Charles d'Albert better than that of his Queen.

I knew a little about Charles d'Albert because there was a great deal of talk about him around the nurseries.

'Another of those Italians,' I heard one of the attendants say. The man was standing beneath my window at the time and even though I had to take a few paces back to hide myself, I was able to hear what was said.

The man to whom he was talking replied: 'We have had our fill of them since the King went to Italy for a wife.'

'And married one of the Medicis at that! It would have been better if he had stayed with La Reine Margot.'

They said something about La Reine Margot which I did not understand and they laughed heartily. I could tell by the sound of their feet on the gravel that they were pushing each other to make their point.

'Well, we wouldn't have had a new King if he had not married her.'

'No, no. For all her tricks Margot was no hand at producing the goods.'

More laughter and jostling.

'They say he's getting a real hold on the young King. . . .'

'Won't do him much good with Maman in control. Concini will see to that.'

'Another Italian! Isn't it time France was for the French?'

'Yes, I agree. But don't worry about Albert. The King is in leading strings and likely to remain there as far as I can see. He's no Henri Quatre.'

'Ah, there was a man!' There followed what I guessed to be more shuffling and jostling, but to my chagrin they moved away. I should have liked to hear more about Charles d'Albert.

I was interested though and kept my ears open. It was no use asking questions – everyone either considered I was too young to understand or they did not want to waste time on me.

So I listened and at the time of the wedding I did know that Charles d'Albert was originally Alberti and he had come to France from Florence to make his fortune. When he found he could do this he decided to become French and changed his name to Albert. He came to the King's notice because he was clever with birds and trained hawks. He loved to hunt with them and as the King did too that made a bond between them and they soon became very friendly. My brother made him his very special falconer and they were constantly in each other's company training birds and making nets and thongs for hawking. Albert could train other birds and he was very clever with little sporting birds like *pies grièches* which, I discovered later, in England, were called butcher birds.

It was very interesting to see the young man of whom I had heard so much. He was considerably older than my brother Louis and he had certainly made his fortune at the Court of France. He had married, through the King's graces, Mademoiselle Rohan Montbazon, who was recognized as one of the beauties of the Court.

Watching them now it was easy to see that he was on very familiar terms with the King.

I sat on a stool close to them. It was sometimes an advantage to be so young that one was ignored. I listened to their talk. They were discussing hunting and Albert was asking the King to come as soon as he could to see a new falcon which he had acquired and of which he had high hopes.

They talked of falconry for some time and then Albert said suddenly: 'Look at Concini over there. What airs that man gives himself!'

'You are right,' said my brother. He was not stammering now that he was talking to Albert which was a sign that he was completely at his ease.

'Your royal mother seems besotted by the man. I believe he thinks himself more royal than she is.'

'I dislike him, Charles. He tries to tell *me* what to do.'

'What impertinence! You should not allow that, Sire.'

I looked up and saw the pleased look on my brother's face. He loved people to recognize his royalty. They did in the streets, of course, and cheered him as the King out of loyalty to our father, Christine said; but there were always those to tell him what to do. It must be a trial to be a King in name and not old enough to be one in fact.

'There'll come a time,' said Louis.

'And I pray the saints it will not long be delayed,' added Charles d'Albert.

'Concini and the Queen Mother will delay it as long as possible you may be sure.'

'Indeed they will. They want to rule, and how can they do that if the King is in his rightful place?'

'I won't always be a boy.'

'If you will forgive my saying so, Sire, you have the attributes of a man already.'

I could see why Louis was fond of Albert. This was the way he liked people to talk to him. 'The time will come . . .' he said.

'Soon, Sire, soon.'

Someone had come forward and was bowing to Louis. I slipped away.

I realized later that I had been listening to the beginning of a plot.

Those wedding festivities were a turning point in my life. My mother seemed to realize that I was growing up, and because I was dainty and pretty and could sing and dance well, the people liked me. It was necessary for her to be seen with us children because the people always cheered Gaston and me and she could pretend the cheers were for her. In fact the only way she could get the people to cheer when her carriage rode by was to have us in it.

My mother loved displays of any sort – banquets, ballets, any kind of dancing and singing; she loved fine clothes too and was determined to have them because she believed that entertainments of a lavish nature made the people forget their grievances. It was no wonder that she had forced the Duc de Sully into retirement. He would have been horrified to see the exchequer, which he had always kept under his control and that of my father, dwindling away.

Paris was becoming a very beautiful city; and my mother liked to call attention to all that she and the late King had done to make it so. She wanted to give balls and fêtes throughout Paris. This she did and the people certainly loved to see the carriages passing through the streets and to catch glimpses of the nobility in all their splendour. On summer evenings the whole Court would go to the Place Royale where my father had begun to build what he intended to be a bazaar, lined with shops rather like St Mark's in Venice. My mother was very enthusiastic – possibly because of its Italian associations, and as my father had died before it was completed, she had had it finished in time for the wedding. There was a promenade known as the Cours de la Reine because she had planted several rows of trees along it and in an attempt to win the people's favour had opened it to the public.

They thronged there and were delighted to catch glimpses of the grand seigneurs and ladies walking in the gardens.

Alas, it needed more than that to win the people's favour, and even if my mother had been the best of rulers, she could not have hoped for great popularity because she was an Italian.

Many of the nobles lived in the houses of the Place Royale and they all had magnificent gardens with wonderful examples of the skill of topiary, and the sculptured figures and glistening fountains were a splendid sight.

'See what a wonderful city we have given you!' That was what my mother was saying.

But the people continued to dislike her and they complained bitterly about the rise of Concini.

It was about this time that Mamie was brought into the nurseries to help her mother with the children. That meant chiefly Gaston and me, for Christine was at that time nine years old and so considered herself to be very grown up.

Mamie did not seem old to me although most people over fourteen usually did. She was even older than that – in her middle teens, I believe – and I loved her from the moment I set eyes on her.

She exuded an air of wisdom; she was serene; and she did not treat me as a child, so that I could ask her questions without fearing to expose my ignorance as I did with most people.

Then there was Anne, the new Queen, who was only thirteen and not quite old enough to be a wife, so I saw a great deal of her too.

We liked each other in a mild kind of way – not as I liked Mamie, of course, but although Anne gave herself certain airs and was a little coquettish in a rather prim way, she was not clever and hardly ever looked at a book, and this endeared her to me; she was lazy and did all she could to evade lessons; and she loved dancing and singing and we discussed ballets and danced and sang together; and she, with Gaston and me, arranged a

dance which we said we would perform together whenever we
had the opportunity to do so.

So I had two welcome additions to my life in Anne and dear
Mamie. The days seemed to have become full of pleasure. I had
no notion of the storms which were gathering in the country.

Then I began to learn, through Mamie, something of what was
going on.

'You should know,' she told me. 'It is a time of great events and
as the daughter of a King you may well have your part to play in
it.'

That made me feel very important.

It was then that she told me about the murder of my father and
that ever since his death my mother had been Regent and would
doubtless remain so until it was considered that my brother Louis
was of an age to rule.

'When will that be?' I asked. 'Poor Louis. He is not much like a
king.'

'It might be sooner than you think.'

She pursed his lips and looked mysterious, glancing over her
shoulder in a manner which I found most exciting. That was
Mamie's way. She created intrigue and made mystery around it.

I remember flinging my arms about her – it must have been
some six months after she had come to the nursery – and making
her promise that she would never go away.

She had stroked my hair and rocked me to and fro. 'I'll never go
until they force me to,' she promised.

For all her exciting outlook on life, Mamie was a realist. 'It could
be that the time will come when I shall have to go. But for now
. . . we are safe. I don't think anyone wants to part us. To tell the
truth my mother finds me too useful here with you children.'

'Gaston loves you too,' I told her. 'And Christine also . . .
although she doesn't show it as I do.'

'Poor Christine! She thinks a great deal about the Princesse
Elizabeth, and she fears that one day what has happened to her
sister will happen to her.'

'Will it?'

Mamie nodded slowly. 'Almost certainly,' she said. 'Princesses
usually marry.'

'I am a Princesse. . . .'

'A little one. You have a lot of growing up to do.'

She was comforting me, but I knew what was in store for me although it had not yet appeared on the horizon. But it would come, because it came to all Princesses.

'We shall always be together,' I said fiercely.

And she did not deny that we should.

She changed my life for me. Although it would soon have changed after the wedding in any case, she put something beautiful into it. I realized for the first time that I wanted a mother – someone to care about me, to scold me at times, to tell me about life, to comfort me when I needed comfort, someone who was the most important person in the world to me – and I to her. I felt I was beginning to get somewhere near that relationship with Mamie. And how strange it was that only then I knew that I had missed it.

She began to make me aware. She told me what was happening all around me. It was by no means what it seemed, and sometimes it was a little frightening, but as conveyed by Mamie always exciting.

'Who is Concini?' I asked, and instead of telling me it was no concern of mine, and that I should know all I needed to know when I was older, she told me.

My mother had brought Italians with her when she came to France. It was inevitable. Usually attendants were dismissed when a young princess came into a new country, but Marie de Medicis had kept some of hers, and many were saying that it was to the detriment of France.

'She brought with her Elenora Galagaï,' Mamie told me, 'who was the daughter of her nurse and who had been brought up with her. They grew up to be very fond of each other . . . like two sisters.'

'As we are . . . you and I, Mamie,' I put in.

'Yes,' agreed Mamie. 'It is very like that. Well, when she came to France to marry the King, your mother refused to be parted from Elenora Galagaï and brought her with her. Then because she wanted to see her settled she arranged for her to be married to a man for whom she had the greatest regard. This was another Italian who had come with her to France – Concino Concini. He was the son of a notary from Florence and she had made him her secretary. They were married and, of course, being such favourites of the Queen, they planned to make their fortunes.'

'And did they?' I asked.

'My dear Princesse! Did they indeed! Concini became the Maréchal d'Ancre. You know of him.'

'I saw him at the wedding celebrations with my mother. Charles d'Albert, who was with my brother, did not seem to like him very much.'

'Oh Charles d'Albert! It is said that the King listens to him more than he does to his mother.'

Gradually I began to learn more and more of what was going on outside the nursery. Mamie was such a vivid talker and I never ceased to marvel that she had made me her special friend. That honour might so easily have been reserved for Christine who was so much older than I, or even Gaston who could give me a year. But no! *I* was the one, and for that I promised myself that I would be grateful to her for ever more.

'At times,' she said, 'I forget how young you are. Never mind,' she went on as though to excuse herself. 'You will have to play a part in all this one day so it is as well that you should be prepared.'

I remember the great excitement just after the wedding. The Prince de Condé was at the centre of it. Mamie had already told me how he had married Mademoiselle de Montmorency when my father had wanted her to be his 'little friend' and how the Prince had turned out to be not quite the indifferent husband my father had hoped he would be. Apparently when my father had died, the Prince had brought his wife back to Paris because there was no need then for him to keep her hidden away.

'It had been a very stormy marriage,' Mamie told me. 'Many marriages are.'

I was not surprised to hear this and remembered what I had heard of my father's marriages to La Reine Margot and to my mother.

'The Princesse was very angry because he had taken her away from Court. She had quite looked forward to being your father's 'little friend'. She would have had all the advantages of being a queen and none of the disadvantages. And what had Henri de Condé done? Dragged her away. For what? His indifferent attentions? She has held that against him ever since.'

I had seen them at one of the *fêtes* at the time of the wedding. The Princesse was very beautiful and I could understand why my father had been attracted by her.

A week or so after the wedding festivities the Prince de Condé was arrested.

'He has plotted to overthrow the Maréchal d'Ancre,' said Mamie, 'and has tried to assemble the nobles of France against the man he calls the Italian Schemer.'

'Arrested!' I cried. 'But he is a royal Prince!'

'Royal Princes can be arrested for plotting against the Queen Mother.'

'He has really plotted against my mother?'

'Dear Princesse, he has plotted against the Maréchal d'Ancre, and that can be said to be plotting against the Queen Mother. There is a great deal of excitement in the streets. They are saying that a great many wish the plot had succeeded. But the Italian is too wily for that.'

'What will happen to the Prince?'

'I doubt they will dare execute him. He may well be sent to prison.'

'At least,' I said, 'the Princesse de Condé will be rid of him now.'

She hugged me suddenly. 'Oh, my dear Princesse, we live in dangerous times.'

Everybody was talking about the coup that had failed and there was a surprising sequel. The Prince was exiled to Vincennes and instead of congratulating herself that she was rid of him, the Princesse de Condé declared her intention of joining him there in captivity and living with him as his faithful wife.

'People are very strange,' commented Mamie. Then she laughed and kissed me. 'It is good that they are,' she went on. 'It makes life more interesting.'

About this time Mère Magdalaine, a Carmelite nun, was chosen to look after my spiritual welfare. I spent long sessions with her; we prayed together; we asked for help; and she made me realize – as my mother did – that the most important motive in one's life was to promote the Catholic Faith, bringing all those who were outside it to the Truth.

The days sped by . . . religious instruction from Mère Magdalaine, lessons from François Savary de Breves, playing

games with Gaston and the children of noblemen, dancing, singing, happy hours with Mamie . . . they were the pleasant days.

It was only just beginning to occur to me that they could change.

There was more talk than ever about Concini after the Prince de
Condé went into confinement.

'There is a great deal of dissatisfaction with Concini,' Mamie
told me, 'and the King is getting older. He is with Charles
d'Albert more than ever, but Albert is only as powerful as the
King is, whereas Concini walks with the Queen Mother.'

'You talk as though my mother and the King are enemies.'

'Perhaps that is because they are,' said Mamie.

Then she went on to tell me about Concini's vast possessions.
'He has several beautiful *châteaux* in the country as well as two in
Paris. He has vineyards and farms. They say he is one of the
richest men in France and the people do not like that because they
say that when he came here he had nothing.'

'He has worked hard for my mother,' I said.

'And for himself,' added Mamie.

One day, in an unguarded moment, she said: 'There is something in the air. I feel it in the streets. There are two factions now:
the King with Charles d'Albert and the Queen Mother with
Concini. Albert and Concini . . . both Italians . . . and the people
don't like either of them.'

'Well,' I pointed out. 'My mother is Italian so both I and my
brother are half Italians.'

'You are French,' cried Mamie fiercely. 'You are your father's
children and he was one of the greatest Frenchmen who ever
lived.'

It was all very puzzling to me but I enjoyed hearing the news
and I must confess to a certain disappointment when life continued smoothly. Sometimes I felt I wanted things to happen,
and even tragic horrible things were better than nothing. They
brought excitement into the monotony of my daily life.

'Concini and his wife are shipping their wealth to Italy, so I
heard,' Mamie told me one day. 'That looks to me as though they
intend to flit. It would be a wise thing for them to do that from
what I hear in the streets. The people are gathering against them
. . . sharpening their knives. . . .' She laughed at me. 'Oh, I did
not mean that literally, my child. I mean they are preparing to
drive him out of the country.'

It could only have been a few days after that when the trouble started. Secretly Charles d'Albert had been plotting with the King and their idea was to get rid of Concini, for without him the Queen Mother would be powerless. She was not interested in statecraft – which had been obvious since the Regency – and she looked to Concini to see to all that for her – with the aid of his friends, of course. She liked food and had grown fat; she liked gaiety, religion, and parading her royalty. People said unkindly that that was all that could be expected of a banker's daughter.

It seemed that Charles d'Albert had decided that the moment had come to strike. The King was growing up. He should exert his rights or he would remain a puppet for years.

The King signed a warrant for Concini's arrest, which was delivered by six of the King's guards. I can imagine Concini's astonishment when he – who had been supreme – was suddenly confronted by the King's men. He must have wished that he had followed his inclination and left for Italy. We learned afterwards that he would have gone but for his wife who had insisted that the time was not yet ripe and that there were many more pickings to be had and thus they could augment their wealth.

Elenora Galigaï was proved wrong.

It was natural that such an important person as the Maréchal d'Ancre should demand to know on what grounds he was being arrested, and that when he was told to be silent and that they must leave right away, he should resist arrest. He drew his sword and that was the signal for which they had all been waiting. The guards fell upon him with their daggers and within seconds it was a bleeding corpse which lay at their feet. In the meantime, having seen the guards going into the residence of the mighty Maréchal d'Ancre, a crowd had gathered and when the guards appeared on the balcony dragging out the dead body of the once-powerful Maréchal, the mob became frenzied with excitement.

One of the guards cried out: 'Here is the body of the Italian Concini, Maréchal d'Ancre, for whose pleasure you have been paying dearly through your taxes.'

With that they threw the body over the balcony and the mob seized it, savagely mutilating it, calling vengeance on all Italian schemers, and declaring that from henceforth France was to be for the French.

That was the signal. The people had spoken.

'Now,' prophesied Mamie, 'there will be change.'

How right she was! My brother lost no time in appointing Charles d'Albert as Chief Minister and created him Duc de Luynes. Concini's wife was arrested. The rumour was that she was a sorceress for only such a person could have such complete control over the Queen Mother. Mamie said it was a waste of time to make her stand trial for her judges had already decided on the verdict beforehand. The charge against her was that only by spells could she have wielded the influence she had had over the Queen Mother.

'There were no spells,' was her rejoinder. 'If I have had the power to influence the Queen, it is that of a strong mind over a weak one.'

My mother would not have liked to hear that, of course, but she had already been sent into exile and was more or less a prisoner in the *Château* of Blois.

Poor Madame la Maréchale, as they called her. She did not long survive her husband. She was judged guilty, and in accordance with the law against sorceresses was beheaded and her body condemned to the flames.

'At least,' said Mamie, 'they did not burn her alive. She was lucky in that.'

Lucky! Poor Elenora Galigaï who had enjoyed such favour and amassed such wealth and power. What were her thoughts when they led her to the scaffold? How she must have reproached herself, for if it was indeed true that her husband had wished to leave France, and it was she who had persuaded him to remain a little longer to make themselves more wealthy, she was certainly in a way responsible.

I remembered well the pall of smoke which hung over the Place de Grève. I thought then how short a time ago it was when we were all rejoicing there among the crowds who had come to see the processions. Now it had become a place of horror. I had never actually seen La Maréchale but I could imagine her horrible death.

I forgot her after a while but I remembered her later, and when I was lonely and filled with remorse, certain incidents from my childhood would flash into my mind and I would see those events more clearly than I had done at the time when they happened.

Louis was now sixteen years old. He had changed. He had looked so happy when my mother was leaving the Court for Blois. He really had been greatly in awe of her and she had never won his affection. He had never forgiven her for being so strict with him when he was a boy for often she had given orders that he was to be whipped for some trivial offence. Kings, she had said, had to be brought up very carefully; they must be chastised more severely than ordinary people. Sometimes she even administered the cane with her own hands. He had hated that more than ever. And when after my father died and she became Regent and he was King and yet not King and so much restraint was put on him, he blamed her for that. I could understand why he responded to people like Charles d'Albert.

So I suppose it was not surprising that he had been so pleased on the day she left for Blois.

He lost his stammer and I heard him say in a clear loud voice, full of the utmost satisfaction: 'Enfin me voici Roi!'

The nobles gathered round the King, and it was clear that they approved of what had happened. The Prince de Condé was released from confinement and he came to Paris to be with my brother.

There was another matter of significance which I think perhaps none of us realized at the time. The Bishop of Luçon, Armand du Plessis, who had held office with the Maréchal d'Ancre, hastily left for Avignon and declared he intended to occupy himself with study and writing.

After all the excitement we settled down to a normal routine again. I did not miss my own mother, for, in fact, she had never given me much loving attention.

'It was very interesting while it lasted,' said Mamie.

Queen Anne had joined her husband and was living with him now. Louis had grown up overnight when my mother was removed from Court. There were fewer entertainments now because it had been my mother who had loved them. Louis had never greatly cared for them, preferring his horses and dogs and hunting. Anne loved dancing so she was not very pleased by the change, and I believed she preferred being a juvenile in our nurseries to wife to Louis.

In her rather impulsive way Mamie whispered to me that they were not really suited to each other and it was not a happy marriage; and then she put her fingers to her lips and said: 'Forget I said that.'

That was the sort of thing which endeared her to me. We grew more and more friendly and I often felt that I was in a cosy cocoon guarded by my dear Mamie. Since she had come, Madame de Montglat had more or less passed me over to her, only making sure that I attended my lessons and was getting my religious instruction. She did not mind so much about Monsieur de Breves. The most important duty was religious study; I had to learn to be an unswerving Catholic, to believe blindly in the Faith and to remember, no matter what happened, that I was the daughter of a King and Queen and that such a state was bestowed by God.

Sometimes I went to Court to enjoy some ball or entertainment devised by Anne. She and I often danced together for we made a very successful pair.

I was to wish in later life that I had paid more attention to Monsieur de Breves and that I had had more than superficial knowledge of the history of my country and of the world. If I had had this I might not have made so many miscalculations. Often in my days of loneliness I look back and think how much I could have learned from the experiences of those who went before me.

But I was impatient with serious matters for I was frivolous by nature and my mind was filled with the tune of a new song or an intricate dance step.

Two years passed. My mother was still at Blois and Armand du Plessis was acting as a sort of go-between. He had been my mother's adviser until the death of Maréchal d'Ancre, and after a spell in Avignon he had emerged and was now professing a desire to serve the King. He was endeavouring to bring about a reconciliation between my mother and Louis. Du Plessis was a brilliant man. We did not realize how brilliant then, but in later years when he became the Duc de Richelieu and later Cardinal, he made his mark on the history of France.

It was two years after Louis' marriage that Christine left us to become the Duchesse de Savoy. She had grown so accustomed to the idea of leaving home that she did not seem to mind as much as Elizabeth had done. There were festivities and banquets, but they

were not as grand as those with which we had celebrated Louis'
wedding – naturally not, I supposed, because he was the King,
but the real reason was that they lacked my mother's extravagant
hand.

I was now ten years old – getting alarmingly near that time
when my own future would be decided. I fancied that I was
beginning to be noticed more. I was next in line for a husband and
I began to dream romantically of what he would be like. I should
like a king if possible. Elizabeth was Queen of Spain, Christine
only Duchess of Savoy. What would be the fate of Henriette
Marie? I talked about it with Mamie. We used to conjure up
bridegrooms for me. It was a great game of mine and I always
ended by saying, 'And where I go, you shall be with me.'

'But of course,' Mamie always said.

I saw less of Gaston now. At eleven years old he was quite a
little man. He was as indolent as I was and liked to be near the
King. Louis was quite tolerant to him and Gaston was longing to
cast off his youth – even as I was.

There was an uneasy situation in the country as I suppose there
always is with a king who is young and inexperienced and who
has favourites jostling for the highest posts. The bitter Catholic–
Protestant antagonism had been kept in check by my father but it
was always simmering near the surface and ready to break out at
any moment.

It was disturbing to have a Queen Mother in captivity and a
young King dominated by a minister who had been born Italian
and was beginning to give himself far too many airs – as such
people always did. The people were getting as irritated with the
Duc de Luynes as they had with the Maréchal d'Ancre.

Soon after Christine's wedding there were rumours and
whispering throughout the Court, so I knew something was
happening, and heard what it was eventually from Mamie.

'The Queen Mother has escaped from Blois!' she said in a
hushed whisper. It was like Mamie to get the utmost drama out of
a situation. She described it to me graphically. 'The Queen
Mother could no longer endure captivity and with the help of her
friends, she made a plan of escape. How could this be brought
about? There were guards all over the place. Well, she had made
up her mind that she was going to try and you know that when
your mother decided on something it was as good as done. A

ladder was placed up against her window and she alighted to a
terrace. But you know Blois. She was still very high up. So they
got another ladder to take her to the next terrace. She was so
exhausted by the first descent that she would not undertake the
second so they let her down by means of a rope. At last she
reached the ground, but she still had to get out of the castle, so
she wrapped herself in a cloak and marched right past the
sentries between two equerries. The equerries winked at the
sentries and whispered something. . . .'

'What did they whisper?'

'That the woman had come in to provide a little light entertainment for some of the men. So as they winked and nodded
and made a few crude remarks, the Queen Mother passed on.
The Duc D'Épernon had a carriage waiting for her and they sped
away to Angoulême.'

'But what does this mean?'

'That your mother is no longer a prisoner. Something will have
to be done now or there will be war.'

'War between my mother and my brother! That's impossible.'

'Nothing is impossible in France . . . or anywhere else for that
matter, little Princesse. Always remember that.'

How her words had a habit of coming back to me during my
troubles. It was no use saying: That could never happen. She had
been right. Anything could happen in France . . . or in England.

We did not know very much of what was taking place in the
Angoumois. It was a very uneasy time. The last thing my brother
wanted was to be at war against his mother and I am sure she did
not want to be at war with him. Fortunately Richelieu was able to
convince them both that what the people wanted was a reconciliation. There were a few skirmishes and a great deal of nego-
tiation and in time a meeting between my mother and brother
took place in Paris. It was an occasion. The people did not want a
civil war. My brother embraced my mother publicly to the
people's cheers and it was another excuse for balls and banquets.

My mother declared that she was delighted to see me and
kissed me more fervently than ever I remember her doing before.
Then she looked at me speculatively.

'You are growing out of girlhood, Henriette,' she said.

I knew what that meant, and the prospect excited me while it
filled me with apprehension.

Elizabeth gone. Christine gone. It must be my turn next.

I was nearly fifteen when I first became aware of the existence of the Prince of Wales. It came about in an unusual way.

Queen Anne was devising a ballet as she so often did and as she and I danced well together she was arranging for a part to be written in for me. I was always excited at the prospect of a new dance and called in the seamstress to make a dress for me which would be suitable for the occasion.

Anne and I practised together and each complimented the other on the lightness of her step and the grace with which she twirled. Earnestly we discussed how we could make the dance more beautiful as – so Mamie said – two generals might plan a campaign which was going to result in the conquest of the world.

I laughed at her. One of the few things about me which she did not fully understand was my passionate commitment to dancing.

We rehearsed together and each time we were more enchanted by our performance. As we neared perfection we would some-times have an audience from people who could persuade or bribe the guards to let them into that part of the palace where we were dancing.

I enjoyed an audience; so did Anne; so we looked forward to these rehearsals almost as much as we did to the grand per-formance in the presence of the King.

I did not know at that time that there was anything unusual about that performance, but it seemed that all the Court was laughing about it and in due course Mamie told me what had happened.

'The audacity!' she cried. 'Guess who was in the audience at your rehearsal?'

'Many people it seemed.'

'There were two gentlemen there calling themselves Tom Smith and John Brown. They asked the Queen's Chamberlain so pleadingly to be given seats for the ballet and, because they were English, he let them in. He said he thought it only courteous to show hospitality to foreigners, and he was so proud of the way in which his Queen danced that he wanted foreigners to see it for themselves. So they came. They applauded the ballet, but somehow it became known who they were. Now, Henriette, guess who our discreet visitors were.'

'How should I know? What did you say their names were? Tom . . . Smith and John what . . .?'

'Their *assumed* names. The gentlemen masquerading under those very undistinguished names were none other than the Prince of Wales and the Duke of Buckingham.'

'Why did they not come as what they are and be treated with the respect due to them?'

'Because, my Princesse, that is exactly what they did not want to do.'

'But why not?' I cried. 'Why did they come?'

'To see the Queen.'

'But they did not make themselves known to her. She would have received them warmly.'

'They did not want to make themselves known and now that the secret has leaked, it is really very romantic. The Prince of Wales is to marry the Infanta of Spain. She is the Queen's sister. He is on his way to woo her because he believes that husbands and wives should know each other before marriage. He thinks they should not be thrust at each other without having a chance to see whether they can like each other or not.'

'*I* think that is right. Elizabeth might have been much happier if she could have seen her husband first.'

'Well, the Prince of Wales was on his way to Spain, and of course he must pass through France and the romantic young gentleman could not resist the temptation of getting a glimpse of the Queen, but he did not want her to know for what purpose. He thinks that her sister must be a little like her, and if the Queen is beautiful, her sister might have a good chance of being so too.'

'Was he . . . satisfied?'

'He must have been because he has gone on to Spain.'

'It sounds very romantic. I wish I had been able to catch a glimpse of him.'

'He caught a glimpse of you no doubt.'

'He wouldn't be looking at me, would he? All his attention would be for Anne.'

'You're pretty enough for him to take a second look.'

The incident was talked of for some time. Everyone was amused by it and thought it was a very daring thing to do.

Anne mentioned it to me when we were at our next rehearsal. She said: 'Did you hear about the outrageous behaviour of the Prince of Wales and the Duke of Buckingham?'

'I did,' I answered. 'Everyone is talking about it.'

'He will now be in Madrid.' Anne looked a little wistful. She enjoyed her position here in France but I sometimes thought she was a little homesick. 'Somehow,' she went on, 'I don't think this marriage will come to anything.'

'Oh surely it will. Such a bold young man will surely succeed with your sister.'

'It is not a matter of succeeding with *her*. I agree she may like him well enough. But nothing is likely to come of this. In the first place the Prince is a heretic from a heretic country. My sister is deeply religious – far more so than I ever was – and one of the terms of the marriage is to restore the Palatinate to Frederick who is the son-in-law of the King of England and brother-in-law to this Prince Charles. They ask too much, and I will tell you something: the Parisians may laugh at two young men who come in disguise on a romantic mission, but the Spaniards will not. They are very formal. No, I feel sure this is a mission doomed to failure.'

'It seems a pity. But you never know what governments will do. They take the strangest decisions sometimes. I think it is rather charming and romantic to come in disguise to court a lady.'

'Oh, I can see he has taken your fancy. It is a pity he did not come to court *you*.'

'Me? What *do* you mean?'

'Well, we shall have to find a husband for you, and don't forget that whoever marries that young man will be the Queen of England.'

'But you just said your sister could not marry him because he is a heretic. I am Catholic too.'

Anne crossed herself. 'As all right-thinking people are. But – apart from his religion – he is the most eligible bachelor in Europe . . . at least one of them. He has a crown to offer. Oh, I wish he had seen you better. The light wasn't very good and he would have been seated rather far away. I wish I had known who they were. . . .'

'But, Anne, he is going to woo your sister. I am only fourteen.'

'I was married when I was fourteen.'

I shivered slightly but I thought that if ever I was married I should like the young man to take the trouble to come and court me.

I often wondered what the Prince of Wales had thought of the Infanta and what happened to him when he reached Madrid. It was strange – almost as though I had a presentiment of what was to come – but I could not get him out of my mind.

War had broken out in France – the sort of war everyone dreaded – with Frenchmen fighting against Frenchmen. When my father had been alive he had appeased both Catholics and Huguenots. It was different now.

The war was remote from Paris and I thought little about it. I was so completely involved with my singing and dancing. I did gather that the King's armies were winning, but as long as what was happening outside did not interfere with my pleasure I dismissed it from my mind.

But there was change in the air and in time even I could not ignore it.

Charles d'Albert, Duc de Luynes, died . . . but not in battle, although he was in camp at Longueville when he was struck down by a malignant fever.

He had been so powerful and so eager that everyone should know how important he was – as people often are when they have risen from small beginnings to high honours. And now he was dead.

I heard that he had been very ill for three days and during that time, because they knew he was dying, his attendants had not bothered to come to his aid. So, as he had been no longer in a position to do them harm or good and was obviously close to death, he was ignored and left to die in agony with no one to give a hand to help him.

I felt rather sorry for the Duc de Luynes.

When he died they put his body on a bier to carry it away and so little did they reverence him that some of the servants actually played piquet on his bier while they waited for their horses to be watered and fed.

Of course his death changed everything. Louis was too weak to reign on his own. My mother came back into power and with her came Richelieu who had done so much to keep the peace between my mother's party and that of my brother.

My mother was jubilant. She saw herself holding the reins again and ruling, with the help of Richelieu.

What she did not see was that in Richelieu, who had now become a Cardinal, she had found a man who was determined to take complete charge and guide a weak King in the way he should go.

It was a blow for my mother, but good fortune for France. But that was later, of course.

In the meantime envoys from the King of England had arrived in France and what they proposed was of the utmost importance to me.

Betrothal

It was a rather bleak February day. I would not be fifteen until the following November so was still very young. Mamie, who was by nature curious and particularly so about matters which concerned me, was the first to tell me about our visitor.

'My Lord Kensington has arrived,' she said, 'and I have heard that he comes to France on a very special mission.'

I replied that when foreign noblemen came to Court it was usually on some special mission.

'I believe he is a great friend of the Duke of Buckingham, and as the Duke of Buckingham is the first favourite of the King of England and known to be a crony of the Prince of Wales, does that suggest anything to you?'

'That his visit might be more than just for personal pleasure.'

'The Prince of Wales is of an age to marry.'

'I believe so and it was for that purpose that he went courting in Spain. Perhaps Lord Kensington calls on us now as the Prince of Wales and Duke of Buckingham did when they were on their way to Spain.'

'The Spanish arrangement no longer exists. The Prince and Duke were not pleased with their reception in Spain.'

'You mean he is not going to marry the Infanta?'

'I do mean that. It is said that he looks elsewhere for a bride.'

I felt myself go cold suddenly, as though – as Mamie would say – someone were walking over my grave.

'Who?' I heard myself whisper.

Mamie took me by the shoulder and replied, smiling: 'Who else?'

From then on my thoughts were in a turmoil. I quickly realized that Mamie's surmise was not without foundation.

I was torn by contrasting emotions. There was pleasure . . . excitement . . . but always apprehension. He had decided against the Princess of Spain. What if he should do the same in the case of the Princess of France.

I knew there was no doubt of what was afoot when my mother sent for me.

All the way to her apartments I tried to tell myself that she wanted to see me about a masque which Anne was devising and in which I was to play a prominent part. As we had a visiting lord from England it might be that she wished us to perform something special.

But, of course, it was nothing to do with the masque.

I curtsied to my mother, who beckoned me to come closer. She laid her hands on my shoulders and said: 'You have grown into a very pretty young woman, Henriette. I am glad. That will please your husband.'

I did not answer and she went on: 'I have good news for you. It may well be that you will be the bride of the Prince of Wales. You understand what that means? You will, in due course, be Queen of England.'

I tried to look greatly impressed but I was only extremely nervous.

'I always wanted crowns for you children. Elizabeth has hers, and now it is your turn, my daughter . . . although of course it is not yet yours. I want you to do all you can to please Lord Kensington who will carry back a report to his master. You are to have a miniature painted and he will take it back with him to England. I am sure we shall get a lovely picture. Stand up straight, child. It is a pity you do not grow a few more inches.' She looked at me critically. I had always been a little self-conscious about my height for I was an inch or so shorter than most people of my age. Mamie used to say: 'Little and good. You are dainty and feminine. Who wants to be a strapping hoyden?' But I could see that my mother did not agree with that and was regretting that my lack of height might be a handicap in the matrimonial stakes.

I tried to stand as tall as I could.

'That's better,' she said. 'Now when you meet Lord Kensington make sure you hold yourself erect. Talk to him confidently. Do not mention that you know about the trip to Spain. It is better to say nothing of that. But it is a stroke of luck for us that it was not successful and it leaves the Prince of Wales free for us.'

I was dismissed and went immediately to Mamie to report the conversation.

'It seems very certain that there will be an offer of marriage,' she said.

'If I go to England you are coming with me.'

'Of course I shall come with you. I'll be the chief maid of honour. You couldn't go without me.'

'I wouldn't go at all . . . unless you came too.'

'There!' said Mamie, speaking more lightly than she felt; knowing the world far better than I she could see difficulties looming ahead, but I did not understand all this until later. 'It will be interesting to be in England,' she said quickly, 'if we go that is . . . to be among strange people. We'll find lots to amuse us, I don't doubt.'

She discovered that Lord Kensington was staying with the Duc and Duchesse de Chevreuse. I liked the Duchesse very much; she was very beautiful and vivacious and had a reputation for being what was called "a little naughty".

'I'll swear my Lord Kensington is enjoying his stay with the Duc and Duchesse,' said Mamie. 'With the Duchesse in any case . . . so rumour has it.'

She made a point of discovering all she could about Lord Kensington, so that when I met him I should not be at a disadvantage. He was Henry Rich, the son of Penelope Rich who was the daughter of the Countess of Leicester – so his step-grandfather was the famous Leicester who had become notorious as the favourite of Queen Elizabeth. Lord Kensington was an extraordinarily handsome man – tall, with very gracious manners, and I could see why he was a temptation to the Duchesse's not very strict morals.

My mother presented me with a certain pride, and he took my hand and, bowing very deferentially, kissed it.

I must forgive him, he said, if he appeared dumbfounded. I might have retorted that he did not appear in the least so. But he was overwhelmed by my charms. He had heard of my beauty but no accounts could do justice to the reality.

Such fulsome flattery should, of course, have irritated me but it did not. I delighted in it and I conversed with him for fifteen minutes before my mother broke up the meeting. She was smiling benignly and I was not quite sure whether this meant that she was pleased with my performance or whether it was merely the facial expression politeness demanded. If it were not the former, I had no doubt that I should hear in due course.

At the masque I had an opportunity of speaking to the Duchesse de Chevreuse who was present with her husband and Lord Kensington. I danced with the Queen and we were very loudly applauded, but I was most eager to have a word with the Duchesse about Lord Kensington.

I said to her: 'Lord Kensington seems to be a very happy guest.'

The Duchesse laughed. It seemed to me that she was constantly laughing; she had reason to be content; she was very pretty and had something beyond prettiness. I noticed how her eyes sparkled as they rested on certain gentlemen, and I was aware of the warm responses she had from them.

'Oh, Madame Henriette, I assure you he is a most contented guest.'

'Does he talk to you much of the English Court?'

'Constantly. He is devoted to Prince Charles and the Duke of Buckingham.'

'So he talks of them?'

'Most glowingly. He says that the Prince of Wales is the most cultivated and handsome gentleman he ever set eyes on.'

'Does he mention that journey to Spain?'

'Oh that. A fiasco . . . nothing more. My Lord Kensington says he is grateful for it. If it had succeeded that would have been an unhappy day for the Prince.'

'Is that what he truly says?'

'Yes . . . now his envoys have come to France. I can tell you this: the Prince is very handsome.'

'How can you know? Did you see him when he came here as Tom Smith or was it John Brown?'

'No. But I have seen a miniature of the Prince, which Lord Kensington keeps on a ribbon about his neck. It is hidden by his coat.'

'But you have seen it!'

She laughed and put her lips to my ear. 'Many times,' she whispered. 'I say to my lord: "Let me see the picture." I declare he grows quite jealous. He demands to know whether I think the Prince more handsome than he is.'

'And do you?'

'Strictly for your ears . . . yes. Though of course the Prince is young but my Lord Kensington is a man well practised in the ways of love.' She evidently thought she had betrayed too much for she put her hand over her lips and giggled.

I was not very interested in her affairs, but I kept thinking about the miniature which hung round Lord Kensington's neck. I longed to look on the face of Prince Charles.

I told Mamie what the Duchesse had said and she herself asked Lord Kensington to show her the miniature. This he did readily and Mamie said that it was indeed a handsome face depicted there. She told me that he withdrew the ribbon from where it was hidden and displayed the miniature to several of the ladies who had gathered round.

'It seems,' I said coldly, 'that everyone has seen this picture except me.'

'I think,' replied Mamie, 'it would be considered unseemly if you showed a great interest in the picture at this stage.'

'Yet how I long to see it. I think I should be the one to see it first.'

'As soon as there has been agreement between the English ambassadors and your mother, you can ask to see it. But I think you can hardly show a great interest before that.'

I grew angry to think that all my ladies knew what he looked like and that I did not, so I decided to act. When I next saw the Duchesse de Chevreuse, I asked her if she could procure the portrait at the right moment . . . and bring it to me.

The Duchesse, who loved intrigue, swore she would do it. 'The very next time he takes it off,' she said, 'which he does . . .' she smiled at me, 'on occasions. . . .'

Within a day or so the portrait was in my hands.

My fingers trembled as I opened it for it was in a gold locket. And there he was! My heart leaped as I looked at it. He was handsome, yes, but there was a fineness – a refinement – about his features . . . something almost ethereal, which I found enchanting.

I could not stop looking at it, and I held it in my hands for the best part of an hour until I knew every part of that handsome face, and the more I looked the happier I felt.

When I gave the picture back to the Duchesse I thanked her for her help. She said that Lord Kensington had missed the locket and she had told him where it was.

'It did not seem to disturb him in the least. In fact I think he was very happy about the matter. He assured me that the Prince of Wales is even more handsome than his portrait.'

Matters were progressing very fast and Lord Kensington asked my mother if she would permit him to have a private interview with me.

After some hesitation she allowed this and I spent a pleasant half hour in the company of the man who, everyone was saying, was not only the English envoy but the lover of Madame de Chevreuse.

He was very courteous to me and implied again that he thought me very pretty. He said he would go back to England and tell his Prince what a charming Princess I was, and that any man who had the good fortune to marry me would be very lucky.

This was the sort of talk which delighted me.

'Doubtless you have some growing to do yet,' he said, and that was the only allusion to my somewhat short stature.

Then he told me about the Court of England. 'Less elegant, I fear, than yours here in Paris, but we manage to enjoy life.'

I replied that I could well imagine *he* did that wherever he went.

He told me that he very much hoped to complete his mission successfully. 'My Prince is a very impatient man where some matters are concerned,' he said, his eyes twinkling.

I liked him very much and during those days I lived in a whirl of excitement.

It was Mamie who told me that everything was not going as smoothly as they had at first expected.

'If you married Prince Charles there would have to be a dispensation from the Pope,' she said, 'because of the difference in religion. Catholic France and Protestant England.'

'If ever I became Queen of England I should try to save my subjects from damnation,' I replied firmly.

'Yes,' said Mamie lightly, 'but what if they should determine to save you?'

'How could they? I am a Catholic and therefore saved.'

She looked at me with her head on one side as she did sometimes but she did not pursue the matter; but when I had interviews with my mother which I did constantly at this time, she impressed on me the need to remember always that I was a Catholic and that it was my duty to bring people to the true Faith.

But Charles, the handsome young man in the miniature, what of him?

"It is the English,' my mother explained. 'They insist on their Kings being Protestant. It is very misguided of them and your first task will be to bring *him* to the true Faith . . . if there should be a marriage.'

I thought about it and burned with zeal. I imagined Charles in time thanking me. 'But for your coming I should have died in ignorance. I should have spent eternity burning in hell.'

It was a pretty picture.

Then there was Mère Magdalaine who was constantly advising me. If it should be God's will that I should go to England I must not give myself up to frivolous pleasures. I must remember that I had a duty there.

There came a time when it seemed that the marriage might not take place. There were too many difficulties, but the main one was the difference in religion. The English were very reluctant to accept a Catholic Queen. They had deplored the idea of a Spanish marriage – for they saw the Spaniards as their greatest enemies; but because an alliance with that country through marriage had been mooted and had come to nothing they were so pleased and almost ready to accept the French proposition as the lesser of two evils. But, of course, the religious aspect still persisted, and it was growing to such proportions that the Duke of Buckingham – who was in charge of negotiations and eager to see them successful – came to the conclusion that Lord Kensington, suave and charming court gallant though he might be, was not capable of handling complicated politics. So he sent out Lord Carlisle.

It was some time afterwards that I discovered why the marriage almost did not take place.

The matter of Frederick and the Palatinate which had put an end to the Spanish negotiations cropped up again. King James wanted the Palatinate restored to his son-in-law, but the French had no wish to support Germany, which was staunchly Protestant.

There was another reason for delay. The French wanted King James to promise to protect Catholics in England and without his promise they refused to conclude a marriage treaty so it certainly seemed at one point that marriage negotiations were about to be broken off and I should have to forget the handsome face in the miniature, which had haunted my dreams since I had seen it.

I suppose my brother and my mother thought that if this marriage did not come about it might be difficult for me to find another opportunity as good as this one and decided that it was better to be a little lenient if by being so they could get me to England where I might be instrumental in doing good work for the Catholic cause.

A great deal of all this I learned later but the fact was that my brother and Lord Carlisle talked together privately and my brother hinted that the English King need not take the religious controversy too seriously. If he would just give his word that the Catholics might practise their religion privately all might be well.

Both sides hesitated. But the English, no less than the French, were eager for the marriage and finally they decided to make concessions to each other.

I was to have full freedom to worship in the true Faith; I was to be given control of the religious instruction of any children I should have up to the age of thirteen; I was to have my own chapel wherever I was, together with my priests and almoners and chaplains.

The next step was to get the dispensation from Rome.

It came at length and with it was a letter for me written by the Holy Father himself. I felt weighed down with responsibility when I read it.

It was simply because I was going to be Queen of a heretic country that he was giving the dispensation. I should have power – perhaps even over my husband – and it would be my duty to devote myself to the salvation of him and his poor sad subjects. I had the opportunity of being like Queen Esther – the Jewish virgin – who was chosen to be his Queen by the Persian King Ahasuerus and who brought about the deliverance of her people, or like Bertha who married Ethelbert of Kent – in that very country to which I was going – and converted him and spread Christianity among the Anglo Saxons. The eyes of the Catholic world would be turned on me.

My fingers shook as I penned my reply to the Holy Father. I assured him that I was aware of the great task which lay ahead of me and that I would endeavour with all my heart to carry out the work assigned to me by Heaven, and to raise my children in the Catholic Faith.

After I had written that letter I knelt and prayed that God would give me the strength to do what I had to do.

So with the Pope's dispensation, there was no longer need for delay. Preparations for the proxy wedding began. It was decided that May would be the best month. It was then March.

News came from England that King James was ill. No one thought he was near to death so therefore it was a shock when on that cold March day news came to Paris that he was dead and his son, my bridegroom-to-be, was King Charles the First of England.

It was a beautiful May morning when I was escorted to the episcopal residence where I was dressed for my wedding. It would only be a proxy wedding and it seemed very strange to be married to a man whom I had never seen, although such an arrangement was commonplace in royal circles. At least I had seen a miniature of him. I wondered if he were thinking the same of me. But perhaps he would have other matters than his wedding with which to occupy himself as he had, only two months before, become a King.

I stood very still while they dressed me. I could not help feeling happy to wear such clothes. Clothes always had an effect on me and I believe I could not have been completely unhappy while I was wearing a beautiful gown. Of course I was very young then and perhaps more thoughtless and frivolous than many of my age. Now I stood patiently while they put on my gown. It was made of cloth of gold and silver and the material was spattered with golden fleur-de-lys and here and there diamonds twinkled on it. My mother had said I must have the most elaborate of dresses to match the Duke of Buckingham, who would most surely be elegantly attired. At that time it had been thought that he would be my proxy bridegroom but he had been unable to leave England because his presence was necessary there on account of the death of the late King.

Strangely enough the choice of proxy had fallen on the Duc de Chevreuse because he was a distant connection of King Charles. I wondered fleetingly if he would be reminded of his own wedding and whether he regretted having married his fascinating wife, who seemed to create scandal wherever she was.

Mamie hovered about me while they placed the little crown on my head. It was very becoming.

'Crowns suit you,' she said.

I smiled happily. I should have to go away but as she would come with me my qualms were considerably reduced.

The morning slipped quickly away and I was glad when we set out for Notre Dame. It was a very slow procession that passed to the west door of Notre Dame for we were to be married outside the cathedral as La Reine Margot and my father had been because marriage in which one of the participants was a Protestant could not take place inside.

The Swiss guards and trumpeters were followed by a great assembly of knights, heralds and marshals. Then I came in my beautiful glittering dress with Louis on one side of me and my brother Gaston on the other – followed by my mother and Queen Anne.

As we neared the platform, which had been placed at the west door, and I stepped under the canopy, my brother Louis stood aside and the Duc de Chevreuse came to stand beside me. He looked very handsome in black velvet with slits in his jacket to show a lining of cloth of gold. Across his chest was a sash covered in diamonds, and as diamonds also sparkled on his coat he glittered almost as much as I did.

So I was married – albeit by proxy – to the King of England.

After the ceremony I went into the cathedral to celebrate Mass with my family, but the Duc de Chevreuse, as proxy for King Charles, did not join us and went off with Lord Kensington, as Charles would have done had he been present. This incident called attention to the differences in my religion and that of my bridegroom and I felt a little sad while I burned with zeal to begin his conversion.

After Mass I could return to the episcopal residence and rest awhile before the banquet began. I spent the time with Mamie, who chattered excitedly about the ceremony and the splendour of my diamonds and those of the Duc de Chevreuse.

It was a merry banquet which took place that evening. I sat at the head of the table on the right-hand side of my brother, and my mother was on the other side of me. I noticed that they paid a new deference to me. I was no longer little Madame Henriette; I had become a Queen.

Afterwards I danced with the Duc de Chevreuse as my partner and I tried to see, instead of his face, the one in the miniature; then I danced with Louis and after that Anne and I did one of our special ballets. I felt excited dancing with Anne because I could remind myself that we were now of equal rank.

It was not an unhappy day by any means though an exhausting one, and I was really rather glad to get out of my splendid gown and lie down to sleep.

'This is my wedding night,' I said to Mamie.

She plumped up the pillows and said: 'It will not be long before you sleep with your bridegroom beside you.'

I was thoughtful and she suddenly put her arms about me and held me tightly.

'He has a kind and gentle face,' she said reassuringly.

And that was my wedding night.

Lord Kensington was made Earl of Holland as a reward for having brought about the marriage and two weeks after the ceremony the Duke of Buckingham came to France. He created quite a stir. He was so debonair and so handsome; and he brought with him a most magnificent wardrobe. 'All the clothes,' said Mamie, 'that he had intended to wear as proxy bridegroom.'

When he was first presented to me he was dressed in white satin covered with diamonds. Mamie heard that the suit alone – considering the number of precious stones on it – was valued at twenty thousand pounds. And that was just one outfit. He loved diamonds and everything he possessed was decorated with them; they were in his hat and even the feather was decorated with them; and they were on the hilt of his sword and on his spurs.

It was as though he wanted everyone to know how rich and important he was. In fact, it has been said that he was the most important man in England. King James had doted on him – but then King James was apt to dote on handsome young men; and now he had become the close friend and adviser to Charles. He had arrived ostensibly to escort me to England but Mamie believed he might have other motives as well. He wanted to make an alliance with my country against Spain.

However, there he was in all his glory and glitter, behaving as though he was an equal of my brother, my mother and the young Queen. There were great festivities to honour him, for we were still celebrating the wedding and it had been decided that after a week of entertainments for the Duke, we should begin the journey to England.

I was not to be torn completely from my family just at first, for my mother with Louis, Anne and Gaston were to accompany me as far as the coast. There I should leave them and cross the Channel in the company of the Duke of Buckingham, and Kensington – now Earl of Holland. The Duc de Chevreuse as my proxy bridegroom was to stay with me until I was passed over to my real one; and as the Duc came, so did his flighty Duchesse. I was quite reconciled to leaving my country – after all none of my family had been very affectionate towards me – as long as I was accompanied by Mamie as my chief lady in waiting.

It was a merry party and as we passed people came hurrying out of their houses to cheer us. There was intrigue afoot – romantic intrigue. This would always occur where the Duchesse de Chevreuse happened to be. What could be more exciting for her than to have a lover actually in the party.

Mamie said that she and the Earl of Holland were quite blatant and she wondered the Duc de Chevreuse was not aware of the flagrant immorality of his wife.

It was not long before the behaviour of another couple in our entourage began to demand our notice. Mamie mentioned it to me.

We had ridden far and she was helping me to bed one night when she said: 'Have you noticed the Duke of Buckingham and the Queen?'

'What of them?' I asked.

'It would seem that the Duke is romantically inclined towards the Queen.'

'Anne!'

'Anne indeed. I must say it does not surprise me. Louis is a most negligent husband.'

'The Duke just admires her.'

'And she likes to be admired.'

'You're imagining this. I believe you do imagine things.'

'Perhaps . . . a little. But I have a sharp pair of eyes.'

We talked of other things, but the next day when we continued
our journey I did notice that Buckingham contrived to ride beside
the Queen and engage her in conversation. There was a great
deal of laughter, and Anne's eyes sparkled with delight while my
Lord Buckingham appeared to be very pleased with himself.

So although I lacked a husband in the flesh, what with the
accomplished affaire of the Duchesse and Holland, which was
carried on quite blatantly in the presence of the cuckolded
husband, and the aspirations of the Duke of Buckingham
towards the Queen, I was beginning to learn a great deal about
existing morals.

We had not gone very far – Compiègne as a matter of fact –
when Louis began to have one of his shivering fits. Our mother
was greatly concerned and insisted that we stop while physicians
were called. This threw a slight gloom over the proceedings and
several of the festivities which had been arranged for us were
cancelled. I was not very disappointed about this, much as I loved
dancing and singing and all that went to make up these entertainments, for it was rather refreshing to have a few quiet
evenings in Mamie's company.

My mother came to my room in the morning looking rather
grave.

'The King is suffering from fever. I don't think it would be wise
for him to continue with his journey,' she said.

I could not believe she was worried about Louis for himself.
They did not like each other. That had been obvious when the
Maréchal d'Ancre had died. At the same time Louis' death or
long illness would plunge the country into disorder. There was
no child of the King's marriage, and I did not know how my
mother felt about my brother Gaston who would be the next in
line to the throne. However, for whatever reason, there was no
doubt that she was deeply concerned about my brother's health.

'I shall rely on what the physicians have to say,' she went on. 'If
they advise him to rest here, the question will be whether to wait
with him or pursue our journey, but I do think it is necessary for
you to get to England as soon as possible.'

I bowed my head. I wondered why she was saying this to me. It
was not as though my opinion would count. But I had forgotten. I
was a Queen now.

'So . . .' went on my mother, 'if the physicians think it is wise

for him to remain in Compiègne, the rest of the party will continue the journey.'

'Yes, Madame,' I said.

'Perhaps a good night's sleep will cure him.'

It did not. And during the next day it was decided that the
journey should continue without Louis.

When we came to Amiens, my mother was very tired and
admitted that she found the journey exhausting. It was not only
the arduous travelling conditions which she had to endure, but
there were the festivities which had been arranged in the villages
and towns through which we passed. She looked very pale and
when we arrived at the *château* where we were to spend the night,
she fainted.

There was no doubt that she was ill. We called the doctors and
the verdict was the same with her as it had been with my brother.
Rest was needed.

There followed a conference. The Duke of Buckingham seemed
to welcome a little delay, which I was sure had something to do
with his pursuit of the Queen, and he said there was no need for
great haste. He would send messengers to the King to explain
why our progress was interrupted. He was of the opinion that we
should not proceed without the Queen Mother, for we had
already shed the King on the way and it would seem as though
the journey were ill-fated if we had to go on without another such
important member of the party.

The Earl of Holland warmly agreed with this. Their reasons
were identical, but the Duke of Buckingham's were more urgent
than those of the Earl of Holland for the latter's mistress would
accompany the party to England so he would not be deprived of
her company for some time. It was different with Buckingham;
the Queen would leave us when we sailed; and he still had his
courting to do, it seemed.

'At least,' commented Mamie, 'we hope so. I would not like to
think that the royal House of France might have a little cuckoo in
the nest . . . even though the little bird had the blood of such a
noble Duke.'

'For shame!' I cried.

And she laughed at me. Her attitude had changed since 'my

marriage'. She referred to me often as 'Your Majesty' and 'the Queen,' and she behaved as though I had suddenly become experienced of the world, which was far from the truth of course.

However we stayed at Amiens and, without the strict supervision of the Queen Mother, morals became more lax than usual.

Ladies and gentlemen paired off and not always with their legal partners. We were lodged in a large mansion surrounding which were beautiful grounds and in which there was a walled garden. It was rather overgrown but there were paths through the trees, and it soon became the favourite haunt of lovers.

One of my mother's elderly women brought this to her notice and as a result orders were given that this garden should be kept locked at night. This could be quite easily managed for there was a gate leading to it. The key of the garden was left with the Captain of the Guard, who was ordered to make sure it was locked at dusk and not opened until the morning.

I did not know what happened exactly, but it appeared that one night the Queen with some of her ladies ordered the Captain of the Guard to give her the key of the garden. He did not know what to do. The Queen Mother had said he was to keep it in his possession, but here was the Queen ordering it to be given up. Anne cajoled – she could be very persuasive – she threatened and she could be ominous. Poor man, he did what most men would have done in the circumstances; he gave up the key.

Several ladies with their gallants were in the garden that night and among them was the mischievous Duchesse de Chevreuse with the Earl of Holland. In fact it was she who had put the idea of getting the key into Anne's head. The Duchesse was a woman who lived dangerously, and like so many of her kind, not content with going the way she wanted to, she was anxious that others should follow her example. I believed she had urged the Queen to encourage Buckingham while her lover Holland did all he could to help the Duke to success with the Queen.

I was not present on this occasion, of course. Why should I want to walk in the darkening gardens? I was in my bed so only heard of the incident from my usual source; but I could be sure Mamie would get the entire story.

'It was like this,' she said. 'The ladies and gentlemen were in the garden walking through the paths to sequestered spots where they settled down to rest for a while. The Queen soon discovered that the Duke of Buckingham was her companion. Imagine them . . . wandering in the darkness. He would put his arm through hers and tell her how beautiful she was and mention that it was a great shame that the King should be so neglectful and seem unaware of her dazzling charms.'

'Anne would like to hear that,' I commented.

'Most young people would – particularly those who have an indifferent husband. The Queen is very young and my Lord Buckingham . . . well, he is not so young. He is thirty-three if he is a day and experienced in all ways of making love, so I have heard. Therefore one would have thought he would have been more subtle on this occasion. He had misjudged his . . . I was going to say victim . . . but perhaps it is *lèse majesté* to talk thus of the Queen.'

'Oh, get on with the story,' I cried impatiently.

'Well, suddenly a shrill scream rent the air. Imagine it! A moment of silence and then all the attendants running to the spot where the Queen stood . . . wide-eyed, hands across her breast as though to protect herself . . . and standing close by looking as near sheepish as such an arrogant Duke could look . . . my Lord Buckingham.'

'What did it mean?' I asked.

'It could mean only one thing. Our Duke made a mistake. He must have attempted to force his attentions on the Queen. He did not realize that all she wanted was words . . . gestures . . . certainly not actions. I will tell Your Majesty something: This will be the end of that little affaire. Perhaps it is as well that it was only a little one. Queens, Your Majesty, must be beyond reproach.'

The next day everyone was talking about the scream in the garden. I was glad no one mentioned it to my mother. I wondered what would have happened to the Captain of the Guard who had relinquished the key if she had known.

My mother's health improved a little but her doctors thought that the journey to Calais would be too tiring for her and bring on a recurrence of her malady so it was decided that she should come no farther. Gaston was the only member of my family who would go with me until I left French soil.

Our waiting in Amiens had therefore been unnecessary for my mother rose from her sick bed and accompanied the party through the town and then took her leave of us.

She embraced me with what seemed like real affection on parting. She told me that her thoughts would always be with me and she would follow my progress with the utmost attention. She entreated me to be a good wife and she trusted I would bear many children. I must always remember that I was royal – the daughter of a King and Queen of France. I must never forget the country of my birth, and there were no matters as important as my faith and my royalty. I was going to a heretic land. God had selected me as he had St Paul and St Peter. I was to carry on with my duty and never cease until my husband and the whole of England were saved for the Truth.

It seemed a daunting task, but I promised that I would do what I could and would always remember my faith, my loyalty and my country.

As she embraced me she thrust a letter into my hands.

That night I read the letter. It was long and it stressed her love for me. She reminded me that I had lost my earthly father and only had God for my father now. I must never forget what I owed Him. He had given me to a great King and had sent me to England where He would require my services, and this would mean that through what I did there I could attain eternal salvation.

'Remember that you are a daughter of the Church by baptism and that it is indeed the first and highest rank which you have or ever will have, since it is this which will give you your entrance into Heaven. . . . Be, after the example of St Louis from whom you are descended, firm and zealous for religion, which you have been taught and for which your royal and holy ancestor exposed his life. Never listen to or suffer to be said in your presence aught in contradiction to your belief in God. . . .'

I read and reread that letter. I knew what was expected of me. I was going to a strange country. I was going to a husband whom I must strive to bring to the true Faith. I had a great responsibility.

As I read the letter I swore to God and to myself that I would do everything in my power to bring the true Faith to England.

The next night news was brought to us that there was plague at Calais and it would be dangerous for us to go there, so we must divert our course to Boulogne.

Before we could set out next morning, the Duke of Buckingham came to me in a state of great urgency.

'Your Majesty,' he said, 'I have this morning received communications from King Charles. It will be necessary for me to
return to Amiens that I may present these papers to the Queen
Mother.'

I was very well aware that he had received no papers, and I did
in fact confirm this later when I discovered there had been no
messenger from England. But Anne had stayed behind in
Amiens with my mother and for that reason he wanted to go back
to see her before he left for England.

'You must admit,' said Mamie, 'that our Duke is no laggard
when it comes to love.'

I was angry at the delay. It seemed that our journey was ill-
fated. First there was my brother's ill health, then my mother's,
and after that, plague at Calais, and now Buckingham was
darting off to suit his whims.

It was too much to be endured.

I abused Buckingham in no quiet voice and it was some time
before I would listen to Mamie's pleas to calm myself.

Then I began to wonder whether I was in any great hurry to
leave my native land, and the enormity of what was happening to
me was brought home to me. I felt there was a vague menace in
the air. I was going into a strange land among strangers.

So when Buckingham did return I was not so very eager to
resume our journey, for every day . . . every hour that passed
carried me farther away from the life I had known.

At length we came to Boulogne. The ship was waiting for us
and as I stepped aboard there was a discharge of ordnance to
mark the significance of the occasion. Mamie was close beside
me. She smiled at me reassuringly.

I was on deck watching the coastline of my country slowly
disappear from view and I felt afraid and very vulnerable on that
seething grey sea. The ship lurched and Mamie persuaded me to
go below.

The uncomfortable journey seemed to go on interminably, but
I think I was too emotionally disturbed to notice the discomforts
as some of the others did.

In due course we came close to land. I went on deck and had
my first glimpse of the white cliffs.

My new life had begun.

Discord in the Royal Apartments

It was seven o'clock on that Sunday evening when I set foot on English soil. An assembly of gentlemen was waiting to receive me and an artificial bridge had been set up so that I could disembark easily. This, I was told, had been ordered by the King who was at that time at Canterbury, which was not very far from Dover, and there he was eagerly awaiting news of my arrival.

I wondered then why he was not at Dover and would have impulsively asked this if I had not had to speak through an interpreter, for I felt more than a little annoyed that he had not been there to greet me.

I was informed that a message would be sent to the King immediately to tell him of my coming and he should be with me in less than an hour.

I replied – somewhat imperiously, Mamie said afterwards – that I was too tired to receive anyone that evening. The journey had been exhausting and I needed food and rest.

I was told that it should be as I wished and we proceeded at once to the castle where it had been arranged that I should spend the night.

The castle was near the coast and I hated it from the moment I saw it. It was very gloomy, quite unlike the Louvre, Chenonceaux, Chambord . . . those castles to which I was accustomed, and as my footsteps rang out on the bare boards I noticed how shabby everything was.

I said that I would retire to my apartments without delay for more than anything I needed rest. Perhaps some food could be brought for my lady of honour and myself. I made it clear that I wished to see no one until the morning.

At least they seemed eager to comply with my wishes and I was immediately conducted to my apartment. I gasped with horror when I saw it. There were tapestries on the walls but they were dingy and dusty. Mamie went to the bed and felt it. It was hard and lumpy. I had never seen such a bed in any of our French castles or palaces. And this was the room they had prepared for the Queen of England!

'Never mind,' said Mamie. 'Don't get angry. You can change everything later. But just for tonight accept it.'

'Don't they want me here?'

'Of course they want you! You have to remember that they do not live in the style that we do. They are barbarians compared with us.'

'What of men like the Duke of Buckingham and the Earl of Holland? They are as elegant as any Frenchman.'

'Perhaps it is just their castles which are different. But never mind about that now. We need rest. Everything will look better in the morning.'

'I don't think this place will ever look better. It will be worse when the sunlight picks out the horrors and shows them to us more clearly.'

But as usual she soothed me. We ate a little together and then she helped me to bed.

Tired as I was it was not easy to sleep. All the excitement I had felt through the wedding and festivities had disappeared and in its place was a growing apprehension.

But Mamie was right. I did feel better in the daylight, for even though it showed up the threadbare state of the bedcurtains, it lit up those dark corners and eliminated the shadows which had been so disturbing on the previous night. Breakfast was brought to the apartment and Mamie and I were eating it when a messenger came into the room.

He bowed respectfully and said: 'Pardon the intrusion, Your Majesty, but the King has arrived from Canterbury and he wishes you to know that he is waiting to see you.'

I stood up. I would see him without delay. This was the moment for which I had been waiting ever since I had seen the portrait of him and knew I was to be his wife.

Mamie was looking at me anxiously, warning me not to be over-impulsive. I smiled at her. 'He is my husband,' I reminded her, 'and I am naturally all eagerness to meet him.'

She tidied my hair and smoothed my gown. 'You look enchanting,' she whispered and kissed me.

Then I descended the stairs to the hall.

I was aware of a figure standing there and I went forward swiftly and was about to kneel and say what I had been taught I must say on our first meeting, that I had come to His Majesty's country to be commanded by him . . . but the words would not come, my voice broke with emotion and I felt the tears gushing to my eyes, while he caught me up in his arms.

He was very tender. He took his kerchief and wiped my eyes; then he kissed my forehead and my tear-stained cheeks . . . not once but several times.

'Why,' he said softly in French, for I had no English, 'I must kiss you until you cease to weep. You are not with enemies and strangers, you must know. It is God's will that you and I are here and does He not tell you to leave your kindred and cling to your husband?'

I nodded in agreement.

'Well then,' he said gently. 'All is well. As for myself . . . I will not be so much a master to you as a servant to cherish you and make you happy.'

It seemed to me that no husband could have used kinder words and I began to feel better.

'Now we will sit down and talk together,' he said. 'You shall get to know me and you will realize that this marriage of ours is not a matter for sorrow but for joy.'

He took my hand and led me to a window seat where we sat side by side.

I was able to take a glance at him. He was of medium height and I was relieved that he was not very tall as that would have accentuated my low stature. He was not as handsome as the picture in the miniature, but he was pleasant looking. There was, however, a certain melancholy aspect about him which had not been apparent in the miniature and which alarmed me faintly.

It might have been that I was a trifle disappointed in his looks but his kindness was comforting. He clearly did not seem disappointed in my looks, for I caught a glimpse of admiration in his eyes, and as others thought I was pretty I guessed he did too.

It occurred to me then that my portrait might have under-rated my attractions, for Mamie had often said that my vivacity was a very large part of my charm. I think a little liveliness might have improved him. I definitely had the impression in that first half hour that he was inclined to be morose.

He told me that we should leave for Canterbury later in the day and stay the night there. He had been there when he had heard of my arrival and had set out immediately, accomplishing the journey in half an hour, which was something of a record and showed his eagerness to be with his bride.

'You must present me to your attendants who have come with you,' he said. 'And I will present your English ones to you.'

'I daresay I shall make mistakes,' I replied. 'Matters are conducted differently here from the way they are in France, and I do not even know the language.'

'You will quickly learn,' he reassured me.

'If I make mistakes you must tell me.'

He smiled at me very gravely and tenderly. I wished he had joked a little though, brought some lightness into the conversation; but of course that was not his nature. I thought then, they could not have found a partner for me more different from myself.

He took my hand and I stood up. I came up to his shoulder and I saw by the way he looked at me that he suspected I was wearing high heels to give me height. He must have heard exaggerated reports of my low stature.

I said at once: 'My heels are flat.' I raised my skirts and held out a foot to confirm this. 'I stand on my own feet and have no help through art to make me taller. This high I am . . . neither taller nor lower.'

He took my hand and kissed it.

'You are beautiful,' he said. 'I think ours will be a happy marriage.'

I wondered even then. There was so much I did not know about England and I had already been amazed – as had my attendants – that they could have housed their Queen even for one night in that shabby old castle. And Charles my husband? He lacked the gaiety of Englishmen like the Duke of Buckingham and the Earl of Holland; there was something very serious indeed about him which I had already detected. Perhaps I should have rejoiced in that. I was not sure.

I presented my attendants to him and he in turn introduced those whom he had chosen to attend me. These meetings passed off comfortably and it was not until the carriage arrived to take us to Canterbury that the trouble arose.

I was walking with Charles, and Mamie was a pace or so behind, for I had told her to keep close and not lose sight of me.

'I want to see you there all the time,' I had said, 'that is until I get used to these people.'

'Don't worry,' she had replied. 'I will be there.'

The King's coach was waiting and he took my hand and helped me in. I sat down and Mamie got in beside me. The King stared at her as though thunderstruck.

'Madame,' he said, 'pray leave the royal coach at once.'

Mamie turned pale while I looked on disbelievingly. At home the chief lady of honour always rode with my mother and the chief gentleman with the King.

She rose uncertainly but I cried out: 'She shall ride with me.'

'There is no place for her in my coach,' said the King.

Mamie gave me an appealing glance and prepared to step out of the coach, but I caught her skirt and would not let her go. I never could control my temper and it was rising now. It seemed desperately important to me that Mamie should ride in the coach. Charles must learn what she meant to me, and I would not have her insulted in this way.

Poor Mamie! For once she did not know what to do. The King was glaring at her, ordering her to go, while I held her skirts firmly in my hands and ordered her to stay.

I looked steadily at my husband and there must have been defiance in my eyes – more than that, hatred. He looked back at me . . . coldly, but a little bewildered I noticed.

I said coolly: 'If my chief lady of honour does not ride in the coach then I will not either.'

'She shall travel with the rest of the attendants,' said the King.

'She is my special friend and she has always ridden with me in my carriage and she shall do so now and if she does not I shall stay in this dirty old castle until I can return to my country.'

It was wild nonsense really. As if I could return! As if *that* would be allowed! I was irrevocably married to this cold-eyed man and in that moment I hated him. But I was never very logical in my rages. Mamie had pointed that out to me many times.

The King was white with anger. And this was the first day of our meeting! I knew that it did not augur well for the future.

There was deep silence all about us. I saw the Earl of Holland looking on in disbelief while in the face of the Duke of Buckingham there was the flicker of a smile. I had an idea that he was enjoying looking on at this – my first conflict with my husband.

I glared at the King. Mamie said afterwards that I looked like a wild-cat and she thought I was going to fly at him. I knew my eyes were blazing and I spat out my words so fast that many of the English had no idea what I was saying, which was perhaps just as well.

I suppose I was a little hysterical. I was like that when one of my rages took possession of me, and I knew that there was more to this than appeared on the surface. It was because I was so frightened that I let my anger get the better of me.

Charles had stepped out of the carriage. I thought he was going to drag Mamie out so I clung to her skirts. She looked at me entreatingly and muttered under her breath: 'Let me go. We must stop this scene. . . .'

But I would not let her go. I felt the hot and angry tears in my eyes and willed them not to fall. I was trembling but determined. If Mamie left the carriage, I told her fiercely, I should go too.

Several of the King's ministers had come to him. They seemed to surround him and there was a great deal of whispering going on. The incident could not have lasted more than a few minutes but it seemed much longer.

Then those about the King parted and Charles stepped into the carriage. For a few seconds I waited in trepidation for what would happen next. He seated himself next to me and signed for Mamie to take the seat opposite, which she did. Then the horses began to move forward.

For a few seconds I felt exultant. I had won. And then a mood of foreboding settled on me while I saw the King's glance sweep over Mamie. There was an implacable hatred in his face.

On the way to Canterbury we came to a place called Barham Downs. There pavilions had been set up and a banquet awaited us, and among those who greeted us were several English women whom the King presented to me as the ladies of my household.

I greeted them somewhat regally because I had brought the ladies of my household with me and I could not see that I should need more than I already had. But at least I was experienced enough to know that this was not the time to raise the question. We had had enough for one day in the upset over Mamie and the carriage. So I smiled and played the gracious Queen and my husband's expression grew a little less frigid. I was hungry and I did full justice to the food which had been prepared and I did feel it was rather pleasant to be in the open fields and watch the pennants fluttering in the light breeze and thinking that all this had been set up in this green field in honour of me.

My spirits continued to rise as the ancient town of Canterbury came into sight, for the approaches to the city were beautiful with the entire scene dominated by the cathedral's magnificent tower.

It was dusk when we arrived and a splendid feast awaited us. The King now seemed to have recovered his good humour and he smiled and talked to me at table, insisting on carving the meat for me himself, which was a great honour.

Father Sancy, my confessor, was watching me, and I knew this was because as it was a fast day I should not be eating meat – but I was hungry and I felt rebellious against authority no matter from what quarter it came. Moreover I was a little triumphant after my victory in the carriage, and while I ate heartily of the meat, which seemed to please the King, I avoided the eyes of my confessor. I would be ready with my excuses when I received his reprimand – as I surely would – and I would explain to him that as I had come to live in this country I must respect its customs. I hoped my confessor had not heard of the incident in the carriage.

After we had feasted the King said there would be a small personal ceremony of marriage. We *were* married it was true, but only by proxy and he wished to be present at his own ceremony. It would be quiet and quick . . . but nevertheless a ceremony of marriage.

So this was performed in the great hall of the city and everyone could be satisfied that we had taken our vows to each other personally.

I was appalled by the state of my apartments and the bed was certainly no better than the one I had slept in on the previous night. How strange that was, for this was my marriage bed which I was to share with the King. Were the English savages? How should I ever grow accustomed to living in such conditions?

Mamie helped me undress and dismissed the rest of the women so that we could be alone. I could see she was still shaken by the incident in the coach.

'It was wrong,' she said. 'You should not have insisted.'

'I do insist and I shall go on insisting that you ride in the carriage with me as you did in France.'

'We are not in France now,' she reminded me. 'When you live in a country you must conform to that country's customs . . . particularly if you are its Queen.'

'I shall conform to none . . . but my own. I will tell you what is wrong with these people. They are heretics . . . and that means they are little better than savages.'

'Be careful,' said Mamie.

'Am I the Queen or am I not?'

'You are the King's consort, which makes you a Queen, but your title comes through him.'

'You talk as though you are on their side.'

'I am always on your side. You know that well enough.'

Then we fell into each other's arms and hugged each other.

She was very serious. 'You know that tonight you will share the King's bed,' she reminded me. 'You know what is expected of you?'

I nodded.

I saw the worry in her eyes. 'You know you have to love your husband,' she said.

'I am not sure that I am going to do that. This afternoon in the coach I hated him.'

'Oh, my little Queen, I can see trouble for you if you do not control your rages.'

'My rage worked well today did it not? You rode in the carriage because I insisted.'

'I think it would have been better if I had quietly alighted and murmured apologies about not understanding the English customs. The King would have understood and that would have been an end to the matter.'

'The matter ended in triumph for me.'

'Let us hope that we have seen the end of it.'

'What is wrong with you? Why are you different today? You would have laughed in the old days.'

'These are not the old days. Try to remember that we are in a new country . . . and remember, too, that from now on it is our country.'

'I shall change it.'

'You talk like a child.'

I narrowed my eyes. 'Do I? My mother and the Pope himself have told me that I must change it. Are they children?'

'Oh take care, dear child, take care.'

I could not shake her out of her gravity, which was so unusual with her. I should have been quite angry with her if I hadn't known that the change in her was due to her concern for me.

But she could not rob me of my triumph over the carriage incident. I had won. There was no denying that. I did realize though that my own mother would have taken a very different view of my tantrums. I should have been lectured, punished and denied what I had demanded if that incident had taken place in France.

Now I had the night ahead to think of.

How different this from the royal *coucher* at the Louvre. The King was undressed by only two of his gentlemen which would have been considered very odd indeed and quite unroyal by the standards prevailing in France.

He came to me in that shabby old room and looked round it. At first I thought he was going to comment on its shabbiness – and perhaps apologize for it – but it seemed he was only making sure that we were alone.

Then he went to the door and locked it.

He looked different in his night attire – not nearly so formidable as he had in the carriage. He seemed to have forgotten all that now and in any case he had not appeared to be displeased with me but with Mamie, which struck me as very unfair.

He lay down on the bed and made me lie beside him; then he put his arms about me and began to tell me how happy he was that I was there and how my appearance pleased him and that it was our duty to have children.

I listened and waited.

I was passive in his embrace and found I was able to endure

what followed with a certain fortitude for I knew that it was part of the duties which were required of me.

I lay bewildered afterwards and wondered what people like Madame de Chevreuse, Buckingham and Holland found so exciting about it.

The King seemed rather pleased. I was tired out by all the emotions of the day and fell asleep quickly.

In the morning when I awoke the King had already left the bed and the door was unlocked. My ladies came in to help me with my toilette and Mamie looked at me questioningly.

I nodded. 'Yes. It happened.'

'And you . . . ?'

I shrugged my shoulders. 'It was no worse than I expected.'

Mamie said: 'I knew the King was kindly.'

But she continued to look uneasy and I guessed she was remembering the incident in the coach.

I burst out: 'I don't like England. I don't like the King. I want to go home.'

'Hush,' said Mamie. 'Don't let anyone hear you say that.'

Then I threw myself at her and refused to let go; she rocked me as she might a baby. I wanted to tell her how only she made it bearable here, how I was tired of being the Queen of England and wanted to go back to being merely a Princess of France.

'I want to go home!' I cried.

'Hush,' she said. 'Don't be a baby.'

We spent another night in Canterbury which was very like the first and I was glad to leave the dingy old apartments for the fresh country air. I had to admit that the landscape was very beautiful with green meadows and majestic trees. I felt better when we were riding away from Canterbury and although I did not like my husband very much, I hoped I should not have to see a great deal of him. During the days I would be with Mamie and my ladies and we could dance and sing together and share our jokes and contempt for our new country while we talked nostalgically about the one we had left. Yes, I thought I could bear that.

We came to Gravesend where we were to stay as the guests of the Countess of Lennox. She was waiting to greet us and paid great homage to the King; then she turned to me and bowed very low. She said she was greatly honoured that we should be her guests and added that she had grave news which she thought should be imparted to the King immediately.

He looked very serious and she went on: 'It is the plague, Your Majesty. It will be most unsafe for you and the Queen to travel through the streets of London.'

My husband said: 'But the people will be expecting us. They will want their processions and all the pageantry which goes with them.'

'Nevertheless that is how it is, my lord. You will hear more of this but I thought I should tell you without delay.'

How serious the King was! He never seemed to laugh spontaneously. Perhaps that was why I found it so hard to like him.

Now instead of the pleasant welcome I had been looking forward to there was great concern and people were gathering round the King deciding what should be done.

I was taken to an apartment to rest and Mamie came with me. While we were there Father Sancy came to us and said he wished to have a word with me, so Mamie retired and left me alone with my confessor, which was the last thing I wanted.

He then began reprimanding me for eating meat in Canterbury and I said what I had prepared myself to say which was that I had only been following the customs of my new country.

'Following the customs of heretics!' he thundered. 'That is a fine way to begin! What will you do? Deny the true Faith because it is the custom of savages among whom you live?'

'That is very different from eating meat, Father.'

'You have gone against the laws of Holy Church.'

'I shall not do it again, Father.'

He seemed faintly mollified. His eyes shone with zeal and as he looked round the room his expression changed to one of contempt, although the apartment was an improvement on those I had had at Dover and Canterbury.

'And now,' he went on, 'there is consternation about your ride through the streets of London. Plague, they say. Let me tell you, my lady, there is constant plague in this accursed country and there will be until these misguided people come to the Truth. It is God's way of punishing them. It was a sad day for us when we came to this land.'

'My mother did not seem to think so. Nor did the Holy Father.'

Father Sancy wagged a finger at me. 'The Holy Father gave the dispensation most reluctantly, and for a reason.' He brought his face close to mine. 'The work must begin without delay. You have been chosen for a great task, my lady, and that is to lead these people back to the true Faith.'

I tried to look solemn. I was longing for him to go. There was so much I had to say to Mamie. I cast down my eyes and folded my hands demurely together. What should I wear for my procession into London? I was asking myself.

'And,' he went on, his voice growing louder, 'you will not do it by eating meat on a fast day.'

The simplest way to be rid of him was not to argue although it was hard to resist the temptation to do so. I murmured a prayer with him and he left.

Mamie came running in.

'I have heard that we have to go to London by barge which will prevent our having to go through the plague-ridden streets,' she cried. 'And you are to wear green. The King will wear green also. I suppose it must be an emblem of spring.'

Then I dressed and we laughed as I told her about Father Sancy and I added: 'If I want to eat meat I shall eat meat. I shall be ordered by no one, Mamie, neither priest nor husband.'

'You are a wild rebellious creature,' she said, 'and,' she added, 'you always were.'

'And always will be,' I assured her.

'We shall wait and see,' said Mamie, which made us laugh because that was what she used to say to me when I was very young.

The next morning I went with my husband and our attendants onto the state barge. The river seemed to be crowded with craft of all kinds because many of the nobility who could had come to join the escort into London, and as we stepped on board there was a volley of fifteen hundred shot which was quite deafening.

I enjoyed sailing down the river. The King beside me seemed very benign though still serious. I wondered if he ever laughed out loud. It should be another of my tasks to make him do so, but that appeared to be almost as formidable as turning Protestant England into a Catholic country. I loved the big ships of the navy which the King pointed out to me with pride as we passed. I had never seen anything like them in France and as we passed them and they fired their ordnance, it was the most thrilling moment that had come to me since my arrival in England.

It was late afternoon when I saw the great Tower of London looming up before us – not beautiful as our buildings are, but formidable and very impressive. The gay flags fluttering from its towers looked rather incongruous and as our barge approached the guns fired so loudly that I almost cried out in half terror, half delight.

The King was amused. He smiled faintly, which was a good deal for him to do; the river banks were crowded with people and they were shouting 'Long live our little Queen,' which my husband translated for me and which so pleased me that I waved my hand in acknowledgement. They seemed pleased by that, and as the King still wore that rather reluctant smile I guessed I was doing what was right.

As we progressed along the river we came right into the city and here the crowds were even greater. People not only lined the river banks but had climbed on ships lying in the river and they were shouting and waving from ships' hulls and craft of all kinds. There was one event which might have been disastrous and it happened just as we were passing. One of the ships capsized suddenly. I suppose too many people had scrambled onto it. It went down into the water and I heard afterwards that there were more than a hundred people on board.

I heard screams and cries of consternation and the attention of the crowd was turned from us to the people struggling in the water. Fortunately there were plenty there to effect a rescue and everyone was eventually brought safely out of the river and all they suffered really was a terrible fright and a ducking.

Along the river we sailed until we came to our destination, which was Somerset House. The grounds ran down to the river and here we alighted and I was conducted ceremoniously into the house. It was grander than those in which I had stayed so far in England but I still found it lacking in the elegance of our French palaces. However the journey by river from Gravesend had been refreshing and the cheers of the people – who seemed to have taken a liking to me – were still ringing in my ears so I felt a little happier.

We spent the night here in a bed which I thought very odd because I had never seen the like. But I was supposed to regard it with some awe as it had once been Queen Elizabeth's and she had slept in it many times.

Queen Elizabeth was the arch heretic and I certainly did not feel the respect that they seemed to consider due to her. In fact I found the idea repulsive and I made no attempt to hide the fact. Charles ignored my hints and behaved as though I were perfectly contented.

We stayed only a few days at Somerset House, which was too near the city for us to be safe from infection, but during that time the King went to Parliament to make his opening speech. I gathered it was not a great success though he did not tell me so. He never spoke to me on serious matters. I suppose I did not encourage confidences at that time. He must have thought me a frivolous and rather stupid little girl – which I suppose I was.

It was Mamie who told me that he had asked for money from the Parliament which would mean taxing the people, and the people hated to be taxed.

'There are many things they don't like,' Mamie told me. 'They don't like Buckingham much.'

'I don't blame them,' I retorted. 'Why don't they like him? Do they know how badly he behaved with my brother's wife?'

'Oh, they wouldn't care about that. It is not a matter of morals. People in high places can do exactly as they like in that respect. The old King doted on him. . . his Steenie as he called him because he said he bore a resemblance to St Stephen. He was his favourite young man, and he had lots of young men around him. But Buckingham is too ambitious. He fancies himself as a states-man and a ruler more than he does a lap dog . . . which was what most of the handsome young men were content to be. Well, the old King has died and now they say that Buckingham is getting a hold on the new one.'

'A hold on Charles!'

'Well, he listens to him. He's his greatest friend. They went to Spain together, didn't they, when Charles was courting the Spanish Princess? And then he came to France when it was your turn.'

'So the people don't like Buckingham. Do you know, I don't think he likes me.'

'Nonsense. It's not for him to like or dislike you. You represent the alliance with France and he worked for that, didn't he?'

'Oh, I am glad the people don't like him. It shows they have some sense . . . even if they are heretics.'

Mamie laughed at me and said I should have to grow up.

The plague was getting worse so it was decided we should leave Somerset House for Hampton Court.

I was impressed by Hampton Court from the moment I saw it. This was more like a royal residence. Approaching it from the river was to see it in all its imposing glory. When I stepped ashore and crossed the splendid gardens to the entrance of the palace I felt I was indeed a Queen of a great country.

I think there were about fifteen hundred rooms in the palace which had been built by Cardinal Wolsey at the height of his glory and taken from him by King Henry the Eighth who could not bear that a subject should live more grandly than he did. The rooms were vast – each of the fireplaces was big enough to roast an ox. The furnishings were drab but I was fast discovering that the English lacked the refined tastes of the French. They seemed either drab or garish in my eyes. But they could not detract from the splendour of Hampton Court.

'This is where we shall stay for a while,' Charles told me. 'Here we shall spend our honeymoon.'

A honeymoon meant getting to know each other and as the days passed I realized that our relationship did not grow warmer as we began to know each other more intimately.

Mamie urged me to try harder to like my husband.

'I think,' she said, 'that he is ready to love you. He finds you very attractive physically.'

'I don't find *him* so.'

'But if you tried. . . .'

'Mamie, don't be silly. How can you *try* to love someone? You either do or you don't.'

'You can be understanding. Try to see what it is that you don't like and then try. . . .'

'He never laughs. He is so serious. He doesn't approve of so much that I do. And, Mamie, he doesn't like you.'

'That matter of the coach was very unfortunate . . . happening as it did right at the beginning.'

'It is over and forgotten.'

'Some things are never forgotten.'

'Well, he had better stop disliking you, for I shall not like *him* until he does.'

'Dearest, you are very wilful.'

'I am as I am . . . and I will not change for anyone.'

'You are very young. When you grow older you will learn that we all have to change sometimes . . . we have to adjust ourselves to circumstances.'

'I will not. I will be myself and any who don't like that can do as they please. I don't care.'

Mamie shrugged her shoulders; she knew it was no use trying to make me see reason when I was in a certain mood.

I was incensed when Buckingham came to me, and from that time I hated him more than ever.

It was downright impertinent and when I realized that Charles had sent him, I hated them both and determined that I would do everything I could to annoy them.

Buckingham tried to look severe. He more or less demanded an audience, which I should have refused, but I didn't out of curiosity to know why he should come to see me.

I expected him to pay compliments and treat me as though I was a pretty woman as well as a Queen. I might have relented a little if he had. He was bold; he was blatant; and I remembered the manner in which he had tried to seduce the Queen of France right under my brother's nose.

He looked at me coolly, rather as though I were a recalcitrant child, and said: 'The King is displeased.'

'For what reason?' I asked.

'Because of your conduct to him.'

'And the King tells you this?'

'I have volunteered to convey his displeasure to you.'

'That,' I said with sarcasm, 'is noble of you.'

'The King says you show no affection towards him.'

'And what concern is that of yours, my lord?'

'It is my concern because the King tells me and has asked me to speak to you on this matter.'

'So you are to plead with me to love him? Why? Are you such a clever supplicant? You were not particularly successful with my sister-in-law the Queen of France.'

Buckingham's handsome face flushed a dull plum colour. I had touched him on a vulnerable spot and I rejoiced. He looked at me steadily while the flush on his face slowly faded, leaving it rather pale.

'I have to tell you that if you do not show more affection to the King and conform more with his wishes, you will be a very unhappy woman.'

'Pray do not concern yourself, my Lord Buckingham. I can manage my own affairs.'

'It would be wise for you to show a little pleasure in the King's company. You laugh and sing with your French companions and as soon as the King arrives with his English ones you become sullen and silent.'

'Then it is for the King and his English attendants to amuse me as my own friends do.'

'It is for you, Madam, to please the King. We are all his subjects . . . even you . . . and it would be wise for you to remember that.'

'My Lord Buckingham, I no longer have need of your presence.'

He bowed and for a moment our eyes met and I knew in that moment that he hated me as much as I hated him.

Mamie was very upset when I told her what had happened. She chided me a little for the way in which I had received him.

'I will not pretend,' I said fiercely.

She shook her head and answered: 'Dearest, you will have to curb your temper. You must, you know; it could lead you into difficulties.'

'Again you seem to be on his side.'

'Never . . . never. But you are wrong, my love. You must learn to be diplomatic.'

'I hate them all. Heretics! Savages!'

Mamie looked very distraught. 'This will not help at all,' she said.

A few days later Buckingham came to see me again. I was on the point of refusing to see him but Mamie was with me when he was announced and she advised me against a direct refusal. 'Try to be calm,' she said. 'Listen to what he has to say and reply to it with tact and calm.'

'I shall grant him nothing.'

'Perhaps not, but do it as a Queen would, not as a rebellious schoolgirl.'

Buckingham came in looking elegant and handsome. It is a pity

I cannot like him, I thought. He dresses with such taste that he looks almost like a Frenchman.

'Your Majesty!' He bowed low and kissed my hand. I could feel the anger surging up in me and I guessed my eyes were beginning to blaze as they did at such moments. 'May I say,' he went on, 'that you are looking even more beautiful than ever. The air at Hampton suits you.'

'You are good to say so,' I replied, so far quite calm.

'I come from His Majesty.'

'Oh? Is he so far away that he cannot come himself?' My temper was beginning to rise. I must remember Mamie's warning and try to keep calm.

'He has given this commission to me,' he replied suavely, 'and I have a special request to make.'

I thought: What insolence! You to make a special request to me . . . after our last meeting. But I said nothing and he went on: 'His Majesty thinks that now you have become his wife and Queen of England you should have Englishwomen in your bedchamber.'

'I am very satisfactorily served at the time,' I replied.

'I am sure of that, but His Majesty is hoping that you will soon master the English language and adopt some of our English ways. Therefore he thinks that if certain ladies came into your bedchamber they would be of service to you . . . if you would graciously allow them to.'

'Oh? And whom does he suggest?'

'He has been most gracious to me and declares I have done him great service. As you know I was the main instrument in arranging this most desirable marriage. His Majesty cannot thank me enough for bringing him such a beautiful bride, and I hope that you too, Your Majesty, feel a little gratitude towards me.'

I was seething with rage and I knew I could not contain it much longer. He did not give me time to speak but went on: 'The King has honoured me by agreeing that my wife, my sister and my niece should occupy these coveted posts.'

I stared at him disbelievingly. He would put his women about me. For what purpose? Their aggrandisement certainly . . . but to spy on me!

I burst out: 'My lord Buckingham, I already have three ladies of the bedchamber. I do not need more.'

'They are Frenchwomen,' he said, 'and the King would like your ladies to be English.'

'You may tell the King that I am perfectly satisfied with what I already have and I intend to remain so.'

He bowed and left me.

Seething with rage I sought out Mamie and told her what had happened. She was greatly distressed. She saw farther than I did. She did not want to worry me but I did make her tell me that she feared she, among the others, might be sent back to France. It was the custom when a Princess married into a foreign country that the attendants who accompanied her went back to their own country after a few days or weeks at the most.

'This is different,' I cried passionately. 'This was the arrangement. I am not to be surrounded by heretics. It was agreed that my own people should stay with me.'

Mamie comforted me and assured me that I had nothing to fear and that I had done right in refusing to accept the Englishwomen into my bedchamber.

I felt very relieved when the Bishop of Mende, who had come with me among my clergy, called on me with Father Sancy and told me that he had had to make my position very clear to the King.

'It was decided,' said the Bishop, 'that you should have English ladies to wait on you in your bedchamber. I have explained that this is quite out of the question.'

I clasped my hands together in delight, which I tried to make appear as religious fervour.

'We cannot have heretics living so close to you,' went on the Bishop.

'They might attempt to corrupt you,' added Father Sancy.

'I would never allow that,' I assured him.

'Nevertheless we cannot afford to run risks,' said the Bishop. 'I have made it clear to the King that my masters in France would take a very grave view of having these Huguenots in your bedchamber.'

'Thank you, my lord,' I said, 'I am grateful for your care.'

'You must never forget your duty to the Church,' said my confessor.

And I assured them both that I would not forget. I would keep about me my own French attendants who were good Catholics. I would fight with all my might against the heretics.

'Let us kneel and pray that you will be successful in that which God has sent you to England to bring about,' said Father Sancy.

The Bishop was less fanatical, but he was determined – even as Father Sancy was – that I should keep the Protestants out.

I was very cool with the King in our bedchamber at Hampton on the night following the visit of the Bishop and Father Sancy. He knew why, of course, and he was very anxious to placate me. I think he enjoyed those intimacies of the bedchamber far more than I did, and I thought it was perverse of him to show a little rancour because I could not share the same pleasure as he did. The fact was that I should have preferred to go home and live as I had before my marriage. True, to be a Queen was gratifying, but I sometimes felt it was not worth all that it entailed.

The King stroked my hair and said it was beautiful. He loved my flashing dark eyes and my clear complexion, even my short stature. I was feminine, he said, all that a woman should be . . . save in one thing. I did not love my husband enough.

I was silent and he sighed deeply. He said: 'It is only because I wish you to learn to speak English . . . and to love this country that I want you to have English ladies about you.'

'I would not love it the more for that,' I said. 'I can accept life here because my friends are with me.'

'But I would be your friend,' he said, 'the very best friend you have. I am your husband.'

'I would not lose those who have come with me from France for anything.'

He sighed. He did realize that it was never any use trying to convince me. He believed now that I was the most illogical, unreasoning young woman imaginable, a creature of whims and fancies, lacking completely in control of my feelings.

I know I was the main cause of all the unhappiness of those years. But I could not see it then.

So we retired to bed for our nightly ritual, which I longed to have done with so that I could sleep.

The discord between us continued and it seemed impossible to find an end to it. I knew there was a great deal of comment about the way I and my French friends behaved. We were allowed to celebrate Mass because that was part of the agreement between our two countries and my religious entourage made sure that this was carried out. But it was accepted with resentment. Mamie said the English could never forget that Mary Tudor had burned Protestants in Smithfield and at that time they had made up their minds that they would never be ruled by Catholics again. Then some of their sailors had become prisoners of the Inquisition and brought back tales of torture. The country had turned its back on Catholicism and forgotten, said Mamie, that the Protestants had not always been so kind to the Catholics among them. The English, she decided, were not an intensely religious nation. They were said to be tolerant, but their tolerance was in fact indifference. But although they might not object to Catholics on religious grounds, they were determined not to have another monarch like Mary Tudor, who was fiercely Catholic, having been brought up by her Catholic mother, Katherine of Aragon.

'It is well,' said Mamie, 'to understand the people with whom you have to live. Sum them up. Don't be afraid of them but don't underrate them.'

I don't know whether she was right but that was her assessment of them. However, I was allowed to celebrate Mass in the royal palaces with my attendants and we took advantage of this – perhaps a little blatantly. I was too careless then to see that we must inevitably be working towards a climax.

Mamie tried to explain to me what was happening, but I am afraid I found the subject rather boring and only half listened. I knew that she said something about the King's finding it difficult to fall in with the terms of our marriage treaty without offending his own people and I should really try to be more understanding towards him. He was naturally preoccupied having state matters to think of and my little tantrums must be trying to him. Moreover he could not get French help to fight Spain, and the hope of doing so was one of the reasons why the marriage had been so pleasing to him. It was all very wearying and I shrugged it aside. I did listen a little more intently when she told me that Catholic services were banned in England – except in my household.

'He had better not try to stop me and my servants worshipping God,' I cried.

'He would not. That would be going against the marriage treaty.'

'Well, let us talk of something more interesting.'

She sighed and shook her head over me. Then I rushed to her and kissed her and she was laughing at me.

When the King dissolved Parliament he looked more stern than ever and said that he was going to the New Forest to hunt for a while. He thought I might not wish to go with him and he was right in that. Perhaps, he said, I would like to stay at Tichfield, which was the estate of the Earl of Southampton.

I was delighted to be relieved of his company and was very merry surrounded by my French attendants, riding with Mamie beside me to Tichfield; but I was a little put out on reaching the house to find that the Countess of Denbigh was there. I was prepared to loathe anyone connected with the Duke of Buckingham and she was his sister. Moreover she was one of those women whom he had tried to force me to accept into my bedchamber.

In the solitude of my apartment, Mamie and I discussed her. Mamie thought she was a very strong-minded woman and advised me to be careful in my dealings with her.

'Don't show that you dislike her. Don't forget that although you may dislike the Duke of Buckingham, he is the most powerful man in the country under the King, and it is unwise to offend him too much.'

But when had I ever been wise? I always listened to Mamie's advice but I only took it when I wanted to.

'What is this Buckingham family?' I cried. 'They were nothing before little Steenie attracted King James – and in a manner that is a disgrace to morality.'

'Hush,' said Mamie.

I snapped my fingers at her. 'Don't tell me to hush. Remember who I am.'

'Oh,' said Mamie, 'on our high horse now, are we? Shall I bow low to Your Majesty and walk out on all fours?'

She could always make me laugh and that was why I loved her so much.

I went on: 'It shows they were nothing . . . otherwise she would never have married William Feilding. Who was he, pray, before the earldom was bestowed on him? A commoner who had the good fortune to marry Susan Villiers. He would not have been allowed to unless he had done so before her brother caught the King's eye with his pretty face and made the family fortunes.'

'My word, you have probed into the family history.'

'Well, I happen to be interested in these odious connections of Buckingham's, and don't forget they tried to force Susan Villiers into my bedchamber.'

'The Countess of Denbigh now.'

'A title bestowed by the good graces of her brother who wants to see all his family in influential places. Oh, he has to be watched, that one.'

'And you will do the watching?'

I said: 'You are laughing at me again. I forbid it.'

'Then I will hide my laughter and present always a serious countenance to Your Majesty.'

'That is what I could not bear. There is too much solemnity around me already.'

I will admit, when looking back, that I behaved in an unseemly fashion towards the Countess of Denbigh; but then she was hardly within her rights in her conduct towards me.

She professed to be very religious and it was quite clear that she deplored the fact that Mass was celebrated at Tichfield. I will not try to pretend that I did not arrange for our services to take place as ostentatiously as I could, and those about me – perhaps with the exception of Mamie – did all they could to encourage me.

It was Mamie who told me that the Countess of Denbigh had decided that she would arrange a Protestant service to take place in the great hall at Tichfield. All the household should assemble and take part – with, of course, the exception of mine.

I was rather pleased because courtesy would demand that as the Queen was in the house her permission would have to be asked.

I discussed it with Mamie.

'I shall refuse it,' I said.

'You cannot,' replied Mamie, shocked.

'I can and I will.'

'It would be a grave mistake. Listen, my dearest, you are a fervent Catholic, but you are in a country where the Protestant religion is maintained. You must graciously give your consent and while the service is going on remain in your apartments. There is nothing else to be done.'

'Why does she arrange this while I am here?'

'Perhaps to show that while the country has a Catholic Queen, it is staunchly Protestant.'

'Then I shall refuse.'

'Please do not. It would be folly. They would hold it against you. It would get to the King's ears . . . worse still, to those of his ministers. It would not be tolerated to forbid these people to worship in the accepted religion of the country.'

I pressed my lips firmly together. In my heart I knew that she was right, but I could not stop myself rehearsing what I would say to Susan Villiers when she came to ask my permission.

Mamie was not with me when one of my attendants came rushing into my apartments.

'My lady,' cried my attendant breathlessly, 'what do you think? There is a service going on in the great hall. The whole household . . . the Protestant household. . . is gathered there.'

I was aghast.

So, she had not bothered to ask my permission. This was a double insult. First to arrange the service while I was under this roof, then to carry it out without asking my permission.

What could I do? I was not going to ask Mamie this time because I knew she would say 'Nothing.' But I was enraged and I wanted it to be known.

I had an idea. I would not go down and demand that it be stopped, which was my first reaction. I would disrupt it in such a manner as I could not be called to task for.

I gathered together a group of my attendants and told them we were going to take out the dogs. We all loved our little dogs and most of the ladies had several. We put them on their leads and I led my party down to the hall where the assembled company was kneeling in prayer. I walked across the hall to the door, my attendants following me. The dogs yapped and barked and ran about; we laughed at their antics and chatted animatedly, behaving as though we could not see the people at prayer.

At length we came out into the courtyard, laughing together. But I did not intend that it should end there. I sent about six of the ladies back to bring a kerchief for me. They went, taking their dogs with them, and I stood at the door exulting in the noise they made.

When they returned, I cried in a loud voice, 'The air is a little cold. I think I will not walk today.' Then we all trooped back. Someone was preaching but his voice was drowned in the commotion we made.

Of course everyone was shocked by what had happened – Mamie as much as anyone.

They were all talking about it. I said that I should have been consulted and that to conduct such a service without my permission was a breach of good manners; but I think that most people thought that her fault in not asking my permission was slight compared with the way in which I and my attendants had acted.

Deep shock was expressed about my behaviour. Mamie was the first to tell me that I should never have behaved as I did and that it would be remembered and held against me. Perhaps the Countess had been remiss but what I had done amounted to an insult to the Protestant religion.

I said I did not care and would do it again, which made Mamie despair.

When the King returned from his hunting trip he said nothing about the incident but I felt sure he had heard of it. There was a certain determination added to his usual sternness, and I wondered whether he was planning something.

In many ways he was delighted with me. I believe he could have been passionately in love with me then; but I was so unsatisfactory to him in many ways and a man of his nature could never quite forget that.

I did not understand this then. It is only now that I do when I have so much time – too much time – for reflection. There was consternation between the Courts of France and England. Nothing was going as anyone had wanted it to. There was so much conflict that Mamie feared my husband and my brother might be on the brink of war with each other. My brother – or I expect it was Richelieu – sent the Sieur de Blainville to try to bring some accord between the two countries. The King did not like him very much and that made it difficult for any understanding to be reached. Blainville came to see me and told me I should try to understand the English, to learn their language, to mingle with them at Court and not keep myself isolated with my French household.

Buckingham was out of the country, which always made me feel happier. He was trying to persuade Richelieu to join him against the Spaniards, so he said. I wondered whether he was still hankering after my sister-in-law Queen Anne and whether his little jaunt was to try to win her favour. After that incident in the gardens when she had had to scream for help, I believed Buckingham was capable of anything.

The Duchesse de Chevreuse provided a little bit of liveliness to the scene when she gave birth to a child. Whose? I wondered, and so did many more.

She was quite blatant about it and the Duc de Chevreuse acted as though the child were his. He must have been used to her little ways and that they should sometimes produce consequences should not be a matter for surprise.

Then Buckingham returned, apparently somewhat deflated. His plans had gone awry. I guessed they would. He could hardly win favour in France after his disgraceful conduct with the Queen. Moreover I think he was not the man to succeed at anything but winning the doting affection of men like King James and the friendship of young inexperienced men like King Charles. I wished that Charles was not so devoted to him. I believed they discussed me and my relationship with my husband and I began to suspect that Buckingham sowed seeds of discord in my husband's mind. Not that Buckingham would dare openly attack me. But he must be a master of the subtle suggestion, and I had noticed that when he was absent there seemed to be less conflict between me and Charles.

When we were alone in our bedchamber Charles would be quite affectionate; he would even smile faintly and express his satisfaction with my person and forget for a while how unsatisfactory I was in other ways, so when I wanted to make appointments in my household I decided that the best time to approach him was during one of those bedtime tête-à-têtes. I wanted to assure the position of some of my attendants and I could only do this by appointing them to vacant posts.

I had taken a great deal of trouble to draw up a list, and I had been careful to add some English names to it. In fact I had rather cleverly – I thought – intermingled them skilfully which had the effect of diminishing the number of French I had included.

I was in bed and Charles had just joined me. He had turned to me and laid his arm about me when I said: 'I have a paper here which I want you to look at.'

'A paper?' he said in astonishment. 'Now?'

'It is just a small list of those I wish to be officers in my retinue.'

'Well, I will look at it in the morning. But you know that according to the agreement with your brother which we made at the time of our marriage, it is my right to name such people.'

'Oh, you will agree to these,' I said lightly. 'There are a number of English names there as well as French.'

He raised himself on his elbow and looked at me and although I could not see him very clearly in the dim light, I knew that he had assumed that stern and suspicious demeanour.

'There will be no French in your retinue,' he said coldly. 'It would be quite impossible for them to serve in that capacity.'

'Why not?'

'Because it is my will that they should not.'

'But,' I retorted angrily, 'it is *my* will that they should. My mother wishes these people to be admitted into my retinue.'

'It is no affair of your mother's.'

'And none of mine?' I asked defiantly.

'None of yours,' he said. 'If it is not my will then it cannot be yours.'

I was so angry. If I could have done so I would have risen from the bed and made my preparations to return to France. We sat up in bed glaring at each other.

I cried: 'Then take back your lands. Take them all . . . lands . . . castles . . . everything you have bestowed on me. If I have no power to act in them as I wish, I have no desire to possess them.'

He said slowly but very distinctly: 'You must remember to whom you speak. I am your King. You are my Queen but also a subject. You should take heed of the fate of other Queens of England.'

I could scarcely believe my ears. Was he reminding me of the ill-fated Anne Boleyn and Catherine Howard? Could it be that Charles, whom I had always thought of as gentle and kindly-meaning, was telling me that if I did not behave as he wished I might lose my head.

I felt enraged and insulted. I began to weep – not quietly but stormily. I said I was utterly miserable and longed to be back in France. I was nothing here. I was insulted and maltreated. I was given a household but I had no power in it. I wanted to go home. While I was saying all this he was trying to placate me.

'Listen to me,' he said.

'I want to hear no more,' I cried. 'The more I hear the more miserable I become. Why do you use me so? Am I not the daughter of a great King? My brother is King of France. If my family but knew!'

He said: 'Your family know full well that you are being treated here in accordance with your deserts. Your brother has sent Blainville here to try to reason with *you*.'

'I have been unused to such treatment,' I wailed. 'I hate it here. I want to go home. I will write to my brother. . . .'

'Much good that will do you.'

'To my mother. . . . She will understand.'

He was silent for a while and I grew tired of talking to what seemed like no one. I slid down and buried my face in the pillow.

There was a long silence. Then he sighed and lay down too.

After a while he said: 'I will say this and that is an end to the matter: You cannot fill posts in your retinue with your French servants. These posts must be filled by English people. You have become the Queen of England and the sooner you realize it, the better for you and all concerned.'

With that he pretended to sleep and I ceased to cry.

Later he turned to me and was very tender.

But I knew I had lost the battle.

The next climax which arose was due to the coronation. Charles of course had only become King just before our marriage and in accordance with custom his coronation should take place soon after he came to the throne. His had been delayed because of the plague but with the beginning of the next year London seemed safe again and plans went ahead with great speed, for a coronation has a special significance. It is only when a King has been anointed and crowned that the people feel he is truly King.

So Charles was of course eager to be crowned.

I was the Queen and I should be crowned with him, but I could see all sorts of difficulties, for how could I – a Catholic – be crowned in a Protestant ceremony.

I discussed the matter with my French attendants and of course with Father Sancy. He was adamant. I most certainly must not be crowned in a Protestant church and indeed I should not even *attend* the coronation.

'Then I shall not be crowned Queen,' I pointed out.

'Only when you receive the crown in the true Faith,' he said.

Charles was bewildered at first when he heard my views on the matter; then he was very angry.

'Do you mean to say you refuse to be crowned?'

'In a Protestant church, yes.'

'You are mad,' he said. 'Do you value your crown so little?'

'I value my faith more,' I replied dramatically.

'You must be the first Queen who has refused to be crowned,' he said. 'Do you realize that it will be said you have no firm hold on it?'

'What would God say if I allowed myself to take part in such a mockery?'

That was when he became really angry. 'Be silent,' he cried. 'Don't dare talk so in my presence.'

He was really rather frightening then. He went away and left me. I think he was afraid he might do me some harm.

It was an extraordinary state of affairs and everyone was talking about it. The Queen would not have a coronation! The English thought I was mad; and they were annoyed with me, too, looking upon my attitude as some insult to them; but my own attendants applauded me. Even Mamie did not condemn the action, but she did say she thought it was unwise.

As for the Comte de Blainville, he was astounded, although Catholic as he was he should have understood. It meant, of course, that if I did not go he could not either. He said he would have risked the small strain to his conscience, which was meant I supposed to be a mild reproof to me. But he did add that as I was not to be crowned he could hardly be there.

Charles tried once or twice to reason with me but I refused to listen.

'The people may well take this as an insult to them and their Church. It will not make you very popular with them.'

'I care nothing for their regard,' I said.

'Then you are even more foolish than I thought,' was his terse reply.

On another occasion he tried to persuade me at least to be present in the Abbey. He would have a latticed box made where I could sit unseen.

'No,' I cried vehemently. 'It would be wrong for me to *be* in such a place.'

He spoke to me no more of the matter, but I knew that he was very displeased and that the people in the streets discussed it and said some very unflattering things about me.

However I refused to be dismayed. In those days I had the gift of persuading myself that what I did was always right. Coronation Day was the second of February, which was Candlemas Day, one of the festivals of our Church, so while the coronation was in progress, we celebrated that; but I have to admit that afterwards I could not resist watching the procession from a window in Whitehall Palace.

The King was very cool to me and I was beginning to feel a little uneasy because, although I was in fact Queen of England, I had not been crowned and I did not see how I ever could be until that day when I brought the whole country to the true Faith.

It was about a week after the coronation when the second Parliament of Charles's reign was about to be opened and that meant a grand procession. Father Sancy said I might watch it from one of the windows of Whitehall Palace, but Buckingham in his interfering way suggested that I should see it better from his family's house and his mother would be very happy if I joined her and the ladies of the Buckingham household.

I was very annoyed about this and wanted to refuse but I was feeling a little nervous because of all the fuss over the coronation.

Charles said he would escort me to the Buckingham residence and I was waiting for him to come, inwardly fuming because I had agreed to go to those I hated so much.

When it started to rain I saw through this a way out and when Charles came I touched my headdress, which was very elaborate, and looked melancholy.

He asked what was wrong and I said: 'The rain will ruin this.'

He gave one of those faint smiles of his and I knew that he was thinking I was rather an adorable child in spite of all my naughtiness and he touched my shoulder gently and said: 'Very well, remain here and watch the procession from Whitehall.'

I was delighted and settled down to do so, but very soon the Sieur de Blainville arrived. He looked very disturbed.

'Is it true, my lady,' he asked, 'that you have refused to go to the Buckingham house to see the procession as arranged?'

'It is raining.'

'It has stopped.'

'Well, it *was* raining and I told the King it would spoil my headdress.'

'That will not be acceptable to Buckingham.'

'The King accepted it. He did not want me to spoil my head-dress.'

'You must leave here at once,' he said. 'I will conduct you there. Do you realize that the situation between our two countries is very uneasy. The King your brother, your mother, the Cardinal . . . they are all seeking friendship with your husband. You must forgive my saying so, my lady, but your conduct does not help to bring about what we want.'

He looked so serious and still a little worried about my action over the coronation that I said I would go with him at once.

So he immediately conducted me to the Buckingham house.

It is strange that when one does not mean to annoy one can do so more deeply than when one does. I had no idea that there could be such a storm over such a trivial matter. But of course it was Buckingham who made the mischief. When he saw that I was not with the King – so I heard from those present who had witnessed the scene – the Duke expressed great concern. He would know the real reason for my refusal to leave Whitehall Palace and that the rain had little to do with it. He was heard to tell the King that he could not hope to make much impression on Parliament if he allowed his own wife to flout him.

Charles was rather angry then. He took a great deal of notice of Buckingham and the Duke was on such familiar terms with him that he never hesitated to give him a hint of criticism if he wanted to. The result was that Charles sent a messenger back to Whitehall to say that I was to leave at once, but by the time the messenger arrived I had already left with the Sieur de Blainville.

I knew what Buckingham's comment was. He would point out that although I had refused the King's request, I left immediately when commanded to do so by my fellow countryman.

In those days Charles was unsure of himself. He was very shy and always afraid of losing his dignity. Looking back I see it all so clearly now. Buckingham had been his father's favourite and had made himself Charles's mentor, so he always listened to him and took great heed of what he said. Now, because of Buckingham's suggestions, Charles sent a message to me telling me I was to return to Whitehall Palace for if I could not come when he was there to escort me I should not remain there.

I was so thoughtless. It never occurred to me to try to understand the situation. I sent the messenger back to say that I preferred to remain where I was now, having made the journey in the company of the Sieur de Blainville.

There was no doubt of the sternness of the command which was brought back to me. I was to return to Whitehall without more ado.

I did realize then that this was blowing up into a storm and I thought it advisable to obey immediately, so back to Whitehall I went and with my attendants watched the procession from there as I had originally planned to do.

That was not the end of the matter.

I did not see the King for the rest of the day and that night he did not come to our bedchamber. In the morning there was a note from him stating that he was most distressed by my behaviour and did not want to see me again until I begged his forgiveness for my conduct.

I was astounded. 'What have I done?' I demanded of Mamie. She understood how the incident had been misconstrued. It was much ado about nothing, she said. I could easily explain my innocence to the King, tell him that I really had been concerned about my headdress and when the Sieur de Blainville had explained to me that I would be offending the Buckinghams I had taken his advice and gone with him.

'But it is all so silly,' I cried, stamping my foot in irritation. 'What a fuss . . . and all about nothing. What did it matter *how* I went to the Buckinghams. I went, did I not? It was not that I wanted to, I can assure you.'

'There is so much formality to be observed in your position.'

'And wherever the Buckinghams are, there is trouble. Have you noticed that?'

'I have. But surely you can explain exactly how it happened. The King will believe you. Go to him and tell him.'

'Why shouldn't he come to me?'

'He is the King and your husband.'

'I don't intend to be his slave. He may be the son of a King, but I am the daughter of one . . . and my father was greater than his. . . .'

'Hush, child. You talk too wildly. You must remember where you are. Remember your position. Oh, my dearest, sometimes you frighten me.'

'*I* will not be frightened by Buckingham, who is trying to make my husband hate me. Why, Mamie, why?'

'I think the Duke of Buckingham held complete sway over the King's father and now seeks to be in the same position with regard to your husband. I think he sees how the King's affection for you is growing and seeks to undermine it, lest you should have more influence on the King than he does.'

'The King's affection for me! My influence on him! You are laughing at me, Mamie. What affection has he for me? What influence have I on him?'

'Both could grow. I am sure of that. The King is ready to love you. It is for you to cherish that love. Now go to him and explain what happened and I am sure he will forgive you.'

'But there is nothing to forgive, Mamie. Why should I grovel to him. Let him come and ask *my* pardon.'

'Kings do not ask pardon.'

'Nor do Queens.'

Mamie sighed. She knew my obstinacy.

A few days passed and still the King made no move to see me. I was surprised to find that I was somewhat piqued and that I missed him a little. I was impatient always and impulsive, and I hated long waiting and silences. So in due course I asked if he would see me.

The answer came back immediately. He would be most pleased to receive me.

When I stood before him I saw that his eyes shone with a certain pleasure. I knew that he was getting ready to forgive me when I told him I had done wrong, but I had done no wrong and I was not going to say so. All I wanted to do was end the waiting. I hated going to my apartment at night and not knowing whether he was going to join me. I did begin to wonder whether I wanted him to. All I knew was that I did not greatly enjoy those lonely nights of uncertainty.

I faced him boldly. I said: 'I do not know what I have done to merit your displeasure. I had no intention of doing so. But if I have offended you I would ask you to forget it.'

I think he was as eager for reconciliation as I was, for he

smiled that faint smile and embraced me.

'The incident is over and done with,' he said.

It was not, however, the end for poor Blainville. He was first of all not permitted to come to Court and as this was an impossible situation for an ambassador to find himself in he was recalled to France. I was very sorry for him. It had come about through no fault of his and I knew that he would be accused of failing in his duties when he returned home.

The Maréchal de Bassompierre was sent to England in his place. He had been a very old and faithful friend of my father and was in fact the man who had been betrothed to Charlotte de Montmorency and had given her up when my father had wanted to make her his mistress. He had served France well and I soon realized that I should get frank speaking from him. He made it clear that my behaviour was not what it should be and that I would have to improve.

It was a trying time. In spite of all my protests, three English-women had been made ladies of my bedchamber though none of my French servants had been dismissed. The English ladies were the Duchess of Buckingham and the Countesses of Denbigh and Carlisle.

Mamie felt it was ominous and I became aware of how worried she was.

I was less so, still confident of getting my own way. I was very sullen with the three new ladies in waiting for the first week or so and refused to speak to them except when it was absolutely necessary, but gradually I began to take notice of them for they were, I discovered, three unusual ladies.

Buckingham's wife seemed to be quite interested in the Catholic Faith and began to ask me questions about it. She was by no means sceptical and I found that I quite enjoyed talking to her; I often wondered how she came to marry her odious husband but marriages were arranged for us poor females and we had to make the best of what came our way. Her sister-in-law the Countess of Denbigh also questioned me about the Faith, and they both listened attentively and were really interested in what I had to tell them. They were very deferential too and in spite of the fact that one was the wife of Buckingham and one his sister, I quite liked them. Best of the three though, I liked Lucy Hay, the Countess of Carlisle. She was a very interesting and beautiful woman. She was about ten years older than I and came from the Percy family, her father being the Earl of Northumberland. She had made a very romantic marriage after falling in love with James Hay who became the Earl of Carlisle. Her family had objected to the marriage and it would never have taken place but for the fact that her father had become a prisoner in the Tower of London and the Earl of Carlisle brought about his release, making it a condition that he marry Lucy. I liked her because she was outstandingly beautiful as well as being witty and amusing.

It was suddenly borne home to me that I could like some of the English and as long as none of the friends I had brought with me from France was sent away, I could welcome these three interesting ladies into my household.

In spite of the fact that I was growing quite fond of Buckingham's wife and sister I hated him more than ever. I was convinced that he made the King dissatisfied with me and I became even more sure of this when Mamie came to me in some distress and told me he had talked to her.

'Of what?' I demanded.

'Of you and the King.'

'How dare he!'

'He would dare anything. The King can see no wrong in him. The fact is that Buckingham tells me the King is not at all satisfied with you.'

'You mean he has told Buckingham to inform *you* of this?' I could feel my temper rising.

'Now you must calm yourself. He says that you disappoint the King in the bedchamber.'

I felt myself go hot with shame and anger.

'How dare he!'

'He says it is what the King has confided in him. He says you seem affable enough during the day but at night you become distinctly cold, and that does not please the King.'

'It is for the King to *make* me affectionate towards him. I shall tell him he will not do so through his ambassador Buckingham.'

'I pray you be calm. Let us think of this clearly. How . . . how is it with you and the King?'

I burst out: 'I should have thought that was a matter between the King and me . . . and us two only.'

'It is. It is. But you see the King has spoken to Buckingham.'

'Mamie,' I said, 'do you really think the King has spoken to Buckingham . . . or is it one of the Duke's fabrications?'

She was thoughtful. Then she said: 'If you tell me that all is well between you and the King . . . at night. . . .'

'As far as I know. I submit . . . though I do not like it very much.'

'Perhaps that is not enough.'

'But to tell Buckingham. . . .'

'If he did,' put in Mamie.

'Mamie, I know that the King and I will never be happy together while Buckingham is here. I am certain that he is going to do everything he can to drive us apart.'

'And if there were no Buckingham . . . do you think that you could grow to love the King?'

'I don't know. Life seemed so much happier when Buckingham was not here.'

'You are not dissatisfied with your new bedchamber ladies?'

'No. I like them very much. Particularly Lucy.'

'We must not allow Buckingham to influence the King.'

'How shall we stop him?'

'I don't know but we can pray for a miracle.'

I was deeply disturbed that the King had spoken of our most intimate relationship with the Duke. But had he? I could not be really sure of this and for once I did not jump to conclusions. But I was more and more wary of Buckingham and I was beginning to believe that but for him we might have avoided quite a number of the storms which had blown up and were threatening to wreck our marriage.

That last affair was, I was sure, a result of his interference.

His determination to harm me was becoming even more obvious. One day he dared ask for a private audience with me. Reluctantly I gave it and immediately wished I had not. He was an extremely handsome man – indeed he owed his rise to power to his personal appearance – and his confidence gave him an air of royalty. I was sure he thought himself of far greater importance than anyone at Court – even the King himself.

He quickly threw off the formalities and began to talk to me very intimately in a manner which infuriated me more and more every second.

'I know, my dear lady, that the relationship between you and the King is not quite what it should be. Oh, you are beautiful, there is no doubt of that . . . and you are regal being the daughter of a king, but you are young . . . so very young. . . .'

'I grow older every day, sir,' I told him with some asperity, 'and my vision grows clearer.'

He laughed rather heartily.

'Dearest lady, you are enchanting. I know where the complaint lies.'

'Complaint, sir. Of what complaint do you speak?'

'You are so fresh, so young, so innocent. Naturally, I tell the King you need to be guided in the ways of love.'

I was too astonished to speak.

'Love!' he said. 'Ah, one needs to be skilled in the art to discover its full delights. Perhaps the King is more practised in the realms of state than in the bedchamber. Perhaps. . . .'

He had moved nearer to me and there was no mistaking the gleam in his eyes. Was this, I wondered, how he had approached my sister-in-law? What was he suggesting? That I learn how to be what he called satisfactory with Charles through Buckingham?

It was monstrous. What would Charles think of this subject of his if I told him what Buckingham had suggested to me . . . well not so much suggested as implied.

'My Lord Buckingham,' I cried shrilly, 'stand away from me. Your conduct is atrocious. I wonder what the King will say when I tell him what you have suggested to me.'

He stood back, his eyebrows raised, his face a mask of bewilderment. 'My lady, I do not understand you. Suggested? What do you think I have suggested?'

'Your remarks about matters which are completely between the King and myself are offensive.'

'Forgive me . . . I just thought a little word – That was all that was in my mind. I swear it. What could you have imagined? You must realize that I have no idea why you should be so offended.'

The man was a monster, a snake in the grass and I must beware of his venom.

'I merely wished to talk to you about your attitude to the faith which prevails in this country. I merely wanted to advise

you. The matter of the Countess of Denbigh's service at Tichfield. . . .'

'That is long ago. The Countess bears no rancour and has now
become my friend.'

'I am happy about that as it brings me to another matter which I
know gives the King a great deal of concern. He wants you to
send your French attendants back to France.'

'That is something I shall never do.'

'You would find many English ladies who would be happy to
replace them.'

'I am very happy as we are. Thank you for your concern. But it
is my affair as to whom I shall choose to serve me.'

'I trust that you speak a little English now that you have three
English ladies of the bedchamber.'

'I do, but there again I do not see that it is any great concern of
yours.'

'I speak only for your own good. My great wish is to please you.'

'Then,' I said firmly, 'I will tell you how you may give me the
greatest pleasure. It is very simple. All you have to do is go.'

With that he went, leaving me very uneasy.

I should have realized that we were working towards a climax,
but my trouble in those days was that I never looked beyond the
immediate moment. If I scored a little victory I thought I had won
the war – though why there should be a war between husband
and wife I cannot now see.

It was June and we were at Whitehall. The afternoon was warm
and beautiful – just the day for taking a walk in the park near the
palace. Father Sancy walked with me and he was admonishing
me for some petty demeanour. I was not listening to him but
thinking how beautiful the trees were and what a lovely day it
was. Mamie was walking on the other side of me when we
strayed away from the park. We came to the gallows at Tyburn,
which had always filled me with horror because so many people
had died miserably there – some I knew for their faith. It was not
long ago when those good Catholics who had set out to blow up
the Houses of Parliament had died most brutally. All they had
wished to do was establish the Catholic Faith in this heretic land,
which was what I wanted to do.

I mentioned this. Mamie frowned. She hated me to speak in this way. She was a good Catholic, of course, but she was more ready to respect the beliefs of others than I was. Father Sancy grew rather fierce talking of the people who had died for their faith at Tyburn and suggested that we approach and say a short prayer for their souls.

So I agreed and we did so.

I suppose nothing a Queen does can go unnoticed. Of course I was seen and as I appeared to have enemies everywhere, the incident was embellished and distorted out of all proportion to what had actually taken place. Stories were circulated about the Court and the city. I heard that I had done penance at Tyburn; I had walked barefoot carrying a candle. I had set up an altar there; I had said Mass; I had prayed to the Virgin and the saints for the souls of those I called Martyrs and whom the English called criminals.

'Lies!' I cried. 'Lies . . . it is all lies.'

But it was strange how many people were ready to believe it.

The King questioned me about it. I told him what had actually happened.

'Unfortunate,' he said. 'Most unfortunate. Why did you have to walk to such a place?'

'I don't know,' I cried. 'We just arrived there.'

I could see that he did not believe me.

He took me by the shoulders and shook me gently. 'You must try to understand,' he said with mild exasperation.

I said: 'I won't go near the place again. It's horrible. I hate it. I feel as though I hear the cries of all those who suffered there.'

'They suffered there because they were criminals,' he said tersely.

'Not all,' I cried. 'Not all. Some suffered for their faith.'

'It would be considered quite amusing for a Catholic to complain about the wrongs done to others for the simple reason that they are of a different faith from their persecutors.'

I was silent then. I was only trying to explain what had actually happened at Tyburn.

He muttered: 'It is that priest of yours. He is nothing more than a spy. He shall be sent away. Your entire retinue encourages you to behave as you do.'

Then he left me. He was really very angry but I thought it was such a shame that he should be prepared to listen to the stories about me and seem to believe those who circulated them rather than me, his own wife.

I was very angry and hurt. To cheer me my friends said that we should have a little entertainment in my apartments at Whitehall and so they brought in their music and we tried some new dances, becoming very merry.

I suppose we made a fair amount of noise. I know we were all laughing rather loudly and I was dancing with one of the gentlemen of my household when the door opened suddenly and the King stood on the threshold.

Everything stopped and the silence was so intense that it made me want to scream out for them to start the music again. I looked at him. I was holding my partner's hand, for that was what the dance demanded, and I could see that the King thought my conduct most indecorous.

He did not speak immediately but stood still looking at us. Then he walked over to me. Everyone watched because he seemed to walk very slowly. He took me by the hand and said 'Come.' That was all. Then he led me to his apartment, which was next to mine, and when we were there he locked the door.

I looked at him questioningly.

He said: 'I have something to say to you. I have been meaning to tell you for some little time that those who came with you from France will now be returning there.'

I stared at him in astonishment. I stammered: 'What? When. . . ?'

He answered: 'Immediately. It is all arranged. I am sure the trouble between us comes from their influence. The sooner they are back in their own land the better for us all.'

'No!' I cried.

'But yes,' he answered, and added soothingly: 'You will see that it is the best thing.'

'I will not allow it,' I said fiercely.

'Now,' he went on in the same soothing manner, 'you must not be so foolish.'

I moved towards the door. 'It is locked,' he said. 'I have the key.'

'Then open the door. I want to go to them. I want to tell them what you are preparing for them. It was agreed at the marriage settlement that they should stay with me.'

'The French have not always adhered to the terms of the marriage settlement, and I am weary of these people who do nothing but cause trouble. Your confessor is all the time stirring up strife. It was he who took you to Tyburn and advised you to act as you did. He is going back to France at once . . . and the whole pack with him.'

'No,' I said faintly, for a terrible fear was gripping me and I was thinking of all my dear ones but most of all my beloved Mamie.

'Let me go to them,' I pleaded.

'You will not see them again,' he replied firmly.

I stared at him aghast, and he went on: 'They are leaving Whitehall today. Even at this moment the carriages are waiting to take them.'

'To . . . take them where?'

'Where they can be housed until arrangements are made to ship them back to France.'

To ship them to France! He talked of them as though they were bales of wool . . . my beloved friends . . . the people who made life here tolerable for me.

'I will not let them go,' I cried.

'My dear wife,' he said, 'try to be reasonable. It is better that they go. It is better that you and I learn to love each other so that no others – save the children we shall have – can be of the same importance to us.'

'I cannot believe this. You are doing it to tease me.'

He shook his head. 'It is true. They must go. There will never be peace between us two while they remain. Come with me.'

He took me to the window. Carriages were drawn up there and I saw that my friends were being directed into them.

'No. No.' I began to cry. I wrenched myself away from him because I had seen Mamie down there being put into a carriage.

'Mamie!' I whispered. 'Oh . . . Mamie . . .' Then I started to call her loudly, but she could not hear me. She looked desperately unhappy.

Frantically I beat on the window.

'Don't go. Don't go,' I screamed. 'Don't let them do this.'

The window pane cracked. I heard the sound of tinkling glass and there was blood on my hands.

Charles had me by the shoulders. 'Stop it,' he cried. 'Stop it.'

'I will not. I will not. I hate England. I hate you all. You are taking away from me those I love.'

I slipped out of his grasp and sat on the floor sobbing as I heard the carriages drive away.

I was alone. Charles had gone and I heard him turn the key in the lock. I sat there on the floor, my hands covering my face, more desolate than I had ever been in my life.

I don't know how long I sat there before the door opened quietly and Lucy Hay came in. She did not speak for a moment but helped me rise and putting her arm about me led me to the window seat. She smoothed back my hair as though I were a child, and when I put my head on her shoulder she held me tightly, saying nothing but somehow giving me the comfort I sorely needed.

After a while I said: 'They have gone . . . my dear, dear Mamie has been taken from me.'

She nodded.

I said: 'I hate those who have taken her from me.'

Still she did not speak though she knew I was referring to the King.

We just sat there in that room with the broken window and I told her how Mamie had been with me since I was a child and how she had taught me so much and how we had laughed together.

Finally she said: 'It happens to Queens. It is their sad fate.'

I knew then that she understood perfectly and that I could not have borne it if she had told me I must try to forget them. How could I ever forget Mamie?

She went on: 'They are being taken to Somerset House and they will stay there until arrangements are made. They are being well looked after.'

A little later she led me back to my apartments and I asked her to stay with me, which she did.

I blamed Buckingham, my arch enemy, the author of my sorrows. It was true that he was in France at this time, making trouble there, but I knew that it was he who had instilled in Charles's mind the need to rob me of my friends and that he taunted him with allowing me to have too much of my own way. Oh yes, Buckingham was the enemy.

I missed Mamie so much. I realized what wisdom she had tried to pass on to me and I bitterly regretted that I had not paid more attention.

I was turning more and more to my three ladies – oddly enough the Buckinghams – but most of all to Lucy. She was a great comfort to me during those days. She was so much wiser than I and she reminded me very much of dear Mamie. Her advice was very similar. Be calm. Think before you act . . . before you speak even.

I knew it was sound advice. I wondered if I could ever be disciplined enough to follow it.

When I saw the letter Charles had written to Buckingham I was so incensed that I almost tore it into pieces and threw it out of the window. I wished I had done so and then I should have delighted in telling Charles of my act.

I don't know how he could have been so careless, but I supposed he had thought it was safe in his own apartments. It was lying on a table just as he had written it, and slipping into the room I saw it.

'Steenie,' he had written.

'Steenie!' I said aloud scornfully. It was absurd how Charles doted on the fellow. He was as weak as his father. What was wrong with these Stuarts? Weaklings, that was what they were. Mary, the Queen of Scots, Charles's grandmother had been foolish – so much so that she had lost her head at Fotheringay.

I went on to read the letter.

'I writ to you by Ned Clarke that I thought I should have cause enough, in a short time, to put away the monsers . . . '

I ground my teeth. He meant by 'monsers', monsieurs, my French attendants.

'either by their attempting to steal away my wife or by making plots with my own subjects. For the first I cannot say whether it was intended; but I am sure it is hindered; for the other, though I have good grounds to believe it, and am still hunting after it, yet seeing daily the maliciousness of the monsers by making and fomenting discontents in my wife. I could tarry no longer in advertising to you that I mean to seek for no other grounds. . . . Advertise the Queen Mother of my intentions. . . .

'I pray you send me word with what speed you may whether ye like this course or not. I shall put nothing of this into execution until I hear from you. . . . I am resolved it shall be done and shortly. So longing to see you, I rest

'Your loving and constant friend

'Charles R.

I was furious. They were talking about my friends, my happiness. And he would do nothing until my Lord Buckingham gave his permission! Oh yes, Buckingham was the evil spirit who had ruined my happiness. I hated him.

It soon became clear that Buckingham approved of the measure Charles was taking against me, for it was not long before all my dear friends left for France.

Lucy took the trouble to send someone along the river to Somerset House that I might know how my friends left.

There was a little trouble, she told me. When all the barges were there to take them away, the people crowded into the streets and along the river to watch them go. At first my dear friends declared they would not leave for they had not been properly discharged and were here on the terms of the marriage treaty. The King had to send a strong body of yeomen with heralds and trumpeters and they were told that His Majesty's orders were that they were to leave without more ado. Mamie was very upset. She wept and explained that she had sworn never to leave me.

Dear Mamie. I knew she would do that.

'One of the mob threw a stone at her,' Lucy said.

'At Mamie!' I cried in horror.

'It was all right. She was not hurt. It just knocked her cap off and the man who had thrown it was killed on the spot. One of the soldiers drew his sword and ran it through the man's body. Then, weeping, Mamie allowed herself to be put into the barge.'

So that was the end. They had left me.

I could not eat. I could not sleep. I could only think of my dear friends who were lost to me and most of all of my beloved Mamie who, I knew, would be heartbroken.

When Charles came to me I refused to speak to him. I see now how patient he was, how sorry that this had happened; but he was firmly convinced (and Buckingham had made him certain of this) that all the trouble between us came from my French retinue.

I would let him see that their dismissal had made everything more difficult between us.

He told me that all my servants had not gone yet and he was arranging for one of the nurses and Madame Vantelet to stay – also a few of my servants. It was a slight concession for none of these people was particularly close and all held minor posts, so this did little to alleviate my grief.

'I want to see my confessor,' I cried.

I knew that Father Sancy had either gone or was going. He would have a fine story to tell them when he returned to France.

'I will send Father Philip to you,' said Charles.

I brightened a little. I was fond of Father Philip, who was much less stern than Father Sancy, and I would be pleased to see him.

He came and talked to me and we prayed together; he said that there were many crosses to bear in this world and I had just been presented with one of them. I must carry it bravely and keep my eyes on the goal, which was to spread the truth wherever I was and always remain steadfast in following the true Faith.

I felt much better and later Charles told me that Father Philip might stay.

I was pleased to hear that, but I did not tell Charles so. I felt in no mood to give him any satisfaction.

One of the hardest things to bear was that François de Bassompierre was not entirely on my side. I had expected condolences from him when in desperation the King sent for him to try to reason with me.

'Your Majesty,' he said, 'I must talk to you most frankly. I know you will allow me – as a loyal subject of your father and one whom he regarded as a close friend – to say exactly what is in my mind.'

My spirits sank. My experience told me that when people declared they were going to speak frankly something unpleasant was certain to follow.

'I have seen you in the presence of the King,' he went on, 'and it appears to me that His Majesty has tried to do everything within his power to make you happy.'

'Such as depriving me of my friends,' I cried petulantly.

'It is the custom when a princess comes to a new country for those who accompanied her on the journey to return in due course to their native land.'

'Why? Why shouldn't anyone . . . most of all a Queen . . . keep her friends about her if she wishes to.'

'Because, Majesty, they do not always understand the customs of the new country and it is the duty of the princess to adopt those customs as she has become a member of that country.'

'I am French. I shall never be anything else.'

He sighed. 'That I fear is at the root of the trouble.'

'How can you ask me to become one of these people? They are heretics.'

'Adequate arrangements have been made for you to worship as you wish, and I see that the King has kept his word in seeing that these are carried out.'

'And taken away my confessor!'

'I did not think you cared greatly for Father Sancy and Father Philip is left to you.'

I was silent. It was true that I greatly preferred Father Philip to Father Sancy.

'Oh,' I cried. 'Can't you see! I have been robbed of those I loved most.'

'You are thinking of your governess. She understands. She is sad, but she is not lost to you. You can write to each other and no doubt she will pay a visit to these shores at some time and you may come to France. Then you will have an opportunity of meeting.'

I felt exasperated. What compensations were letters and the occasional visit for the hours of confidences and fun which Mamie and I had shared?

Bassompierre went on to lecture me. He could see that the trouble between the King and myself was largely due to my attitude. If I could only be reasonable . . . try to adjust myself . . . much progress could be made. The King was fond of me. He wanted to be more fond. He would do a great deal to make me happy, but my demands were childish and he was the King on whom state duties weighed heavily. I was not helping him nor myself by my conduct. I was self-willed, said Bassompierre. My father would not have been pleased with me if he were here today. I was impulsive; I spoke before I thought what I was saying; I must try to curb my temper.

I scowled at him and he went on: 'It is not merely yourself you have to consider. Do you realize that your actions are causing strife between France and England?'

'They do not need me to bring strife between them. It has been there for centuries.'

'There was friendship. The marriage was meant to make that firm, and it should have done so, had you behaved in a manner which your great father would have expected you to. Instead you have made this petty war betwen your faction and that of the King with the result that they are all dismissed . . . banished . . . because they have been fomenting strife betwen you and the King.'

'You think I and my friends are to blame. You should be on my side. I thought you were French and would stand by me.'

'I am French and I will stand by you but there is much you must do for yourself. You must change your attitude towards the King.'

'Shouldn't he change his towards me?'

Bassompierre sighed. 'He is willing to do much for you.'

'Will he send back my friends?'

'You know you ask for the impossible.'

'I never thought you would turn against me.'

He was on his knees, taking my hand and kissing it. He was for me, he declared. He would do anything for me. That was why with great temerity he was telling me exactly what be believed without subterfuge, and he hoped I would see it in the way it was meant and forgive him if he had offended.

He was so handsome, and contrite in a way while adhering to his principles, that I smiled and said: 'Get up, François. I know that you do what you do and say for my good. But if only you knew how tired I am of having things done for my good.'

He smiled. I was the dear, adorable child once more.

I was sure he thought that now we had passed through the emotional preliminaries he could talk seriously to me. This he began to do. The situation between England and France was becoming dangerous. The English were very unpopular in France and the return of my attendants had made them more so. Some of them who had served me were circulating rumours about the way in which I was treated in England and my countrymen were becoming incensed.

'If the Duke of Buckingham set foot in France now he would be torn to pieces by the mob.'

'A befitting end for the monster,' I commented.

'And imagine the effect that would have on the King. Why, it could result in war.'

I was silent.

'You see, my dear lady, many eyes are on you and this marriage. Your mother . . . your brother . . . they look to you to strengthen the bonds of friendship between the two countries. They will be very sad to hear the stories which your attendants are circulating.'

'It is well that they should know.'

'But you have nothing of which to complain. You have been treated royally. The King has shown you every consideration.'

'By taking away from me those I loved best!'

He was exasperated. 'I have explained, my lady, that it is the custom for attendants to return home after a certain period. You cannot say that you – or they – have been ill treated here. Now let me explain what is happening in France. In the villages and the towns they are talking about the ills which have befallen their Princess. They speak as though you have been confined to prison and kept on bread and water.'

'I wouldn't mind that if I could have Mamie with me.'

'Do try to understand. Let me explain to you that one girl, obviously deranged, has been to a convent in Limoges and asked for shelter there. She called herself the Princesse Henriette de Bourbon and told some garbled story about having escaped from England and cruel King Charles because she was persecuted there in an effort to make her give up her Faith. I can tell you this: Thousands of people are flocking to Limoges to see this girl. They believe her and are crying vengeance on King Charles of England.'

'Surely it is easy to prove she is a fraud.'

'To any who have knowledge of Courts, of course, but these are simple people and she is succeeding in deluding them. The King, your brother, is extremely angry. He has other matters with which to occupy himself. The Huguenots are causing a great deal of trouble.'

'Tell me more of the girl. I should like to see her. Is she like me?'

'She passes herself off well, I hear. She has a certain dignity and seems to know something of the English Court. Your brother has made a declaration that the girl is an impostor and that you are living amicably with your husband in England where you are given every dignity due to a Queen.'

I was silent.

He went on: 'She has been proved in a public trial to be a fraud. She has done a penance through the streets carrying a lighted taper and is now in prison. But that does not mean that certain people do not continue to believe her.' He bent towards me. 'Please, Your Majesty, will you try to do your duty here. Do you see how easily great trouble could arise from your actions. I am sure you would not wish to be responsible for a war and to know that innocent blood was being shed because of your wilful actions.'

He did succeed in making me realize how important some trivial actions of mine might be. I said I would remember what he had told me and he went away a little happier than he had been on his arrival.

After my talk with François de Bassompierre I did try to be a little more affable to Charles and I must admit that he was only too ready to meet me in this. We became friends again and without Mamie to confide in and Father Sancy to point out the iniquities of heretics we did seem to be happier together.

He was very preoccupied at this time with affairs of state. He was more serious than ever and wanted so much to rule the country well. I heard him say that he and Steenie could manage very well without a parliament. It was Kings who had been chosen by God to rule not men who set themselves up – although they declared they had been elected by their fellow men – to say what should and should not be done.

Looking back now I can see quite clearly the danger signals even at that time beginning to show. I was not very interested in politics, but I did know that there was a great deal of trouble in France and that somehow the English were not exactly aloof from it.

Cardinal Richelieu had more or less taken over the reins of government, and it seemed that my brother – who had never been a very forceful character – was glad for him to do this. But my mother, who was a born intrigante, had become the centre of an opposing faction. The Cardinal was a very strong man but even he had his difficulties when he was surrounded by those who would be ready to stab him in the back.

I thought a great deal about Buckingham, whom I hated violently for I really believed he was the cause of the unhappiness I had endured since I came to this country.

He was very unpopular I was glad to note. I always said he owed his rise to power to his good looks and certainly not to his performance in state matters. He would have been impeached if Charles had not saved him. He had failed in an expedition to Cadiz. Why he should have imagined himself as a military commander I could not say. He had no talent for command. He could hardly be impeached for failure in war, but accusations of other crimes were brought against him. Charles saved him by dissolving Parliament. What did he want a parliament for? he would say. He could govern on his own.

Buckingham loved the applause of the crowd and wanted to regain his popularity so he began making a great show of his sympathy for the Huguenots who at that time were being a nuisance to my brother. In fact they were more than merely vociferous and the country was becoming weakened by civil war.

Buckingham wanted to send help to the Huguenot citizens of Rochelle who were being blockaded by my brother; this naturally meant a declaration of war between France and England.

I was most distressed. What a terrible position for a Queen to find herself in: her husband at war with her brother! I thought constantly of my dear friends who had been torn away from me and although I was generally able to shut my mind to what I thought of as stupid politics, it was hardly possible to do so at this time.

Charles and I were becoming more friendly, and he even talked a little about what was on his mind. He was always against the Parliament. What right had these men to tell a King what he should do? He was constantly asking that question.

'I would go without a parliament altogether,' he said, 'but I have to get them to grant me money. How can we carry on the country's affairs without money?'

He believed that he and his beloved Steenie could manage very well without those dreary men who were always putting obstacles in the way.

He tried raising money without the aid of Parliament by making every one of his subjects pay a tax. If they refused they were imprisoned. He raised an army and the men were billeted in

private houses whether the owners wanted them or not. Fortunately they blamed this on Buckingham. How they hated that
man! I would laugh inwardly every time I saw a sign of this.
Charles, however, continued to love him. It used to make me so
angry when I heard his voice soften as he said his name.

In spite of all his efforts Charles found it necessary to call
Parliament, which immediately made him surrender his right to
billet soldiers in private houses and to exact loans without the
consent of Parliament.

How he raged against them! But he needed their help if he was
going to take part in the siege of Rochelle, and he was forced to
accept their terms.

I was relieved when the siege of Rochelle was over and ended
in triumph for the French, partly because in my heart I liked to see
my own countrymen triumphant and because it was another
failure for my old enemy Buckingham. I was so delighted when I
heard him reviled. There were satires and pasquinades written
about him and stuck on buildings all over the country.

To try to make the people like him again and to show how he
upheld the Protestant Faith he started to plan a new expedition.
This time it was to relieve the people of Rochelle.

He came to see Charles, and I don't think he was very pleased
to realize how much better we were getting on. He was delighted,
of course, that I had lost my friends; and I wondered what fresh
unpleasantness he could plot against me when he was free from
his present project, for at that time he was concerned with little
else but his expedition to Rochelle and he was going down to
Portsmouth to make sure that all the provisions and ammunition
they would need were on board.

Charles came to me after he had left.

'Steenie is in a strange mood,' he said. 'I have never seen him
gloomy before. He is usually so sure of success.'

'His lack of success has probably made him doubt his powers
after all. In which case it would be a good thing, for it is always
well to see oneself as one really is rather than how one would
wish to be.'

Charles was a little hurt as always when I criticized his beloved
Steenie, but he refused to be drawn into an argument and ceased
to talk of Buckingham and became my loving husband.

It was not long after that when it happened.

The King was prostrate with grief and I was very sorry for him because I knew what it meant to lose someone one loved perhaps as deeply as one had ever loved anyone. Had I not lost my own beloved Mamie?

It was ironical that the King who had robbed me of my dearest companion should now find that fate had robbed him of his.

William Laud brought the news from Portsmouth. Laud was a priest and a great favourite of both Charles and Buckingham. My husband had shown him great favour and perhaps because Buckingham had thought so highly of him, he had made him a Privy Councillor and promised him the Bishopric of London. He was already Bishop of Bath and Wells. He had grown very friendly with Buckingham because Buckingham's mother had shown signs of becoming too interested in the Catholic Faith and Charles had sent Laud to be her priest and bring her back to Protestantism. This Laud had tried to do, and while he was under Buckingham's roof had formed a great friendship with the Duke, and as the King liked to share everything with his Steenie, Laud was his friend too.

So it was Laud who came with the news.

There was tension throughout Whitehall. I had never seen the King look as he did then. His face was quite devoid of colour and his eyes stared ahead disbelievingly as though pleading with someone – the Almighty, I suppose – to tell him that it was not true.

But it was true.

'He had a presentiment that death was close to him,' Laud told us. 'He called me to him the night before. He was very serious and Your Majesty knows that was not like him. He begged me, Your Majesty, to commend him to you and request you take care of his wife and family.'

'Oh, Steenie,' murmured the King, 'as if I would fail you!'

'I said to him,' went on Laud, "Why do you say this? You have never before suggested that you are going to die. I have never seen you, my Lord, but when you are full of high hopes and good spirits." He answered me, "Some adventure may kill me. Others have been killed before me." I said to him, "Is it an assassin you fear?" And he nodded. I suggested that he wear a shirt of mail under his clothes, but he laughed the idea to scorn. "That would not protect me against the fury of the mob," he said. So he would take no precautions.'

'Oh, Steenie,' moaned the King.

I wanted to know how it had happened, every detail. The King covered his face with his hands while I asked the questions. Laud whispered to me that the King could not bear to hear more.

I could very well bear to hear more. I could listen and exult so insisted that he proceed.

'He was staying at the house of Captain Mason in the High Street,' said Laud. 'It was convenient for the supervision of the loading. His Duchess was staying at the house with him before he sailed. He had come down to breakfast and partaken heartily of it. Then he went into the hall and paused for a moment to exchange a word or two with Sir Thomas Tryer who had come to see him. Suddenly a man stepped forward. He cried out: "God have mercy on thy soul!" and brandishing a knife he thrust it into the Duke's left breast.'

The King moaned softly and I went to him and took his hand. He pressed mine warmly.

'The Duke himself withdrew the knife,' went on Laud. 'He was bleeding profusely and there was blood spattered everywhere. My Lord Duke took two steps as though to go after the man. He cried, "Villain!" and then fell to the floor. The Duchess came running into the hall. Poor lady, she is three months with child. She knelt beside him, but he was dying and I could see there was nothing we could do. I gave him what comfort I could and it was then that he again begged me to commend him to you and ask you to look after his family.'

The King was still too overwrought to speak.

I said: 'Have they caught the assassin?'

'Yes, a certain John Felton – a discharged officer who thought he had a grievance, and when the House of Commons showed their disapproval of the Duke he believed he was doing his country a service.'

He was, I thought. Oh good John Felton!

But I had learned my lessons. I said nothing; and then devoted my time to attempting to comfort the King.

How strange it was that the man who had done so much to drive a wedge between us in life, in death should be the means of bringing us together.

I understood Charles's grief so much and because for once I could see through someone else's eyes, I could console him, because his was the greater pain. Steenie had gone for ever but I could still write to Mamie and I hoped to see her one day.

He talked to me a great deal about Steenie and I had to control my impulses to say something derogatory about him, and then after a while I saw how comforting it was for him to talk about this beloved friend whose faults he could not and never would see.

Life for him had lost its savour and it seemed that I was the one who could make up for that. I took a great pleasure in this and he could hardly bear to be away from me. I felt tender towards him. I sensed a certain weakness in him and instead of being critical of it, it endeared him to me.

I treated him as though he were my child instead of my husband and he was grateful for that. Charles was not a man who enjoyed exerting his will. He was serious in his intentions to do right; he wanted to be a good ruler and a good husband. He had not enjoyed sending away my attendants but he had done so because he had thought it was the best for us all.

I began to understand so much and each day I looked forward to our talks, and at night, in the privacy of our bedchamber, I think we truly became lovers.

I began to wonder whether there had been two reasons why we had had such a stormy beginning to our married life. One was undoubtedly Buckingham and the other . . . could it really have been my attendants? Sancy had led me into some difficult situations culminating in the visit to Tyburn; my ladies had always reminded me that I was a Frenchwoman among the English, and a Catholic in an alien land.

Of course Mamie had done her best to help me, but she was apart from the rest.

A few weeks passed while Charles mourned Buckingham deeply, but I knew his sorrow was passing because he was finding great pleasure and the deepest satisfaction in the new relationship which was springing up between us.

Then I discovered that I was with child.

I was very excited at the prospect of having a baby, and Charles was delighted.

'It must be a boy,' I said. Then he smiled gently at me and told me I must not be disappointed if our first child was a girl. We would get boys in due course, he was sure.

I talked about the child practically all the time with my women. One of them said she was sure it would be a boy by the way I was carrying it.

'How I should like to know for sure,' I said.

One of them whispered to me: 'Why not consult Eleanor Davys.'

It was the first time I had heard the woman's name and I had no idea then that she would be the cause of frictions between Charles and me.

I talked over the matter with those three who had become my special friends among the English ladies of the bedchamber: Susan Feilding, Countess of Denbigh, Katherine, Buckingham's widow, and my favourite of the three, Lucy Hay, Countess of Carlisle. Poor Katherine was very sad at this time; she could not get over the shock of losing her husband. It was strange to me that anyone could love that man, yet she had apparently done so – as had my own husband. She told me how she would never forget coming down the stairs and seeing him lying there in the hall with his blood spattering the walls. I could quite understand why she had nightmares nowadays. We did our best to cheer her and somehow that brought us all closer together.

'Why not call in Eleanor Davys?' said Susan. I think she looked upon it as a diversion for me as well as for Katherine.

Lucy said that Eleanor Davys had foretold her first husband's death. 'She said he would die in three days,' she added, 'and he did.'

We were all awestruck.

'She would know then whether I was carrying a boy or a girl,' I said.

'Why not wait and see,' suggested Katherine. 'Wouldn't it be nice to surprise yourself?'

'I should like to know now,' I said. 'Moreover I should like to put this wise woman to the test.'

'Let us bring her in then,' suggested Lucy.

'Who is she?' asked Katherine.

'She is the wife of Sir John Davys, the King's Attorney General,' Susan told us.

'Her second husband,' I added, 'since she foretold the death of her first husband. I wonder if she has told Sir John how long he has to live.'

We were all laughing together and even Katherine managed to raise a smile.

However it was arranged that Lady Davys should be brought to me and she was only too delighted to come. In the meantime I had found out certain facts about her. She was the daughter of the Earl of Castlehaven and was quite renowned for her prophecies. If the letters of her name – Eleanor Davys – were arranged differently and her first name spelt with two lls as it often was and her surname Davie instead of Davys (which one could say was used occasionally) the result would be 'Reveal O Daniel'. This seemed very significant.

We all became very excited thinking of the revelations to come and when the lady was presented I was greatly impressed by her. She was a big woman, dark-haired with enormous luminous eyes – just the sort, I said to Lucy afterwards, which a seer ought to have.

She was not in the least overawed by me. I supposed as a prophetess a Queen did not seem so very important in her eyes.

She told us that she had a mission; she was in touch with powers. She could not explain them; she merely knew that she had been selected by some great force to be able to look at that which was not revealed to ordinary people.

I made her sit down and I told her that I had heard of her miraculous powers and there was a question I wanted to ask her. She folded her arms and looked at me steadily while I asked about the child I was to bear. There was a breathless silence round the table while we all waited for her words. She did not hurry. She sat back for a while and closed her eyes. When she opened them she gazed steadily at me and said: 'You will have a son.'

There was a gasp of delight round the table.

'And,' I cried, 'shall I be happy?'

She said, speaking very slowly: 'You will be happy for a while.'

'Only for a while? How long?'

'For sixteen years,' she replied.

'And then what will happen?'

She closed her eyes and at that moment the door opened and the King came in.

Although I was so much fonder of him now I was irritated by the interruption, particularly as he assumed one of his most serious looks. I thought then what fun it would have been if he had joined us and listened with us and giggled and enjoyed the excitement of prophecy. But that was not Charles's way.

He stood by the table and my ladies all rose and curtsied.

He was looking straight at our soothsayer and he said almost accusingly: 'You are Lady Davys.'

'That is so, Your Majesty,' she answered with pride, and I must admit showing very little deference to the King.

'You are the lady who foretold her husband's death.'

'Yes, Sire. I did that. I have the powers. . . .'

'I can scarcely believe that he welcomed the news,' said Charles coldly. 'Indeed it might well have done much to hasten his end.' He turned to me and offered me his arm.

There was nothing I could do but rise and leave with him, though I was fuming with irritation at having that interesting session cut short.

When we were outside the door he said: 'I do not wish you to consult that woman.'

'Why not?' I cried. 'She is clever. She told me that I would have a son and be happy.'

He was a little uplifted but persisted in his condemnation of her.

'She probably hastened her husband's death.'

'How could she? He did not die of poison. He just died . . . as she said he would.'

'It is dabbling in the black arts.'

I was afraid that he was going to forbid me to see her and I knew that if he did my temper would flare up and I should disobey him. It was a pity. We had been getting on so happily until now.

Perhaps he was thinking the same for he said no more. But there was an outcome. Left alone with the ladies, Eleanor Davys talked a little more and what she said was not nearly as pleasant as that which she had told me. When I returned to my women I noticed that they looked very grave.

I said: 'Did Lady Davys stay long after I left?'

'A little while,' Lucy replied, not looking at me.

'I was so annoyed to be taken away like that. I felt quite angry with the King.'

'He certainly did not like her,' said Susan.

'Did he forbid you to see her?' asked Katherine.

'He did not. And I would forbid him to forbid me. I will not be told, You must not do this and you must not do that.'

'Yet it would be awkward for her, I suppose,' suggested Susan, 'for he could forbid her to come to Court, and of course there is her husband to be considered.'

'Do you think Lady Davys is a woman to be told by her husband what to do?'

'No,' said Susan. 'She would probably tell him he had three days to live if he offended her.'

'That isn't fair,' I protested. 'I think her prophecies are true ones. She promised me a son.'

There was a strange and ominous silence round the table which immediately aroused my suspicions.

'What's the matter?' I cried. 'Why are you looking like that?'

They remained silent and I went to Lucy and shook her. 'Tell me,' I said. 'You know something. What is it?'

Lucy looked appealingly at Susan and Katherine shook her head.

'No,' I cried stamping my foot. 'You had better tell me what is wrong. Is it something Lady Davys said . . . eh? Was it about me?'

'She er . . . ' began Katherine. 'She . . . er . . . said nothing of importance.'

'And that is why you look as though the heavens are about to fall in? Come on . . . I command you . . . all of you . . . tell me.'

Susan lifted her shoulders and after a few seconds of silence Lucy nodded and said resignedly: 'Well, it is just talk, you know. It doesn't mean anything.'

'What?' I cried. 'What?'

'It is better to tell the Queen,' said Lucy. 'If it should come true . . . and I do not believe for a moment that it will . . . it is better for her to know.'

'Know what?' I screamed, my patience at an end; and now a certain fear was creeping into my mind.

'I think she made it up because she was angry about the King's interruption,' said Susan.

'If you don't tell me soon I'll have you all arrested for . . . conspiracy,' I shouted.

Lucy said quietly: 'She told us that you would indeed have a boy.'

'Well, go on. That's what she told me. There is nothing new in that.'

'But that he would be born, christened and buried all in one day.'

I stared at them in horror. 'It can't be true.'

'Of course it can't,' soothed Lucy. 'It is just that she was angry. She was so annoyed that the King came in and showed he did not approve of her.'

I stared ahead of me. I was seeing a little body wrapped in a shroud.

Susan said: 'Don't tell the King what she said or that we told you.'

I shook my head. 'It is such nonsense,' I cried. 'She is a mad woman.'

'That is what so many people say,' said Lucy quickly. 'Your son will be a beautiful child. How could he be otherwise? You and the King are both handsome.'

'My son!' I murmured. 'There will be a son.'

I had so firmly believed her when she said I was to have a son but if the first prophecy was correct, why should the second not be?

Now I began to be haunted by fears.

I don't know whether that prophecy preyed on my mind but whenever I thought of my baby, instead of seeing a laughing lively child I saw a little white one in a coffin. I could not eat much and at night my dreams were disturbed. The King was very anxious about me.

'Perhaps,' he said, 'you are too young to have a child.'

Too young! I was eighteen and would be nineteen in November. That was not so young to have a child. I did not tell the King about the prophecy. He would have been very angry with Lady Davys and I am sure he would have made some complaint to her husband. I tried to disbelieve her. After all, how could she possibly know? It had been a coincidence about her first husband. Perhaps he had been very ill and she, as his wife, knew exactly how ill.

The King was most attentive to me. In fact I think he was far more interested in me and my baby than he was in state affairs and was bitterly resentful when they took him away from us.

I hoped that we should have many children. I could see us in the years ahead with them all around us – beautiful children, the boys looking like Charles and the girls like me. They would certainly be a handsome family.

We were at Somerset House. We had arrived on a Monday and I had arranged for a Te Deum to be sung in the chapel there. While I was in the chapel I began to feel very unwell. It could not be the child yet, because it was not due for another month.

I was very glad to get out of the chapel and to my chamber. I told Susan and Lucy that I was not feeling well and that I thought I should retire to bed.

'You are certain to feel tired,' they said. 'You are getting close to your confinement.'

'Oh, it is a month away,' I reminded them.

But during the night I began to feel pain. I shouted and very soon people were crowding round my bed. I was in agony and I knew that my child was about to be born.

I cannot remember much of that night. I think it was rather fortunate for me that during much of it I was unconscious. In the evening of the next day my child was born . . . prematurely. It was weak, not having reached its full time and I heard afterwards how Charles and my confessor argued together over its baptism which had to take place immediately as it was ominously clear that speed was necessary. My confessor said that as I was to have charge of my children's religious upbringing until they were thirteen, the baby should be baptized according to the rites of the Church of Rome. Charles retorted that this was a Prince of Wales and the people of England would never allow a child who was destined to become King of England to be baptized as a Catholic.

The King, of course, had to be obeyed, and the little boy was baptized according to the Church of England and named Charles James.

Scarcely had those rites been performed when he died.

I remember waking from my sleep of exhaustion to find the King at my bedside.

'Charles,' I whispered.

He knelt by the bed and taking my hand kissed it.

'We have a son?' I asked.

He was silent for a second and then he said: 'We had a son.'

I felt the desolation sweep over me; the waiting months, the discomfort . . . the dreams . . . they had all come to nothing.

'We are young yet,' said the King. 'You must not despair.'

'I so wanted this child.'

'We both did.'

'Did he live at all?'

'For two hours. He was baptized and we christened him Charles James.'

'Poor little Charles James! Are you very sad, Charles?'

'I tell myself that I have you and you are going to be well soon. You are young and healthy and the doctors tell me that in spite of your ordeal you will soon be well again. That is the most important news for me.'

That was my first real experience of Charles in misfortune. He was always able to bear disappointments nobly and with few complaints. These qualities were to stand him in good stead later.

I soon recovered, though I learned that I had been very near to death. There had been one point where they could have saved the child at a cost to my life and the doctors had actually asked the King whom they should consider first . . . me or the child. I was told that he had answered immediately and vehemently: 'Let the child die but save the Queen.'

Perhaps I started to love him then. There was something so good about him; and if there was a vulnerability, a certain weakness, that only endeared him to me the more. Young, frivolous and impetuous as I was, there was a certain maternal feeling in my emotions regarding him. Perhaps it was born at that time.

As I lay in bed I remembered the prophecy. What had she said? I should have a son and he would be born, baptized and die all in a day.

The prophecy had come true.

It is amazing how news like that is circulated. Everywhere people were talking about Lady Davy's prophecy. She was indeed a seer. The King was very angry, particularly when it was suggested that the prophecy had so upset me that it was due to it that I had given birth prematurely.

It was nonsense. I was sure that Lady Davys really had the powers of prophecy.

Charles wanted her to be dismissed from Court.

'You can't do that,' I said. 'You are being like a petulant King who punishes the messengers for the message.'

He did see that. 'But I want no more of these prophecies. They are evil.'

'She promises good things sometimes.'

'First her husband. Then our child.'

'It was ordained that they should die. She just had preknowledge of it.'

'I want her out of the way.'

'You would never get a woman like that out of the way. You could burn her at the stake for a witch but she would curse you or prophesy something evil on the very scaffold.'

Charles was a little superstitious. I think that was why he was so angry.

He did not dismiss her from Court, but he did send for her husband Sir John Davys and asked him to put an end to his wife's prophecies. But Sir John explained to the King that his wife was a forceful woman and could not be forbidden to do anything. 'She believes she has a mission, Your Majesty. She says she will fulfil it no matter what humiliations and punishments the ignorant press upon her.'

Charles was a very understanding man. He knew what Sir John meant and he thought he was very brave to have married Eleanor Davys after what had happened to her first husband. Sir John, however, did burn some of her papers for she had been a collector of ancient manuscripts.

I was against this and argued with Charles about it. I said that if anything was going wrong it was better to know about it. I was sure that having heard the prophecy about my son I was more able to face the bitter disappointment because it was not entirely a surprise to me.

We argued and came near to quarrelling as we used to in the old days, but I remembered his tenderness towards me at the bedside and he thought of all I had gone through so we did not actually use harsh words against each other.

He looked at me pleadingly and said: 'It would please me if you did not see this woman again.'

I hesitated. I wanted to say: But it pleases me to see her. I want to know. I don't want to live in ignorance.

But we both compromised.

He said he was sending Mr Kirke – one of the gentlemen of the bedchamber – with a message to Lady Davys. He was to tell her that the Queen did not wish to see her again.

'It would be more truthful to say the King does not wish the Queen to see her again,' I said with a flash of my old temper.

He kissed me lightly on the forehead.

'My dearest,' he said, 'everything I ever do is with your good in mind.'

I knew that was true and I relented. I took an opportunity of waylaying Mr Kirke before he left with the message. One of the attendants brought him to my chamber.

I said to him: 'Mr Kirke, you are going with a message to Lady Davys?'

'That is so, Your Majesty,' he replied.

'When you hand it to her give her the Queen's compliments and ask her if my next child will be a boy and will he live.'

Mr Kirke bowed and went off.

I could scarcely wait for his return.

I set someone to wait at the gates for him and when he arrived back to bring him straight to me. When he came he was smiling happily so I knew that it was good news.

I said: 'Did you ask Lady Davys my question?'

He replied that he had done so. 'She said, my lady, that your next child would be a lusty son who will live, and that you will have a happy life for sixteen years.'

'Sixteen years! How strange! But a son, you said . . . a son who will live.'

'Those were her words, my lady.'

'Thank you, Mr Kirke,' I said.

And he went away to the King to report that he had carried out his mission.

Sixteen years, I thought. That would take us up to 1644 or thereabouts. Sixteen years . . . that was a long way into the future; and in the meantime I was to have my son and my happy years.

I went to the King. Mr Kirke had left him and I was sure he thought the matter was satisfactorily settled.

I embraced him and said: 'Our next son will be lusty and live.'

He looked at me in astonishment.

'You are with child?' he asked.

'Not yet. But Lady Davys says that my next son will live and be strong.'

I saw the joy in his face. He held me close to him and I laughed exultantly.

It was illogical of him. He was not supposed to believe in prophecy.

But he believed in this one though.

I said: 'It is not such a bad thing to believe in prophecies when they are good. It is only when they are bad that one does not want to know.'

Then he laughed and we were very happy. We were both thinking about the strong and lusty sons we would have.

The Happiest of Queens

It was nearly two years later before the promised boy was born. They had been two happy years, with the affection between my husband and myself growing with every passing week. It seemed so strange that out of those stormy beginnings this deep and glowing love had come. Charles seemed to have grown more handsome than when I first saw him. He smiled now more frequently. He had completely forgotten his obsession with Buckingham and I had been quite content with the letters Mamie and I exchanged. She was married now and had become Madame St George. Her husband was of the noble house of Clermont-Amboise so it was a very worthy match. I knew she was happy and had found consolation for our parting and I was glad of that. She had become governess to my brother Gaston's daughter, who was known as Mademoiselle de Montpensier, and I believe she was quite a handful. Mamie wrote often of her enduring love for me and assured me that she would never forget those happy years when as Mademoiselle de Montglat she had been my governess and friend. But we both realized now that it was no use grieving and my letters, I know, were just as much a joy to her as hers were to me.

I was happy. I had learned to speak English now, and although I should never be exactly fluent in the language I could converse adequately. It pleased Charles so much and I was always happy pleasing him.

We rarely ever quarrelled nowadays. Occasionally my temper would burst out and he would shake his finger at me but there would always be a smile and I would cry out: 'Oh, you can't expect me to change all at once. My temper has been with me from the cradle. I doubt it will ever leave me altogether.'

He said that he really liked me the way I was, which was very comforting and true lovers' talk.

The only trouble between us was, of course, my religion. I often thought that if I could convert Charles to the Catholic Faith and with him the whole of England, I should be completely happy.

But that was asking too much, and even I was wise enough to realize that I had a great deal.

And now . . . my child was to be born.

I kept reminding Charles of Lady Davys' prophecy and although he pretended to be sceptical, because it was a happy one, he was not really so.

I knew I had a great many enemies in the country. Some people even refused to rejoice at the prospect of an heir to the throne. They called me an idolatress – some even had the temerity to shout after me when I rode out. It was rather disconcerting; but I had always known that it might be necessary to suffer for the Faith. But there were plenty of people to rejoice in the birth and there were prayers all the time for my safe delivery and that the child should be a boy.

Well, we were not disappointed, for on the morning of May the twenty-ninth in that year 1630 I was brought to bed in the Palace of St James's and within a comparatively short time my son made his appearance. This time he was strong, lusty and clearly healthy – just as Lady Davys had said he would be.

I shall never forget the moment when they laid him in my arms. He was the ugliest child I ever saw. He was big and very dark and looked much older than one day.

'Why,' I said, 'he is a little monster.'

Charles came in and looked at him. He said: 'He is a perfect child. The doctors say he is in excellent health.'

'He is so dark . . . almost like a blackamoor.'

'Babies get lighter as they grow.'

'But,' I said, 'you are handsome. I am not considered ill-looking. Why should we get the ugliest baby in the world?'

But we were not really concerned with his ugliness. He had arrived and he was by no means sickly. Doubtless he would grow prettier with age.

The King was most excited. He held the baby and marvelled at him. 'Perfect in every way,' he kept saying. Everything which ought to be there was there; he made his presence felt with lusty yells and showed from the first his determination to survive.

We were all delighted with him; better a strong ugly child than a frail pretty one.

On the very morning of the child's birth Charles rode to St Paul's Cathedral to give thanks for the birth of his son and heir. The people cheered wildly; they liked him far better than they did me.

According to the custom my baby was baptized within a few days of his birth. I knew there would be some controversy about this because of the difference in the King's religion and mine. I had been promised that I should supervise the religious upbringing of my children until their thirteenth year and that meant of course that I could educate them as Catholics.

However, I did see that the ceremony could not take place in my private chapel because it was fitted as a Catholic sanctuary. The King said firmly that the baby must be baptized in the chapel of St James's and I was too tired and too happy to argue.

The Bishop of London, William Laud, conducted the service with the help of the Bishop of Norwich and the sponsors were my brother, the King of France, and my mother; they could not, of course, be present, and the Duchess of Richmond and the Marquis of Hamilton were their proxies.

My baby went through the ceremony without too much protest and was christened Charles.

The next thing we had to concern ourselves with was his wet nurse. She must be from Wales, Charles told me, for it was a tradition that the first words the Prince of Wales spoke must be in the Welsh language. After that he could speak his own tongue.

How I enjoyed those days. Sometimes I try to live them again through my memories. It was such a joy to have a child and a devoted husband. Charles could scarcely tear himself away from us. He tried to please me in every way and I was very happy to accept his attention and feel proud of myself because I had given my husband and the country this ugly boy.

Young Charles grew apace but his looks did not improve. His wet nurse said he was the liveliest and hungriest child she had ever known and was going to be tall; he was already big for his age. He was so forward and was more like a three months' child than one of a few weeks. I used to look at him in his cradle and he would return my gaze steadily. His nose was too big for a baby, I thought; but his lively eyes were darting here, there and everywhere.

'You are going to be a remarkable man,' I said to him; and he looked at me so intelligently that I could delude myself into thinking that he understood.

I had to write and tell Mamie all about him. She had a child of her own so she would fully understand the pleasures of motherhood. Writing to her was like talking to her and our letters had been a great solace to me since she left.

'Mamie,' I wrote,

'The husband of my baby's nurse is going to France and I am writing this letter believing that you will be very glad to ask him news of my son. . . . He is so ugly that I am ashamed of him, but his size and fatness supply the want of beauty. I wish you could see the gentleman, for he has no ordinary mien; he is so serious in all that he does, that I cannot help deeming him far wiser than I am myself. . . .

'I assure you that if I do not write to you as often as I might it is not because I have left off loving you but because – I must confess it – I am very idle. Also I am ashamed to admit that I am on the increase again; nevertheless I am not yet certain.

'Adieu. The man must have this letter.

'Your affectionate friend,

'Henriette Marie R.'

Yes, I was indeed pregnant again. I was not displeased about this as my wise little Charles had made me long for another child.

The King was delighted too. It was well for us to have several children, for although little Charles already looked as though he would be able to give a good account of himself, with plagues and other troubles one could never be sure.

Kings and Queens should have large families. Well, it seemed as if, now I had started, I might live up to what was expected of me.

Being a mother and a contented wife did not change my nature. I still loved to dance and although being pregnant did restrict me in many ways I did enjoy entertainments, ballets and banquets. I was very fond of dwarfs. The little people fascinated me and I was delighted when the two I possessed decided to marry. I declared we should have a celebration for them, which we did, and I took great pleasure in arranging the wedding. I had a masque written for it, a musical entertainment. Our great poet Edmund Waller wrote lyrics for it which were set to music. I sang some of the songs but not those, naturally, which were written in praise of my beauty. There were many of those sung at Court and I was vain enough to enjoy them.

How the dwarfs amused us as they tumbled about the room and when they danced on the table, I thought I should laugh so much that it would be bad for the child I was carrying.

Charles and I made a short journey soon after that and were entertained at the house of the old Countess of Buckingham. It was amazing how, since the death of the Duke, I had become quite fond of his family.

This was an occasion I shall always remember. I was seated beside the King in the place of honour and dinner proceeded in the usual manner with the musicians playing all the time, for the Countess knew how much I enjoyed music.

During a short pause in the playing a great pie was carried in and placed in the centre of the table. All eyes were on it as slowly the pastry began to crack from within, until there was a great hole in it and it was scattered over the table. Then out of the enormous dish there stepped a man. He was eighteen inches high, beautifully dressed in miniature garments and with a face which was quite handsome. He advanced along the table taking mincing steps between the dishes. When he came to me he bowed low and said in a very pleasant voice that he trusted I liked him well enough to appoint him my devoted servant.

Everyone was laughing and clapping. Even the King was smiling benignly. I think they were all aware of what was going to happen. For me, of course, it was to be a surprise.

I begged the little man to come and stand beside me. He did so, delicately brushing scraps of pastry from his elegant coat. I said I should be delighted to take him into my service for I liked well his looks and, as he would have heard, two of my little people had married. Oh, they were still in my service but married people were apt to be more devoted to each other than those they served.

He nodded knowingly and said he would dedicate himself completely to his Queen.

I kept him by me and thanked the Countess for giving me so much pleasure.

My little man told me his name was Geoffrey Hudson and that it had long been his ambition to serve me.

So he came into my service. He was extremely intelligent and capable of performing all sorts of errands for he was quite a little statesman; and I became very fond of him and was so pleased that he had come to serve me.

That November, a year and five months after the birth of my swarthy gentleman, I produced a daughter. We decided to call her Mary and like her brother she was baptized in St James's Chapel by Bishop Laud.

A few weeks after her birth my daughter became very ill, and Charles and I spent an anxious time during the days which followed. I had been so happy to have a pretty baby and now reproached myself that I had ever complained about my son's lack of good looks. Healthy children were what we wanted; beauty could take second place.

The Countess of Roxburgh had been chosen as little Mary's governess and Mrs Bennet was her nurse; the child had the usual dry nurse, watchers, rockers, a gentleman usher, two grooms of the backstairs as well as a seamstress and a laundress and other menial servants which were the requisites of a royal infant. I greatly feared during those first days of her life that she was not going to need them.

Prayers were said in my private chapel but not all over the country because we did not want the people to know that we feared for the baby's life.

But in a week or two Mrs Bennet came to me beaming with delight. 'My lady Princess is demanding nourishment, Your Majesty. It is a good sign. She is coming through this.'

And she did.

Charles and I were so happy then. We went to the nurseries and he held young Charles, and I my frail little Mary, and Charles said with that faint stammer which was there when he was over-emotional or very shy that he would be the happiest man in Christendom if this little girl lived and I continued to love him.

Dr Mayerne, the Court physician, was soon declaring in his rather sombre way that Mary would live, and I expressed my overwhelming gratitude to him, and Charles did so more quietly but none the less sincerely.

It was not long after when, one night, as Charles was disrobed in our bedchamber that I noticed some spots on his chest. I was not alarmed at the time, but in the morning I remembered and looking at them again I saw that they had multiplied and were spreading up to his neck.

Dr Mayerne was sent for and diagnosed small pox, which threw us into a panic. He told me to remove myself at once while he looked at everyone in the palace to make sure none was suffering from the dreaded disease.

'But,' I said, 'it is my place to look after my husband.'

Dr Mayerne gave me one of his withering looks. I often laughed with Lucy about him for he was no respecter of persons and always treated me as though I were not only a child but a somewhat stupid one. Strangely enough he was French, having been born at Mayerne near Geneva of Protestant parents, and his real name was Sir Theodore Turquet de Mayerne. Ever since he had practised he had been a pioneer and had invented several cures, and he considered his work more important than anything else on Earth and did not care whom he offended in practising it. Charles's father, King James, had thought so highly of him that he had made him Court physician and Mayerne had looked after Charles ever since he was a boy.

'Anyone who goes into the sick chamber is liable to risk his or her life,' he said.

'He is my husband,' I replied, 'and I shall allow no one else to look after him.'

'You are too fond of drama,' he told me. 'This is not to be confused with play-acting.'

'I assure you I do not think of it as play-acting,' I cried indignantly. 'I am deeply concerned for my husband and I shall be with him in case he needs me.'

Mayerne shook his head but I did see a gleam of something in his eyes which I could not exactly construe. It might have been a faint glimmer of approval.

Charles did not feel very ill, which was unusual in such cases, and tried to persuade me to leave him, but I stood firmly and refused.

He said: 'You are a stubborn woman.'

'I am . . . where I love, and I can tell you, Charles Stuart, that no one is going to tear me from this room while you need me.'

He was deeply moved and turned away so that I might not see the tears in his eyes. All the same, he kept urging me to go.

I would not and I was the only one who nursed him through those days. Fortunately it was only a mild attack that he suffered; we spent the time playing games together, and but for my anxiety about him I could have been completely contented for within a few weeks he was well again. I suffered nothing, although all through his illness I had been in his bedchamber and had even slept in the same bed.

Mayerne said it was a miracle and implied that I did not deserve such good fortune since I was capable of such folly. But I think he admired me, although he considered me foolish. As for Charles, he loved me more than ever. He said he was the luckiest of men and no matter what happened to him in the future everything would be worthwhile because life had brought me to him. For a man who was not inclined to talk extravagantly that was saying a good deal and I told Lucy that I was happier than I had ever been in my life.

Alas, there was one of whom I was fond who was less fortunate. Poor Lucy retired to her rooms in great distress. The dreaded plague had struck her and for a woman like her, one of the beauties of the Court, it was the greatest blow which could befall a woman, for even if she survived, the chances of her being disfigured far outdistanced those of her immunity.

Lucy was not only one of the beauties of the Court, she was chief of them all. Edmund Waller and the poets said I was, but I think some of the beauty attributed to me was homage to royalty. To be honest, I had never been classically beautiful; my nose was too large, so was my mouth; of course I did have magnificent dark eyes and because of my nature, which so many thought frivolous, they sparkled with more vitality than most people's. My features were rarely ever in repose long enough for people to notice the length of my nose; so I gave the impression of charm, which may have been mistaken for beauty. But Lucy Hay was beautiful by any standards. Poets wrote verses to her; and she was lively and intelligent and liked to dabble in politics, she was rightly considered to be the most attractive woman at Court.

The thought of all that beauty being dimmed by the aftermath of the small pox cast a shadow over the Court. I was delighted when I heard that she was recovering, but she refused to admit anyone to her chamber; and only her closest attendants were allowed to see her, so I feared the worst.

For some time she would not emerge from her bedchamber and we all waited in trepidation for her to appear. Some of the poets were disconsolate. I believe they thought they had lost their main source of inspiration.

Then she sent word to me that that night she intended to join the company in the great hall for the evening's entertainment. I was planning some special celebration to give thanks for Charles's recovery. I was not sure whether Lucy's was going to be a cause for rejoicing or not.

I remember that occasion so well. I was wearing a dress of white satin with a large collar trimmed with points. It is strange that when I remember certain occasions I see my clothes clearly. I suppose it is because in those days I paid great attention to them. I had a slight curvature of the spine which had to be disguised by clever dressmaking. I hated anyone to know of this and often had large collars made which hung over my dresses like shawls. Because my dresses were like that it became one of the highest fashions. This was a charming dress and I remember it in detail because it was one of my favourites and that was such an outstanding evening. I often wonder whether it is good to remember so clearly. Such memories come back and back again and I can project myself into those times and relive them. Whether it is a clever thing to do I cannot say. Sometimes the sorrow such recollections bring is greater than the joy.

There was a hushed silence when Lucy appeared. She was magnificently dressed and she had a superb figure, and that was certainly unaltered except perhaps she was a little thinner, which only made her look more elegant.

She was masked and we feared the worst. The mask was black velvet and it covered the whole of her face; through the slits, her eyes glittered. She walked up to Charles and me and bowed low.

I put my arms about her. I knew it was indecorous but I couldn't help it. I was so distressed. My beautiful Lucy, the shining light of our Court and forced to wear a mask!

I fancied I sensed despair in her. I tried words of comfort. I kept saying: 'Lucy . . . *dear* Lucy' again and again.

Then she stepped back and said in a voice which everyone could hear because there was such silence: 'Your Majesties, have I your permission to unmask?'

'Only if you wish, Lucy,' I said.

She replied: 'I do. It is well for all to see.'

Then dramatically she threw off the mask. There was a gasp. Lucy was revealed, her skin dazzling pink and white, completely unmarred.

There was a rustling throughout the room and then everyone was rushing up to look at her and congratulate her.

That scene was typical of Lucy Hay.

I said that we must celebrate the King's recovery – and Lucy's – and the manner in which we should do so would be by having a play or a masque performed. I wanted one written specially for the occasion so I summoned a writer whose work we liked. This was Ben Jonson, an ageing man but one who had a light touch, and I had engaged him on several occasions to write a masque for me; and the best of our designers of scenery could work with him; this was an architect called Inigo Jones. Before I came to England the banqueting hall in Whitehall Palace had been destroyed by fire, and it was Inigo Jones who had designed the new one. He was the only son of a cloth-maker but he had done very well and there was evidence of the fine quality of his work throughout the capital. Unfortunately he and Ben Jonson did not like each other and were constantly quarrelling. Jonson had once said that if he wanted to name a villain in one of his plays he thought it would be a good idea to call him Inigo. I should have known better than to engage the two of them to work on the same production. It was not long before they were refusing to work with each other because Jonson had put his own name before that of Inigo Jones on the title page of the work.

I was so angry with them both that I dismissed them and called in Walter Montague to start all over again and give us a play we could act, which had dancing and singing in it. Wat Montague was the son of the Earl of Manchester and had lived a great deal abroad in France and Italy, and although some people said he had not the wit and panache of Ben Jonson he had a good idea of the sort of entertainment I wanted.

Consequently he produced a masque called *The Shepherd's Paradise,* which all my attendants declared was a masterpiece.

Many were going to perform in it and of course there was a part – the main one – for me. I was glad to have a big part but I did flinch when I saw the amount of words I should have to learn. I almost wished that I had retained Ben Jonson who for all his quarrelsome ways was able to say a great deal in a little space.

However we laughed over it and heard each other's words and there was a great deal of talk of the play we were going to perform both in and outside the Court.

We had an enormous audience because people were allowed to come in from the streets if they could get in. It was not always easy and the Lord Chamberlain had made several rules which kept out certain people. But it was natural, I said, that the people should want to see their Queen perform in a play so I asked the Lord Chamberlain not to be too harsh.

The play went on for eight hours; and there was singing and dancing, which I liked, and in spite of the fact that many people had to sit cross-legged on the floor and quite a number of us forgot our lines and had to be audibly prompted, it was a success and I liked to see the people laughing and having a good time. It would make them like us, I said to Charles afterwards.

Then we heard of the odious Mr Prynne.

He took this very time to publish a book which he called *The Histriomastrix;* it was over a thousand pages in length. It was a diatribe against immorality, for William Prynne was a Puritan of the worst kind, which I hated so much and grew to hate so much more than any other type of man. Play-acting was unlawful, he wrote. It was an incentive to Immorality. Plays had been condemned by the Scriptures and he was condemning them now.

The book was brought to Court and we all pored over it.

Saint Paul had forbidden women to *speak* in churches. He 'Dares any Christian woman to be so more than whorishly impudent as to act or speak publicly on the stage (perchance in man's apparel and cut hair) in the presence of sundry men and women.'

He went on to rant about women actors who were nothing more than strumpets. As for dancing that was worse still. It should be a criminal offence, and those who performed should be thrust into prison and do penance for their wickedness.

We might have laughed at such fanaticism but he did quote the
bible and the writings of many illustrious Christians; and we all
new that the attack was directed against me because I had acted,
had sung, and more than anything I loved the dance.

When the King read it he was very angry – not because he
onsidered it important but because it was an insult to me. He
nought the author should be brought before him and made to
pologize. I think that would have satisfied the King, but Dr
aud, who had become Archbishop of Canterbury, saw some-
ning significant in this attack.

He believed it was directed not only against the Court but was a
riticism of the vestments of the clergy and ceremonies of the
Church.

'Prynne is a dangerous man,' said Archbishop Laud.

As a result Prynne was arrested and stood trial in the Star
Chamber. He was sentenced to prison and fined; his degree was
aken from him and he was to stand in the pillory and have his
ars lopped off.

Charles thought it was a harsh sentence for writing a book but
ne Archbishop was stern in his condemnation. 'Men such as this
ould ruin the Church and all it stands for,' he said. 'There are too
nany Puritans in the land and inflammatory literature such as
nis could increase their number. Let them see what happens to
nyone who dares criticize the Queen.'

That silenced Charles but I could not sleep for some nights – the
ast upset gave me insomnia – and I kept seeing that man in my
nind's eye standing in the pillory with his ears dripping blood.

Of course he was an unpleasant creature. He was miserable old
poilsport and he wanted to make us all like him. But his
ars. . . .

Charles knew that I was worried about him, and Charles was
oo, for he was a just man. On the other hand Prynne had
ttacked royalty, for there was no doubt that the Court was his
arget, and Charles said that he was going against the Lord's
nointed – although, of course, I had never been anointed owing
o my firm adherence to my own Faith.

Charles said he would order that pen and paper be taken to
'rynne in prison. 'That will comfort him,' he said.

'And enable him to write more words directed against us?'

'Poor fellow! He has suffered,' was all Charles said; and I

agreed with him that he must let Prynne have pens and paper. H
would have learned his lesson and not write any more against us
was sure.

Soon after Lucy had appeared to the company so dramaticall
without her mask a rather unusual contretemps sprang u
between some of the notable men of the Court. I was particularl
interested because it concerned a letter of mine and one of m
favourite friends was involved.

This was Henry Jermyn who had always seemed to me a mos
amusing gentleman and we had found a great deal to talk abou
when we met for, although he was quite humble in station, h
had most excellent manners and I felt at home with him perhap
because he had spent a great deal of time in Paris, where he ha
been sent on an embassy. He was able to give me news of m
family and to talk knowledgeably about the life I remembered s
well from my girlhood.

Henry was very tall, inclined to be somewhat on the heav
side; he was as fair as I was dark, with a lazy look which I foun
diverting. Some years before he had been appointed to the pos
of Vice Chamberlain and before that he had represented Liver
pool in Parliament.

He was an inveterate gambler and as different from Charles a
one man could be from another. Everything Charles did must b
right in his own eyes. I sensed at once that Henry would not hav
the same regard for duty but liked to do what was most comfort
able to him and which did not demand too much effort. As I wa
equally lazy and pleasure-loving there was an immediate bond
between us. He was the sort who slipped in and out of trouble
with easy grace, usually relying on his charm to extricate him
from anything which interfered too much with an easy life.

There had been a little trouble on the tennis courts of Whitehall
when he accused one of the men of attacking him with tennis
balls. Henry had become really violent for like many people who
are not easily aroused, when he was he seemed to make up for his
periods of quietness.

That was a small matter compared with two other scrapes
which followed closely on each other and resulted in a term of
imprisonment and then banishment.

The first incident rose through the new French ambassador,
the Marquis de Fontenay-Mareuil, to whom I had taken an

instant dislike as soon as he arrived to replace my dear Marquis de Châteauneuf, who had been in England for some three years. There was at Court at this time a very charming young man, the Chevalier de Jars, who had come into conflict with the devious Cardinal de Richelieu and been exiled. He had come to me and as I knew that Richelieu and my mother were now enemies, naturally I made the Chevalier welcome. He was young, handsome and charming; he danced beautifully and played tennis so well that Charles – who was an excellent player – enjoyed a game with him. I was glad to see my compatriot fitting in so well at Court.

There was one man whom I greatly disliked and that was Richard Weston, Earl of Portland, who was the Lord Treasurer. Now when I try to reason out why I disliked him so much, I suppose it was because Charles thought so highly of him and I could never forget Buckingham and what a hold he had had over the King, and I think I was always afraid that someone else would rise up and manoeuvre himself into a similar position. Moreover, Weston was always refusing to give me money and at times made me feel like a pauper. When I complained of this to Charles, he gave me his slow smile and said it was Weston's duty to look after the exchequer and make sure there was always enough money for the country's needs. I said that was all very well but need he be so parsimonious? In any case there was enough money for the country's needs so why be so miserly about my little request.

Charles said that was female logic and kissed me.

However, I was not to be put off so easily and I talked to my friends like Lord Holland and the Chevalier de Jars about it.

The Marquis de Fontenay-Mareuil was aware that I confided in the Chevalier de Jars, and men such as he always imagine that conspiracies are being hatched. One day the Chevalier came to me in great distress. He told me that his chambers had been ransacked and his papers taken away.

I took him to Charles at once, who looked very grave and asked him who he thought was responsible for this action.

'I feel sure it is someone who wishes to do me harm,' said the Chevalier.

I said: 'We must find this thief, Charles, and he must be punished.'

Charles said the best thing to do was summon the French ambassador. This he did and I begged to be present at the interview because I thought that it might be necessary to defend my dear friend, the Chevalier.

I was right. Not that there was much I could do; and the effect of this was a near quarrel between Charles and myself.

Fontenay-Mareuil was very haughty. He admitted at once that it was on his orders that de Jars' chambers had been ransacked and his papers removed.

'This is stealing,' I cried out.

'Your Majesty,' replied the ambassador, turning to me and bowing, 'I am in the service of his Gracious Majesty, King Louis, and it is on his orders that I investigate the actions of the Chevalier de Jars.'

Charles nodded, seeing the truth of this.

'I have therefore removed the Chevalier's papers,' went on Fontenay-Mareuil, 'and in view of the fact that he is now without them, it will be necessary for him to return to France.'

'For what reason?' I demanded.

'That, Your Majesty, will need to be discovered.'

He then asked Charles if anything more was required of him.

When he had gone I turned to my husband. 'You are not going to let him tell lies about the Chevalier. He is a friend of mine.'

Charles spoke tenderly. 'Oh, I know he dances very well and is a merry companion, but if he is working against his King he must answer for his actions.'

'But he is *my* friend.'

'He is first the subject of the King of France.'

'Does this mean he will be sent back to France?'

'He cannot stay here if he has no papers.'

'Why not?'

'Because they have been removed by the ambassador and I have no doubt that in a few days we shall hear from your brother that the Chevalier is to return to France.'

I begged and pleaded, but Charles said that much as he wanted to give me all I desired he could not interfere with matters of state, particularly between a King and a subject of another country.

'It is *my* country,' I cried.

But he reminded me that I was now English.

I felt my temper rising, but Charles looked so distressed, and I did not want to do anything to spoil our happy life together so I curbed my irritation and made up my mind that I would be wiser to be silent as long as I did everything I could to help my dear friend.

But there was little I could do, for within a week or so the Chevalier received orders from my brother to return to France. I was very worried about him for I was certain that the odious Fontenay-Mareuil would have told tales about him.

I was right for as soon as the Chevalier set foot in Paris he was arrested and sent to prison.

After that there was a series of arrests. Châteauneuf was sent to Angoulême and kept there; even the frivolous Duchesse de Chevreuse, who I believe had numbered Châteauneuf among her admirers, was sent into retirement. Not that she endured it long for in due course we heard that she had captivated her guards and with their help, dressed as a man, she escaped into Spain.

But that was later. Meanwhile I had to think of my dear Chevalier de Jars.

This was where the trouble started for I wrote to my brother, begging him to release the Chevalier and assuring him that the young man had never been anything but a good friend to France. Unfortunately Weston's son, Jerome, was acting as a courier and had been sent to Paris with important papers to be delivered to Louis and on his way back to England with further communications he happened to spend the night at an inn where the courier taking letters to Paris was staying. They fell into conversation and Jerome, who took his duties very seriously and, as the son of his father, was well aware of plots against him, thought he was within his rights to examine the letters which were being taken to France.

Thus it was that he came across the one which I had written to my brother and another written by Lord Holland. These were private letters and the custom was to send them separately; and the fact that they were in the diplomatic bag raised the officious Jerome Weston's suspicions. He took the letters and brought them back to England to present to the King.

It was not difficult to imagine my fury when I heard what had happened. Charles did his best to restrain me, but this time he did find it impossible.

'It is an insult,' I cried. 'How dare this . . . upstart treat me like this? Am I the Queen or am I not?'

Charles tried to calm me. 'He was doing what he thought was his duty.'

'His duty . . . to insult me!'

'It was not intended to be an insult. Private letters should not be put into the diplomatic bag. Don't you see that if someone wanted to make mischief how easily it could be done. There has to be a close watch on this. All young Weston was doing was his duty.'

'Lord Holland is furious,' I cried. 'He will do that young man an injury.'

'He will be foolish if he does for that would be an offence whereas Jerome Weston has committed none.'

I was exasperated and left him. I dared not trust myself to stay longer for I should have started to abuse Charles himself very soon.

I went to my own apartments. Lucy was there with Eleanor Villiers, a niece of Buckingham, who had joined the ladies of my bedchamber some little time before.

I told them what had happened and they both expressed their astonishment that young Jerome Weston could have behaved so; that comforted me a little.

It was Eleanor Villiers who brought the news to me. She seemed very upset.

'Henry Jermyn has been arrested,' she said.

'Henry Jermyn! But why?'

'Holland challenged young Jerome Weston to a duel because he said he had insulted you and himself. Henry delivered the challenge and that is an offence.'

'What of Holland?'

'He is also arrested.'

I said: 'I will see the King at once.'

I found Charles with some of his ministers and they were already discussing the matter which had sprung up between Holland and the Westons involving Henry Jermyn.

'I must see you at once,' I said, glancing haughtily at the ministers, and adding: 'Alone.'

I could see that they thought Charles a most uxorious husband for he immediately told them he would see them later.

They left and I burst out: 'I have just heard that Henry Jermyn has been arrested and Lord Holland with him.'

'That is so,' said the King.

'But why?'

'For disobeying the law. They know duelling is forbidden and ny connected with it are guilty of breaking that law.'

I said 'Holland has challenged young Weston. But why Henry :rmyn. . . .'

'I will not allow the laws to be broken.'

'He is my friend.'

'My dearest, even your friends are not friends of the crown if ley break the laws.'

'This is a plot.'

'I think,' said Charles, 'that there is a plot and it is directed gainst my Treasurer. The young man did right to intercept the :tters. He suspects that some people are working against his ather and I am of the opinion that he may be right. He was acting vithin his duties in searching the diplomatic bags. You must nderstand that, my loved one. We cannot have plots within our nidst and we must be ever watchful of those who foment them.'

'Do you mean that Holland and Jermyn will be punished?'

'They must answer to the law. There have been murmurings gainst the Treasurer, who is a good and honest man. He is areful with our money and that is what we need.'

'So you are determined to be on his side!'

'My dear, I am on the side of right.'

I could see that no amount of pleading could change him. He vas the most obstinate man alive and while he thought he was loing what was right he would continue to do it.

He explained to me that it was offensive that a member of his ouncil – as Holland was – should send a challenge to a man in the King's service who was merely carrying out his duties.

Of course neither offence was very great and all that happened vas that Holland was confined for a while to his house in Ken-ington and Henry Jermyn was sent away from the Court for a hort time to stay in a private house.

It was typical of both men that they should make the most of heir captivity. Holland gave parties and it was said that he ttracted all the most amusing people from Court to visit him. I leard that his parties were the most exciting thing that was happening. The Court certainly seemed a little dull without those wo. I particularly missed Henry Jermyn. I did not realize how nuch he had amused me until I had lost his company.

Charles had become more friendly than ever with the Earl c
Portland since the incident and with his son – the little spy,
called him. They were both high in Charles's favour.

I said to Charles, rather bitterly: 'It is clear that you will neve
listen to my desires. You punish my friends and cherish m
enemies.'

'You rule my heart,' said Charles, who could be very senti
mental at times, 'but, my dearest love, because God made m
King I have to rule this kingdom. Those whom you think are you
friends are not truly so for if they work against me and m
ministers they cannot be mine, and you and I are as one, an
therefore what is evil for me is evil for you also.'

I was so happy with Charles and the babies that I did not reall
want anything changed; but I did think a great deal abou
Holland and Henry Jermyn, and after a few weeks, because
missed them so much, Charles said they could return to Court
So they came back and I was delighted. But Charles was cool t
them both and his trust in the Earl of Portland seemed not to hav
decreased.

Charles said that Holland was unreliable and I should no
become too friendly with him. I reminded him that he ha
arranged our marriage and I added: 'He will always have a speci
place in my regard because he did that.'

Charles was touched and very soon these two gentlemen wer
as much in evidence as ever, though I did believe they saw hov
useless it was to try to shift the King's trust in his Treasurer.

It was soon after that that the second trouble arose.

I noticed that Eleanor Villiers had been looking a little straine
lately and it gradually dawned on me that she was in a certai
condition which I myself had been in more than once so I wa
very much aware of the signs.

I called her to me one day, making sure that we were alone an
I said: 'Eleanor, are you feeling quite well?'

She looked startled and then blushed a fiery red, so I knew
had not been mistaken.

'Who?' I asked.

She would not say at first and I thought I could not press he
. . . just yet.

'How soon?' I asked.

'Five months,' she replied.

'Well, Eleanor,' I went on, 'it is a good thing I know. Your
arriage will have to take place without delay.'

She was silent and I feared the worst.

'He is married?' I asked.

She shook her head.

'Then that is good. There must be no delay. Why did you wait
) long?'

'He does not want to marry.'

'Does not want to marry! But he will have to keep his promise.'

'He made no promise.'

'You mean that you . . . a lady of the Court . . . without a
romise of marriage. . . .'

'Yes, Your Majesty.'

I said angrily: 'Who is this man?'

And then she told me. 'Henry Jermyn.'

'Oh, the rogue,' I cried. 'Leave this to me. The King will be
most put out. You know what a high standard of morality he sets
pon the Court. I will speak to Jermyn at once. Go and leave this
) me.'

I sent for Henry. He looked as jaunty as ever – not in the least
ke a man who was heading for trouble. He took my hand and
issed it.

I said: 'I have just been talking to Eleanor Villiers.'

Even then he did not look in the least disturbed.

I went on: 'She had some distressing news to tell me. I think
ou must know what it is.'

He put his head on one side in an amusing way he had and
egarded me with earnestness. I said severely: 'It is no use
ssuming innocence. You know what you have been doing. You
aave got the poor girl with child.'

'Most careless,' he said.

'I agree with that. There is nothing you can do but marry her.'

'That I cannot do.'

'What do you mean? You cannot marry her! You are a bachelor,
re you not?'

'A very impoverished one.'

'I cannot see that that should prevent your marriage.'

'Alas, the lady is also impoverished and now that her uncle is
dead and blessings have ceased to flow on the family, she is as
poor as I am and such poverty should always be a bar to marriage.'

'You are a wicked man,' I said.

'Who sometimes amuses Your Majesty. If I can do that I mu
be content.'

'The King will hear of it and be most displeased.'

'I regret that.'

'He may well order you to marry the lady.'

'I do not think the King would step outside his rights.'

'No. He always does what is right. Well, Henry, there will |
trouble over this. She is after all a lady of the Court and a memb
of the Buckingham family at that.'

'I know,' he said mournfully.

'You *should* marry her.'

'It would not be a good marriage for either of us. She is
charming girl . . . but penniless, and I am a rogue as you say ar
not worthy of her.'

In spite of his light manner I could see that his mind was mad
up.

The King was most distressed. 'I will not have this immorali
in my Court,' he said.

'You cannot make them marry though. Do you think Elean
Villiers would want to marry a man who did not want to mar
her?'

'As there is to be a child, yes.'

'But I do see Henry's point. If he marries her he will have r
chance of retrieving his fortunes.'

'If he doesn't what chance has she of making a happ
marriage?'

I looked at him helplessly and thought again how fortunate
was in my happy marriage.

I flung my arms round him and told him so. He smiled quiet
and indulgently at my demonstrative behaviour, which was s
unlike his own; he patted me and said that he would consider th
matter and decide what should be done.

The King saw both Eleanor Villiers and Henry separately.

He was determined then that Henry should marry Eleanor. F
said he must have promised marriage before she agreed
intimacy with him but Eleanor, who was a very honest girl, sai
there had been no talk of marriage.

The King was horrified, but she said; 'I loved him too much.'

Charles was touched and that made him all the more ang

with Henry. He said that as there had been no promise of marriage he could not insist on it, but he would not for one moment give his approval to what Henry Jermyn had done. He did not demand that there should be a marriage but he said that Henry would not be welcome at Court until there was one.

That meant banishment. Henry went abroad and once more I was deprived of his company.

In the meantime I had become pregnant again. I often thought that Buckingham must have laid a spell on me because during the time of his ascendancy over Charles, I remained barren; and no sooner was he dead than I became as fertile as any woman in England.

When I told Charles that I was expecting another child he was overjoyed.

'We must go to Scotland soon,' he said, 'for you will not be able to travel when your pregnancy is advanced.'

'Scotland!' I cried in dismay. I had never liked what I heard about the place. It was cold and the people were dour, so said my informants. I thought some of them in our own Court were solemn enough so I did not relish going among those who were more so.

'It is time I was crowned there,' said Charles. 'The people expect it.'

I was immediately apprehensive. I had refused to be crowned with the King in England. How could I possibly be in Scotland? I was in a very difficult position as my French advisers had pointed out. For a Queen not to be crowned was to place herself in a position which could be dangerous. On the other hand, how could I, a fervent Catholic, bow to the doctrines and customs of the Protestant Church?

'I cannot do it,' I said. 'I should hate myself if I did. It would be wrong. I cannot deny my Faith.'

Charles tried to explain patiently that there was no question of denying my Faith. All I had to do was stand beside him and be crowned. But I knew there was that in the coronation ceremony which obligated the sovereign to swear to live in the Reformed Faith. I knew what that meant. It was flouting the Holy Church, and I could not do it.

In the old days there would have been a quarrel. There was none now.

Charles looked at me sadly and tenderly; he said that he understood the depth of my feelings and would do nothing to distress me.

So he went to Scotland without me and I stayed at home to await the birth of my next child.

When I look back in the light of hindsight, and perhaps because I have become wiser than I was, I think perhaps the first seeds of disaster were sown during that visit to Scotland. I now understand the character of my husband as I never did then. Then I loved him for his concern for me, his devotion and the knowledge that he was one of the few faithful husbands at Court and because he made me feel cherished and beautiful. Now I can love him for his many sterling qualities and at the same time for the weaknesses which would destroy him.

I thought then – and I think now – that Charles was one of the most noble and virtuous men ever to sit on the throne of England; he was a good man, but to be a good man is not necessarily to be a good King; some of the greatest Kings who ever lived have been far from good in their private lives. I see now that the two lives are different and one cannot be judged against the other. We do not judge a man but a King. As a man Charles was noble and good; as a King he was often blind, often foolish, unable to see beyond his own vision, which was misted over by the firm belief that Kings are chosen by God and rule by the Divine Right.

I can see all this now; but I could not see it then. In fact I did not give much thought to it. If I had been asked I should have said that of course we should go on living as we were, raising our children, and in due course my eldest son would take the crown. There were outcries about taxes and Charles said the exchequer was in a sorry state but that had often happened before and as it never made any difference to my way of life, I ignored it.

Now I look back at Charles and try to see him as he was – a smallish man, fastidious and very reserved; he took a long time to make friends, but when he did he became devoted to them, as I had seen through Buckingham and, once he had really grown to love, with me. He was the sort of man whose friendship was to be completely trusted. He was very steadfast in his opinions, and if he liked or disliked a person it was hard to shake either his trust or his suspicion. He loved art in any form and once told me how he would have enjoyed being able to paint, write verses, or compose music; he lacked the talent of performance yet that did not mean he was not a good judge and he did a great deal to encourage painters, musicians and writers at our Court.

'I want a cultivated Court,' he once said to me.

I enjoyed these things, too, so that was an added bond between us.

Dear Charles! He could not make friends easily and he never really understood the people whom he was so anxious to govern well. Later I read a great deal about Queen Elizabeth. This was when I was trying to understand what had gone wrong. I remembered those pilgrimages she made through the country – getting to know the people, always pleasing the people; she had been much more careful in her treatment of them than she was of her intimate friends. Oh, she was a clever woman – a great Queen and a great ruler . . . but she lacked the noble personal character of my Charles.

He would become less aloof in the hunting field. He loved horses and understood them far better than he did people. Perhaps that was why he liked to be with them and avoided human contact – except with those few whom he loved.

He was so constantly reading the book his father had written called *Basilicon Doron* that he must have known it off by heart for it was not very long. It was a kind of guide book for kings and had been intended for Charles's elder brother, who had died leaving Charles to bear the burden. The theme of this book was that a King had received his crown from God. Charles never forgot that and he always believed firmly in the divine right of anointed Kings to govern their people.

I realize that I was in a great measure responsible for the people's dissatisfaction – but perhaps I should say my religion was. There were, it was true, many Roman Catholics in England, but the country as a whole was solidly behind the Reformed Church. And here was I, the Queen – a Catholic.

Charles did everything he could to make things easy for me. He never tried to make me give up my Faith and I had my chapel, which was as Catholic as anything I had in France. But the people did not like it. He had introduced certain ceremonials into the Church of which the people did not approve and Charles,

believing that he had Divine guidance in this, had directed the
clergy to keep silent on the matter. There was trouble with the
people they called Arminians, who were followers of a
Dutchman, Jacobus Arminius. He had published a book which
opposed some of the teachings of Calvin, and the Commons had
wanted the Arminian theory to be suppressed and were annoyed
with the King's attitude. This was disastrous for him because he
needed their support over the tonnage and poundage matters
which could provide funds for the Treasury.

I paid very little attention – I wish now that I had paid more. I
might have seen the storm clouds gathering and done something
to protect ourselves from them.

Charles had dismissed that Parliament and not called another.
For eleven years he had ruled without a parliament. How blind
we were not to realize what forces we were building up against
ourselves.

Meanwhile the King went to Scotland. There he angered the
Scots by being crowned by five bishops all ceremoniously
dressed in white rochets and sleeves and copes of gold and shoes
of blue silk of which the Scots did not approve; moreover the
communion table was arranged after the manner of an altar with
a tapestry set up behind it on which the crucifix was put up.

This was bringing something which the Scots called near-
idolatry into their Church and they did not like it. Moreover they
strongly resented it and there was a very dangerous moment
during the Parliament which Charles was forced to call in Edinburgh after his coronation, when the matter of imposing appare
on churchmen was raised.

The majority of members voted against it, but Charles, who
was certain he could manage very well – in fact much better
without Parliament, instructed the clerk of the court to announce
that the matter had been carried in the affirmative.

Charles then said that the decision must be right since the clerk
had made it, and since it was a capital offence to falsify the
records were some members going to accuse the clerk? None was
prepared to put the clerk into such a dangerous situation, for how
could they know what would be proved against him; but the
Scottish nobles were not the kind of men to allow this to pass
There were objectors and the chief of these was John Elphinstone, Lord Balmerino, who was consequently arrested and pu

into Edinburgh Castle. Charles had returned to England before he was tried. It was imperative that Elphinstone should be found guilty and, when he was, the people gathered in the streets of Edinburgh, threatening to kill the judge and jurors, swearing vengeance on all those who had connived against their hero Elphinstone. He had to be reprieved but was made a prisoner in his castle at Balmerino and finally he was freed.

I mention this because I think it was one of the pointers to the King's eventual fate and was the beginning of Scotland's disenchantment with him.

The King returned from Scotland in time for the birth of our next child. There was great joy on that October day for we had another boy. We called him James after Charles's father and a pretty boy he was – so different from his brother. Poor Charles, his looks did not greatly improve, but he was certainly bright and clever enough to demand attention. Beside him James and Mary looked beautiful, but a little frail.

When the King pointed this out I replied: 'All children look frail beside our dark gentleman. He is already twice as big as other children of his age. Don't worry about the others because they lack his undoubted strength. They have the consolation of being beautiful.'

The arrival of a new baby was certain to arouse the controversy of religion. If Charles had not been a King who took his duties so seriously I was sure I could have made a Catholic of him by this time. But of course the English were a stubbornly Protestant people. I had always maintained that they were not deeply religious. They were Christians; they worshipped God, but they were a lazy people and they did not greatly care to bestir themselves until some issue was presented to them which they considered worth fighting for. How formidable they could be when this happened I did not learn until later. At this time I saw only their lazy indifference. Another thing which I had not seen was that there was a Puritan element beginning to arise in direct defiance of the beautiful church ceremonies and the gracious way of living which I flattered myself I had introduced with the help of Charles, who was such a great lover of art and all its beauties.

The trouble started with the baby. A boy was more important

than a girl and, as he was a possible King, next in line to the dark gentleman, he must be baptized by the King's Protestant chaplain. James was christened and created Duke of York and Albany. I was very proud of him because he was a good and beautiful baby, but I did feel that as he was mine I should not give way to the Protestants on every point, so I engaged a wet nurse knowing that she was a Catholic – in fact choosing her for that reason. It was soon being whispered about the Court that the nurse would inject the baby with idolatry and Charles's advisers warned him that the nurse must either be converted to Protestantism or go.

Charles came to me in some distress. He told me about the complaints and said that if the woman would only make certain statements she would be allowed to remain.

I protested. 'She is a good nurse. The baby has taken to her. I might not be able to find another as good.'

But Charles was adamant as he could be on some occasions, and I could see that in a matter like this my wiles would avail me nothing.

He sent for the nurse and gently explained to her that she had done her work well and that the Queen was highly satisfied with her as a nurse but she must remember that the baby could in some circumstances become the King of England and the English thought he should not have a Catholic nurse. All she need do was take an oath to the effect that the power of the Pope to depose princes was impious, heretical and damnable.

'Take this oath,' said the King, 'and all will be well.'

The nurse started to scream in horror: 'Deny the Pope. Deny the Holy Father his rights. Never . . . never . . . never. . . .'

The King said: 'Then you will leave this palace at once.'

I was very distressed and although the King tried to comfort me I refused to listen to him. I said that every woman in the country could choose the nurse for her own child but a Queen, a daughter of Henri IV, was denied that right.

The King went on trying to comfort me, making allowances for my state, I know; but I was really distressed, not only because of the nurse, but because I had believed till then that I was making some headway and that Catholics were treated much more leniently in England than they had been before my arrival. I had strong hopes that I was beginning to make the King see the rightness of the Catholic Faith and I had thought how wonderful it would be if I could convert him, and, through him, the nation. I should go down in history as another St Augustine or Bertha of early England. And now I could not even have a Catholic wet nurse for my baby!

I refused to eat and I lay sullenly in my bed and was so despairing that I became really ill. The King sent for doctors who could not put a name to my malady. 'The Queen is depressed and so upset that she has lost her vitality and her interest in life,' said the doctors.

Charles was beside himself with anxiety. He really did love me, and I hated to worry him; but I was upset for I did see in this dismissal of the nurse the hopelessness of my dreams.

As I lay there, one day Charles came to the room and with him was the Catholic nurse.

'She is to come back,' he said simply. 'I have given permission. I will silence the gossipers. I hope that pleases you.'

I just held out my arms and we clung together. I was so happy – not only to have the nurse back but because of this further sign of his love for me.

I was better within a day.

There was another little trouble a few days later. The King's Protestant chaplain came to me and explained to me what great good I could do the King and the country by renouncing the Catholic Faith and embracing Protestantism.

What a proposition to make to an ardent Catholic! I denounced him and his Faith vehemently but he persisted; he went on his knees and prayed. This angered me. As if I did not know the meaning of prayer!

I cried out: 'It is you who are mistaken. You will burn in hell. God will never forgive you for renouncing the true Faith.'

I became hysterical and ill again.

The King came and soothed me. I must be calmer, he said. He knew how strongly I felt about my religion and he had done everything he could to make life easy for me. He had relaxed the laws against Catholics and that was making the people displeased. A great deal of our unpopularity was due to that. I must know that he would do everything he could to please me.

'Anything?' I asked.

'You know that I would.'

'Then there is one thing I want more than anything in the

world. Dear husband, I want you to stand beside me in worship.'

He sighed and said: 'Ah, little one, I would that could be.'

I was confident then that one day Charles would see the light. I threw off my lethargy, my fury against those who had taken the nurse – but I had her back, had I not? – and I determined to fight as never before for the conversion of my husband to the true Faith.

There were many people to report what was happening in England and I realized that the general opinion abroad was that I had a great influence on the King and was bringing him round to my Catholic point of view. I think there was some truth in this and perhaps it was the reason why I was becoming more and more unpopular in England. I ignored this in my heedless way, believing with Charles that Kings were the Lord's anointed and the common people at length must realize that they had no right to do anything but accept this. However, there were high hopes in Rome because I was regarded as the Pope's good ambassadress.

Baby James was just over a year old when Gregorio Panzani came to London. He had been sent by the Pope to visit England in particular to talk to me. I was greatly flattered and I really did feel that in spite of a few steps backward I was making some progress.

Father Philip presented Panzani to me as soon as he arrived in England and Panzani was most gracious.

'The Holy Father himself thanks you for what you have done and what you are doing for the Faith in this misguided land. You have been as a mother to these ungrateful people. Can you, do you believe, bring them to true understanding?'

I was filled with emotion.

'I cannot tell you how much I esteem the good opinion of His Holiness,' I answered. 'Tell him to rest assured that I will do everything within my power to please him and God.'

'His Holiness is aware of this but will be overjoyed that you have confirmed it.'

My impetuosity took charge. I was so pleased that my efforts were recognized and I wanted to get the ultimate credit, so I said confidentially: 'I firmly believe that before long I shall have converted the King to the Faith. He is a saintly man; he appreciates what is holy. Yes, I am convinced that ere long I shall bring about his conversion.'

'That,' replied Panzani, 'is the best possible news I could have heard and exceeds my expectations.' He went on to say that he greatly desired a meeting with the King and I told him I would arrange it without delay.

When Charles heard that Gregorio Panzani was in England and had actually visited me informally he was greatly disturbed. He looked at me with that tender exasperation which I knew so well and said: 'This could be dangerous. What will be said if the people hear that you are secretly receiving messengers from the Pope?'

'If you receive him his visit will not be secret,' I said logically.

But Charles merely shook his head at me.

I then said that I had promised Panzani should meet the King, so Charles could not humiliate me by not receiving him.

Charles demurred. He was far more worried about the people who surrounded him, and many of them were his enemies, than I realized then.

At length he said that a meeting should take place, but it would have to be in secret . . . not official.

I was delighted. That would do very well, I cried and embraced him and told him I was the happiest and luckiest of women to have such a husband.

A meeting was arranged and Panzani and Charles met without any fuss. I was not present at their meeting but I knew it was an amicable one.

It was impossible to keep the arrival of Panzani a complete secret. Several members of the Court knew he was in England; however, realizing the King wished that the visit should not be considered an official one, they kept quiet.

But these matters cannot long be kept secret. There is certain to be someone who cannot resist talking too much, and one day when Charles and I were together playing some parlour game a guard came in to tell us that there was a man outside who was begging an audience with the King on a matter, he said, of grave importance.

'He does not look in the least dangerous,' said the guard, 'and he carries no weapons.'

'Then bring him to me,' said the King.

The man was brought in. He proved to be one of that sect which was becoming more and more prominent in England during the last year or so: a Puritan. He was very plainly dressed and his hair was cut in an odd fashion which made his head look round.

I was convulsed with amusement when the man said in a very confidential whisper: 'Your Majesty, I thought you should know that a dangerous man has arrived secretly in England.'

The King said: 'A dangerous man! Who is this?'

'Your Majesty, it is one of the Pope's men. I have information that his name is Panzani. I decided it was something you should know at once.'

Although I could scarcely keep a straight face, the King managed to.

'Thank you for warning me,' he said.

And our round-headed Puritan went on his way convinced that he had done his duty.

How I laughed about that afterwards – but not with the King. He admired the man for coming to tell him that he thought he was in danger.

'I could see that he thought the manner in which we live somewhat sinful,' I commented. 'I saw his eyes roaming round the tapestries and some of the furnishings. I think he thought they were symbols of the Devil.'

'Poor fellow,' said Charles. 'It must be a sad thing to be blind to beauty.'

I laughed over the incident with Panzani. He was a very sophisticated gentleman, and pious as he was, could still compliment me on my gowns and scents. Father Philip was very pleased with me and he told Panzani that he reckoned in three years or so the King would become a Catholic and then it would only be a short time before the country followed. When this happy state of affairs occurred the religious world would have to be grateful most of all to the Queen of England.

They were intoxicating words, and foolishly I believed them. How was I to know that it would be a very different story and that I should play quite a big part in bringing about not triumph but disaster?

But it really did seem as though we were going to succeed because, although Panzani did not come until December, the following March Richard Weston, Earl of Portland, the Treasurer who had been at the heart of the trouble over my letter, died and in his final moments he sent for a Catholic priest to administer the last rites.

Then there was Wat Montague, the poet who had written *The Shepherd's Paradise*, which had caused Prynne the loss of his ears. Wat had been abroad and recently returned to England announcing that he had seen the light and become a Catholic. He was proposing to go to Rome and join the Fathers of the Oratory.

Ah yes, I thought, we were indeed making progress.

Then I discovered I was pregnant again.

While I was awaiting the birth of my child, my new chapel in Somerset House was completed. What a joyous day that was when it was consecrated. It was so beautiful with a wonderfully painted dome in which archangels, cherubim and seraphim appeared to be floating above our heads; and it was my happy task to draw the curtains and reveal all this beauty.

I was so moved when Mass was celebrated that there were tears in my eyes. It seemed to me the ultimate triumph that I had made this corner in a land alien to the Truth. Soon, I promised myself, there should be chapels everywhere – not so grand as this, of course, because this was a royal chapel, but places where Catholics could go freely to worship. I would not rest until I had turned the heresy of England to true belief.

Charles could not be there to worship with me, of course, but as a connoisseur of art and beauty he came to admire the work, and his eyes glistened with appreciation.

Panzani congratulated me in private. 'But,' he said, 'this is not enough. What we need is conversions . . . of men in high places.'

I was a little cast down for I thought I had done very well. He comforted me and said that the Holy Father was delighted with my efforts. I had done more than he had thought possible at the time of my marriage, but there was a great deal to be done yet and we must not be complacent.

To tell the truth I was not feeling any great desire to do anything but rest, for my baby was shortly due to arrive, and however frequently one gives birth – and in my case it seemed to be an event which began again as soon as one was ended – one does every time have to face an ordeal.

It was a cold December day when Elizabeth was born. I had spent an exhausting day in labour and as night was falling – at ten o'clock to be precise – my daughter made her appearance.

However irksome the waiting has been, it always seems worthwhile at that moment when the little one is there and one's inconvenience is over . . . for the time being. I loved the child at once and I was rather glad that it was a girl. The only one who gave me cause for anxiety was Mary, who seemed to be delicate and had given us one or two frights. My eldest, Charles, flourished, although he did not grow any less unprepossessing. Perhaps that is the wrong word, but he was definitely lacking in beauty, though it did seem that he had a great deal of charm to make up for that. I had never seen a child win people to his side as Charles did. James, for all his innocent beauty, could not compete, and I could not be anything but surprised and delighted by my still rather swarthy eldest. He said the most amusing things and he was so serious contemplating the world with those large dark eyes and clearly finding it diverting.

I sometimes wished that I could go right away to Oatlands with the children and Charles and live like a simple noblewoman. Should I really want that for long? I was not sure. My frivolous nature did enjoy the masques and balls and all the beautiful clothes and jewels that seemed part of them. I was by nature an intriguant, I suppose. I loved to be in the thick of adventure. I had so enjoyed Panzani's visit and that enjoyment had been greater because of the secret understanding between us which I knew would be against the wishes of those serious puritanical people who were springing up everywhere.

A new baby was an additional expense. She was put into the care of the Countess of Roxburgh, who was already looking after her elder sister Mary; but she had to have her suite of attendants befitting a royal child – her dresser, her watchers, her nurses, her rockers and quite a number of minor servants. Moreover, Charles's nephews – the sons of his sister Elizabeth – came to visit us and that meant lavish entertainments. Charles Louis, the elder, was a little dull, but Rupert was a very attractive young man of about seventeen. Charles took a great fancy to him and he to Charles. It was fun to have the young men at Court and there was one entertainment which stands out in my memory. Lady Hatton gave a wonderful show at her place in Ely Court, and the masques, plays and balls and firework displays lasted for a whole month. Lady Hatton closed her entertainment with a ball for the citizens of London. It was not for people of the Court, she said.

It was Henry Jermyn who suggested that we go incognito and I thought it was an excellent idea.

'But how?' I asked.

'We shall have to dress as citizens,' said Henry. 'I'll be a merchant. Your Majesty can be a shop-keeper's wife.'

What fun we had! I instructed one of the seamstresses to make me a suitable gown and a bonnet which hid my face to a certain extent because it was just possible that someone might recognize me. I sent for my lace woman who kept a shop somewhere in the city and let her into the secret. She promised to take us in with her.

It was so amusing dancing with the citizens and interesting to listen to their talk although a little disconcerting that there were some who had harsh things to say about the way in which Catholics were getting a footing in the country. There were even one or two comments against me, but I didn't take them very seriously. They only seemed to add to the fun as I was intent on enjoying the evening and Henry Jermyn was so amusing posing as a merchant and Lord Holland – always good for adventure – was excellent company.

Charles was at this time in good spirits, for to celebrate the birth of the new baby, Louis and Rupert had brought with them presents from Charles's sister Elizabeth and the Palatine her husband, and these happened to be four paintings of great beauty and nothing could have pleased the King more. He was delighted to add the two Tintorettos and Titians to his collection, and I often found him gloating over them. The Arab horses – snow white in colour – which had accompanied the paintings, Charles had presented to me.

'I am sure you will enjoy them more than I would,' he said fondly. 'And I have my pictures.'

It was hardly likely that with a new addition to the family making us the proud parents of four healthy children and all the merrymaking we were going to worry ourselves about the depleted state of the exchequer.

It was certainly not in my nature to do so.

I was a little saddened to hear that Lady Eleanor Davys, who

had prophesied that my first child would be born, christened and
buried on the same day, had become a widow. She had prophesied Sir John's death, which she had said would take place within
three days of her prophecy and it did. It was reported that when
she had looked sombre and worn something dark in mourning
for him, he had said: 'Don't weep while I am alive and I will give
you leave to laugh when I am dead.'

There was a great deal of talk about her and her prophecies at
the time of Sir John's death. I should have liked to consult her
again, but I knew that Charles would not be pleased if I did and I
was so happy in this wonderful relationship which was growing
between us and which was becoming stronger every day, that I
did my best not to upset him now.

Only recently Lady Eleanor had been committed to the Gate
House Prison and fined three thousand pounds. I don't know
exactly what she did but she had been accused of some crime
through her writings. She did not care about this but continued to
write. Whether she was in league with the Devil I cannot say, but
she sincerely believed in her prophecies and that it was her duty
to make them.

A new Papal agent had arrived in England. This was George
Conn. He was a Scotsman of great charm and good looks who
had been sent to the Scots' College in Paris and Rome and gone
on to complete his education afterwards at Bologna, where he
had become a Dominican friar.

His mission, I learned later, was to mingle with the people of
the Court and persuade them – with the utmost subtlety of course
– to embrace the faith of Rome. Panzani had been too ambitious.
He had planned to convert the whole country. The new idea,
which came with George Conn, was to convert the important
people of the Court; and this was what George was setting out to
do.

Having travelled a great deal he was possessed of a sophistica-
tion which made people forget he was a priest. Charles enjoyed
his company very much indeed – almost as much as I did; and he
was very soon popular at Court. He had some rooms in the house
he had acquired made into what he called the Pope's Chapel, and
Catholics from all over the neighbourhood went there to
worship. George Conn told me that the Pope was delighted with
what I was doing in England and as a symbol of his approval sent

ne a beautiful gold cross studded with exquisite gems. I wore it
proudly and told my friends that I regarded it as my most
precious possession.

One day George Conn showed me a beautiful picture of St
Catherine which he said he was going to have framed for me. I
loved it on the spot and asked if I might see to the framing myself.
I then decided that I would not have it framed after all but have it
attached to my bed curtains so that the first thing I saw on
opening my eyes was the beautiful serene face of St Catherine.

George Conn was very pleased with me but he pointed out that
as there was a great deal of work to be done we must not be
complacent. I was so delighted that Charles enjoyed talking to
George almost as much as I did.

Once Charles said: 'I think I am a Catholic at heart.' And
George and I exchanged glances of triumph for I at last believed
victory was in sight. I suppose George was too wise to think so.

But there was no protest when one of the preachers said in a
sermon which he gave for the King and the Court that the people
who had brought about the English schism were like tailors who
cut out garments and find themselves unable to piece them
together and become so bemused that they do not know what
they are doing.

I began to feel very proud of myself for there I was, a happy
wife and mother, and upon my shoulders had descended the
great task of leading the country of my adoption back to salvation. I was seeing myself at that time as one of the great figures of
history. I should be remembered as that Bertha of whom some
people were fond of reminding me.

There were set-backs of course. I was sure Charles wanted to
become a Catholic. There was nothing of the Puritan in him, but
he had at his coronation vowed to uphold the Reformed Faith as
all anointed sovereigns must do and which was one of the
reasons why I had refused to be crowned with him.

I had made a habit of taking my son Charles to Mass. It had,
after all, been one of the clauses of the marriage settlement that I
was to have charge of the children's religious education until they
were thirteen. Charles was only six years old but he was very
interested and asked a great many pertinent questions as he did
about everything, and he happened to mention something of this
when he was with his father.

Charles was taken aback. 'Surely,' he cried, 'you did not take the boy to Mass?'

'But, of course, he must go to Mass,' I said. 'He is six years old. want. . . .'

Charles laid his hands on my shoulders and looked at me with that half-exasperated, half-tender look which I seemed to inspire so often.

'My dearest,' he said, 'you cannot take the Prince of Wales to Mass.'

'But why not?'

'Because, my love, he will one day be King of this country. He will take his oath, as I have, to adhere to the Reformed Faith.'

'But I am to have charge of his education until he is thirteen.'

'You must not take him to Mass.'

'And if I insist?'

'I hope you will not, my dearest, because if you do I shall have to forbid you and you know how it grieves me to forbid you anything.'

So of course I had to obey, but in my heart I knew that Charles leaned towards the Faith and, if he had not been the King who had sworn to adhere to the Reformed Faith, I am sure he would have admitted it.

It was only later that I realized that all these small incidents were like a smouldering pile in which the smoke is only seen in occasional escaping wisps. But the fire is there waiting to break out. I could not see it then though. I was foolish and frivolous, congratulating myself on the work I was doing.

Quite a number of the ladies of the Court were becoming involved with religion. George Conn was so persuasive and he never talked religion openly, only in the most subtle manner. I had the greatest admiration for him.

Lucy Hay professed interest, but I thought in my heart that she did so lightly. In fact she had a fondness for George Conn's company. Quite a lot of the women were like that. They flirted with the ideas as they did with the men, while they had no intention of becoming involved in anything seriously.

It was different with Lady Newport. She became very involved and I think she had always been a little inclined towards Catholicism, for her sister was a Catholic. George Conn had made a special effort with her and so had Wat Montague, an old favourite

of mine who had now returned to England with Sir Toby
Matthew, a much travelled and zealous Catholic. We all believed
that a little persuasion would bring her to the decision she was
longing to make.

Lady Newport's husband, who was Master of the Ordnance
and a stern Protestant, had forbidden his wife to dabble in
idolatry, as he called it; but Anne Newport was a persistent
woman and she was growing more and more certain that the true
Faith was that of the Catholic Church. Her conversion was
delayed, for oddly enough she had become greatly influenced by
her glover who, humble though he was, was something of a
preacher and a Protestant belonging to that sect of Puritans which
had become more and more prominent since such efforts to bring
back the Catholic Faith had been made in the country.

She said to me: 'I know he is humble and merely a glove-maker
but he has a power . . . a way with words which can only be
inspired.'

I replied: 'Bring him along and let George Conn talk to him.
We'll see how his inspiration stands up to that.'

Lucy, with the rest of my ladies and friends like Wat Montague
and Toby Matthews, was always excited when I proposed something unconventional, and in due course we all assembled and
summoned the glover, George having already consented to talk
to him.

When I saw the glover I disliked him on sight simply because
here was another of those Puritans in plain black garments and
that ridiculous haircut which made their heads look round.

George Conn looked elegant and handsome and so worldly
that I was sure he confirmed all the glover's suspicions about
idolatrous Catholic priests. The result was as we all predicted.
The poor man had a certain eloquence, it was true, but to watch
him in verbal conflict with George was like watching two com-
batants fighting with a spade and a sword. George's rapier
thrusts were soon getting home and the poor glover was growing
more and more bewildered.

At length he cried: 'Pray give me leave to retire. I must think
. . . think . . . You bemuse me. I am mazed. . . .'

George smiled and laid his hand on the poor man's shoulder.
'Go in peace, my friend,' he said. 'Go and ponder what I have
said. You will find yourself confronted by the truth at every turn.

Never forget that when you leave the tanglewood of ignorance, I shall be the first to welcome you to the paths of truth.'

I had rarely seen a man so bewildered. He left us in a daze and we all clustered round George and congratulated him.

'You were so clever,' I said. 'Poor man! It was most unfair of me to set you against him.'

'It was right for you to do so, Your Majesty,' replied George. 'Another of your good deeds.'

'You were so clearly the victor,' added Lucy.

'The truth will always prevail,' answered George.

That interview was to have startling results. A few days later the glover went mad. He could not reconcile himself to either form of religion and, as religion was the centre of his life, he was lost in a maze of beliefs and disbeliefs. We were all very sad to hear of his tragedy, for he was a worthy man and a most excellent glove-maker.

But the event which caused the greatest stir was the conversion of Lady Newport. She came to me in great uncertainty one day.

'Madam,' she said, 'I need your help. I have been talking to my sister and I am now convinced which is the true Faith. I want to be reconciled to the Church of Rome. I want to make my confession and proclaim my beliefs, but how can I do this? If my husband discovers what I am about to do, he will shut me away, send me out of the country . . . do anything to prevent my conversion.'

Intrigue ever fascinated me and I was delighted to help her, for bringing people to the true Faith was my great purpose. I was longing for everyone to know that we had a convert in Lady Newport because I guessed that would bring quite a number who were wavering to make a decision.

So I consulted George Conn.

He came up with an idea. 'Let it be a secret until it is actually done,' he said. 'Otherwise there may be powerful people who will do everything within their power to prevent it. Let her visit one of your Capuchin friars at that time when she would normally be returning from some entertainment perhaps.'

Anne Newport thought it was a good idea and she said that she could go to a performance at Drury Lane and on her way home call at Somerset House and see the friar there.

So that was what we arranged. Lady Newport went to the theatre and on the way home visited the chapel and made her confession to the Capuchin friar; and then she was reconciled to the Catholic Church.

Another convert! I congratulated myself that I was winning my war against heretics. I was, however, unprepared for the storm which the conversion of Lady Newport brought about. The fact that his wife had become a Catholic enraged the Earl of Newport. He was a clever man, which was not surprising considering that his mother was Penelope Rich, the daughter of Lettice Knollys, Countess of Leicester. Even now people talked about that forceful woman. The fact that Penelope's son was illegitimate – his parentage was shared with Charles Blount, Earl of Devonshire – had not stopped his inheritance or impeded his advancement. Not only had he been made Master of the Ordnance for life, but he had made considerable profits out of the office and he was not the sort of man to stand quietly by while his wife defied him on a matter which he considered of great importance.

He went himself to see Charles. He ranted and raged and was clearly distressed. Charles expressed deep sympathy. Newport, of course, dared not say anything to Charles about me, but his implications were that I and my little coterie were infiltrating mischievously and undermining the accepted Faith of the country. He blamed several of my close associates, naming Wat Montague and Sir Toby Matthews.

'Your Majesty,' he begged, 'I pray you send Montague and Matthews out of the country. I am sure that they and some of their friends are at the root of this disaster.'

Charles was very sorry for Newport's distress but he knew that I would be rejoicing in my convert. However, he did not think it was good for such a fierce Catholic as Montague to remain at Court in view of growing resentment, but he did nothing for he knew how upset I would be if Montague were sent away.

Very soon a bigger issue grew out of the matter. When he found the King reluctant to act, Newport went to Archbishop Laud to complain that he feared the King was too much influenced by his wife to take any action which might not be in accordance with her wishes.

This was the beginning of the antagonism between myself and Archbishop Laud. There had been times when I had had hopes of Laud for he was a man who loved the ceremonies of the Church. I had mentioned to George Conn that if the Pope would give him a

Cardinal's hat he might become our man. I am not sure now whether I was right about that, but in any case he did not get his red biretta. On the other hand he said that he 'laboured nothing more than that the external public worship of God – too much slighted in most parts of the kingdom – might be preserved and that with as much decency and uniformity as might be, being still of the opinion that unity cannot long continue in the Church when uniformity is shut out.' This implied that he loved all the ceremonies of the Church and it was natural that I should think he was leaning strongly towards us. Had he not amended the Prayer Book and imposed it on Scotland in place of the liturgy which had been prepared by the Scots bishops?

The son of a Reading clothier, Laud was indeed a clever man to have climbed so far; such are always the most difficult to bend to one's wishes. I have always recognized that they are possessed of a very special cleverness to have risen up and overcome their handicaps and one must in assessing them – particularly as an enemy – have a special respect for them.

There was another point: many people suspected that his attitude to the ceremonies of the Church meant that he was a secret Catholic and as he was aware – far more than I was – of the growing resentment in the country, he was eager to prove himself staunchly Protestant. He therefore complained at a meeting of the Council that since the coming of the Papal agents, Panzani and Conn, there had been many conversions to Catholicism and there was too much favour shown to Catholics and he thought that both Walter Montague and Toby Matthews should be prosecuted.

When I heard this I was enraged, and from then on the Archbishop was my enemy. Poor Charles was in a dreadful dilemma. He could quite understand Lord Newport's fury; he saw the Archbishop's point; but he was very eager not to upset me.

I realized then – and I think so did many others – how important I was becoming in the country. I had had such success with the Pope's agents; I had done so much to make life easier for our Catholic subjects that I was beginning to be thought of not so much as the frivolous pleasure-loving Queen as the power behind the throne. My husband listened to me because he loved me so much and hated to disappoint me so that I was almost in the position of being his most favoured and influential minister.

I heard that Laud had said to Thomas Wentworth, whom the King greatly favoured and who had just returned from his duties in Ireland: 'I have a very hard task and God, I beseech Him, to make me very good corn, for I am between two great factions very like corn between two mill stones.'

I was made fully aware of the importance of this by George, who came to me in great haste to tell me what was happening at the Council.

'I think we have gone a little too far too quickly,' he said. 'Laud has suggested to the Council that the Catholic chapels should be closed down, including yours of Somerset House, and the counsellors have agreed with enthusiasm that this should be so.'

'I will never allow that,' I cried.

'I beg of you be careful,' begged Conn. 'Do not ruin the good work we have done so far.'

'Nothing can ruin that,' I assured him. 'We have saved souls and that is our endeavour. Do not take this threat too seriously. I know Charles. He would never agree to a step which he knows would make me very unhappy.'

When Charles came to me he was really distressed. 'Laud wants all the Catholic chapels to be closed down,' he said.

'What!' I cried. 'That man is a monster. Let him go back to his father's clothier's shop.'

'He is the Archbishop of Canterbury,' he reminded me gently.

'But he loves the ceremonies of the Church. He hates these miserable Puritans as much as I do.'

'He supports the Protestant Church, my love.'

'I will not allow him to shut my chapels. Charles, you will not allow this. You have promised me. . . . Oh, Charles, promise me now. Not my chapel. . . !'

He soothed me and swore that my chapel should not be closed, although he added: 'There is no alternative for the others. They will have to be closed wherever they have sprung up.'

The controversy went on for a long time and it did show how thoroughly the people disliked the Archbishop. It has always amazed me to see how the common people dislike to see one of their own rise to great heights. One would have thought they would be delighted. But no. His humble birth was continually flung at Laud, more so by the common people than by the nobles. It was said that he was at heart a Catholic and ought to admit it. At

least, they said, the Catholics like myself and George Conn made
no secret of their idolatrous beliefs.

Poor Charles, he did not know which way to act. He was
advised that he could not ignore the growing feelings against the
Catholics, and on the other hand, how could he hurt me?

In the end he compromised. He agreed that there should be a
proclamation threatening Catholics in the country; but at the
same time he had so weakened the laws against them that they
did not amount to very much. He tried to do what he had to do
without offending either protagonist.

I laughed and told him he was very clever. He was serious
though and seemed to be looking into the future with very
melancholy eyes.

Dear Charles! He was only vaguely aware of the dangers which
were springing up around him – but he was not quite so blind as
was.

There was sad news from my mother. She was in great
distress. It seemed that she had quarrelled irrevocably with
Richelieu, and that he governed France. He had made it clear to
her that she was not wanted there; in fact he had actually sent her
into exile.

I worried a great deal about her. It was dreadful that she, who
had always been such an imposing figure during my childhood
should now be reduced to this.

'Who is this Richelieu?' I cried to Charles. 'Merely a priest – a
Cardinal it is true – and yet he has set himself up as the ruler of
France, and he has decided that there is no place there for my
mother.'

The King said something very strange then. It was almost like a
prophecy, but he did not know that, and I certainly did not. 'Yes,'
he said slowly, 'it is strange. And what is happening here? I often
think there are some who would like to do the same to me.'

I laughed disbelievingly, but he went on seriously: 'There is
trouble brewing, my dearest. Scotland. . . .'

'That awful country,' I cried impatiently. 'Haven't the Scots
always been troublesome?'

He agreed with that. Then he went on: 'There is something
about these Puritans. I can understand the situation when there

a desire to supplant one king by another who it might be
ought has a greater claim to the throne. But these people seem
have set themselves against kings and all that Kingship means.
hey seem as though they want to abolish that rule and set up
eir own.'

I continued to laugh and Charles managed to smile. It was such
n incongruous idea. There had always been kings; and who
ere these people who went about looking like black crows with
eir ridiculous haircuts?

If only we could have looked into the future then, perhaps we
uld have done something to prevent the holocaust. I think we
ight well have. When I look back I see the way we came was
rewn with warnings which we ignored.

But for the time there was the problem of my mother.

Charles knew it would be a mistake to give her refuge in
ngland, but he also knew that it was what I wanted. I could not
ar the thought of her going about Europe like a beggar pleading
r sanctuary. I wondered how my brother could allow her to be
eated so, but I supposed he was under the thumb of that hateful
d Richelieu. At least he gave her a pension but he was adamant
out her leaving France. To be turned away from one's home
ust be horribly humiliating, particularly when one had in the
st been its ruler.

She was now in Holland and one of Charles's agents there had
nt a message to tell him that be believed she had plans for
ming to England.

'The people would not like it,' said Charles, and he looked at
e sadly. It was a great sorrow to him that the people had turned
ainst me. I think he would rather have heard them cheer me
an himself. He rarely ever did. I was not only a foreigner, I was
Catholic and that was enough to turn a great many people in
ngland against me. 'And,' went on Charles, 'you know the state
the exchequer. We can hardly afford to entertain your mother
the manner she would expect.'

'Poor dear lady,' I said. 'I daresay she would be pleased to
ceive any warm welcome from someone who cared about her.'

Charles was very depressed and I knew this was because he
ad sent a messenger to Holland to tell his agents to do every-
ing to dissuade my mother from coming to England.

She must have known that she was unwanted but, being my

mother, that did not deter her. I was her daughter; she imagine
that I was rich and powerful. I was after all the Queen of Englan
Perhaps she did not know that there were certain difficulties
the country now, but even if she did she would sweep tho
aside. I knew her well. She was the sort of woman who ma
circumstances fit her needs.

I wondered how she felt about the new baby at the Court
France. There had been great excitement there for month
because Anne of Austria, after twenty-three years of infertilit
had given birth to a boy.

However I knew that the King was probably right in n
inviting her to England but on the other hand I did feel that I ha
failed her. I decided I would try to persuade Charles to let h
come if only for a brief visit. But that would mean that if she lik
it here her visit would not be a brief one.

This was the state of affairs when we heard that my mother ha
actually set sail from Holland and was making her way to tl
English coast. Moreover she was bringing with her one hundre
and sixty attendants and servants, six coaches and seven
horses, which was a clear indication that she expected to l
received in a manner worthy of a Queen.

Charles was nonplussed. 'But I have not invited her,' he cri
in despair. 'I have not given her permission to come here. . . .'

I knew that he was thinking of what it was going to cost
house my mother and I hated to see the furrows in his brow, b
what could I do? I went to him and slipped my arm through h
while I looked up at him pleadingly. 'I could never be happy if v
turned her away,' I said. 'She is my mother. . . .'

He tried to explain to me the cost and the attitude of the peop
– but eventually I won. The fact that I was pregnant again ma
him very anxious not to upset me. He promised that he would g
himself in state to meet her to show everyone that she came as
honoured guest. I should prepare rooms for her and have thr
thousand pounds to spend on any alteration or new furnitu
which I deemed necessary. She was my mother and for th
reason, naturally he must welcome her.

I hugged him and told him he was the most wonderf
husband in the world and my mother would be so happy to s
what a perfect marriage I had made.

He was as good as his word and set out for Chelmsford an

went to St James's, where the children had their apartments, and chose fifty rooms for my mother.

My baby was due in four months' time and I was feeling heavy and tired but exhilarated by the thought of seeing my mother. I had told the children that she was coming and the elder ones were very interested. Charles was now aged eight and different from the others, with his black hair cut into a fringe which almost covered his black brows, under which his flashing dark eyes were the most lively I ever saw in a child of his age. Mary, only a year younger, was beautiful and so was James; Elizabeth was three and Anne only a baby. She had been born in March of the previous year and within a few months I had become pregnant again. And I was not thirty yet! I often wondered how many children I would have. I was happy to be the wife of an ardent and loving husband and to have produced a growing family but frequent childbearing was often taxing and I certainly did not feel well at this time.

However, I tried to forget my own discomforts and prepare for my mother. Riders came in breathlessly to tell me that she had had a good reception in London, that people had hung out banners in the streets and that the Lord Mayor in all the splendour of his office had greeted her. I was immensely relieved because one could never be sure of the people of London and, with all those horrid Puritans about, they might have decided to become hostile. But they did love pageantry and it may have been that they found that more entertaining than a stupid riot. But I liked to think they did homage to my mother as a woman who had once been Regent of France and was still mother of their Queen.

I heard the sound of trumpets which meant that the cavalcade was approaching St James's. Young Charles was right beside me and the others came toddling up. I hurried into the courtyard. I could not think of ceremony at such a moment.

I ran to my mother's coach, the children at my heels, and I tried to pull open the door. One of the coachmen opened it for me and as my mother stepped out, I was so overcome with emotion that I dropped to my knees and begged her to give me her blessing.

With great joy I took her into the palace and showed her the apartments I had had made ready for her. I was rather shocked by her appearance. It was, after all, a long time since I had seen her. I

had been the fortunate one. I had learned to love my husband
and had made for myself a family life so felicitous that I could not
believe many people were so blessed. Poor Queen Marie! She
was sixty-five years old and her life during the last years had been
very uncomfortable. She had never been beautiful and events,
with the aid of time, had ravaged such looks as she had had. But I
was quick to realize that the indomitable spirit had remained
intact, and so had the determination to manage the lives of all
those about her.

She talked incessantly. She was poor . . . yes *poor*! She, the
Queen of France, now lived in abject poverty. She had her jewels
. . . oh yes, she had been clever enough to bring those with her
and it had occurred to her that she might have to sell some of
them.

'I will buy them, dear Mother,' I cried. 'That will give you some
money and you will know the jewels are safe.'

She patted my arm. She said I was a good girl and as I was rich
she would be glad to accept the money for the jewels and know
that they were safe in the family.

I said: 'I am not really rich, my lady. There is always trouble
about money. There is never enough. Charles is always wanting
money and unable to get it except by unpopular taxation.'

'The perpetual cry of Kings!' replied my mother. 'Of course
there is money, dear child. There always is in a country. It is a
matter of knowing how to extract it. You shall have the jewels. I
may not be here long, you know, to burden you.'

'Burden us!' I cried. 'Dear Mother, how can you talk like that?'

'I did not mean I am going to die,' she replied. 'I know you are
pleased that I have come to be with you. It was far too long that
we were apart, Henriette chérie. I will stay with you and help
you. But I may be called back to France.'

'Do you think the Cardinal. . . .'

'The Cardinal!' She spat out the words. 'He is plagued by a
terrible cough. He can't keep warm. I hear he sits by the fire
drinking that sickly strawberry syrup which is the only thing
which gives his throat some relief. He crouches over the fire
because he cannot keep warm. How long do you think he can last
like that?'

'You really think he is desperately ill?'

'I *know*, my child. You don't think I have been idle. I know what

going on. One advantage of being in exile is that one can send
out one's spies and no one can be absolutely sure who they are.
There are always advantages in life, child.'

'I cannot understand my brother's turning you away.'

'Oh, he is a weakling, Louis. He always was. He is guided by
his wife and the Cardinal. He is nothing . . . a puppet . . . a
cypher.'

'And the baby?'

She nodded, smiling. 'A healthy boy. Another Louis.' She came
close to me. 'No, I shall not be here with you long, dear child. A
breathing space, that's all I need. My astrologers have told me
that Louis cannot last more than a year or so. He is a sick man. He
was never strong. And then when he is dead . . . can a baby rule?
Little Louis XIV will be still in his nursery. Then it is for me to
return and take over the reins as I did when your father died.'

'And this is the prophecy?'

'It is and I have had the best astrologers in Europe. Their
verdict is always the same. So it would be advisable for your
Charles to make me happy here. I could be of great importance to
him later on.'

I was overawed. It all seemed so plausible and I had seen the
evidence of astrologers and soothsayers. I should never forget
Eleanor Davys and her prophecy about the first baby I had had.

My mother's presence at Court did mean that I must spend a
great deal of time with her, which gave me less time for my
husband. She loved the children and was most impressed by
Charles. She even liked his looks and said he had inherited them
from some of my father's ancestors – The Brigands of Navarre she
called them.

'He has a look of your father,' she said. *'Mon Dieu*, how he
reminds me! Quick, lively, eyes everywhere. Let us hope they do
not linger on every woman in the vicinity as your father's did. I
had to shut *my* eyes to his infidelities and I did so without
complaint . . . for the sake of the crown. You, my dear Henriette,
have no such trouble with your husband. He seems a mild man
. . . but devoted to you. There seems to be nothing but pregnancies for you. I know what that means. Your father always took
me off from his lights of love to fill the royal nurseries. How
different you are with your Charles. You are a very fortunate
woman, Henriette.'

I told her I realized that and if only Charles would stop worry
ing about the troubles of the country and those wretched Protes
tants – and worse still Puritans – I could be completely happy.

'It appears there is always trouble for rulers, but you have don
well and I believe even the Holy Father is pleased with you.'

'How is Madame St George? Have you heard?'

'I haven't seen her since I left France, of course. I think she i
happy with that little tyrant. Gaston dotes on his daughter. It is
pity he could not get a son. Little Mademoiselle de Montpensier i
very rich, for Gaston's wife, as you know, left everything to he
when she died. It is a pity it did not go to Gaston. It is a mistake, i
my opinion, for young people to inherit large fortunes.'

'She will find it easy to get a husband.'

'My dear child, they are waiting to pounce. Gaston will have t
be careful. I should be there to make sure no mistakes are made
Well, perhaps soon . . . according to the prophets. . . .'

I was a little sad at the thought of Louis' dying. After all, he wa
my brother and although I had seen very little of him and I di
think of him more as the King of France than a relation, the bon
was still there. My mother was so sure that he was going to di
and I couldn't help feeling a little horrified that she seemed to b
looking forward to the event.

Power! I thought. How people crave for it! I didn't think I did
What I really wanted was to be with my husband and family in
peaceful country where there were no troubles – but of cours
that must be a country which had turned to the Catholic Faith.

My mother was saying: 'I could have returned to Florence.'

'Oh, my dear lady, that would have been wonderful,' I replied
'You could have gone back to your family.'

'Oh yes. The Medicis would have welcomed me. They have
strong family feeling. It would have been strange to be ir
Florence again, to stroll along the Arno and to live in the olc
palace. But think how I should have gone back. A Queen yes, bu
one who had been turned out of her adopted country by her owr
son and a Cardinal. No, I could not do that.' For a moment the
mask of optimism slipped from her face and I glimpsed a rather
fearful old woman. Fleetingly I wondered how much she really
believed in those prophecies. She added slowly: 'I could not gc
back to Florence . . . a failure.' Then the mask was back again
'One day, I shall be very busy. If I have to return to France – I am

re the message will come before long – then I shall be fully
gaged with affairs in Paris.'

While she was waiting for all that, she concerned herself with
fairs in England.

The children were very interested in her and I was delighted to
e how well they got on. She wanted to take charge of the
rseries. Charles, oddly enough for such a precocious child,
d always taken a wooden toy to bed with him. He had had it
hen he was about two years old, had formed an attachment to it
d his nurses told me that he would not go to sleep without it.

'Nonsense,' said my mother. 'Of course he must give it up. It is
t becoming in a Prince of Wales to need toys to go to bed with.'

She talked to Charles very seriously and somehow made him
e that it was childish and not worthy of a future King.

When that argument was put to him he allowed them to take
e toy away. He was very interested in the fact that the would
e day be King and was already talking now and then of what he
ould do, and it was only this which made him relinquish his
y.

He was a shrewd, often devious little boy. We were amused by
e incident of the physic, but at the same time it did show that he
d a clever, if crafty, nature. The fact was that he had refused to
ke some physic which his Governor, Lord Newcastle, thought
e needed and Newcastle had complained to me, so I wrote to
harles telling him that I had heard he had refused to take his
ysic and if he persisted I should have to come and make him
ke it as it was for his health's sake. I added that I had told Lord
ewcastle to let me know whether or not he had taken his
edicine and I hoped he was not going to disappoint me.

Lord Newcastle visited me next day with a note which he said
e Prince had sent him.

'My Lord,' Charles had written in his still childish script and on
led lines to keep the writing straight, 'I would not take too
uch physic for it doth always make me worse and I think it will
the like for you. I ride every day and am ready to follow any
her direction from you. Charles P.'

I could not help laughing and was so impressed by the wit of
y son that I told Lord Newcastle that we would not impose the
ysic for a day or so and if the boy was well enough without it he
served to escape.

How could I help being proud of such a boy? And I was su▪
that even my mother could not succeed in getting the better ▪
him.

My mother was complaining now that Mary ate too much ▪
breakfast and must expect to be sick if in addition to manchets ▪
bread and beef and mutton she took chicken as well. Also s▪
drank too much ale.

It was true that when her rather large meals were curtail▪
Mary did seem better.

My mother was not popular. People thought she was t▪
extravagant and that too much money was being spent on h▪
entourage and entertainment. It was true that she expected to li▪
like a Queen – but then she was a Queen.

The weather had changed as soon as she arrived, and th▪
southern half of the country was engulfed in storms and gal▪
which caused a great deal of damage. The people, always supe▪
stitious, said it was a sign and meant that the Queen Mother w▪
going to be a menace to the country. It was very upsetting and ▪
was afraid my mother would hear these rumours. But if she di▪
she brushed them aside. I had forgotten her capacity to acce▪
only what she wanted to happen.

Whenever the weather was bad during my mother's stay ▪
England, the Thames watermen would shout to each other th▪
this was more of the weather the Queen Mother had brought ▪
England, as though she used some malicious influence in th▪
heavens to make us uncomfortable.

As a Queen she looked upon luxury as her natural right an▪
maintaining her household was a drain on the exchequer. Sh▪
did not, however, see why the people of England should not pa▪
for it. They did, and complained bitterly about her in the stree▪
and now and then I overheard unflattering comments. It was sai▪
that she was a trouble-bringer and there was never tranquillit▪
when she was nearby. There was grumbling about the people ▪
England being taxed to pay for her "shaggrags" – by which ▪
presume they meant her household.

Charles grew worried and told me he had sent a message t▪
King Louis urging him to invite his mother back to France. 'It ▪
the best way,' he said. 'She pines for the old life in Paris. I kno▪
that she has entered into intrigues in the past, but I feel sure sh▪
would promise not to if you would only have her back.'

Charles explained to me that, apart from the expense of
keeping her in England, her presence was an irritation to the
people and that was something he wanted to avoid because he
was growing more and more uneasy about the state of the
country.

I hated to see him worried so I made no protest, but Louis
wrote back to the effect that however much his mother promised
not to meddle she would be unable to prevent herself doing so
because she was a meddler by nature; and he would not give her
permission to return to France. He was sorry for his brother-in-
law but he must be as firm as Louis himself was and explain to
Queen Marie that her presence was no longer wanted in England.
But how could Charles do that! She was after all my mother and
in spite of those traits of hers which I had to admit were there, I
loved her. Charles could never do anything to hurt me if he could
help it, so she remained.

It was true that she meddled. One day she said to me: 'I was not
idle in Holland. All the time I concerned myself with your good
and that of the children. I sounded them on the possibility of a
match between the Prince of Orange and one of your girls.'

'The Prince of Orange!' I cried. 'He is of no great importance.'

'I didn't mean for Mary, of course. Perhaps Elizabeth.'

'She is three years old!'

'My dear daughter, we have to think of the alliances of our
children when they are in their cradles. I will discuss the matter
with the King.'

'No, my lady,' I said firmly. '*I* will discuss it with the King.'

'Oh,' she said, a little huffily, 'you two seem to talk nothing but
lovers' talk. State matters have their place too, remember.'

'They will be the state matters of England,' I retorted coolly,
and wondered if I was becoming as hard towards her as Louis
was. We must show her that she could not interfere in English
affairs any more than she could in French. Hadn't she learned her
lesson? Surely being turned out of her home must have made her
realize something. But no doubt she blamed Louis and Anne . . .
and the Cardinal of course, for turning away one who could have
been – as she would see it – a great help to them.

At the first opportunity I told Charles what she had suggested.

'The Prince of Orange!' he said. 'Oh, he is too petty a prince to
mate with a princess of England.'

'So thought I,' I replied. 'But my mother talked of it when s
was in Holland and she tells me that the Prince of Orange wo
be very happy with the match.'

'I have no doubt he would. No. Not even for one of
younger daughters would he be good enough.'

There was one other point which seemed to have escaped th
all and of which I was very much aware: the Prince of Orange w
a Protestant. When my children married I wanted to make s
that they married Catholics.

I was getting bigger but still able to walk a little in the garden
loved those of St James's with the deer park and the terrace
enjoyed walking there with Charles and the children. Char
was always so tender and affectionate and everyone marvelled
his care of me . . . especially when I was in the condition I wa
this time.

Charles and I would sit on one of the seats and the childr
would run about making a great deal of noise with all the d
yapping round them; and the ladies and gentlemen made suc
charming sight walking on the paths round the palace.

Happy days they were, when Charles looked so handsome a
was so different from the rather shy young man whom I had fi
met. I rarely heard him stammer now; he didn't when he wa
peace and happy; and he certainly was with his family. He lik
to hear little domestic details. He answered young Charle
questions gravely and gave his attention to James when
accused Mary of taking his share of the custard tart they had h
for dinner. I was sure he would have been happier being just w
us than coping with his ministers.

Why couldn't everyone stop complaining? I asked mys
Why could they not enjoy life as we did walking in the garden
St James's.

Winter came in fiercely. 'Queen Mother weather,' said
boatmen.

It was at the end of a bitter January that my baby was born
was a little girl and she was hastily baptized and christer
Catherine, for she died a few hours after her birth.

The Human Sacrifice

After the death of Catherine I think happiness was over for me, although perhaps I did enjoy snatches of pleasure when I was able to convince myself that all was well; and even when I was most apprehensive I could not have conceived the magnitude of the horror which was waiting to spring on me, crushing my joy for ever and making me wait each day for the release which only death could bring.

Where did it start? It is difficult to say. Scotland – I sometimes think – that land of trouble which I hate, with all the squabbling over a prayerbook. But who am I to talk? Who was more sternly religious than I? Had I not from the moment I had set foot in England worked to bring the country back to Rome from which it had been so ruthlessly torn by that monster Henry VIII, simply because he wished for a new wife? But the succeeding monarchs had had their chance and had done nothing. I see now that the Protestant Faith suited the English – not the Puritan branch, which was as intense as our Catholic – but the easy going, not too demanding Church of England.

Was it religion? Perhaps to some extent. Then if it were, I was indeed to blame.

But no. That was not the real reason. I was not the only one.

I suppose Archbishop Laud with his rigid insistence on the ceremonies of the Church, the correct vestments of the clergy, all the ceremonies which were akin to the Church of Rome, had done much to bring about the Puritan strain, and consequently to result in what was tantamount to a new party composed of solemn men who thought it was a sin even to laugh; as for dancing and singing, to take pleasure in those meant to them to be on the road to hell. Laud was anxious not to be called a Catholic, but he resembled one in many ways, and he had become the most unpopular man in the country.

Charles respected him very much and Charles was always loyal in his friendships, but I think the man he preferred above all was Thomas Wentworth. Charles admired him enormously for he had often in the past proved himself to be an honest man. He had recently returned from Ireland, where he had done well by promoting the growth of flax, opening up trade with Spain and abolishing piracy in St George's Channel. His aim had been to make the Irish as prosperous as the English and dependent on England while they realized that it was in their interest to be loyal to the English.

Wentworth's conduct of affairs had led Charles to believe that it was men like him whom he wanted at home and he sent for him. Soon after his arrival in England, Thomas Wentworth was created Earl of Strafford.

That year came in on a rather melancholy note. I knew that Charles was very worried although he was cheered by Strafford who, he confided to me, was one of the ablest men he had ever come across and loyal too. For that reason I tried to like the man and I found I could when I rid myself of a certain jealousy for he was a most elegant, gallant and courtly gentleman.

I was beginning to see myself a little more clearly than I had before. I had had time for reflection during my pregnancies and to my dismay (although I did not let Charles know this yet) I was pregnant again. The experience with Catherine had been so distressing that I had hoped for a little respite. To suffer the discomforts of nine months only to find there is no result, or that it is snatched away from you almost before you have received it is a devastating experience for a woman. The point was that realized I had been jealous of Charles's appreciation of Strafford. Buckingham had a great deal to answer for; I suppose that during my happy life with Charles I was always looking out for some clever man who might try to snatch him from me . . . not that anyone could do that now but they could diminish the regard he had for me and that was something I could not bear.

But it was not so with Strafford and when I overcame my initial dislike, I was grateful to him for the comfort he brought to Charles; and then I found I liked him for himself. There was someone else in my household who liked him very much. That was Lucy Hay. Lucy was ten years older than I which made her bordering on forty, but no one would have believed it to look at

er except that the years of experience – and I suspected very
reat experience – had made her more fascinating than ever; in
ite of being no longer young she was still the most attractive
oman at Court.

Katherine Villiers and Susan Feilding attended services at
omerset House and were coming out into the open and declaring
eir conversion to the Catholic Faith, which endeared them to me.
ut fond as I was of them both, it was Lucy whom I liked best to be
ith. She was so amusing and bright, and was always in the midst
f some intrigue which sometimes she would talk about and at
thers be so secretive that she fascinated me more than ever.

It was no secret that she had become Strafford's very good
iend. They were a magnificent pair – the cleverest man and
oman at Court, I guessed. I wondered what they talked of in
eir intimate moments.

I impressed on Charles that it was no use letting people know
ow anxious we were about everything. We should make life
em as normal as possible, and to celebrate the coming of the
ew Year I arranged a masque and a comedy in which I was
ing to take the most important part.

Charles thought it was a good idea and we had an amusing
me discussing the play and the part I would take – and, of
urse, my costume. Lewis Richard, who was Master of the
ing's Music, composed the songs and we ordered Inigo Jones to
ake the scenery and design the costumes so that we could make
ire to have a dazzling spectacle.

That masque stands out vividly in my memory. I suppose it
as because it was the last one I played in at Whitehall. It was a
rave attempt and Charles, no less than I, determined to make it
emorable. I really did enjoy prancing about the stage dressed as
1 Amazon in silvery armour and a helmet which sported a
agnificent feather.

The winter was harsh and the New Year came in grimly. I was
eling ill because of my condition and my spirits suffered
rough memories of Catherine's birth and death.

Strafford called at Whitehall one day and when he left Charles
as very depressed. He came to me as he always did to tell me the
ews for, bless him, he always behaved as though I had a grasp of
ate matters, which was far from the truth, although I must say
at I did try my best to understand.

'Strafford wants to call a parliament,' he said, 'because w
must have money to prosecute the war against the Scots and th
is the only way to set about getting it.'

I frowned. I hated both parliaments and wars against the Scot
One was hard enough to bear but the two of them together wei
intolerable. Wars took Charles away from me and that was trag
for us both; parliaments made laws and they were nearly alway
aimed at the Catholics, which meant myself.

'Need it be called?' I asked. 'Parliaments always mean trouble.

Charles agreed that they did. There had always been confli
between him and them because he could never see why a Kir
should not be an absolute ruler since he had inherited the crow
through birth and was therefore God's chosen ruler. No
certainly Charles had no wish to call a parliament. But he neede
money to carry on the war and a parliament would have to find
means of raising it.

'I wish they would let us live in peace,' I said.

'I could not agree with you more,' replied the King. 'But
suppose Strafford is right. He usually is.'

'So you will call this parliament?'

'I have no alternative.'

'Well then, call it, and let us hope it does not last long.'

As a matter of fact it did not. It lasted only three weeks and
was that one which was called the Short Parliament. Charles wa
uneasy. There were three men he mentioned to me. One wa
John Pym, a strict Presbyterian, who was evidently a man of grea
powers and was becoming the leader of that party in th
Commons which was opposed to the King; then there was Joh
Hampden, who had endured a spell in prison for refusing to pa
what he called the forced loan – an act which had made his nam
known throughout the country and turned many a man to h
favour; and the other – a man whose name I had not heard befo
but which was to become engraved on my mind for ever – was
connection of Hampden's for I believe Hampden's mother wa
his aunt; he came from Huntingdon and was the member fo
Cambridge. His name was Oliver Cromwell.

These were the men whom Charles feared. They were not i
favour of imposing a tax to raise money for war on Scotland an
they carried the House with them. Charles was in desperation.

At first I was delighted that the Parliament was so short-live

ut it seemed there was little to rejoice about. Then Strafford
ame forward with a suggestion. Because of the good work he
ad done in Ireland he had been made Lord Lieutenant of that
ountry and he said he could raise an army there and bring it over
o fight for the King.

That was where the mischief started. I do not know even now
who our enemies were. Perhaps there were so many of them that
was impossible for me to know them all. I believe that Richelieu
as at the heart of many of the conspiracies against us. As a ruler
f the French it was to his advantage to see a weak England; he
id not want to see the English helping friends abroad who were
e enemies of France. It was devious politics – far too involved
or me, and I had not then learned the art of unravelling these
ysteries. I saw life in bright light and dark shadow . . . with
ttle shading between. For me there were the good and the bad
nd there was no wrong in the good, no right in the bad. I am
raid my emotions not my mind guided my thoughts.

Charles was a saint; I was his devoted wife; and any who were
gainst us were villains. It was as simplified as that.

If we had our enemies abroad, heaven knew we had enough
ving close.

Strafford was firm beside the King and there were many who
greed that he was the most able statesman in the land. For that
eason there were many more waiting to destroy him.

They seized their opportunity. Soon after the dissolution of the
hort Parliament rumour was sweeping through the country like
rildfire. Strafford was going to bring over an army of Irishmen
n a pretext of fighting the Scots but actually to subdue the
nglish.

London was in an uproar. Charles came riding with all speed to
Vhitehall where I was, for being six months with child, and
omewhat melancholy, not only worried about the country's
ffairs, but still brooding on the death of little Catherine, I was
pending a great deal of time resting.

Charles told me of his fears. 'They are against Strafford,' he said.
And if they are against him it is because they are against me.'

'You are the King,' I reminded him.

'That is so,' he answered, and looking at me fondly he asked
pout my health and said he wanted to go over to St James's on
he next day to see the children.

We spent a pleasant evening until one of the guards came in with a board he had found attached to the gates of the palace. On it was written: 'Whitehall to Let'.

There was a sinister implication in the message which made Charles turn pale.

He said: 'I think you should leave for the country while you are still able to travel.'

'I wanted the child to be born in Whitehall.'

'No,' said Charles gently. 'It would be better to go to the country.'

While we were talking a letter was brought to him.

'Who sent it?' he demanded of the guard.

'One of the serving men said it was passed to him by one of the guards at the gate who did not recognize the man who handed it to him.'

I looked over Charles's shoulder and read: 'Chase the Pope and the Devil from St James's, the lodging of the Queen Mother.'

Charles and I looked at each other for some seconds without speaking. Then I said: 'What does it mean?'

'Our enemies have done this,' said Charles.

'It is a threat . . . to my mother.'

'Someone is raising the people against us,' said the King.

'I must go to St James's without delay,' I cried. 'They are unsafe there.'

'We will go together,' said Charles.

We rode to the palace and were relieved that we met no hostile crowds on the way. I think we were prepared for anything.

When we arrived at St James's it was to be greeted by my distraught mother. She looked wild-eyed. 'I have not been fed,' she cried. 'How could I be? They have been sending notes calling us idolaters. They should be hanged, all of them. Charles, what are you thinking of to allow such conduct from your subjects!'

I silenced her, bidding her remember that she spoke to the King, but Charles just smiled and said: 'There are times, Madam, when a king . . . or even a queen . . . is not powerful enough to stop the cruelty of enemies. They must first be found and then condemned.'

She turned away. I guessed she was wishing herself far from here and I could not help thinking that there was a little good in all evil for if this decided my mother that she could not live in

roubled England that was not entirely to be deplored. This
ounds heartless. I loved my mother. I wanted to see her happy
nd comfortable, but I did realize that she was causing friction
.ere; she was interfering with the way in which the children were
rought up and I knew she was in secret teaching them to become
Catholics. I had turned a blind eye to this but recent events had
aught me to be a little more watchful; and I could guess at the
ury which would be unleashed if it were thought that the Prince
f Wales and his brother and sisters were being brought up
utside the Church of England.

The children were concerned, particularly Charles, who was
ery solemn. Lady Roxburgh told us that he had had several
ightmares and she thought he had something on his mind. She
ad asked what troubled him and he would not answer though
e did not deny that there was something.

Charles and I were determined to find out what was worrying
im and I said that I did not think he could possibly be aware of
he depressing state of affairs outside St James's; but it seemed he
vas.

Charles called the boy to him and my son stood before his
ather, his dark eyes alert, his expression attentive.

'What is wrong?' asked the King. 'You know you can tell me or
our mother anything. Come. Don't be afraid.'

'I am not afraid,' said Charles.

'Then what is worrying you?'

'How many kingdoms did my grandfather leave you?' He did
ot wait for the answer but supplied it himself. 'Four,' he went
n. 'There are troubles in the country. I know of them. I listen to
he people talking. They think I am too young to understand and
hat is an advantage because they do not lower their voices or
hoose their words. Yes, I am anxious because although you, my
ather, were left four kingdoms, I greatly fear that I, your son,
nay find myself without one.'

I broke in and cried: 'What a wicked thing to say to your father!'

Young Charles regarded me from under that black fringe and
aid: 'You asked for the truth, Mam. I but gave it. If you do not
wish to hear the truth it is best not to ask for it.'

The King put his hand on the boy's head and said: 'You do
well, my son, to speak what is in your mind on these matters. I
am having trouble. That is true. I have enemies who send out

rumours. People listen to them and learn half truths. Have no
fear. I shall fight for this kingdom, so that when the time comes it
shall be yours.'

I was too overcome to speak, for when my son talked of what
he would inherit I could only see the figure of my beloved
husband lying dead before me and that was more than I could
bear at that moment.

Charles saw this and understood. He said: 'I shall take your
mother to her bedchamber. She is not well.'

'She is pregnant,' said young Charles. 'I hope it is a little girl. I
would prefer a sister.'

'Now you go back to the nursery,' commanded the King. 'I can
assure you that I know how to defend my kingdom and when the
time comes it shall be handed . . . intact . . . to you.'

'Thank you, sir,' said young Charles gravely.

When we were alone the King said: 'He is a bright boy. One to
be proud of.'

'I liked not his words.'

'Sweet wife, do not blame the boy for looking to his inheritance. I would rather he did. He would be ready to fight for his
rights, though I pray he will never have to. Oh God, how I pray
for that! And now, my love, all this unpleasantness is bad for you.
Will you promise me that you will make preparations to leave
London at once?'

'I promise,' I told him, 'and I have already decided where.'

'Where is that?'

'Oatlands. I like it and it is pleasant to be close to the river.'

'Could not be better,' said Charles. 'Soon then . . . you will
leave for Oatlands.'

I was very fond of Oatlands, perhaps because it was just far
enough from London to make access to the capital a not too
strenuous journey and in addition had the charm of the river.
Moreover Charles had granted me the estate for my life and I felt
it was therefore my very own. I was always excited when I passed
through the beautiful arched gateway designed by Inigo Jones,
who had also built the silkworm room which had been planned
by my predecessor, Anne of Denmark, Charles's mother. There
were two quadrangles and three enclosures with the garden

yond; and the principal quadrangle had a battlemented
:eway with angle turrets and bay windows. Everything about
tlands pleased me. It was not large, as palaces go, but there
s royal dignity about it. Oh yes, I was very fond of Oatlands.

should have been serene during those last months of preg-
ncy, but I could not think so much of the coming child as of
arles. I fancied he had anxieties which he did not always
part to me – not because of a lack of trust or because he thought
:h matters would be beyond my understanding, but because
feared to worry me. Perhaps, though, I worried more being in
 dark.

was not the sort of person who could sit and wait. I was
npletely without patience and always felt better when I was
ing some action, and I was apt to take it without due thought
nply because I was eager to do something.

t was while I was waiting for the birth of my child that I wrote
the Pope. It was a daring thing to do, but I remembered how
ased he had been with me and what Panzani and Conn had said
ut his appreciation of my efforts to bring people to the Faith. I
d my beautiful cross which I wore constantly to remind me.

Sadly poor George Conn had died. He had had to leave
gland because the winters were too damp for him, but he did
t live long when he returned to Italy. I now had Count Rosetti
his place and was quite fond of him, but he could not be such a
nd as George had been.

However, greatly daring and not telling Charles for I was sure
 would have forbidden it, I wrote to his Holiness telling him
t the Puritans of England were trying to destroy my husband,
o desperately needed funds to fight against them. Would the
pe come to our aid?

When I had despatched the messenger, I felt better. I was sure
 Pope would do something for us. After all, he had been so
ased with me.

The weather had grown hot and I was dreading my confine-
nt. I was haunted by memories of the last and I wished
vently that Mamie could have been with me. There were times
en I missed her sorely. I should have loved to have her wise
nments on the situation now. Of course there was Lucy. Lucy
s amusing, vital but different from Mamie. She lacked that
therliness which I had always sensed in Mamie and which had

been such a comfort to me. There would never be another Mam
She had three little children of her own now and had not be
very well of late. I longed to tell her of our trouble but ever
realized that it would be dangerous to write letters about su
secret matters.

Every day now I looked for a messenger from the Pope
imagined myself telling Charles what I had been able to achiev
How delighted he would be with his clever little wife!

In the meantime there was the baby and the time for its arri
was getting nearer and nearer.

It happened on the eighth day of the month. The birth was ea
and the child healthy. This time it was a boy, and I was
delighted when they put him into my arms. The ordeal whic
had been dreading was over and there seemed to be no fee
about this one.

'I do declare,' I said to Lucy, 'I never felt so well after havi
given birth to a child.'

'It's a good sign,' Lucy told me. 'The boys always come mo
easily than the girls.'

I forgot everything else in the next few days and just lay in i
bed. Charles came to see me and the boy and we were very hap
for a while. I had only one regret. I had no good news from t
Pope to give him.

Never mind, I told myself, it will come and it will be a furth
reason for rejoicing.

Then he had to leave for the Border because the Scots were
their mischief again.

It was about a week after he had left when the messenger car
from the Pope. Eagerly I read what he had written and I ha
rarely been so disappointed in my life. The Holy Father would
willing to help and could send as many as eight thousand me
He would do so as soon as the King of England embraced t
Catholic Faith. Until then the Holy Father regretted that he wou
be unable to do anything to help.

My disappointment was so bitter, I just buried my head in i
pillows and wept.

After that I suffered such a tragedy that I forgot all my anxiet
about everything else.

My little Anne fell ill. She had always been the delicate one and
d been troubled by a cough from her birth, but after the arrival
my son, whom we christened Henry, she seemed to grow
rse.

was with her night and day towards the end and I prayed
stantly that her life might be spared to me. She was three
rs old and although I had lost Catherine this was not the same.
therine had died within a few hours of her birth. She had
rcely lived at all and was just a baby to me; but Anne . . . she
s my child . . . my little daughter . . . for three years I had
ed and cared for her and now . . . she was dying.

She was too good for this world, I thought. I shall never forget
se last moments at her bedside and in spite of everything that
mory is one of the most tragic of my life. I can see her lovely
le face, the gravity of it, the knowledge in the beautiful eyes
t death was close.

I cannot say my long prayer,' she said, meaning the Lord's
yer, 'so I must say my short one.' She paused awhile to collect
breath. It was pitiful to watch her. 'Lighten mine eyes, oh
rd,' she prayed, 'lest I sleep the sleep of death.'

Then she closed her eyes and that was the end.

flung myself down by her bed and gave myself up to bitter
rs. Charles came to me and we sat together in silence for a long
e. Then he took my hand and reminded me of the beautiful
lthy family we had.

We are singularly blessed,' he said, 'not only in our children
t most of all in each other.'

Then we clung together almost as though some premonition
d come to us that we might not always be together and we must
erish what time was left to us.

After a while we talked of Anne, and Charles said he wanted to
ow the cause of her death, so he ordered that there should be a
st-mortem. He feared that death might have been due to some
ident – perhaps a fall about which we had not been told. Our
l friend, Sir Theodore Mayerne, presided over the examination
ich revealed that Anne had died of a suffocating catarrh with
inflammatory disposition of the lungs, accompanied by con-
ual fever, difficulty in breathing and a constant cough.

The doctors said that she could not have lived long no matter
at had been done for her.

This satisfied us in a way because we knew that we had n
failed her.

We laid her to rest in Henry VII's Chapel in Westminster Abb
and the memory of the sweet child lingered with us to sadden o
days.

So grief-stricken had I been by the death of our little daugh
that I had temporarily forgotten the troubles which were sprir
ing up all around us.

The Scots were giving us trouble as usual and Charles said th
as he had no money there was nothing to be done but call anoth
parliament. I was against it. When had parliaments ever done
any good? I assured Charles he could govern better withou
parliament.

At least I was right about that, for no sooner was the Parliame
installed – led by the odious Pym – than it acted in such
dastardly way that even I would not have thought it capable of

I might have seen that those men were determined to destr
the King, and they were beginning to do this by robbing him
his most able supporters. They were accusing Strafford
criminal acts against the State. This was such arrant nonsen
that it made me laugh them to scorn at first; but I was wror
They were wily, powerful men, and they were well aware of wh
they were doing.

Poor Charles was beside himself with anxiety.

'They are accusing him of treason,' he cried. 'Pym is instituti
an enquiry into Strafford's conduct in Ireland.'

'But that could only be to his credit!' I cried.

'They will say he was planning to bring over an Irish army
England to fight against the English.'

'That's nonsense!'

'Of course it is nonsense but they are determined to bring hi
down. Don't you see, they are in truth striking against *me*?'

I put my arms about him and kissed him tenderly. I assur
him that we would overcome our enemies and save Straffo
from their venom.

'We will prove them wrong,' I declared. 'We will teach a less
to those wicked men who are trying to work against their King

'My little love,' he said, 'what should I do without you?'

I often thought of that and the irony of it. I know now that he ould have done so much better without me. Who knows, he ight even have been saved!

Impetuous, unworldly, without even the smallest understand- g of the situation, I plunged in to save him. How much better it ould have been for him if I had left him to his own devices! Dear arles, he was the best man and husband in the world. But as a ng – and I must be truthful now – he was weak. He was sessed by the desire to do right and this gave his unscrupulous emies power over him. Moreover be believed that whatever he d *was* right because he was King. But because of this determin- on to choose the right course he vacillated, not taking action en he should and then hastily plunging in and doing what was wise.

I blush now to think of the months that followed. I had always en foolish; now I added recklessness to my folly. I loved arles so dearly, so intensely. I was not a sensual woman; my e for him was protective, almost maternal. In different circum- nces I could have been a happy and contented mother, but a een does not have the same opportunities of being with her ildren as other women have. They are kept from her by a guard nurses, governesses, rockers, servants of all sorts. Tradition ced them there and there they must be. I thought of Charles as e of my children, particularly during those days when, prived of Strafford and fearful for him, he seemed so bewil- red. I could have been perfectly happy living somewhere like tlands, walking with the children and Charles, listening to eir chatter, watching over their meals. But that was not for me. Now I saw my Charles in distress and I was going to do erything in my power to take the burden from him.

I tried to placate those stern men of the Parliament – those mbrely clad gentlemen, many of them with the plain round ir style which I so hated. I wrote several letters addressed to the rliament. I apologized for my chapel at Somerset House. I told em I would be very careful only to act as was necessary. I knew at the Pope's envoy Rosetti was not approved by some of them d if it was their wish I would have him removed. If there was ything they wished me to do I should be glad to listen to it. I s grovelling and that was against my nature; and my humili- on was increased because they ignored me.

Father Philip came to me.

'Why will not the Holy Father help me?' I demanded. 'A gre
deal of this trouble has come about because I worked so zealous
for the Holy Church.'

'You know the Holy Father's price. Charles must embrace th
Catholic Faith. Let him do that and he can be assured of the Ho
Father's help.'

'If he became a Catholic the Puritans would immediate
depose him,' I reminded him.

Poor Father Philip! What could he say? As for me, I was begin
ning to see how dangerous everything was becoming. I w
certain now that we must show the people that we were n
fanatical Catholics, that we were quite ready to accept their alle
iance to the Protestant Faith and it seemed to me that the best w
of doing this was to make approaches to the Prince of Orange.

Recently he had wanted our daughter Elizabeth for his so
Although Elizabeth was a second daughter we had thought t
match demeaning. The Prince of Orange was of small cons
quence in the world and we were the ruling family of a gre
country.

I said to Charles: 'They are Protestant and many have said tha
was against the match because I wanted Catholic alliances for n
daughters.'

'Which you did, dear heart,' replied Charles.

'Of course I did. But the Prince of Orange is very eager.' I la
my hand on his arm. 'Let us do this. Let us show the people ho
ready we are for a Protestant alliance. Let us give Mary – o
eldest – to the son of the Prince of Orange.'

He stared at me in disbelief. Then I saw the realization of wh
this would mean dawn in his eyes.

Charles was a man who needed someone to rely on – Buc
ingham, Strafford . . . men like that. Buckingham had been de
patched by the assassin's dagger and it could well be th
Strafford might go by the executioner's axe. I was left to him
might not be clever and shrewd and have little knowledge
affairs but I was more staunchly loyal to him than anyone in t
world could be.

He clung to me and that made me all the more determined to
everything I could however much others might disapprove
would do anything . . . just anything for him.

When Archbishop Laud was arrested, Father Philip and osetti came to me and talked very seriously about the Puritans in arliament.

'The time has come for the King to declare his conversion to the atholic Faith,' they said. 'Now is the moment. The Parliament is eady to rise against the King. If the King would announce his onversion, the might of the Pope would be behind him and the arliament with its Puritans would be quickly subdued.'

'The King will never do it. He has sworn to govern the country the Reformed Faith.'

'A man can change such an oath if he has the might of an army ehind him. How many of his subjects would be ready to follow im?'

'Not so many as would be against him.'

'Let him say then that he wants liberty of conscience to think d worship as he pleases.'

'He will never do it. I will speak to him but even I could not rsuade him to that.'

'They have Strafford. They have Laud. Who next?' asked osetti.

'I do not know,' I cried in despair.

They would be horrified when they heard of the proposed arriage with the House of Orange. But the people were not, though it did not have the impact I had hoped for.

Strafford and Laud were still in the Tower.

Of course the Prince of Orange accepted with alacrity and there as a lull in our unpopularity because of the coming marriage.

Mary's wedding should have been a wonderful occasion but it as not. Our first daughter to marry – and her husband a petty rince! But that was not really why we were depressed.

The trial of Strafford had begun and in our hearts we knew that was really a quarrel between the Throne and the Commons. It as King against Parliament. Charles was wretchedly unhappy. e had always been loyal to his friends and he had loved rafford who, he knew, had been condemned not for his etrayal of his country but for his loyalty to his King.

Charles had written to him. I had been beside him as he wrote d mingled my tears and prayers with his.

'The misfortune which has fallen upon you,' wrote Charles
'being such that I must lay by the thought of employing yo
hereafter in my affairs, yet I cannot satisfy myself in honour o
conscience without assuring you now in the midst of you
troubles, that upon the word of a King you shall not suffer in life
honour or fortune.'

We were both happier when he wrote that, for those wicke
men who accused him would do their best to bring him to th
scaffold, but it would be the King who would have to sign th
death warrant so Strafford could not go to the block unless th
King agreed to his death. 'And that,' declared Charles, 'is some
thing I will never do.'

They had set up a great tribunal in Westminster Hall and th
peers and Lord Chancellor on the Woolsack were there with th
judges – and also the Commons. How I hated them in their blac
clothes. Cruel Roundheads, I called them.

I watched, with the King, behind a trellis. I had said that th
two elder children should go with us – so Charles and Mary came
I shall never forget the intent look on the face of my serious sor
Young Charles was determined to learn how to be a king. Mar
was a little apprehensive. I supposed she was thinking of th
young bridegroom who would soon be coming to claim his bride

We sat there throughout the day, and at night returned t
Whitehall Palace. We grew more and more depressed as the day
passed. I had to do something for I could not endure inactivity.

I wrote again to the Pope. I begged him to let me have fiv
hundred crowns for I believed that if I had this money I coul
bribe the members of Parliament. It was a wild idea and as soon a
I had done it I regretted it and saw the folly of it. But watchin
those horrible Roundheads in the hall with the cruelty on thei
stern pale faces and knowing that they were doing their best t
hound dear Strafford to his death made me desperate and I wa
sure that they were such villains that they would be open t
bribes.

That was not the height of my stupidity. I knew that Lucy wa
rather interested in their Puritan doctrines. It was laughable
Lucy a Puritan! Her main preoccupation was with her gowns an
her complexion. But Lucy was like that. She favoured contrasts
and oddly enough she had become quite friendly with the odiou
Pym.

guessed that she was worried about the Earl of Strafford and
must be believing that Pym might help to get him released.
w clever of her! Pym carried great weight in the Commons. He
s their leader, and of course the best way to serve Strafford
s to be friendly with men like Pym, to try to make them
derstand that in no way could he be called a traitor.

told Lucy that I too would like to meet some of the Parliamen-
ians that I might talk to them and attempt to make them see
son.

he said it would have to be in secret.

'Could you bring them to Whitehall?' I asked.

'Well, you know I am talking to Pym quite a lot nowadays.'

Yes, I know. You are so clever, Lucy. What could you arrange
me?'

Lucy loved intrigue. She said we could use one of the rooms in
palace. One of the ladies was away for a time so why should
not use hers? Lucy would see whom she could bring to the
ace.

So there I was creeping through the corridors of Whitehall after
k, lighted by the taper I carried, meeting those men whom
y arranged should talk to me. They were astonished; they
re overawed although they held their stupid uncurled heads
h; they were respectful; they listened; but they did not commit
mselves to help Strafford, which was what I wanted them to

did not tell Charles what I was doing. It was unconventional
l he liked to do things by order. But after a while I began to see
t the operation was useless and told Lucy so. She agreed with
.

So the Strafford trial went on and, listening to it every day
ind the trellis, I was certain that those men down there were
ng to insist on his destruction, no matter what the verdict.

But we held the trump card, I told Charles. He had promised
afford that he would never sign the death warrant and they
ld not kill him without the King's authority.

hat thought sustained us during those days.

owards the end of the month our bridegroom arrived with
ne pomp, escorted by a fleet of twenty vessels in charge of the
ous Dutch Admiral van Tromp. Charles despatched the Earl
Lindsay to welcome him in his name when they arrived at

Gravesend and in due course the Prince rode into London in t
carriage Charles had sent for him. As the Prince came close to t
Tower one hundred pieces of ordnance were discharged a:
welcome, and it was about five o'clock in the evening when th
arrived at Whitehall. Charles was worried because of the stran
mood of the people, who were overexcited by the trial
Strafford and taking sides with the Parliament against the Kin;

It would have been disastrous if they should riot and attack c
visitors, so he had ordered the guards to be out in full force
which looked like a guard of honour but which was really one
protection.

I liked the look of the young Prince. He was fifteen years ol
Mary was only ten – and quite good looking. Moreover it w
obvious that he was pleased by the match and it was only natu
that he should be. He had the sad state of affairs in England
thank for it; it would never have been made in happier circu
stances.

Mary was at Somerset House so she was not present at our fi
meeting and the Prince immediately asked our leave to visit I
there. Charles said that the permission was readily granted a
he felt sure that the Prince would want to pay his respects to t
Queen Mother at St James's before making the journey
Somerset House.

The Prince bowed and said that he would first call on t
Queen Mother although I knew he was all impatience to :
Mary; but as Charles said to me, he thought we should be the
when they met and while William was visiting St James's
could go privately and with all speed to Somerset House, wh
we did; and I was so pleased to see the first meeting between t
young couple.

It lifted my spirits for they liked each other on sight and I kn
from experience how terrifying it can be to be sent to a bri
groom whom one has never seen.

I said to Charles: 'I have one prayer to make at this moment a
that is that Mary may find almost as great a happiness with I
husband as I have had with mine. . . . I would say, as great, I
my dearest, there can be only one most perfect husband in t
world and I have already taken him.'

Charles smiled in that rather embarrassed way he had wh
face to face with my extravagant words and deeds, but he w

eatly moved and he did say that his prayer would be worded in
actly the same way except that he would substitute wife for
sband.

Whitehall chapel was prepared for the ceremony and the bride-
oom appeared looking very handsome in red velvet, adorned
 a collar of Vandyke point lace. Mary looked beautiful. She was
mewhat simply dressed in a gown of silver tissue and her
wellery was all pearl. Her hair was tied with silver ribbons so
at she gave an impression of absolute purity. I myself had
osen her dress and I was glad that I had insisted on such
nplicity for I thought that, standing beside her red-velvet-clad
idegroom, she looked elegant, while the poor boy looked over
essed, *nouveau riche* . . . and to tell the truth a little crude.

I did not participate in the ceremony. How could I since it was
otestant? I sat with my mother and my daughter Elizabeth in a
rtained-off gallery from which we could watch the scene below
thout taking part in it.

The Bishop of Ely performed the ceremony. Our Archbishop, I
as reminded with a pang of fear, was a prisoner in the Tower.
e King gave his daughter away and the Prince put the ring on
r finger.

Then the entire company proceeded to the great chamber
ere the banquet was to take place. It was an impressive scene
th the magnificent tapestries on which was depicted the defeat
the Spanish Armada lining the walls. How different England
d been then! I reflected ruefully. How the brave men rallied to
eir Queen and fought for their country. And my Charles is such
good man. Queen Elizabeth was not always a good woman.
w was it that she had bound men to her when my beloved
arles lacked the power to do so?

There followed the farcical ceremony of putting the bride and
om to bed. There was to be no consummation as Mary was too
ung and she would not go with her bridegroom when he left
: home, but stay a little longer with her family.

My little girl was undressed, put in a night robe and lay down
the beautiful state bed adorned with blue velvet which was in
y chamber. Then the Prince of Orange came in. He looked very
easant in a robe of blue and green satin lined with silver. He
s put into the bed where he kissed Mary and the two children
 there together, one at each end of the bed with a considerable

distance between them. They stayed there for fifteen minut
then Prince William kissed Mary and left the bed.

The ceremony was completed. My daughter was married to t
Prince of Orange.

Now we must return to the dismal way of life which we h
temporarily left to celebrate the marriage.

During those dark days which followed the wedding I w
constantly looking for some ray of hope. I thought I had found
when George Goring came to me with what seemed like
splendid idea.

I liked George Goring. He was the son of the Earl of Norwi
and was exceptionally handsome and charming. His looks l
him into temptation, however, and he was somewhat profliga
and because he was so extravagant he had had to go and li
frugally abroad for some time. But he had good friends – amor
them the Earl of Strafford – and a place was found for him in t
Army where he had the rank of colonel with the command
twenty-two companies. He was shot in the leg in battle, whi
had resulted in his being a little lame.

When he asked for an audience I was delighted to grant it ar
even more delighted when he laid his plans before me.

'The trial is going against Strafford,' he said, 'and the Parli
ment is striking at the King through the Earl.'

I replied that I feared this was so.

'Well, Your Majesty,' said the dashing man who was about t
same age as I was, 'are we going to sit back and let them lead us
the nose?'

'It is the last thing I want to do.'

'Well, we must act,' said Goring. 'The Army should be
London and the first thing to do would be to seize the Tower.'

My eyes gleamed and I clapped my hands. Action at la
Positive action. It was what I had craved for.

He talked excitedly about how he would achieve the desir
effect. He would want to be made Lieutenant General of t
Army. That would be essential.

I agreed that this should be.

'Madam,' he said, 'I came to you because I know what weig
your word carries with the King. I knew I could be sure of yo

understanding and sympathy. Will you put this plan to the King?'

I said that most certainly I would and I could scarcely wait to see Charles.

When I did see him I was so excited that I began by telling him that we were going to defeat our enemies because we had the Army on our side and I would prove this to him.

He looked rather abstracted. Then he said: 'First I will tell you my news.'

'Yes, yes,' I said impatiently. 'What is it? Be quick for you will be so excited by *my* news.'

'I want to tell you of a plot which involves the Army.'

At first I thought he was talking about the same one and that George Goring must have gone to him after all. But that was not so. It seemed that there was another plot which involved four Members of Parliament – all officers of the Army – who were disturbed by the course events were taking.

'They tell me,' said Charles excitedly, 'that the Army does not like the Parliamentarians and is eager to rise against them.'

'This is wonderful,' I cried. 'Who are these men?'

'They are all in Parliament and that is significant. You know them: Henry Percy, Henry Wilmot, William Ashburton and Hugh Pollard.'

'And George Goring. . . ?'

The King looked surprised and I could contain myself no longer. 'George Goring has been to see me. He has a wonderful idea for seizing the Tower and bringing down troops from the North to take London.'

'George Goring . . . ' murmured the King. Then he turned to me, his eyes alight with hope. 'So there are two separate plots afoot. This shows well the feelings of our friends. Oh, my love, at last I see some light in the sky.'

I hugged him fiercely; then I was serious and so was he, I could see that we both had the same idea. There must not be two plots. The conspirators must join up and work together. Taking the Tower was an excellent idea; the four noble gentlemen must be informed of it.

'We shall link up the two parties,' I cried excitedly.

'With the greatest care,' replied Charles. 'You know we are

closely watched. It would not do for us to be seen with either party yet.'

'We need a go-between,' I said, my eyes sparkling.

'Someone whom we can trust. Who is the most loyal supporter we have. Jermyn, I think.'

I was very fond of Henry Jermyn. The slanders which have been uttered regarding my relationship with him are utterly false, but that does not mean I did not have a great regard for him. To be involved in these plots was dangerous and, for someone who was outside both of them and would have the delicate task of linking them up, it could be doubly dangerous.

'Not Jermyn,' I said firmly. 'He is too close to us. Any unusual movement on his part would be immediately noticed.'

'We must have someone we can trust.'

'I know, but I don't think it would be wise for Henry Jermyn to do this.'

'I think it would be most unwise to trust anyone else to do it.'

'Jermyn is *not* the man.'

'Jermyn *is* the man.'

In the past there would have been a stormy scene but we did not have those now; we were both too emotionally involved with danger and each other for quarrels. I did not want Henry Jermyn to involve himself in danger. I relied on him a good deal and he had been a great comfort to me. He was such a merry man and Charles was so sober. Of course my feelings towards Jermyn were those of a Queen to a dear friend and were quite different from my relationship with Charles.

At last I agreed that Henry Jermyn should meet both sets of conspirators and persuade them to work together. Henry willingly undertook the task but after a while he came to me and I could see that he was a little worried.

'Goring is a very ambitious man,' he said, 'and you know the King is really more in favour of the Percy and Wilmot plan to get the country to declare for the King against the Parliament. Wilmot confessed to me that he thought the capture of the Tower would prove too difficult and if it failed the entire enterprise would fail with it. Goring is not very pleased. He is set on being in command. Wilmot however wants that role for himself.'

'Oh, these petty quarrels,' I cried. 'They should forget about them at such a time.'

I thought they had, for Goring gave way to Wilmot and went to Portsmouth to make preparations as we had decided.

It was Lucy who broke the news to me. She was very well informed of what was going on and I talked to her a great deal, although Charles had warned me not to mention the Army Plot to anyone . . . simply not anyone . . . and I had obeyed him in this.

I knew by her face as soon as I saw her that something dramatic had happened. I cried: 'What is it? What is it?'

'There has been a plot,' she told me. 'The Army is involved. They planned to take the Tower and march on London.'

I felt my heart beating wildly as the colour drained from my face. 'A . . . a plot?' I stammered.

'Yes . . . against the Parliament. Wilmot is one involved, with Percy.'

'No!' I cried.

'This will decide the case against Strafford.'

'Why Strafford? He has nothing to do with it.'

'He is against the Parliament and for the King.'

'I . . . I don't understand.'

'John Pym spoke in the House about it. He has all the details and a list of the conspirators.'

I thought: Can we never succeed? Then I thought of Henry Jermyn whom I had allowed to become involved. They would be called traitors . . . all of them and I knew what sort of death awaited traitors. I was sick with fear and worry and while we were talking a guard come to the door of the apartment.

'Your Majesty,' he said with his usual respect, 'I have orders that no one shall leave the palace.'

'Does that include the Queen?' I asked ironically.

'My orders were no one, Madam.'

'Young man,' I said. 'I am the daughter of Henri Quatre, the great King of France. He never fled in danger nor am I about to.'

The guard looked ashamed and murmured that he must obey his superior officers.

'I do not blame you,' I told him. 'It is your masters who will have to pay for this.'

There was one thought in my head. I must get a message to Henry Jermyn. He must get away quickly as, of course, must all the conspirators.

I smuggled a message out to him and was relieved when I

heard that he had already left London and was on his way to Portsmouth to warn Goring of what had happened. They would have no alternative but to leave the country and from Portsmouth they would have a good opportunity of doing so.

Meanwhile I remained at Whitehall but I did see that it was dangerous for me to stay there. The best plan would be for me to leave secretly and to make my way to Portsmouth. If I could get there and across to France I could see my brother and perhaps raise money and gather an army to fight for Charles.

I think I might have got away for the guards had now been withdrawn. I had gathered together my jewels and a few things and arranged for the coach to be ready, but just as I was about to leave, the French ambassador arrived at the palace. He regarded me with some dismay when he saw that I was on the verge of departure.

'Your Majesty cannot leave now,' he cried. 'That would be disastrous.'

'How can I stay here? The people are murmuring against me. It is not safe for me . . . my mother or my children.'

'Nevertheless to go now would be the worst thing possible. Do you know what is happening?'

I covered my face with my hands. 'I only know that everything we do results in failure. I have to get away. I have to find money and men. I must save the King.'

'Your Majesty, the Army Plot was betrayed to the Parliament by George Goring.'

'George Goring! No! Never!'

'That is so. He wanted to be in command and there was conflict with Wilmot on this issue – so to take his revenge he informed against the plotters.'

'I cannot believe it.'

'Whether Your Majesty does or not it is true,' he said. 'The conspirators have escaped to France. I will say this for Goring. He let Jermyn go . . . Jermyn came to warn him that the plot was betrayed and, not knowing who the traitor was, urged Goring to get away quickly. Goring could have arrested Jermyn on the spot but apparently he had enough decency to desist from that.'

'And Jermyn?' I asked anxiously.

'Is safely on his way to Rome.'

'I thank God for that.'

'And, Madam, do you know what is being said about you and rmyn?'

'I know people will tell any lies about me.'

'They are saying that he is your lover. If you fled now and ined him and the others what is now speculation would be ken as certainty.'

'Oh, the wickedness of it!' I cried. 'How dare they!'

'They would dare much,' said stern Montreuil, 'and I beg you give them no more cause to do so. Some of your ladies have een questioned and they speak of nocturnal visits to meet men f the Parliament.'

'It was to persuade them to help the Earl of Strafford.'

'The actions of a Queen who made midnight assignations with arious men could be misconstrued.'

'I never heard such nonsense. I am the King's loyal wife and ubject.'

'We know, Madam, and those close to you have no doubt of it. ut a queen must not only be beyond reproach but be seen to be, nd your behaviour has scarcely been restrained.'

'This is no time for restraint. It is time for action. Oh, why is veryone against me!'

'That is untrue. As your brother's ambassador I am here to erve you and I can do that best by giving you the truth.'

He had gained his point. I knew that I must stay for a while yet.

That very day news came. The revelation of the Army Plot had ecided them. Strafford was found guilty – among other charges of attempting to bring an army over from Ireland to fight the nglish.

He was sentenced to death.

I know that Charles has been blamed for what happened next nd I know too that he had no alternative but to do it.

What terrible days they were! They marked the beginning of e débâcle.

The King came to Whitehall. He was strained and more un-appy than I had ever seen him. His thoughts were all for trafford. He had loved that man, and I had been fond of him too. leither of us could bear to contemplate what would happen to im.

'He must not die,' Charles said again and again. 'I have prom
ised him that he shall not die.'

'You are the King,' I reminded him. 'You will refuse to sign th
death warrant and they cannot kill him without that. You are sti
the King, remember, though these miserable Puritans try t
pretend otherwise.'

'No,' said Charles firmly, 'I shall not sign the death warrant.'

London was afire with the desire to see Strafford's hea
severed from his body. Why did the common people love suc
sights? Was it because those whom they had envied might nov
be envying them since, in spite of lack of wealth and standing
they at least had life. Perhaps. But in any case the mob wa
howling for Strafford's blood.

There were rumours coming from every direction. Some sai
the French fleet had seized the Channel Islands. That made ther
curse me . . . and my mother. Poor Mother, what a choice sh
had made when she insisted on coming to England!

The night that followed was one of the most terrifying of m
life. The shouts and screams of the mob can reduce even the mos
brave to fear; it is the sound of those who are like baying animal
intent on destroying their prey; there is no reasoning; there i
nothing but the desire to inflict pain and torture on those whom
they have decided to attack.

The wicked scandals about me, the accusations against tha
good man, the King, the demand for Strafford's blood, when a
he had done was be a loyal statesman – all these were excuse
those blood-crazed men and women had fed to themselves. I
they had had any power to think and paused awhile to do so the
must have seen them as false. But the very thin layer of civiliz
ation had been broken apart and they had emerged like animal
in a jungle hunt. They were worse. Animals hunt for food; the
hunted just for the lust of revenge on those who had enjoye
what they thought of as the luxuries of life. How I hated them
The feeble-minded, unwashed, envious bloodthirsty dregs of th
human race.

They were clamouring at the gates of Whitehall. I coul
vaguely hear the shouts of 'Justice! Execution.' Justice! Wha
justice was there for a good man like Strafford? Execution? Yes
They wanted blood. Strafford was to appease them first. They
were like hungry wolves following a sleigh. Throw out Straffor

so that we can feed on him. That will satisfy us . . . for a time.

Catholics were crowding into my chapel to pray, for they saw this as something more than the mob's fury against Strafford. My name was bandied about too freely for their peace of mind. Some of them collected their valuables and were making efforts to get to the coast.

I sent a messenger to Pym, as the leader of the Commons, asking him for protection. Lucy helped me. She professed friendship with Pym and he must have been rather flattered by the attention of such a beautiful lady of the Court. I knew of her relationship with Strafford and I was sorry for her, guessing what she would be suffering now.

Pym's answer was that I should prepare to leave the country for that was the only way I could be safe.

Charles arrived at Whitehall. The people did not hate him so much. If he would sign Strafford's death warrant doubtless they would cheer him.

He was distraught.

'What can I do?' he cried. 'Strafford has been loyal to me. He was my friend . . . my good friend. I have promised him that although it may be necessary to remove him from his post, I will never let him die.'

We clung together. He stroked my hair. 'This is a sorry state of affairs,' he murmured. 'It grieves me that I have brought you to this.'

'You brought me only happiness,' I told him. 'Always remember that.'

Then we sat together, holding hands and in a way comforting each other.

'Whatever happens,' said Charles, 'you and I have known such a happy life together as few people experience.'

It was true and it was wonderful how, even with the mob howling at the gates, we could feel a certain happiness as long as we were together.

Suddenly there was a quietness from without and Charles sent one of the guards to see what was happening. What they had to tell made me shiver with horror. Someone in the mob had said that the Queen Mother was the real culprit. Nothing had gone well since she had come to England. She even had a malevolent effect on the weather.

'To St James's!' they had cried.

I buried my face in my hands. I would have been glad if m
mother had left England but she was still my mother and I love
her in a way. I could not bear the thought of her being subjecte
to humiliation. It was true she had meddled: she had tried t
make Catholics of the children; she had urged me to take a stron
line with those who had gone against me and perhaps I had bee
influenced by her; she had openly flouted her adherence to th
Catholic Church and her contempt for that of the Protestants
she so often forgot that she was a guest in this country and sh
had cost Charles a great deal of money by keeping an establish
ment for which she could not afford to pay. Yet she was m
mother.

And the younger children were with her at St James's. Onl
Charles was with us at Whitehall and Mary was at Somerse
House.

The long night seemed as though it would never end. Charle
and I sat hand in hand hardly speaking, worn out with exhaus
tion but unable to sleep.

In the morning several of the bishops called on Charles.

'There is nothing to be done other than sign the death warrant,
they said. 'The people have made up their minds that they wan
Strafford's blood.'

'I cannot do it,' Charles insisted. 'I have given my word.'

'My lord,' said one of the bishops, 'there comes a time when
certain action must be taken. It is better for one man to die than
thousands.'

'Thousands . . . ' echoed Charles.

'The people are in an angry mood. I fear they would attack the
palace first.'

'My wife . . . my children . . . ' cried Charles.

'My lord, none of them is safe. It is Strafford's blood they want
He is a symbol. If you refuse to sign the death warrant you are
going against Parliament for they have passed the sentence. To
refuse to sign it is defiance against Parliament.'

'I do defy them. I will not sign away the life of a man who has
shown me nothing but friendship and loyalty.'

The Bishops were dismayed. 'We fear the consequences. They
will break into the palace. The Queen. . . . ' They looked at me
solemnly. 'The people murmur all the time against the Queen.'

I looked at Charles and saw the frank terror in his face. It was fear for me and the children.

He said: 'Give me time . . . time . . . ' And I knew that he was wavering.

The Bishops left and Charles turned to me. 'What am I going to do?' he cried in despair. 'You are in danger. The children. . . . '

I said: 'Charles, you must not think of me. You must do what is right.'

'How could I not think of you? I would do anything . . . anything rather than that harm should come to you.'

Then we kissed tenderly and were silent for a long time. His resolution was wavering. He was going to give them what they wanted, not out of fear for himself – he was the bravest man on earth – but because he dreaded what they would do to me. I think we both remembered that queens had been beheaded before. Worse still, if I fell into the hands of the mob, they would tear me to pieces before the judges could condemn me.

Our son came to us. He was very grave for he was fully aware of what was going on. Young Charles had always been precocious. He looked at his father questioningly and the King said: 'They are crying for Strafford's blood. How can I sacrifice one who has served me so loyally?'

Our son surveyed us solemnly and I thought how serious and kingly he looked – tall, commanding even at his age – he was eleven years old but already looked like a king. His dark rather saturnine looks gave him an air of authority. He was the sort of child whom none could ignore.

The King said: 'My son, you shall take a message to the House of Lords. I will appeal to their sense of justice. It will be our last attempt to save the Earl of Strafford.'

Young Charles was eager to play his part in the drama and all night the King and I sat up drafting the letter which our son would take. We were sure he could not be ignored and would attract sympathy by his very youth.

In the morning young Charles put on robes of state and took his seat in the House of Lords. There was I heard a stir of interest as he entered and I could imagine that gravity, that kingly dignity which was so impressive in one so young.

He presented the letter. If the matter had not gone so far it might have had some effect. But it was too late and our last attempt failed.

The King was deeply moved to receive a letter from Strafford himself. Strafford realized what was at stake. He could perhaps see more clearly than I or the King. He knew that this struggle was between the King and the Parliament and there was still time to save the country from civil war. The Parliament had decided on his death; if the King did not agree to accept their verdict they would rise up against him and try to destroy all that the monarchy stood for. Strafford must have seen that, and loyal subject that he was to King and country, he released the King from his promise.

Charles was deeply moved and I think that helped him to his decision. All next day the people were filling the streets. They made for Whitehall and St James's. The situation was becoming very dangerous.

I had been urging Charles not to give way but now I saw that if he did not it would be the end of us all. I thought of my mother, my children, the King himself . . . and my commonsense told me that Strafford would have to go.

Charles was beside himself with grief. He had given his word to Strafford, but Strafford had released him from his promise. He believed in his heart, though, that the King would never agree to his execution.

'You have done all you could,' I reminded Charles. 'No one could have done more.'

The King nodded. 'But I gave my word. Perhaps . . . I should keep it.'

'At what cost?' I asked. 'Your children . . . me. . . .'

'Don't,' he begged. 'I could not bear life if you were harmed.'

'We must be reasonable, Charles. I was fond of Strafford. I know he was our loyal friend . . . but many lives are at stake.'

He embraced me. He was calm and cold and I knew he was thinking of me and the children.

Then he said slowly: 'There is no other way out. I must sign.'

Strafford's execution was fixed for the next day – the twelfth of May – a day I shall never forget. Charles insisted on knowing what Strafford had said when he understood that Charles had signed the death warrant.

Charles never got over it. I am sure to the last he remembered

Strafford and in his mind's eye saw the man whom he had tried to save being given the news that the King had betrayed him – for that was how Charles saw it and would not see it otherwise, however much I pointed out to him that it was not betrayal for Strafford himself had advised him to do it. But he heard that Strafford had murmured: 'Put not your trust in princes.' Poor man, he must have been overwrought. Not so much for himself but wondering about his family.

He had sent a message to Archbishop Laud, who was also lodged in the Tower, to be at his window as he passed and give him his blessing. Laud was there, and blessed him as he passed and then fell fainting to the floor as Strafford went on to the scaffold on Tower Hill.

Crowds came to see the deed, and there was a hushed silence when he raised his hand and spoke to them.

There were plenty to tell us what he had said and this was the gist of it.

'I had always believed parliaments in England to be the happy constitution of the kingdom and the nation and the best means under God to make the King and his people happy. Do not let the beginning of the people's happiness be written in letters of blood.'

There was a warning there, but the people would not see it.

He died nobly as would be expected of such a man, refusing to have his eyes bound and asking for a moment of respite to say a silent prayer, promising that when he had prayed he would lift his hand as a sign to the executioner to wield the axe.

Thus he died and so ended the troubles of his earthly life.

Ours were just beginning.

The Spy

When I went to see my mother she was in a state of panic. She had faced the fury of the people of her own country so was no stranger to unpopularity which was reaching danger point.

'I must get away,' she said. 'I must leave this country. I tell you this, Henriette. I picture those people storming the palace. They would have no respect for queens. I did not think this could happen here. I had thought you were well settled. These people are barbarians. They hate the King. They hate you. And it seems that most of all they hate me. Savages! Like uncivilized people they turn on those who are foreigners to them.'

'They turned on Strafford,' I reminded her. 'He was no foreigner. And yes, dear mother, I think you should go . . . if that is possible.'

'You should come with me, my dear.'

'And leave Charles!'

'Come with me. Perhaps we could go to France.'

'My brother would not welcome us.'

'Shame on him! His own mother and sister!'

'He is first of all King of France.'

'He has no mind of his own. Between Richelieu and that wife of his. . . . She gives herself airs now that she has produced the heir to the throne. *Mon Dieu*, she took long enough to do it.'

'Charles thinks that no hindrance would be put in the way of your going.'

'Then I shall leave as soon as possible.'

'I have thought of something. We have a new ally now in the Prince of Orange. This marriage might not have been so degrading after all. I know that Orange has little standing in Europe, but he is very rich. It may be that he will help to raise an army for us and I could bring it back to stand with the King's. And then we could make war on these Puritan Parliamentarians and t them see who is the master here . . . they or their anointed ing.'

'It is a good idea. I want to leave as soon as possible. I shall ever sleep peacefully in my bed until I am out of this country.'

I said that I would consult Charles. 'He would not want me to ,' I added. 'He would hate my being out of the country.'

Oh come,' said my mother impatiently, 'you talk as though he a passionate bridegroom and you plan your honeymoon.'

'Our being together is a long honeymoon. There is no restric-on that I know of as to how long they shall last.'

My mother lifted her shoulders in exasperation. She was not e sort of woman to understand love like ours.

I left her then and when I saw Charles I told him what was in y mind. He always listened to what I had to say with as much tention – no more – than he listened to his ministers.

'Mary is too young for the consummation but the Prince of range is urging us to send her to Holland. Why should she not ? She will be safer there than here. I can take her . . . perhaps avel with my mother . . . and then I could say that I am going to e spa in Lower Lorraine because I am in poor health. Of course I ould not go there, but be in Holland and perhaps try to see my other. Who knows? If he were actually face to face with me he ight not be able to refuse my pleas for help.'

On consideration Charles thought it a good idea.

'We should be separated in any case,' he said, 'as I have to go to cotland.'

'Scotland again!'

'I plan to placate them, to give them what they want and to list their help against those in England who are against me.'

I clasped my hands. Any new project filled me with hope even ough, had I pondered more intently, I might see that it was omed to failure befire it began. But my nature was such that as ng as I was feverishly putting some plot into action I could see othing but success. Charles was a little like that too. Perhaps at was why we plunged into wild schemes without giving them ue thought.

When Parliament heard that my mother was planning to leave ey gave their wholehearted permission for her to go. No one uld have said more clearly: Good riddance. They even helped er on her way by giving her a sum of money for the journey.

As to my leaving, they were very suspicious about tha
Naturally they suspected my trip to the Continent had bee
arranged for a purpose other than my health. They were insul
ing. They gave orders that my jewels were not to be taken out o
the country and they instructed Sir Theodore Mayerne t
examine me and decide whether the waters of a foreign spa wer
necessary to preserve my health.

Old Mayerne could be one of the most irritating men I knew. O
course he was a Huguenot and not very sympathetic towards th
Catholic cause. I think he looked upon me as a wayward child. H
could not bring himself to say that my health would be endar
gered if I did not take the waters. I was annoyed with him when
heard what he had reported and the verdict was that I was not t
be allowed to leave the country.

I raged at Mayerne, who surveyed me sardonically. I could ne
threaten to dismiss him from the royal service. He was to
valuable for that and Charles would never have agreed. H
admired Mayerne as the best doctor in Europe and he ha
often said that his frankness was symbolic of his nature. 'H
is incapable of dissembling,' said Charles, 'and those are the so
of people we need about us, those who tell the truth for i*
own sake and do not suppress it out of fear or in the hope o
favour.'

So I had to accept his judgement, knowing of course that it wa
the truth. But I stormed at him. I had suffered a great deal durin
the uncertainty over Strafford and I was worried every hour o
the day for our future.

'I am afraid I shall go mad,' I said to Mayerne, at which h
looked at me steadily.

'You need have no fear,' he replied, 'for you already are.'

I could not help laughing at him. What a way for a subject t
speak to his sovereign! But he did not see me as a queen. In hi
opinion I was an hysterical overwrought woman who was eithe
imagining or pretending she suffered from ailments which woul
be cured in a foreign spa.

So with Charles in Scotland and my mother on the way t
Antwerp, I went to Oatlands. There I would work out how
could get Mary to Holland and accompany her; and even if I wer
not allowed to leave the country it would be better for Mary to go
She would be much safer in Holland.

I was trying to find a little peace while I waited for Charles to
return. If he could please the Scots, if he could get them on his
side, who knew, we might put an end to this miserable Parliament. Parliaments had always caused trouble. I agreed with
Charles that a king had been chosen by Divine Right to rule and
surely that should be enough without parliaments interfering.
They always caused trouble. Why could they not leave us in
peace?

But they could not . . . even at Oatlands. Word was sent to me
that the Prince of Wales was visiting me too frequently and that I
was endeavouring to instruct him in the Catholic Faith.

My reply to that was that the King had chosen his governor and
was well aware that it was not the King's will that any of our
children should be brought up in the Catholic Faith.

That had to satisfy them, but an extraordinary thing did
happen while I was at Oatlands. One day the local magistrate
came to me and asked to see me in private. I saw him at once and
he told me that he had received an order from Parliament to get
together all the militia of the district and bring them to Oatlands
by midnight. They would be met by a company of cavalry officers
and would be told what was expected of them.

'I came to Your Majesty,' said the magistrate, 'because I feared
that it was a plot against you and I would have you know that it is
my desire to serve Your Majesty with my life.'

I was always deeply moved by such expressions of loyalty and I
thanked the magistrate warmly. I told him that there might well
be a plot to capture me or my children . . . all of us perhaps. 'I
have many enemies, my friend,' I said. 'They are those grim-
faced men who think they are holier than God Himself. We have
many of them in Parliament, I fear, and they plan to do me a
mischief. I thank you for your warning. Now I shall be ready.'

And I was ready. The day passed quickly and I was exhilarated
in spite of everything, because immediate action was demanded.
I saw that everyone in the house was armed. Then we waited for
nightfall and the assault.

It did not come.

I wondered why because I was sure of the integrity of the
magistrate and he swore he had received the instructions he had
explained.

I could only think that whoever had planned it had got wind of

the loyalty of the magistrate and his men and did not want t
meet opposition.

But the incident did make me feel that I ought to make plans t
get away; and if they would not sanction my departure I mus
leave secretly.

Plotting, discarding plans, discussing the matter endlessl
with Lucy who, I felt, was the only one I could really trus
planning for the horses I should need on the road to Portsmout
. . . all this made time pass quickly.

I decided I would leave Oatlands for Hampton Court for wor
had come to me that Charles was on his way home. At Hampton
could meet some of the most influential men in the country and
hoped to persuade them to stand with the King.

It was wonderful when Charles arrived at Hampton. We clun
together for a long time as though we would never let each othe
go. The children were there too and they had their share o
affection. But for Charles I was the one who meant most to hir
and so it was with him in my affections.

We talked and talked. The trip to Scotland had not been
success but that did not seem to matter as long as we wer
together again.

Quite a number of people came to Hampton to welcome th
King and it was like old times and, ever ready to hope, I tol
myself all was going to be well again.

We were going to make a triumphant return to Whitehal
Some of our friends told us that there would be a civic welcom
for us. The people were delighted because my mother had gon
and that was a great source of irritation removed; the Papal envo
had left; the King had returned from Scotland without that arm
of Scotsmen which it was feared he might bring with him.

'Our troubles are over,' said the hopeful ones; and of course
was ready to believe them.

And then this unfortunate thing happened. We were all stand
ing at a window looking out – the King, the children, myself an
one or two of our friends – when a gypsy came up and asked fo
money. She had a basket on her arm; she was bent and deforme
and such a strange sight that some of our party began to laugh a
her.

There was a general titter. I did not like it because I neve
laughed at people's deformities. I had my dwarfs, it was true, bu

always treated them with the respect due to normal human beings. It was not their stunted growth which appealed to me but that I saw a certain beauty in them and they were such good servants. *I* was not one who laughed at the gypsy.

She looked up at us and her face was malevolent, evil. I drew back for I saw that her eyes were fixed on the King and myself as well as our children.

She took out a hand mirror from her basket and handed it to the King.

'I don't want it,' he said.

'Look into it,' she commanded, 'and see what you can see.'

The King looked at it and I who was close, looked too. I gave a little shriek. The King had turned pale. Others crowded round and looked into the mirror but they could only see their own faces and that was all I could see now, but just for a few seconds I had seen something else . . . and so had the King.

The mirror had shown us the King's head . . . without his body.

I was almost fainting. The King had put an arm about me and I heard the cackle of the gypsy.

'Did you like what you saw, my lord, my lady? You should give me money. You should always treat the gypsies well or they might show you what it is better for you not to see.'

'Give the woman money,' said the King.

It was thrown down to her. She picked it up and put it in her basket. She took the mirror which had been given back to her. She said: 'In that room in which you stand another will be weeping. He has a dog with him. That dog will die . . . and when he dies the kingdom will come back to the King.'

With that she hobbled away leaving the company twittering with excitement and myself almost fainting in my husband's arms.

He said I needed to rest and he took me to our apartment in the palace.

'It was terrible,' I gasped.

'It was an illusion,' he replied. 'How could something which was not there be seen in the mirror?'

'We both saw it,' I reminded him.

'It could not have been so,' he replied.

Then he tried to comfort me with the good news that the people of London were giving us a welcome.

'They have changed towards us,' he said. 'Those who we
shrieking outside the palace are now going to receive us wi
affection.'

'Can we trust those who change so quickly?'

'They had what they wanted. Strafford dead . . . and yo
mother gone. They will love us again, you will see.'

'I do not trust such fickle love,' I said.

Then he held me fast and thanked God that we were togeth
again.

The weather was cold but there was a new warmth in my hea
as we rode side by side into Moorgate where the Mayor an
aldermen were waiting to greet us. We were presented with tw
richly caparisoned horses and a golden coach. The Mayor told
that the horses were for the King and the Prince of Wales and t
coach for me and the younger children.

Charles was so delighted that he knighted the Mayor and t
Recorder on the spot and when this pleasant ceremony was ov
the merchants of the city crowded round to kiss the King's hand

My two Charleses mounted the horses which had been pr
sented to them and with the children I stepped into the coach ar
we drove down to the Guildhall.

I had not been so happy for a long time as I was when I ro
through those streets under the fluttering banners and the stri
of cloth of gold which they had put up to welcome us.

My husband and son looked so noble on their magnifice
horses. I wondered how any could turn against them for the sa
of those ugly roundheaded creatures with their black clothes ar
miserable faces.

There was a sumptuous banquet for us at the Guildhall and t
city dignitaries had brought out the gold plate which they on
did on the most important occasions.

What a welcome! It showed the mood of the people. We ha
only had to sacrifice Strafford – which I knew still worrie
Charles – and get rid of my mother, who had been one of the ma
causes of our unpopularity. It was a pity that she had ever com
Well, she had gone now. She would be in Antwerp. I hoped sh
was not making trouble there.

All was going to be well. We must be strong. We must star

rm. I would talk to Charles about that. Dear good man that he
as, he was too lenient, too ready to believe the best of everyone.

At last we arrived at Whitehall, tired but jubilant.

All was going to be well in the end.

I talked to Charles that night when we were alone. He had
leas. He was going to dismiss the guards which the Parliament
ad set up in Westminster to look after the Houses of Parliament.

'Their guards will go,' he said. 'Mine will be there. I know you
ink I give way too easily, but I have not been idle. There are
en loyal to me in the kingdom and they have their own trained
ands. They shall guard the Houses of Parliament.'

I clasped my hands in pleasure. 'That is excellent,' I said.

'Of course,' went on Charles, 'they won't like it. Men like Pym
ill have their suspicions.'

'Let them,' I cried. 'We'll make sure that our guards are loyal.'

'I wish that I could arrest certain members of the Parliament.
hey should be impeached for their disloyalty to the crown.'

'Why not?' I asked excitedly.

'I am unsure,' he answered.

'Which would you arrest? Pym for sure, I would say.'

'Certainly Pym; Hampden is another. Then there are Holles,
trode, Haselrig. . . . They are the ones I most distrust. If we
uld be rid of them we might make some headway in Parlia-
ent.'

'You must arrest them.'

'I will think of it.'

'Soon,' I whispered.

Then he lifted me in his arms and said it was time we went to
ed.

I could not sleep much. I was thinking of the wonderful recep-
on which the city of London had given us. It was often said that
London was with you, the whole country would be.

It was changing. Perhaps the panic had been unnecessary and
e had feared too much, become too nervous, let ourselves be led
y fear.

I must keep Charles to his resolution. He would achieve much
he could take those men by surprise. If he could ride into the
ouse of Commons with guards to arrest them, they could be put

into prison before they realized what was happening; and on
they were there it should not be difficult to make the people se
that they were a menace to peace.

He must do it. He must.

I knew he would waver. He was always tormented by his fea
that he might not be doing what was right. This was right . .
absolutely right. What had they done to dear good nob
Strafford? Murder. Judicial murder if they liked, but murde
nevertheless. They should all go to the block for that alone.

I could scarcely wait for morning.

Charles was thoughtful. He was pondering on the enormity
what he proposed to do. It was coming into the open, he said. S
far, although it had been in people's minds, no one had men
tioned yet that such divided opinion in the country was headin
towards civil war. That was a prospect which should mak
anyone who wished the country well pause and think.

Now Charles was pausing and thinking.

I urged him; I persuaded him; I hinted that to let such a
opportunity pass was cowardice as well as folly. If he did n
grasp this chance and use it to advantage he could not blam
anyone but himself if he had to fight for his kingdom.

He looked at me with horror and I cried out: 'Yes, I keep m
eyes and ears open. I keep myself alert . . . for you. I cannot stan
by and see you lose your kingdom. Dearest Charles, you must a
. . . now. This is the time. Let this go and you may not hav
another opportunity.'

At last he made his decision. He knew that he would not b
able to face me if he did not make the attempt.

He was ready. He was going to do it. I embraced him fever
ishly. 'I am so proud of you, my King,' I said. 'Everything is goin
to change now. This is the turning point.'

He whispered to me. 'I will go now. If one hour passes withou
your receiving ill news of me, you will see me when I retur
master of my kingdom.'

I bade him farewell. 'My heart goes with you,' I said.

'I will be back,' he told me. 'Give me one hour.'

I don't think I have ever known an hour take so long to pass.
could not stop myself glancing at my watch every few minute
Lucy was sitting with me. 'You are restless this mornin
Madam,' she said.

No . . . no . . . Lucy. Not restless.'

Well, I declare this is the third time you have looked to see the
e . . . and all in the last five minutes.'

Oh . . . you are mistaken,' I said and she smiled and spoke of
er things.

When I remember that morning, I am so ashamed. I curse my
y, my stupidity . . . my blindness. Why could I not see what
s right under my nose? The burden of guilt becomes intoler-
e when I look back.

t last the hour was over. Now! I thought. It is done. At this
ment those men are under arrest. Everyone is going to see that
King is indeed the King. He will brook no interference from a
of miserable sly-faced scheming Puritans.

jumped up. I could contain myself no longer. Lucy was beside
'Something ails you, I know. It has been worrying you this
hour.'

am not worried . . . not any more,' I cried. 'It is time for
icing. I have every reason to hope that the King is now master
is realm. Pym and his confederates will have been arrested by
v.'

ucy stared at me. 'Is that so?' she said. 'Has the King gone to
House of Commons to arrest them?'

He has indeed.'

Then there is every reason to congratulate the King. I am going
ring a little wine so that we can drink a toast to him.'

Do that, Lucy,' I said.

he ran out of the room. I was astonished that she did not
urn. But I was too excited to bother very much. I went to the
dow and stood there waiting.

waited for a long time.

he King eventually returned . . . dejected. Then I heard the
ible news.

he arrests had not taken place. Pym and his friends had been
rned of what was about to happen and had fled, so that when
King with his guards entered the House of Commons, they
already left.

Charles was desolate. It seemed that fate was against us. Who
ld have warned them? There had been so few of us who knew
at was planned.

'There is a spy close to us,' I said.

'I fear so,' replied the King. He went on to tell me that he |
been delayed when he was about to enter the House
Commons. 'You know what it is like when I go to the Parliame
They are lying in wait for me. They all have some grievance, so
petition to present. I must stay and listen to them. They are
subjects. I did not worry about the loss of time because I thou
that only you and I shared the secret. So I was late going into
House. I believe they had left but a few minutes before.'

'But how . . . why . . . ?'

'Someone knew and warned them.'

'But who could?'

He looked at me sadly. 'You did not mention the matter?'

'Only to Lucy . . . and that after the hour had passed.'

'But Lucy Carlisle has become Pym's mistress.'

'Oh . . . *mon Dieu.*' I felt sick with horror. 'Lucy? Not Lucy. '
is friendly with Pym. She finds out what she can from th
devious Parliamentarians so that she can tell us, help us. . . .

'It may be,' said Charles sombrely, 'that she talks to you
passes on to them what they want to know.'

'You can't mean that Lucy. . . .'

'I was told that a messenger went to Pym. He came from he

'I will send for her immediately.'

I did so, but Lucy was not in the palace.

'What did you tell her?' asked the King.

'Nothing . . . until the hour was up. Then I asked her to rej
with me because you were master of your realm for you had g
to arrest those trouble-makers and the deed was now done.'

'Within an hour! It must have been a good half an hour l
before I was able to get into the House. Time enough for he
warn Pym . . . which she did.'

I covered my face with my hands.

'Oh Charles,' I cried, 'I have destroyed your plan! I, who wo
give my life for you, have destroyed you.'

But he wouldn't hear of it. He tried to comfort me. He told m
was unimportant. All that mattered was that I loved him.
would forget this disaster.

'But it was *my* fault. You may forgive me but I shall ne
forgive myself.'

He rocked me in his arms as though I were a baby ar

rvelled at this love for me and that he should care so deeply for
ᵉ whose folly had dealt him such a blow.

Vhat could I do to convince him of my love for him, to show
 gratitude for his forgiveness of my folly? What could I ever do
ᵗhow him how much I loved him?

 longed for an opportunity to die for his sake. But such oppor-
ᵤities do not come.

Ve did not at first realize how disastrously we – or rather I –
ᵈ mismanaged that affair. The King's intention was now
ɔwn and our little flush of popularity was over. It seemed that
ᵉryone was turning against us. No, that was not true. There
ᵣe some faithful friends. Lord Digby for one suggested taking a
ᵣpany of his cavaliers and pursuing Pym and the rest, and
ᵉn he had found them putting them under restraint. Perhaps
ᵗ would have been the best thing to do. However, the King
ᵇade it.

ᴬt least we were now shown who were our true friends. I was
ᵥildered and quite stunned by Lucy's perfidy though when I
ᵏed back over the last years I can see that a wiser person than I
ᵍht have guessed. Her friendship with Pym should have told
. How could I have been such a fool as to imagine that she was
ᵍning that interest in him and his affairs for the sake of me!
ᵃt hurt me more than Lucy's unfaithfulness was the fact that I
ᵈ been the one to foil Charles's plans. Sometimes it seems to
 that no one could have worked more indefatigably against
ᵐ than I who loved him and would have died for him.

ᵌut as I said we sorted out the good friends from the false. Men
ᵉ the Earl of Holland and the Earl of Essex made excuses to
ᵢre from Court and in my newly found wisdom I knew what
ᵗ meant.

Ve became really alarmed when the mobs started to roam the
ᵉets. They carried placards on which was written the one
ᵣd: Liberty. I did not know what they meant by that. Did they
ⁿk they would have greater liberty under the stern Parlia-
ᵉntarians' Puritan rule than they did under that of the King?
ᴹy mother was gone; the Pope's envoy was gone. What did
ᵉy want of us now?

ℂharles was afraid for me because it was against me that the might of their venom was turned. He thought it better for us [to] leave Whitehall and we prepared to go.

It was a terrible journey. We sat there in the gilded coach wh[ich] had so recently carried us through cheering crowds and as [we] went, faces looked in at us . . . frightening faces, hating, leeri[ng] threatening . . . I knew not what.

How glad I was to leave Westminster behind and come to [the] green fields surrounding Hampton but the mansion its[elf] although always beautiful and a place I had especially loved, n[ow] held memories of a wild-eyed gypsy holding a mirror to our eye[s].

When we entered it seemed dark and unwelcoming. No [one] came out to attend to the carriage. Our guards helped us to ali[ght] and the air struck cold as we entered. There were no fires to gr[eet] us and no apartments had been made ready.

All through the night the King and I, with our three child[ren] Charles, Mary and James, shivered in one room.

'At least,' I said to Charles, 'we are all together.'

'We cannot stay here,' he replied. 'Tomorrow we will leave [for] Windsor.'

This we did and what a comfort it was to see the beaut[iful] castle, which looked so strong and royal that there seeme[d] special significance in it at this time. I was so glad to escape fr[om] the cold unwelcoming ambience of Hampton, which I felt I co[uld] never really like again whatever happened.

'We must be prepared,' said the King. 'Pym and his frie[nds] know that I would have impeached them. They will do eve[ry] thing they can to raise the country against me. It is going to b[e a] matter of deciding between the King and the Parliament. I put [my] faith in my loyal subjects.'

'There are countless numbers of them,' said Denbigh. 'We w[ill] call them together. They will all understand the menace of [the] Puritans.'

I said: 'We must raise money and I am the best one to do tha[t. I] am sure that I could persuade my brother to help us if I could o[nly] see him.'

They looked at me expectantly and I was thinking: If onl[y I] could do something really wonderful! If only I could make up [for] this terrible thing I have done. I was sure that they all blamed [me] for the position in which we now found ourselves. The arrest [of] those ringleaders would have stemmed the tide against [us.]

arles was the only one who tried to pretend that it was not so
ry important.

I was desperate to show him what I would do for him.

It seemed to be a good idea. Help was desperately needed. The
pe's conditions were too harsh. In exchange for helping
arles to keep his throne the Holy Father was demanding that
act in such a manner as could not end in anything but his
sing it. The people of England would never accept a Catholic
ng. I knew that now. Our friends did not forget for one moment
at I was the sister of the King of France and, although they did
t expect altruism from Louis, they knew that he would not
ant to see a monarch deposed. There was a possibility, there-
re, that he would give aid, and who better to plead for it than
s sister?

I rather pinned my hopes on the Prince of Orange. He was so
lighted to have secured our Princess that he might be willing to
ve money or arms. I warmed to the project. I would go to
olland on the pretext that I was taking my daughter to her
sband.

'The Parliament did not agree to your leaving the country
fore,' Denbigh pointed out.

'I will leave this time with their permission or without it and I
ll take valuables with me so that I can barter for what we need.'

The King looked at me with pride. He said: 'I shall have to go to
ull, so we should be separated in any case. At Hull there is the
ore of ammunition which is in readiness for attacking the Scots.
I can secure that I shall be ready to face my enemies if need be.'

This then was to be our plan. The King would go to Hull so that
necessary he would have the means to fight. In the meantime
ith or without Parliament's permission I would take my
ughter to Holland.

'We should first wait for permission,' said Charles, eager to
ep everything peaceful for as long as he could, and to our
nazement no objection was raised to my leaving the country
ith my daughter.

I said we must go with all haste in case they changed their
inds and tried to stop us and everyone agreed that this should
so.

Charles conducted us to the coast. First we stayed in Canter-
ury, where the cold of the February winds was more bearable

than the coldness in my heart. I was to leave Charles and as ev
when he said goodbye to me I asked myself when we shou
meet again.

I tried to smile. I told him that the project was going to I
successful and in time our troubles would pass away. The
would be no black-clad grim-faced Puritans to spoil our happ
ness.

'It is going to be so hard without you,' said Charles. 'When y
are with me nothing else seems of any great importance.'

'I know,' I answered. 'So it is with me. But all is going to con
right in the end. Sometimes I feel that happiness like ours has
be fought for . . . paid for. My love, I am going to bring back su
aid for your cause that we shall beat those rebels into the ground

'My fierce little general,' he said, 'don't stay away too long.'

'Not for a moment longer than I can help,' I assured him, 'ar
our reunion will be the sweeter for our having been parted for th
little while.'

I wished we could have lingered in Canterbury beneath th
shadow of the great cathedral but we had to pass on with
speed, for who knew when our enemies might change the
minds and try to stop my departure?

The next day we left for Dover. It was a brave sight to see t
Dutch ships in the harbour – a squadron of fifteen commanded I
Admiral van Tromp.

I said to Charles: 'How eager they are to have their litt
Princess. I am sure they will want to help her father and mother.

A surprise awaited us, for with the fleet had come Prin
Rupert, who had visited us earlier with his brother, Charl
Louis. We had been amused at the time of Mary's weddir
because Charles Louis had refused to come. He had been sulkir
because Mary was marrying the Prince of Orange instead of hir
Rupert, however, had been there and this bright handsom
young man seemed to be really fond of us.

He greeted us with affection and said that he had heard the
was trouble in England and that he would put himself at th
disposal of his uncle to fight those miserable Puritans.

Charles thanked him and said there was no question of w
and he thought that all sensible people realized that that was th
last thing that would do anyone good. He was thankful to say
had not come to that and he fervently hoped it never would.

Rupert was clearly disappointed and as he did not wish to stay in England if there was no fighting to be done, he said he would go back to Holland with us and protect me and my daughter.

Charles replied that he would indeed be grateful to his dear nephew if he would do that.

'The Queen is my most precious jewel,' he said. 'Care for her and you serve me in the way for which I am most grateful.'

So it was agreed that Rupert should return with us.

The last farewell! I shall never forget it. It is one of those memories which stay with me for ever.

To draw attention from his real purpose, which was to go to Hull where the stacks of ammunition were being held, Charles was dressed in hunting clothes. He had let it be known that after saying goodbye to me he was going north on a hunting expedition.

He kissed first our daughter, then he turned to me and held me in his arms. He kissed me again and again. Then he released me only to catch me up in his arms once more.

'How am I going to live without you?' he demanded.

'In the same way as I must perforce live without you.'

'Oh, my dearest, don't go. Never leave me.'

'I will come back with riches . . . with what we need to fight our enemies. Then, my dearest love, we shall be together and live happily for as long as our lives shall last.'

More kisses. More embraces. We could not bring ourselves to release each other.

But I must go and at last I reluctantly tore myself away. He stood watching me as I went aboard. I stood on deck, he on the shore, and we looked longingly at each other until the ship began to move slowly away.

Then he galloped along the cliff, his hat in his hand waving . . . waving. . .

I could not see him clearly for the tears in my eyes, but I went on waving until he was out of sight.

She–Majesty–Generalissima

I hated the sea. When I was sailing it always seemed to put on it
most malevolent aspect, and we were only a little way off th
English coast when the storms arose. These journeys alway
seemed endless, but at least the stormy weather took my mind o
my parting with Charles. I was in a state of anxiety most of th
time, not so much from fear of drowning as that the ships carry
ing my plate and valuables would be lost.

My fears were not without foundation, for when Helvoetsluy
was in sight one of the ships went down in the rough sea. I wa
grieved to see that it was the one which contained the equipmen
to fit up a chapel for me in the apartments which would be give
to me during my stay.

That seemed a bad omen.

I had very few friends with me. Among them were Lor
Arundel and Lord Goring – the father of George who ha
betrayed the Army Plot but who had returned to us so contrit
that Charles had forgiven him, saying that he would be the mor
eager to serve us because of his lapse from fidelity and woul
want to make up for the trouble he had caused us. I had m
confessor Father Philip and Father Cyprien Gamache; an
among the few ladies Susan, the Countess of Denbigh and th
Duchess of Richmond – and a few of my French attendants.

How wonderful it was to be on dry land. I was immensel
relieved when, with Mary beside me, I stepped ashore a
Hounslerdike. The eager young bridegroom was waiting for u
there and the welcoming cannon thundered out as he escorted u
to the coaches which would take us to the Hague.

There was no doubt of the respect in which the Prince of Orang
held us. I had not been mistaken in his delight at the marriage; I di
not want ceremony though. I wanted to make my transaction
quickly, to build up an army and take it back to Charles.

was met by Charles's sister, Elizabeth of Bohemia, who was
ry beautiful although she took little pains with her appearance
d now seemed somewhat ravaged by the tragedies which had
fallen her. There could not have been two people more unlike.
e made me aware of how she despised that attention I gave to
 appearance and the clothes I wore (something which was
rn in me and which I had never cultivated), my smallness, my
nininity; perhaps she knew that my folly had not helped her
other's cause. She had never forgotten that she was an English
ncess and was angry because of what was happening in
gland. She could not have been more deeply concerned about
t than I was, and the fact that she was inclined to blame me
s something I found hard to bear at that time.

Rupert was kind and respectful; he exuded the desire for
venture and was determined to obey the wishes of the King and
k after me. Charles Louis was still sulking and did not appear.

thought that if only Charles had been with me and all was well
home, what a happy occasion this could have been.

March had set in, cold and blustery, and during the journey-
s and triumphal entry into the capital I was growing more and
ore impatient. But the Prince of Orange was determined to
nour us. How I could have laughed with Charles at the gauche
haviour of these Dutch. They lacked the manners of the
glish Court and I remembered that I had found those far less
icious than the ones I had grown accustomed to in my girl-
od. The Burgomasters kept their hats on in my presence which
home would have been considered an insult, and at first I
ught this might have been intended because some of those
nply clad, unsmiling men bore a certain resemblance to our
rn Roundheads. But it proved to be just ignorance. I thought
en the mistake was explained to me I would break into hyster-
l laughter for one of them kissed the hand of my dwarf,
:offrey Hudson, thinking he was one of my sons.

How indignant my sons would have been at that!

I used to cry at night longing for Charles. The only consolation I
uld find was in writing to him; and as I did so my eyes would
m over with tears which dropped onto the paper making great
ots.

'The marks of love,' I told him they were. They would prove to
n how I wept for him.

It was a great day when I received a letter from him. It co
tained little news of the progress of affairs, but it assured me –
dear heart – that his days were dark without me and that he w
entirely mine.

The weeks flew past. So much time was spent in ceremon
and I realized that I should have come quietly for there were f
opportunities of conducting the business which I longed
complete.

By the time we left the Hague for Rotterdam, May had com
chafed against the delay. Charles was writing regularly and
letters constantly expressed his devotion, but they were
substitute for his presence. We had worked out a little co
before I left and it gave me a delicious sense of intimacy a
opened his letters and read. I lived for those letters and the
when I would return to him.

In the midst of this, one of the daughters of the Prince
Orange died and the ceremonies were brought to an abrupt e
We returned to the Hague and the Prince of Orange joined
army. He insisted that we inspect his troops, which was all
our honour, of course, but I could get no answer to the r
question: How much help could I wring from them? Or perha
could I get any help at all?

At length it was intimated to me that while the Prince
Orange was ready to mediate between the King and the Par
ment it would be unwise to supply arms for Charles to fight
own subjects. The people of Holland were sternly Protestant a
not unlike our own Roundheads. He could not go against
wishes of his people.

Then I must try to barter with the jewellery and plate whic
had brought with me. There followed for me a period which v
something like a dream. I became a kind of saleswoman, a ped
displaying my wares and trying to bargain with people the like
whom I had never known before.

It was a disheartening business. Most of the people who ca
to see me were Jewish and had a keen eye for business. Th
admired the jewels. Who could fail to do so? They were
priceless heirlooms of England.

They were beautiful, one merchant told me and his e
glistened as he touched them reverently. 'But, my lady, th
jewels are not yours to sell. They are the property of the Crow

I was angry. 'My husband gave them to me so I cannot see how
ey are not mine,' I retorted.

'If we bought them they could be demanded back as goods sold
hen the seller had no right to sell.'

'That's nonsense,' I cried.

'It is how it would be,' insisted the merchant. 'And who would
ant to buy a crown like this? Who would wear it but a monarch?'

'You could break it up. The rubies are priceless.'

'Break up such a beautiful thing, my lady! You are asking me to
eak my heart.'

So they argued and the real reason was that if they bought
ose jewels they could be demanded back and a court of law
ould doubtless say they had no right to them. It was under-
andable from their viewpoint.

They were interested, though, in some of the smaller items. I
lew I should not get a very high price for them but supposed
1ything was better than nothing.

My journey was not being a success and I was beginning to
onder what Charles was doing without me there to guide him. I
1ow that sounds conceited and nonsensical too, considering the
istakes I had made, but much as I loved Charles I could not be
ind to his weaknesses, and most of all the easy way in which he
1ve in when pressed. He needed me there to make him stand
m against his enemies.

It was a great blow to learn that Hull had declared against him
1d that when he had sent out little James to occupy the city in his
1me, the gates had been shut against him. Hull! That city where
as stored the ammunition intended for the Scots!

'It is disaster all the time,' I said to the Countess of Denbigh.
Ve are the most unlucky people on Earth.'

A messenger came – not from Charles this time, but from
meone on behalf of my mother. She was living in abject
)verty in a small house in Cologne. Her attendants had all
eserted her because for a long time she had been unable to pay
1eir wages, and she had been forced to break up the furniture
burn in the grate because she suffered so much from the cold.
1e had little longer to live and she wanted to see me before she
ed.

I prepared to leave at once but was told that the visit would be
owned on by Holland for there was a strong republican feeling

here and they did not like queens. While I was hesitating anoth
message came. My mother was dead.

Desolation hit me then. My mother – the wife of the great Her
IV, the Regent who had once ruled France, to die as a paupe
How could my brother have allowed that?

What was happening to everyone and everything around us
could not believe that the world had grown into such a cru
place. There was another death which saddened me even mo
than that of my mother. It was years since I had parted fro
Mamie and during that time Charles had become of such impor
ance in my life that my affection for him was greater tha
anything I could ever feel for another person. But I had love
Mamie dearly and always would. She had been the deare
companion of my childhood. And now she was dead.

I was stunned when I heard the news following so closely o
the death of my mother.

Mamie was too young to die. Her life must have been ve
different after she had left me. Marriage . . . children . . . had sh
been happy? She had given me the impression that she had bee
but how could I be sure? And she had had little children. De
Mamie, how she must have loved them and they her! She ha
become governess to Mademoiselle de Montpensier, who mu
have been a trying charge, and yet she was at Mamie's bedsi
when she died and Mamie had commended her children to her f
her last thoughts had been for them. She had remembered me to

I wept bitterly. I should have been there. Dear Mamie,
thought. I hoped she had been as happy in her marriage as I ha
. . . but that was impossible for there was no man on Earth li
Charles. Mamie had been so pleased that I had found happines
in marriage.

'Dearest Mamie,' I murmured. 'Rest in peace and may Go
bless you.'

In the midst of my mourning for my mother and my deare
friend, there was one piece of good news. Messengers arrive
from George Digby, Earl of Bristol, and Henry Jermyn. The
wanted to join me but first wished to know if they would |
welcome. I sent off at once to say I should be delighted to recei
them.

'There is so much I could do with the help of trusted friends,
wrote.

So they joined me and in spite of everything my spirits were
lifted a little. I often thought how happy I could have been if
Charles were with me and this was a state visit. With the Prince of
Orange and his father away from the Court on military manoe-
vres there were not the same entertainments. Mary seemed to
pine for her husband, which pleased me because I longed for my
children to enjoy the happiness I had found in marriage – or
would have done if our miserable enemies had allowed me to.
Alas, there were not many men in the world like Charles.

Henry Jermyn did a great deal to cheer me. Digby did what he
could but he was too fond of the sound of his own voice and was
constantly declaiming about the wrongs of the Parliament and
such matters which did not make him very popular. Henry
Jermyn was different. He was merry and charming and somehow
made me feel that everything was not as hopeless as it had
seemed before his arrival.

The Princess of Orange gave birth to a daughter and I was
asked to hold the child at the font and as a compliment to the new
member of the family the child was to be given the name of Mary.
But I held firmly to my convictions which could not allow me to be
present at a Protestant church ceremony, so Mary took my place.

There were some – perhaps Henry Jermyn among them but he
was too discreet to mention the matter – who thought that I
should not have risked offending the Prince and Princess of
Orange by refusing to take part in the ceremony, but nothing on
earth would induce me to go against my principles.

With the coming of Henry and Digby luck changed a little. I
discovered that, though I could not sell the royal jewels, I could
pawn them, for there were some merchants who were ready to
advance large sums of money on the understanding that if the
jewels were not redeemed by the payment of this money with
interest they could legitimately claim them.

I was never one to think far ahead. I needed the money at that
time and I needed it desperately and here was a chance of getting
it. Ammunition, an army, ships . . . they were far more important to me than jewels.

Moreover the Prince of Orange who had publicly said he could
not aid me, was less rigid in private. He was very proud of his
connection with the royal family of England and did not want to
see it become of less importance. Unobtrusively ships were

beginning to slip across the North Sea and were lying at anchor
the river Humber. I was really becoming rather pleased with n
mission after all. It had taken longer than I had anticipated and
had not done it in quite the manner which I had believed it wou
be done, but what did it matter as long as the mission w
accomplished.

With what joy I wrote to Charles to tell him of my success, b
whatever news we had for each other was always overshadowe
by our declarations of love. I asked tenderly after his health an
told him he must not worry. *I* was working with him. He w
going to be surprised at what I was able to do. We should so
have those miserable Roundheads skulking away, hiding ther
selves in the country. I was longing to be in England, I told hir
'Holland does not suit me. The air must be different from that
our land which you love because it is yours, and I for the san
reason. I have pains in my eyes and my sight seems sometim
not so good. I think perhaps I have shed too many tears and th
need the balm of seeing you since that is the only pleasure whi
remains in this world, for without you I would not wish to rema
in it one hour.'

Rupert came to me one day at the end of August. He was wild
excited.

He said: 'The King has set up his standard at Nottingham
shall go and fight beside him. This is war.'

So it had come. I had known it would for some time, but to he
it was actually so was a great shock to me. I had to get back
could not remain away any longer.

I began my preparations to return.

It was sad saying goodbye to Mary. The poor child we
bitterly.

'But you understand, my love,' I reminded her, 'that I must g
back to your father. I am leaving you with your kind new fami
and I believe you are already in love with your Prince and I
certainly is with you. In happier days you will come to our Cou
and we shall come to yours. I shall enjoy wandering throug
those lovely gardens of the Hague Palace. The ornamental wal
and the statues and fountains are very fine and the lovely state
hall is almost as large as our own at Westminster. You will so

e with us, dearest child, so don't fret. Pray for us. Your father is
ne best man in the world and we are all so lucky to belong to him.
Jever forget that.'

Poor child, she was so young! It was too much to expect that
he could hide her grief.

I hated the sea. It has never been kind to me. Sometimes I
nought there was some malevolent force which was determined
o make me as uncomfortable as possible whenever I set out on it.
 had my dear old dog Mitte with me. She was always such a
omfort and I would not be parted from her; I dreaded the day
vhen death would take her from me for she was very old. I loved
ll my dogs and had always been surrounded by them, but
harles had given me Mitte and she had been with me so long. So
 talked to her and she nestled against me and I whispered to her
nat we should soon be home.

The *Princess Royal* was a fine old English ship and we set sail
om Scheveningen with eleven ships all full of stores and the
mmunition which I had been able to buy. I must say I was feeling
ather proud of myself and I prayed fervently that I should reach
ngland without mishap. As the great Admiral van Tromp
ccompanied us, I was confident that we had a good chance of
oing this.

I might have known that there would be no easy voyage for me.
t was not in my destiny to have that good fortune. No sooner
vere we a few miles from the coast than the wind arose. What
iscomfort! There we were in our horrid little beds, tied down to
revent our being thrown out by the violent pitching and tossing.

That journey was a nightmare but oddly enough I seemed able
o endure it better than my companions. Perhaps I had suffered
o often at sea that I was prepared for it; perhaps I was so fearful
f the future and of what would happen to Charles and his
ingdom that a storm at sea seemed of less consequence to me.
Moreover I was not so ill as some of the others and found that if I
ould escape from my bed and stagger onto deck, the fresh air
evived me. Everyone thought this was highly dangerous but I
nsisted. My ladies who felt they must accompany me wailed out
heir wretchedness.

'We are all going to be drowned,' they cried.

'No,' I answered. 'Comfort yourselves. Queens of England are
ever drowned.'

I was so elated at the thought of going home and by th
transactions I had been able to make that I could not be down
hearted. They all marvelled at my high spirits and I couldn't hel
laughing to see my attendants attempting to observe the etiquett
of the Court and serve me in an appropriate manner though th
mischievous winds tossed them about and some of them wer
obliged to approach me on all fours.

We had several priests on board. They lost a little of the
dignity for they thought they could not possibly survive, and
could not altogether restrain my mirth to see their fear. They wer
usually so tutorial and I had resented being told even by priest
that I was sinful and that I must make this or that reparation. So
could not help but be amused to see *them* in terror of sudde
death when they might not have time to make their last con
fessions and so die without the forgiveness of their sins.

Some of them shouted to the heavens, detailing what sins the
had committed, so it could not be anything but funny to hea
these men who had set themselves up as our pastors admitting t
such sins as fornication and dishonesty, revealing that they
who had set themselves on such high pedestals the better t
instruct us in *our* duty – had the same acquisitive and prurien
tastes as so many.

After we had tossed on that wicked sea for nine days w
sighted land. Alas, it proved to be Scheveningen from where w
had started out.

As we came into port my daughter, with the Prince of Orang
and Prince William, was there to greet us for news had reache
the Hague at we were being driven back to Scheveningen.

I stumbled on deck, not realizing what a pitiful spectacle I mus
have presented – pale-faced, tousle-haired, my garments, whic
I had been unable to change for nine days, stained an
malodorous.

The gallant Prince drove his carriage into the sea so that I coul
be lifted into it and not have to face the eyes of the curious crow
which had assembled on the shore.

Our terrifying trip was over and had merely brought us back t
the place where we had started, minus two ships; but mos
people thought we were lucky to have lost only two.

The first thing I did when I was bathed and changed was si
down and write to Charles.

God be praised that He has spared me to serve you. I confess I
ver expected to see you again. My life is not a thing I fear to lose
:ept for your sake. Adieu, dear heart.'

was determined to stay only long enough to recover from the
deal so that we could be refreshed and ready to start again.

We landed at Burlington Bay in Bridlington. It was bitterly cold
the snow lay on the ground, but I did not care. I had landed
ely and I had a squadron of ships containing the treasures we
eded. I was exultant. Soon I should be with Charles.

t was a quiet spot but I noticed a little thatched cottage close to
shore and this appeared to be the nearest habitation and the
ly one from which I could watch the unloading of the stores so I
d that was where we would stay.

sent some of the men to arrange this and very shortly I was in
cottage eating food which had been prepared for me. Now
at I had arrived I realized how exhausted I was. During the first
astrous stage of our voyage I had hardly slept at all and now
at I was becoming easier in my mind there was nothing I
eded so much as sleep. And I think this applied even more to
attendants, who had suffered far greater from the ravages of
sea than I had.

We could not begin to unload until I heard from Lord
wcastle, who was in charge of the area and who, I knew, was a
unch supporter of the King. I needed his help in the operation,
we should have to get the arms and ammunition to the King's
ces as soon as possible. So the wisest thing to do was to rest.

went into the little room which had been made ready for me
d I stood for a moment looking out of the tiny window at the
; which was settling on the sea and my eyes strayed to the
pwy-roofed houses of the town. Where was Charles? I
ndered. I should soon know. I could imagine his delight when
heard that I had landed safely in the country.

Then I lay down on the bed and was soon fast asleep.

was awakened by the sound of a shot and as I sat up in bed I
ard voices and running footsteps as the door of my room was
ng open. Someone came and stood close to the bed.

Henry!' I cried for in the dim light I could recognize Henry
myn.

'You must get up at once,' he told me. 'We have to get out this cottage. Four ships belonging to the Parliament have co into the bay. They know you are in the cottage and are openi fire.'

He seized a robe and wrapped it round me.

'Hurry!' he commanded, forgetting in his agitation that he w speaking to the Queen.

I allowed myself to be wrapped up and hustled into the op where my ladies and other attendants were impatiently waitir

'We must get away from the shore,' said Henry; and even as spoke the cannon balls were firing on the village and one hit roof of the cottage I had just vacated. 'Hurry,' went on Hen 'We must take cover.'

Then suddenly I remembered that Mitte was still sleeping my bed. I stopped short and cried: 'Mitte. She is back there in cottage.'

'We cannot think of a dog now, Your Majesty.'

'You may not,' I retorted, 'but I do.' And breaking away fr them I ran back into the cottage.

Although a cannon ball had hit the roof it had not destroyed place and Mitte was curled up and sleeping soundly through the commotion. She was a dear old creature and quite infi nowadays but I always remembered her as the mischievo puppy she had been when Charles gave her to me. I snatched up and ran out of the house to where my party was anxiou waiting for me.

Henry would have taken the dog from me but I would not her go.

The shots were coming faster and one came so near that wh it buried itself in the ground the soil came up and was spatter over our clothes and faces. I was hurried through the village the ditch which surrounded it and Henry made us all lie in this that the shots could whistle over our heads and where, ap from a direct hit, we could be safe.

I crouched there with Mitte in my arms and my thoughts w for the ammunition I had brought to England. It would be endurable if after all my endeavours it were to fall into the har of the enemy.

After about two hours spent most uncomfortably in the di ditch, the firing ceased. Some of the men went out to see w

ıd happened and came back with the news that van Tromp had
nt word to the Parliamentarians that if they did not cease their
ımbardment – neutral though his country was – he would open
e on them.

I was delighted of course but a little annoyed with van Tromp
ɪr waiting so long before making his declaration.

'He took his time,' I commented drily.

How relieved I was to see our attackers had retired! They must
ıve realized that they could not have made much of a show
ainst van Tromp and his mighty squadrons.

Henry Jermyn convinced me that I could no longer stay in the
ttage, even though the damage from two cannon balls had
·en slight.

'Boynton Hall is but three miles from here,' he explained. 'It is
e only mansion in these parts. Three miles is not such a great
stance and you could come to the coast and from there each day
atch the unloading of stores.'

'Boynton Hall? To whom does it belong?'

Henry grimaced. I always told him that his mischievous
ımour would be his undoing – but I liked it all the same.

'I am delighted to tell Your Majesty that it is the home of Sir
alter Strickland,' he said.

I raised my eyebrows and then we were both laughing. Strick-
nd had been the envoy to the Hague at the time I was trying to
ıse money and arms, and as he was a firm supporter of the
ırliament he had done everything possible to frustrate me.

And it was to his estates that Henry was suggesting we go!

'He is far from home serving his masters,' said Henry slyly. 'As
ɔur Majesty well knows, when sovereigns travel through the
alm it is the delight of all loyal subjects to place their houses at
e royal disposal. It is an honour none would want to forgo. You
e not going to deny Lady Strickland that pleasure?'

I ceased to hesitate. I must be near the coast and I could not stay
 the cottage. I must maintain my royalty as best I could if only to
mind myself that I was still the Queen.

'Very well,' I said. 'Let it be Boynton Hall.'

What would have happened if Sir Walter had been there I
nnot imagine, but the ladies of the household were thrown into
lutter of excitement on my arrival at their gates.

Henry went on ahead and explained to them that I had come

and would stay for a few days. He added that he knew that th
were aware of the honour done to Boynton Hall.

Lady Strickland was presented to me and she fell to her knee
Custom dies hard and I was sure she and the ladies of t
household were more pleased to receive the Queen than th
would have been to have some miserable old Roundhead come
stay with them; and after the first hesitation Lady Strickland
her servants working in the kitchens and had the best apartme
prepared for me. She even brought out the beautiful family silv
plate which they used only for their important guests.

The next day men came from the Earl of Newcastle to unlo
the ships and work got under way. There were no more thre
and the operation was carried out successfully. It was wide
known that I was in the country and I could imagine Charle
impatience. I knew that he would come to me as soon as w
humanly possible.

In the meantime, to my fury, I received a letter from Gene
Fairfax, one of the leaders of the Parliamentary cause.

'Madam,' he wrote,

'The Parliament has commanded me to serve the King a
Your Majesty in securing the peace of the northern parts of t
country. My highest ambition and humblest suit is that Yo
Majesty would be pleased to admit me and the forces with me
guard Your Majesty; wherein I and this army shall all of us mc
willingly sacrifice our lives than suffer danger to invade the tru
imposed. I am, Madam,

'Your must humble servant Fairfax.'

When I read that letter I was overcome with rage. Did the m
think I was a fool? And what would he do when he came to gua
me? Imprison me most likely. 'No, Master Fairfax,' I said, 'I a
not as easily caught as that. If you came near me I should imm
diately have you arrested so that you could no longer harm t
King.'

I was longing to get away with the armaments and to march
join the King. What a moment that would be when we met!

I had by this time brought the stores ashore but the difficulty
transporting them worried me a great deal. Ten days passed a
still I could not find waggons in which to carry all that I h
brought. I should have to get help and there was no more ne
from Lord Newcastle. I thought then that if I marched to Yc

with the army I had managed to accumulate I could take some of
the stuff with me and leave the rest at Bridlington with men to
guard it until we could get it removed.

There was a letter from Charles.

'Dear Heart, Although ever since last Sunday I had happy
hopes of thy landing, yet I had not certain news before yesterday.
I hope thou expects not welcome in words, but when I shall be
wanting in any other way according to my wit and power of
expressing my love for thee, then let all honest men have doubt
and eschew me as monster. And yet when I shall have done my
part I shall come short of what thou deservest of me. I am making
all haste to send my nephew Rupert to clear the passage between
this and York. . . . My first and chiefest care shall be to secure
thee and hasten our meeting. So longing to hear from thee I
continue eternally thine. . . .'

I wept over his letter and then prepared to make my way to
York. I had been able to acquire two hundred and fifty baggage
waggons and these I loaded with ammunition, arms and valuables. I had now several thousand horse and foot, for many of the
King's loyal subjects had joined me.

Just as I was about to leave Henry said to me: 'What excellent
silver they have at Boynton Hall. It would be a pity if that were
sold for the benefit of our enemies.'

'What are you suggesting?' I cried. 'That we take the silver?'

'Borrow it. Promise payment when the King is safe on his
throne. It is rather amusing. Sir Walter Strickland's silver . . .
going to help the King.'

The more I thought of it the more I liked it. I hated Sir Walter.
He had made things very difficult for me in Holland, but his wife
was a pleasant creature and I am sure that but for her husband
she would have been entirely with us.

I sent for her and said: 'You live very comfortably here, my
lady. Do you think it right that while the King and I must take
what lodgings we can get it is fitting for Parliamentarians to live in
such style?'

The poor woman blustered and did not know what to say, so I
went on quickly: 'I am, therefore, taking your plate. It is very
pleasant and tolerably valuable. The King needs all the support
he can get and I am sure you will think it goes in a worthy cause
. . . whatever your villain of a husband should believe. I was

never one to blame a wife for her husband's misdeeds . . . so we
are taking your plate. We are not stealing it . . . just holding i
until all is well. When the trouble is over we will redeem the plate
and it shall be given back to you. In the meantime I will give you
pledge . . . as is always done in such transactions. You shall have
this magnificent portrait of me as a pledge for your plate and
memento of my visit to Boynton Hall.'

So we left taking the plate with us and leaving the portrait with
Lady Boynton.

As we travelled westward we met a crowd in the midst o
which was a very disconsolate man seated on his horse with
manacles on his wrists and his legs tied under the horse's belly
The crowd was shouting abuse at him and I stopped and asked
who he was.

'It is Captain Batten, the commander of the squadron which
sailed into the bay, and he is the man who did his best to murder
you,' I was told.

'I am glad to say that he did not meet with success,' I an
swered.

'Thank God for that, Your Majesty,' said Henry who was
riding beside me.

'Thank you too and all my loyal friends,' I replied with
emotion. 'What will happen to this Captain Batten?'

'He was captured by our royalist friends who are incensed that
he did his best to kill you. They'll hang him . . . or worse. It wi
be the end for him.'

'But I have already pardoned him. He was, I suppose, doing
what he thought to be his duty. Moreover he did not kill me
Therefore he shall not die by my wish.'

The crowds who had gathered to see me watched with interes
and I told them that I bore no ill will towards Captain Batten.
have pardoned him,' I said. 'He shall not die for he did no
succeed in killing me.'

When Captain Batten heard that he had been pardoned at m
command he came to see me. The guards did not want to let him
come near me, but I fancied I knew a little more of human natur
than they did.

I said: 'He is a brave man. He will not hate me since I have jus
saved his life.'

And I was right. He threw himself at my feet. He told me tha he would never forget my merciful act and his great desire now was to serve me.

I smiled at him. He had a good honest handsome face.

'Very well,' I said. 'Let us see. You are in command of a squadron. Perhaps you can persuade others to follow your example and turn faithful subjects to the King.'

'I shall endeavour to do so,' he said, and added: 'With all my heart.'

He kept his word and I doubt whether the King or I had a more loyal supporter after that than Captain Batten.

When I arrived at York people flocked to my banner and it was heartwarming to see them. I was very happy when William Cavendish, the Earl of Newcastle, arrived. I had always been fond of him. He was loyal, gallant and handsome and so eager to fight for our cause that he was inclined to be a little reckless. Charles was always wary of such impetuosity but I was inclined to favour it. William gave me confidence and I knew he had his Whitecoats all over the North. It was true that they were not trained soldiers but they were his tenantry and they regarded him as their lord for he was a generous one and I heard that they liked their uniforms made of undyed wool -- hence the name of Whitecoats.

Then there was James Graham, Earl of Montrose, the romantic Scotsman who had suddenly become our friend. He also was very handsome and, although not tall, of a marvellously stately bearing which distinguished him in a crowd. I took a great liking to him in spite of the fact that he had at one time helped the cause of the Covenanters and had commanded their troops. He had been anti-royalist then and defeated those in Scotland who had risen in favour of Charles at both Stonehaven and the Bridge of Dee. But when the Covenanters had refused to make him their supreme commander, he had abandoned them and declared his support for the royalist cause.

I spent a great deal of time discussing the future plan of action with him and William. Henry Jermyn was always present at our conferences and I enjoyed them so much because I found all three men charming as individuals – I had always been rather fond of handsome men – and they were all vital and ambitious and hated indecision, which I fear was a fault in my beloved Charles.

Montrose wanted to go to Scotland and raise an army for the King and said that it should be done before the Parliamentarians got a grip on the country. William had engaged in several skir-mishes with Parliamentary forces; as for Henry he was always anxious for action. I felt that if it were left to us we should soon have some decisive movement.

Charles, however, was against what we were doing. He wrote reprovingly, reminding me that only three years ago Montrose had been an enemy. Charles did not trust what he called turn-coats. I might have pointed out the case of Captain Batten and reminded him that when an enemy turned, through gratitude he very often became a loyal servant. It was no use trying to change Charles's opinions. Although he could never make up his mind quickly, when he did he could not be moved from his standpoint. He would not trust Montrose and sadly I had to explain to the Earl that the King declined his offer.

This made a certain coolness between myself and Charles – nothing much of course; but I could not help being a trifle piqued after all I had suffered and done, and I suppose he was anxious – as he had so often been – about my impetuosity.

Nothing could weaken our love and we were both very contrite when that little storm had blown over and our letters were more loving than ever. We longed to be together and chafed at the delay. From York I made a few little skirmishes and not without some success. I enjoyed riding at the head of my tropps, often with Montrose, Cavendish or Henry beside me.

The Parliamentarians pretended to be sceptical of my endeavours but I believed they were beginning to regard me with some concern. I called myself She–Majesty–Generalissima. I rather liked the term and what it implied and encouraged my friends to use it.

My spirits lifted when I heard people singing one of the songs written by a royalist. My attendants also hummed it as they went about their work.

It was the words I liked:

> God save the King, the Queen, the Prince also
> With all loyal subjects both high and both low

The Roundheads can pray for themselves, ye know
> Which nobody can deny.

Plague take Pym and all his peers
Huzza for Prince Rupert and his Cavaliers
When they come here those hounds will have fears
> Which nobody can deny.

I was astounded one day when news came from France of my ~~brother~~ other's death. He had always been a weakling, but I had not ~~re~~alized that he was near death. Coming so soon after my ~~m~~other's end it shocked me a great deal. I know I had not seen ~~hi~~m for many years and that he had been far from helpful to me in ~~m~~y need; but death is so final. And he was after all my brother ~~an~~d King of France.

Anne had become Regent as little Louis XIV was too young to ~~ru~~le and I did not think she would be a very good friend to me. ~~S~~he was very much guided by Mazarin, who had been a close ~~as~~sociate of Richelieu; so France had once more passed into the ~~h~~ands of a Regent and a wily churchman.

But I had too many troubles of my own to ponder much on the ~~fa~~te of my native land. I should have to wait for events to show ~~m~~e what would happen there and in the meantime those of ~~E~~ngland were such as to demand all my attention.

My mood changed from day to day. If I was exhilarated over ~~o~~ne success, I could be sure that my joy would not last.

Catholic priests were being persecuted in Puritan strongholds ~~an~~d my heart bled for them. Then the Parliament decided to try ~~m~~e for high treason. They did not even give me the title of Queen. ~~I~~ remembered then how Charles had pointed out to me the folly ~~o~~f refusing to be crowned. But did it matter to me? 'Let them find ~~m~~e guilty if they want to,' I cried. And they did. I did not care. I ~~w~~as working for my King; and there were days when I was ~~c~~ertain of victory just as on others I was sunk deep in despair.

In one of these moods I wrote to Charles: 'Being patient is ~~k~~illing me, and were it not for love of you, I would with the ~~g~~reatest truth, rather put myself in a convent than live in this ~~w~~ay.'

I think the enemy were a little afraid of me which showed they ~~v~~iewed with misgiving the success I had had. They attempted to ~~d~~rive a wedge between me and Charles and they could not do this

in any other way than by slandering me in my private life, so th
attacked my moral character. But Charles knew and I knew th
the love between us was too strong to be hurt by these calumnie
He did not belive them for one instant when they said I was mo
fond of William Cavendish than a virtuous wife had a right to b
They had long accused me of being Henry Jermyn's mistress
could shrug all that aside. I hoped Charles could.

Then they began to sneer at my title. They changed it to 'Mar
by the help of Holland, Generalissima.' They always referred
me as Queen Mary – as many people did. I think they found th
name Henriette too foreign although it was people in Englar
who had changed it to Henrietta.

But I was certainly in high spiits when at last we reache
Stratford-on-Avon and were there entertained by a sprightly ar
witty lady in a pleasant house called New Place. This lady was th
granddaughter of the playwright William Shakespeare and sh
had many an amusing anecdote to relate of her illustrious grand
father.

But the great excitement was meeting Rupert there. He ha
grown considerably since I had last seen him and was handsom
vital and seeming to enjoy the conflict. I shall never forget ho
disappointed he had been when we met at Dover and he learne
that the war had not started. He talked excitedly and gave me th
impression that victory was in sight. Best of all, Charles was o
the way and very close now. We were to ride to Oxford to me
him.

In the Vale of Kineton the meeting took place. I cannot describ
my feelings as I saw him coming towards me. Charles, m
beloved husand, and beside him my two sons, Charles an
James. I was too moved to speak as we came close and so was he.
saw the tremor of his lips and the tears in his eyes.

Then he dismounted and came to my horse and taking m
hand kissed it with fervour. He lifted his eyes to mine and all hi
love for me was there for me to see – as I knew mine was for him.

The joy of our reunion was almost like a pain, so intense was
and I wondered how we had lived without each other all thi
time. It was only because I was working for him, waiting for thi
reunion that I had been able to endure the separation.

Now here we were . . . together.

I greeted my sons. How they had grown! Charles still looke

warthy and incredibly wise. James was handsome but somehow
very much in Charles's shadow.

I was so happy and I thought then that it was only because of
the wretchedness I had endured that I could feel this great joy
now.

We rode side by side back to Oxford and all the time we were
talking not of war, not of the parlous state of the country, but of
how we had missed each other every hour of the day and night,
how we had lived only for this reunion.

I sometimes tell myself that those few months I spent in Oxford
were the happiest of my life. It was so wonderful to be with
Charles and to marvel at the intelligence of my sons. Young
Charles at thirteen seemed quite a man of affairs. How quickly he
grasped the situation and although he assumed a somewhat lazy
attitude I knew he missed nothing. I noticed that his greatest
interest was aroused by pretty girls. I mentioned this to the King,
who laughed and said that Charles was but a boy.

The King told me that he had arranged our meeting in the Vale
of Kineton because it was close to Edgehill, where he had fought a
victorious battle against the Parliamentarian forces. The enemy
might say it was scarcely a victory but the Parliamentarian forces'
losses were far greater than those of the royalists and that was the
real test. But whatever the enemy said, the advantage was with
Charles, who had been able to take Banbury and march on to
Oxford without resistance. That old traitor Essex had gone to
Warwick. It was particularly depressing when members of the
nobility ranged themselves against us. What was Essex doing on
the side of the enemy? One could forgive men like Pym more
easily.

My lodgings were at Merton College, in which was a beautiful
window overlooking the Great Quadrangle. I had many of my
attendants in a suite close to the Fellows' Gardens and they were
very happy there. I remember still the old mulberry tree which
had been planted by James I. I often think I should to see that
once again.

The weather was warm and sunny for most of the time – or so it
seems looking back. I loved to sit in my rooms with my dear little
dogs all about me. Mitte had survived her adventures and was

more demanding than ever and although some of my attendar
said she was ugly and bad tempered I pretended not to hear
only remembered the days when she had been an adorable pupp

Many people came to see me. I was still the Generalissim
Nobody could sneer at my efforts now. Hadn't I been to Hollar
and brought back that which we needed more than anything
had ridden at the head of my troops. The Parliament had thoug
it worth while to impeach me. I was a force to be reckoned with

Some said that the King listened too much to me. They ev
likened me to the ivy which clings to the oak and in time destro
the tree. That was something I was to remember in the years
come.

But now the days were made for pleasure. We all believed th
we were going to succeed. We were going to march back
London, take up our residence in Whitehall and fight o
enemies. Charles and I used to walk arm in arm though t
cloisters and sometimes our sons were with us. We talked ar
talked of what we would do, and everything seemed set fair.

There were of course minor irritations and some which up
me a good deal. I could not bear to hear of the break-up of r
chapel, which it had given me such pleasure to erect. The mob
savages had forced their way in and destroyed the place. Ruber
picture over the High Altar had been spoiled; and the seat
which I had been wont to sit had been treated with spec
violence to indicate hatred of me. But what shocked me most w
the thought of those ruffians breaking off the heads of Christ ar
St Francis from their statues and playing ball with them.

There was other sad news too. Edmund Waller, who used
write such beautiful verses for me in the old happy days, plott
in London to destroy the Parliamentarians and bring back t
King. It was discovered and Waller was now in prison. Wor
still, one of my faithful servants, Master Tomkins, who w
concerned in the plot, had been hanged outside his own fro
door in Holborn.

But as Charles said, we must not brood on these matters. V
must look ahead to victory and when that was achieved v
would remember our friends.

'If they have not died in the meantime,' I added.

'We will not forget the families of those who have served u
answered Charles.

Oxford became a very elegant place during our stay there. People came from all over the country to be at Court and almost every house in the town had to take in lodgers to accommodate all who wished to be there. The finest ladies and gentlemen were grateful for the smallest rooms in tiny houses. The citizens of Oxford were delighted for we were bringing prosperity to the town. The colleges were loyal and determined to help us. The tower of Magdalen was loaded with ammunition to fire down should we be attacked. We strengthened the walls, and even the professors came out of their colleges to help dig ditches.

Rupert was there with his brother Prince Maurice and at night they used to go out to see if they could find any of the enemy to fight. The Puritans hated Rupert. They called him Robert the Devil. He was a great asset to our cause for he could not have been more enthusiastic and determined on success if he had been fighting for his own country.

Autumn was on the way and that beautiful summer was nearly over. It was to live in my memory as the last truly happy time I was to know, and perhaps the intensity of my joy in it was the knowledge that it was fleeting. I knew I had to grasp every delightful moment and savour it . . . and this I did.

In September Henry Jermyn was created Baron Jermyn of St Edmundsbury, an honour well deserved. A less happy event was the impudence of the Earl of Holland, who had worked with the Parliament and had the impertinence to present himself to the King and expect to be treated with the old friendliness which we had shown him in the days before his defection.

This time Charles was inclined to forgive and forget, but I never would.

Henry advised me to try to accept Holland because of his importance and he pointed out to me that if such men decided they had wavered towards the wrong side and were eager to make it clear that they were back on course, that was all to the good. It should mean that the general feeling was that we were the winning side.

I could never bow to expediency in that way and I was annoyed with Charles for what I called being duped by such men. Our roles had reversed.

Holland was trying to persuade Charles to make some sort of patched-up peace with the Parliament and I was urging exactly

the opposite. I wanted Charles not only to call himself King bu[t]
be King. And if he were truly so he could not be dictated to
men like Holland, who were ready to give their services to t[he]
other side if they thought it was to their advantage to do so.

I was right as it was later proved because, although Holla[nd]
was with the King at the siege of Gloucester, he soon came to t[he]
conclusion that he could do better with the Parliament and l[eft]
Oxford. He was one of those men who liked to hold themsel[ves]
aloof from complete involvement and watch which way t[he]
conflict was going before leaping to the winning side.

I was aware of this but could not make Charles see it a[nd]
though Henry agreed with me, even he thought we could ma[ke]
use of Holland.

When the Earl left Oxford and took his seat in the Parliame[nt]
guessed that meant he felt the Roundheads had the grea[ter]
chance of success. I had no patience with such men and, howev[er]
much good they could bring when they happened to be on [my]
side, I did not care.

I wanted only faithful friends around me. I was deeply hurt [by]
traitors and still felt the wounds inflicted by Lucy Ha[y's]
treachery.

But as the autumn mists rose over the town I began to expe[ri]
ence certain familiar symptoms.

I was once more pregnant.

It was the worst possible time for this to happen. I was tir[ed]
and ill; the country was in a state of civil war; we had healt[hy]
children and did not need another child. However, it had ha[p]
pened and I should love this child when it was born – if I did n[ot]
die in producing it, for to tell the truth, I felt near death, and as t[he]
months passed I became more and more indisposed. I was suffe[r]
ing badly from rheumatism, which was no doubt due to all [my]
travels and sometimes sleeping in damp beds; and to add to [my]
discomfort was this unwanted pregnancy!

Charles was deeply disturbed. He wanted me to go to Exet[er]
where I could stay in Bedford House and he would entreat [Sir]
Mayerne to come to me. I wondered whether the rather perve[rse]
Sir Theodore would do that even for the King. He was old and d[id]
not want to concern himself in the country's conflicts I was su[re]

t he had always loved Charles and had been his physician
ce Charles was a boy. He may have thought of me as a foolish
man and made no attempt to hide his opinion, but for Charles
had something like reverence and when Charles wrote to him:
r the love of *me* go to my wife,' he could not refuse.

also wrote: 'Help me, or all you have done in the past will be of
use.' Then realizing that this was the kind of statement which
ght make him refuse I added: 'If you cannot come to me in my
reme need I shall always remain grateful to you for what you
ve done in the past.'

he result was that Dr Mayerne came with all speed to Exeter,
ere in a state of considerable anxiety on account of the King, I
aited the birth of my child.

wrote to my sister-in-law Anne of France to tell her that I was
ecting a baby in June. We had never been great friends but she
self had suffered a great deal from the dominance of Cardinal
helieu and that might have made her more gentle and sympa-
tic towards the suffering of others. She was now in a strong
ition as Regent, with Mazarin beside her to guide her, and her
nding must be more firm than it had ever been. I was looking
her for help. Perhaps I could go to France if I ever recovered
m this birth and there raise money and arms as I had done in
lland.

he response was immediate and I knew that I had been right
thinking that success often changed ambitious people for the
ter. She sent me fifty thousand pistoles, which was a good
n, and with it came everything I would need for my confine-
nt. She wrote that she was sending Madame Perrone, her own
e femme, whom she could thoroughly recommend.

was absolutely delighted at both this display of Anne's
ndly feelings towards me and for the money – the greater part
which I immediately sent to Charles for his armies.

t was a hot June day when my daughter was born. She was a
utiful child from the moment of her birth and, perversely,
ause she was the one I had not wanted, I loved her more
rly than the others.

called her Henriette after myself and later I decided on Anne
r the Queen of France in gratitude for past favours and in
pe of future ones. But for the time being she was simply
nriette.

I was very anxious about my new daughter for I feared th
events were not moving as we had imagined they would duri
that flush of euphoria which Charles and I had experienc
during our reunion.

I sent word to Charles at once with the news of our daughte
birth, telling him not to believe rumours which were being circ
lated to the effect that she had been born dead. She was ve
much alive and very beautiful and I was sure that he would on
have to see her to love her.

He sent word that she was to be baptized in Exeter Cathed
according to the doctrines of the Church of England. De
Charles, he was terrified that I would have her baptized in t
Catholic Church!

He was right, of course, and I suppose Dr Mayerne was t
when he implied that a great many of the troubles through whi
England was passing were due to my adherence to the Catho
Faith and my efforts to introduce it into the country.

I immediately complied with Charles's wishes and our lit
one was taken to the cathedral where a canopy of state had be
hastily erected, but the ceremony was naturally conduct
without the usual pomp.

Whatever was happening outside I did feel that joy whi
mothers feel when they have been safely delivered of an infant.
Charles could have been with us – even for a brief time – I cou
have forgotten what was happening in the outside world.

It was just over a week later, when I was still in bed and we
from my ordeal, when Henry Jermyn came to see me in son
agitation.

He cried out unceremoniously: 'Your Majesty is in dange
Essex is mustering troops in the town. He is going to ask for
surrender or there will be a siege.'

'Then we must leave here without delay.'

'That would be unsafe. Essex's army is even now firm
entrenched about us.'

'Can he really be such a brute? Does he not know that I have n
yet risen from child-bed.'

'He knows well and doubtless thinks it is a good time to for
his will on you.'

'Bring me pen and paper. I will write to him asking for sa
conduct. If he has any compassion at all he will give it.'

nry obeyed and I wrote a letter to the Earl of Essex asking
to allow me to go unmolested to Bath or Bristol – a favour I
ly resented having to ask.

hen his reply came back I was furious. The request was
ed. I should have known better than to make it. Essex,
ver, stated that it was his intention to escort me to London
e my presence was required to answer to Parliament for
g levied war in England.

at was tantamount to a threat. I knew then that I had to get
before they captured me.

w could I travel with an infant only a few days old? I was
aught. I did not know which way to turn. I believed that the
ish Essex had contrived this because his main object was to
re me. How I loathed and despised the man. He should
been with us. He had turned against his own upbringing
his own people. I could more readily forgive that traitor
r Cromwell, whose name was being mentioned more and
and who seemed to be responsible for the greater success
h the Roundheads were having now. Yes, I could forgive
He was a man of the people – but when men like Essex
ed against their own, that was unforgivable.

t it was no use wasting time in expressing my fury against
x. I had to think how I was going to escape, for escape I
. If they captured me and took me to London it would be
ultimate disaster. Charles would promise anything to free

ad to escape, and as I could not take my new-born daughter
me, I must, perforce, leave her behind.

ent for Sir John Berkeley, who was the Governor of the city of
r and a tenant of Bedford House where I was living. I
dy had Lady Dalkeith with me, a woman of great integrity
Charles and I had agreed, must be the one to look after our
hter. In this we proved right. I shall never forget what I owe
at woman.

efly I explained that for the King's cause I had no alternative
o escape. The Roundheads were almost at our gates and their
t was to capture me and take me to London, there to accuse
f treachery to the Crown.

is as you know would be such a blow to the King that he
ld do anything to save me, jeopardizing his own throne and

losing it if need be. There is only one course open to me. I k
you understand that.'

Sir John said he did indeed and would do anything I ask
him. Lady Dalkeith joined her loyal expressions to his and
me that she would defend my child with her life if need be.

I took her into my arms and we wept together. Sir John r
my hand to his lips and kissed it.

So fifteen days after the birth of my little Henriette I left
desolate and heartbroken as I was, for I knew it was the
course to take.

I waited until night fell and then dressed as a servant and,
only two of my attendants and a confessor, I escaped
Bedford House.

We had arranged that others of my household who were d
mined to accompany us should leave the house at various t
in disguises so that they should not be recognized. My fai
dwarf, Geoffrey Hudson, who had stepped out of a p
comfort me in no small degree, had begged to be of the party
could not refuse hime. He knew of a wood near Plymou
which there was an old hut, and he suggested that we sh
make this our meeting place and all make our way to
different routes.

When dawn came we were only three miles from Exeter a
was clearly too dangerous to walk about in daylight, for
were so many soldiers about. We found a hut. It was tur
down and filled with straw and litter and we hastened to
refuge in this when we heard the sound of horses' hoofs. I
fortunate that we did for the horses belonged to a grou
Roundhead soldiers who were on their way to join the forces
were gathering on the outskirts of Exeter.

Our dismay was great when we realized that the soldiers
coming straight to the hut and we were thankful for the
underneath which we were able to hide ourselves.

When I heard the soldiers right outside, my heart seemed
it would suffocate me and I had rarely been so frightened as v
I heard the door creak. We all held our breath as a soldier ste
inside the hut and kicked some of the rubbish aside.

I prayed – something incoherent and silent – and on
occasion my prayers were answered for I heard the man s
'Nothing in here but a load of rubbish.' Then the door cre

1 and the soldier was no longer inside the hut.

e waited breathlessly, listening. The man must have been

ing against the wall of the hut. He was talking to another.

e said: 'There is a reward of fifty thousand crowns for her

l.'

new they were talking of mine.

l like to be the one to carry that to London.'

'ho wouldn't? Fifty thousand crowns, eh? A goodly sum and

ng the country of the Papist whore at the same time.'

vas difficult to curb my anger. I wanted to go out to them, to

ounce them for the traitors they were. Traitors, liars,

mers of virtue and my religion. I restrained myself, thinking

narles. I would endure anything for him, discomfort, insults,

, hardship . . . anything for Charles.

vas some time before they passed on, but we did not emerge

the hut until darkness fell; then we sped on our way. We

fortunate after that and reached our rendezvous in the

dland cabin in safety. There I was rejoined by many of my

ful friends including Geoffrey Hudson, who had brought

e and another of my dogs with him, for he was certain that I

ld be unhappy without them.

ow the good friends made up for the treacherous ones!

Pendennis Castle Henry Jermyn was waiting for me with a

ble guard and when he saw how ill I was he immediately

orders that I was to be carried on a litter for the rest of the

ley to Falmouth. How thankful I was for his thoughtfulness!

what a relief it was to see a fleet of friendly Dutch vessels in

ay.

fore I went on board I wrote to Charles explaining why I had

he child behind. It was for his sake for if I had been captured

ur enemies, as I was sure I should have been had I remained

eter, that would have been a great blow to our cause.

m hazarding my life that I may not incommode your affairs.

u, dear Heart. If I die believe that you will lose a person who

never been other than entirely yours and who, by her

tion, has deserved that you should not forget her.'

tood on deck, exhausted almost beyond endurance, but

rmined to remain there until I could no longer see the land

re he was . . . as desolate and unhappy by this parting as I

Murder in Whitehall

Once again the sea proved that it was always my enemy. sooner had I returned to my cabin for a much needed rest th heard cries of alarm and Henry Jermyn came dashing in loo distraught.

'Pray don't be alarmed,' he said, 'but we have sighted t ships which are obviously pursuing us.'

'Enemies?' I asked.

'I fear so,' replied Henry. 'I should stay here. We are equip to fight them.'

'If we stop to fight we shall never escape,' I cried. 'We mu free of English waters as soon as possible.'

'If we do not fight they could take us.'

'They shall not take me,' I cried vehemently. 'I will die firs take me would be disaster to the King's cause . . . far greater my death would be.'

Henry was aghast. 'My dear lady,' he stammered, 'you n not talk thus. Your death would be the greatest sorrow that c befall me.'

'Personal sorrows cannot be weighed against major calami dear friend,' I said. 'Help me up.'

'Where are you going?'

'To see the Captain.'

I would not listen to his protests and tired as I was made painful journey to the deck. The Captain looked amazed whe saw me; and by this time the enemy were drawing very close

'Do not stop to return the fire,' I commanded. 'Let out all s Make all speed ahead.'

'My lady, these ships are determined to take us.'

'They must never do that. When you think it impossibl escape, set fire to the powder. Blow us up. I must not fall their hands.'

When they heard me, all those who were in attendance on me
d who had crowded onto the deck began to cry out in alarm.
e Captain looked startled but he was a man who would obey
ders. I thought Henry was going to remonstrate with me so I
d: 'I shall go to my cabin and there await the outcome of this,
d whether it is to be freedom or death I shall be ready.'

Then I left them and when I reached my cabin I began to have
ious misgivings. It was all very well for me to die if I wished to,
: what right had I to condemn others to the same fate?

For Charles,' I said. 'If I became a prisoner that would be the
d for him. They would use me to subdue him. No, I must either
e to serve him or I must die in the same cause.'

Suddenly I heard shots which were almost immediately
owed by cries of: 'Land!' It could not be France which was
hted. It must be the Channel Islands. So there was hope yet. If
could reach land, if the people would help me. . . . Just at that
ment I heard a loud explosion and the ship seemed to leap in
air and then begin to shiver.

We are hit, I thought. All is lost.

The ship appeared to have stopped.

At any moment I was expecting the Captain to obey my orders.
is must be the end.

waited . . . and then because I could endure the suspense no
ger I came out of my cabin. I saw Henry. He was on his way to
. He told me that the rigging had been hit.

'Are we sinking?' I asked.

'We are very close to the coast of Jersey and the Roundheads
moving away fast because a number of French ships have
peared and are bearing down towards us.'

'Praise be to God,' I cried. 'Once again I am saved and all with
. Oh Henry, how cruel I was. Believe me, I regretted it as soon
I gave that order.'

Henry understood me well. He knew I was near hysteria and
was always calm and somewhat jocular at such times, which
s the best way to soothe me.

'Come up with me,' he said. 'See the Captain. I think he has
cided to make for Dieppe.'

t was like a miracle, but my old enemy the sea had not done

with me yet. Even as we were in sight of Dieppe a violent g
arose. Henry advised me to return to my cabin and this I did a
as I lay listening to the tempest all about us I wondered if Fate w
playing another trick on me, making me believe that I h
escaped the Roundhead ships by a miracle, only to become
victim of the storm.

But after an hour or so of terror and with the knowledge th
my escort had been scattered and my frail ship was battling alon
we were at length thrown up on a rocky coast.

I stared at the land before me. France! The land of my birth.

'A fine way to come visiting it,' I said to Henry.

'You will be an honoured visitor,' he assured me. 'Don't forg
you are the daughter of France's greatest King.'

I could have wept with emotion. I felt so sick and ill, so anxio
about what might be happening to Charles; but there was
certain lifting of my spirits because I was at last in France.

A little boat took me ashore and I stood there staring up at the
rocks. I wanted to feel the soil. I wanted to bend down and kiss
but we could not stay on the narrow strip of sand. We had
climb the rocks. On hands and knees I crawled. I was bruised a
my hands were bleeding; my hair hung about my face and n
gown was torn. I climbed to the top of the cliffs and there befo
me lay the tiny Breton fishing village.

Dogs were barking; fisher folk were running out of th
houses, carrying hatchets and scythes, believing us to
marauding pirates.

'Hold!' I cried. 'We are not pirates. We have not come to do y
harm. I am the Queen of England, the daughter of your own gre
Henri IV. I need help. . . .'

They approached cautiously. But I had come to the end of r
endurance. Henry Jermyn was there to catch me in his arms a
fell.

When I recovered consciousness I was lying in a small roc
and Henry was at my bedside. I struggled up, feeling sick a
dizzy.

Henry said: 'It is all right. The people here know who you a
and will do everything within their power to help you.'

'Oh Henry,' I cried weakly, 'what should I do without you.'

'No need to wonder,' he said, 'because while there is life in my
dy I shall be here to serve you.'

I was weeping with emotion. I felt so helpless and it seemed
at fate was determined to heap one sorrow upon me after
other.

'What now, Henry?' I asked.

He was thoughtful. Then he said: 'The Queen of France has
own herself to be a good friend. I think I should go to her with
speed and tell her that you are here in dire need of help. That
ould be the first move.'

'I shall feel very uneasy without you.'

'You will be surrounded by good friends. You don't have to
ir the Roundheads here. With your permission I will leave first
ing in the morning. You need doctors first, I think. You have
ffered a terrible ordeal and following so close on the birth of
ur daughter it has put a great strain on your endurance.'

I saw that he was right and I told him that much as I regretted to
ie his company for the short time I hoped it would be, he must
.

He left the next day and I was deeply moved when visitors
gan to arrive at the tiny thatched cottage to see me. The gentry,
m miles round, rode into that little fishing village with food
d clothing, horses and carriages.

I thanked them and they knelt to me, eager to pay homage to
e daughter of their great King.

Very soon I was able to move on but I could only travel in short
iges and it took us twelve days to reach Nantes. From there we
ent to Ancenis and when we arrived in that town I was greeted
the Comte d'Harcourt, who told me that Henry had been
ceived by the Queen who was most grieved by my plight and
d sent him to tell me so. With him were two physicians.

I felt so relieved to be among friends and was immediately
tter; but when the doctors examined me they were grave and
id that I must take the Bourbon waters.

It was a great delight to see Henry again, particularly as he was
erjoyed with the result of his mission. The Queen had given
m ten thousand pistoles to defray the cost of the journey and a
tent for a pension of thirty thousand livres.

Why had I ever thought that Anne was not my friend? What a
ppy day it had been when she had joined our family. Now of

course she was virtually ruler of all France. This was the first goo
luck which had come my way for a long time.

One of the most delightful gestures of all was the Queen
understanding of my need for a personal friend, someone
whom I could confide, someone whom I could trust, someon
who could be something of what Mamie had been to me in th
past. She sent me Madame de Motteville and I loved her from th
moment I saw her.

Her mother, a Spaniard, was a good friend of Queen Anne an
had come with her to France when Anne came to marry m
brother. Her father was a Gentleman of the Bedchamber. An
she herself was beautiful and charming, very quietly spoken an
gentle, yet shrewd and understanding. I was as grateful for m
new friend as I was for the pistoles and the livres which we
helping to make my life comfortable.

In Bourbon l'Archambault I began to get better. It was such
beautiful place with an atmosphere of such peace that each da
awoke to a feeling of rejuvenation. So many hideous disaste
had befallen me that I could not single out any particular one
brood on. My greatest sorrow was parting with my husband; b
at least I was here and he was in England and while both live
there would always be the hope of being together again.

It was a hot August. From the window of the castle I could loo
out on waving corn and watch the oxen pulling the carts acro
the fields and through the little lanes. Within the ivy-covere
walls of our castle we were sheltered from the inquisitive eyes
those who were in the town to take the waters, for invalids ha
been coming since the time of the Romans as the waters were sa
to be beneficial. I certainly began to improve and with such goo
friends at hand as dear Henry Jermyn and Madame de Mottevill
of whom I was becoming fonder every day, my health w
rapidly returning.

Dear Madame de Motteville had troubles of her own. Sh
confided in me a good deal. She was a widow now, although on
twenty-three years of age. She had been married when she w
eighteen to a man of eighty but her bondage had not lasted lon
and now she was rejoicing in freedom as, she said, only thos
who had lost it would understand what a pleasant state it was
be free again.

'Without the chains of affection,' I amended. 'Sometimes

k love is a gift bestowed to bring the greatest joy and the
test sorrow. One cannot have one without the other, for an
nsity of love brings constant anxiety, particularly when one
t be parted from the loved one.'

ow right I was! No sooner did I begin to experience a return to
lth and a raising of my spirits than I had news from England.
here had been a fierce battle at Marston Moor – a defeat for the
lists, and although there had been heavy losses on both sides
over four thousand soldiers had been killed, three thousand
hose were Cavaliers. My dear Lord Newcastle's own regiment
Vhitecoats, who had put up such a fierce resistance, had been
to pieces and the whole of the artillery and baggage of
rles's army had been captured with ten thousand arms.

hey were gone now – my hopes of early victory. This was
ster. Charles would be desolate and I would not be there to
fort him.

he Roundheads were jubilant. They owed a great deal, it was
l, to that wretched man Oliver Cromwell who had trained his
n and somehow inspired them with talk of God and ven-
nce, making it almost a religious war.

s for their attitude towards me, it had become abusive, and
y were circulating pamphlets about me.

saw one of them which gave an account of the battle of
rston Moor, and of me was written: 'Will the waters of
rbon cure her? There are other waters open for her to drink in
Protestant Church, the waters of repentance, the waters of
Gospel to wash her clean from Popery. Oh, that she would
h in those waters and be clean!'

wept until I had no more tears. I felt a terrible lethargy come
r me, a hopelessness. Fortune was against us.

ut my moods never lasted long and my dear quiet but wise
dame de Motteville was there to talk to me calmly and give me
help I needed.

lthough I was living quietly in my ivy-covered castle with its
per-pot towers like so many I had known in my youth, storms
hered about me . . . small in comparison with the tempest
ich was raging in England, but they seemed violent while they
ed.

lthough I had begun to feel better, the ordeals through which
d passed had affected my health. I could not see very well and

seemed to have lost the sight of one eye; my body was unna
ally swollen and I developed an ulcer in my breast. When this
lanced I felt better and my body became more its normal size.

Then my favourite Geoffrey Hudson was in trouble. He
often teased because of his size and he certainly had a dig
which he did not like to be assailed. I could understan
perfectly and had always made a point of treating him as I wc
any normally sized man about me. I think that was one of
reasons why he adored me.

There was some joke about a turkey. I never quite knew wh
was. Probably they likened Geoffrey to one and this incen
him more than anything and naturally the more angry be beca
the more they liked to tease.

One day in a rage Geoffrey said he would challenge to a ⟨
the next man who mentioned turkeys in connection with hi
did not hear of this until it was too late. There was a young ma
the household called Will Crofts who could not resist taking
the challenge. Geoffrey was serious and they chose pistols as
weapons. Crofts, treating the matter as a joke, had no intentio
aiming seriously; but to Geoffrey it was no joke and he s
Crofts dead.

I was angry and distressed for I was fond of Crofts and part
larly of Geoffrey, and alas, it was not for me to decide w
should be done. We were on French soil and subject to Fre
laws and the penalty for murder was death. The only one v
could override this was Cardinal Mazarin. I was not sure of
true friendship for me and it occurred to me that I might h
favours to ask of him in the future; therefore I was loth to be
asking for anything that was not for Charles.

But this was poor Geoffrey. He wept with me. I told him he
been a fool and he agreed with me. He was not afraid of death
said, if that was the penalty. He cared very much though th
should be without him to care for me.

I was deeply touched and decided that I must do everythi
could to save him, so I did after all beg Mazarin for leniency.

The Cardinal kept me in suspense for a long time and t
finally sent word that the dwarf could go free if he left
country. Poor Geoffrey! Sometimes I think he would have ⟨
ferred death to leaving me. I certainly had some good frier
even if others betrayed me.

He wept bitterly and his sadness was unbearable but finally he
me. I never knew what became of him for I never saw him
in.

Events moved fast after that. My brother Gaston came with his
ughter to escort me to Paris. It was an emotional meeting with
ston, whom I remembered from my nursery days. We two
ng closer in age than the others had been together a great deal.
did not know this young man in his extremely scented
ments, his quick black eyes and tufted beard and moustaches.
looked at me with some surprise. I was sure he did not
ognize me either for I must have changed a good deal from
t attractive girl who had left for England all those years ago.
ness had tampered with my looks and all that remained to me
them were my large eyes, which if they did not serve me well
d retained something of their former beauty. Gaston's
ughter was a pert miss whom I did not like very much. She was
erly spoiled, having inherited a vast fortune through her
other which had made her the most desirable heiress in France.
t they were my family and it was good to be with them – even
ough I returned to them a wreck of what I had been, a miser-
le exile and supplicant for aid. Not the happiest way to come
me!

As we approached the outskirts of Paris the Queen herself with
r two sons, little Louis XIV, who was six years old and his
other Philippe, the Duc d'Anjou, who was four, came to meet

I was deeply moved to see my little nephews; they were such
autiful children, particularly the younger; their dark eyes
arkled with excitement to see me and they regarded me with
disguised curiosity.

But it was Anne whom I wanted to see. She had changed a
od deal in the sixteen years since we had last met. She had
own fat, but was still proud of those beautiful white hands and
e had forgotten none of the old gestures which she had
ployed to show them off.

But there was such kindliness and compassion in her plump
ce that I wept with joy to see her and there was such warmth in
er embrace as to send my hopes soaring.

'You will ride with me in the coach and the boys will accom-
any us,' she said.

Thus I rode into Paris seated with the Queen Mother, the lit
King and his brother.

We drove through streets which I remembered and now th
were hung with bunting in my honour. How kind Anne wa:
felt remorseful to remember that when she first came to Franc
might not have been so kind to her as I should have been. I
mother had disliked her and coloured my attitude towards h
But that was all past. Anne did not remember – if there w
anything to remember – and now she had only friendship
offer.

We went over the Pont Neuf to the Palace of the Louvre whei
had been born.

'Apartments have been made ready for you here,' said Anne
I turned to her and pressed her hand, too moved for speech

The next day Cardinal Mazarin came to see me. The Cardi
was an extremely handsome man, and I could see at once why
had acquired such a sway over the Queen. There was somethi
quite fascinating about him and, although I had not at fi
believed the rumours about the love between him and Anne
now began to think that there might be some truth in them. La
I was to hear that some people were of the opinion that there h
been a marriage between them. I could hardly accept that bu
was clear that Queen Anne and Cardinal Mazarin enjoyed a ve
special relationship.

He was shrewd – he would have had to be that to have be
selected by Richelieu as his successor – and it was strange tl
Richelieu, who had been Anne's enemy, should have brought
her notice the one who was to become her very close friend.

My concern was not with the intricate relationship betwe
those whom I hoped would be my benefactors. It was to enl
their help and save my poor beleaguered Charles.

Anne, I was sure, would have promised a great deal. Maza:
was cautious; and it occurred to me that he was not altogetl
displeased by the way events were going in England as th
meant that country could not interfere effectively in the polic
of France. Anne was a good-hearted woman ruled by I
emotions, but Mazarin was an astute statesman and he was goi
to make sure that everything worked to the advantage of Fran

He was extremely kind and gentle with me; he told me how
uch he disliked the English Parliament and those traitors who
d risen against the King, but as military help from France
ould be considered an act of war, he reminded me he would
ve to go cautiously.

I could never bear caution and in spite of the warm welcome I
d been given I began to feel depressed. It was true I was able to
nd Charles a part of the pension Anne had given me, but that
as nothing compared with what I had hoped to send in men and
ms.

Eventually Mazarin put forward the suggestion that I should
proach the Duke of Lorraine. The Duke was friendly with
ain and had great resources with which he proposed to help
at country. Now if those resources could be directed to
gland, they could be of inestimable help to Charles.

'The Duke could easily be weaned from Spain,' said Mazarin.
e likes a cause and I am sure yours would appeal to his chivalry
d feeling for the nobility.'

I could not afford to lose any opportunity so I at once sent an
ent to Lorraine. At the same time I put out feelers at the Court
Holland. My son Charles was growing up and would need a
fe. Why should she not be the eldest daughter of the Prince of
ange? I made it clear that the Princess would need a very large
wry if she was to marry the Prince of Wales.

News from home filtered through to me. It was worrying. My
d friend the Earl of Newcastle, on whose loyalty I would have
ked my life, had decided that he could no longer live in a
untry which suited him so ill and had given up his command
d gone to Holland where he proposed to settle down. I guessed
at he had been heartbroken by the decimation of his Whitecoats
Marston Moor.

He was not the only Royalist who left the country. It was
nificant. Those men must have made up their minds that
arles had little chance of keeping his crown.

But Charles had determined to fight on. I worried constantly
out him. I dreamed of him in fearful situations. Men like
irfax, Essex and Oliver Cromwell haunted my dreams.

'Take more care of yourself,' I wrote to Charles. 'You risk
urself too much and it almost kills me when I hear of it. If not
· your sake then for mine, look after yourself.'

There was a rumour that he was suing for peace. This terrifi
me and I wrote to him to take care of his honour and begging hi
to be true to the resolutions he had made. He was the King
anointed in the eyes of God. He must never forget that.

His reply put new heart into me. Nothing . . . no fear of dea
or misery would make him do anything unworthy of my love.

I think our love for each other was greater than it had ev
been. Adversity had strengthened it. We lived only for the d
when we should be together; and it was that hope which kept
both going when disaster stared us in the face.

There was a new ray of hope when the Duke of Lorraine se
word that he would let us have ten thousand men, and the Prin
of Orange offered transport. I was delighted. I was getting som
where; but just as I was about to write off to Charles and tell hi
the good news, the States General decided that to allow the
men to pass through their territory would be considered an act
war by the Parliamentarians and they could not permit it.

How I raged and stormed! Why should it not be an act of w
Why were they afraid of those miserable Roundheads!

I knew the answer. Our enemies were gaining ground ar
many people believed that Charles was already defeated.

I turned to Mazarin but he, too, impressed by the Roundhe
ascendancy, found that he also could not allow us to bring o
men and arms through France.

Disaster on all sides! if it had not been for the hope of seei
Charles one day, I would have asked nothing more than to ret
from the world, to enter a convent and there wait for death; b
while he lived, I wanted to live. I must be ready if ever we shou
be free to be together again.

His letters comforted me. I read them again and again.

'I love thee above all earthly things,' he wrote, 'and r
happiness is inseparably conjoined with thine. If thou knew t
life I lead . . . even in point of conversation which in my mind
the chief joy or vexation in life, I daresay thou would pity me, i
some are too wise, others too foolish, some are too busy, othe
too reserved. I confess thy company hath perhaps made me ha
to please but not the least to be pitied by thee who are the or
cure for the disease. . . .'

It was not until the end of that July that I received news of t
crushing defeat at Naseby. The general view was that this was t

·ginning of the end but I would not allow myself to believe that.
hile Charles was alive and I was alive I should go on hoping and
orking.

Why had it happened? Why was Fate against us? I raged. I
ormed. I shouted. I wept. But what was the use? It would have
emed at the start of the battle that we had a fair chance; but as
ual everything went against us. Charles had chosen his posi-
on on the raised land called Dust Hill about two miles north of
e village of Naseby and we had been stronger in cavalry than
e enemy, but the skill of Fairfax and Oliver Cromwell decided
e issue. Prince Rupert who had had some initial success and
ought he had won the battle went off to attack the Parliamen-
ry baggage and came back to the heart of the battle too late to
ve it. Fortunately both Charles and Rupert managed to escape.
ie Roundheads lost two hundred men and the Royalists one
ousand, but that was not the whole sad story. Five thousand
en were taken prisoner with all our guns and baggage, as well
Charles's private correspondence.

It was disaster . . . the greatest we had had.

Queen Anne very kindly offered me the *Châteaux of St Germain*
r the summer and I was grateful for that, and there in the
autiful castle I brooded on what was happening at home.

There was worse to come. Rupert had surrendered Bristol to
e Roundheads. Bristol . . . that loyal city! Charles said he
uld never forgive Rupert for giving it up. Poor Rupert! Poor
arles! How wretched they must have been! Charles, after
aseby, had lost half his army. What hope had he against
omwell's trained men? Cromwell! That name was on every lip.
w I hated him and yet there was a tinge of admiration in my
nom. If only he had been for us instead of against us. He had
ined men to an excellence which could compare with the
gular army and at the same time he had imbued them with
ligious fervour. He was the greatest leader in the country and
· was against us. None more fervently so. His aim was to
stroy the monarchy, and after Naseby and the loss of Bristol it
oked as though he were going to do it.

My anxiety was intense. Charles was more or less a fugitive
d my children, with the exception of the Prince of Wales, were
the enemy's hands. They were treated as commoners, all royal
nk denied them; and there was a rumour that my little Henry,

the Duke of Gloucester, was to be apprenticed to a trade. Sho
making was being considered.

I wept until I could not see. I thrust aside the comfort n
friends had to offer. I would not listen – even to Henry Jermy
and Madame de Motteville.

But after a while I began to bestir myself. Everything was n
lost. Charles had gone to Scotland; he was going to see if he cou
persuade the Scots to help him against the Roundheads. The
would settle their religious differences; he would promise the
almost anything in return for their help.

It was a desperate situation but just as my spirits had sunk
their very nadir, I was hoping again and beginning to mal
plans.

My hopes were on my eldest son. He had escaped to Jersey ar
I wanted him to come to France to me. He was fifteen years o
and if I could get him advantageously married it might l
possible to raise a fresh army which I could send to England. Tl
suggestion of a Dutch marriage had not been received with ar
great enthusiasm by the Prince and Princess of Orange. Th
meant that they were beginning to suspect that the Roundhead
had almost won the day and that the heir to a throne which mig
not be there was not a very good match. I wanted him with me
did not want to be separated fom all my family. I longed for n
baby more than any of the other children; I worried about h
constantly. She was just over a year old and I wondered wh
would become of her. I knew that when Exeter had fallen to tl
Roundheads she had been removed to Oatlands and was still
the care of Lady Dalkeith.

I wrote to that good and faithful woman and begged her to c
all she could to bring my daughter to me, although before, whe
she had been in Exeter with her at the time of the siege, I ha
abused her for not leaving the city with my child.

Many royalists had come to me in France, which was anoth
indication of how badly everthing was going at home. Some
them did not like the idea of the Prince of Wales's coming
France because they thought that I would endeavour to make
Catholic of him and if he became one that would put an end to h
ever succeeding to the throne. I had other ideas. I wanted a goo
marriage for him.

Lord Digby was one of those who was against my sending f

Prince and I knew it was because of religion, but I managed to
suade him of the necessity to get arms so that the King might
it again, and finally I won their agreement, and they went off
ersey to tell the Prince that I wished him to come to Paris.

hey were a long time gone and in due course I had a com-
nication from Digby to the effect that the Prince was very
ictant to leave Jersey because he had become enamoured of
Governor's daughter. This was the first of Charles's countless
e affairs which were to be talked of all over Europe. He was
y fifteen but he was already showing the way he would go.
it he could dally in such a way when so much was at stake
ered me. I sent urgent messages to Digby, but still Charles
ild not leave the Governor's daughter.

1eanwhile there was news from the King. He was going to
tland. I was frantic. I wrote to him asking him to command
son to come to me at once.

Vhile I was waiting for his arrival, which could not now be
g delayed, I turned my attention to my niece, Mademoiselle
Montpensier or the Grande Mademoiselle as she was often
ed – the richest heiress in France. She was in fact Anne-Marie-
iise d'Orléans – a royal Princess, daughter of my brother
iton and therefore worthy to mate with the Prince of Wales on
ount of her birth and doubly so on account of the money she
inherited through her mother. I did not greatly care for her.
was a haughty, arrogant creature and being fully aware of my
ortunate position she was not going to let me forget it. She
nted her superiority. Her clothes were always so much richer
1 those of others; she scintillated with precious jewels as
igh to say, 'Look at me. The richest heiress in France! The
st desirable wife for some lucky man. He shall be of my choice
igh.' She had been spoiled all her life and now it was too late
orrect that. She was very fair, which made her outstanding in
dark-haired almost black-eyed family. Her large blue eyes
e slightly prominent and although she had not inherited our
kness she certainly had the big nose of the family. She glowed
1 health and I rather spitefully noticed that her teeth were
oloured and spoilt her looks. She had visited me now and
1, having been prevailed on to do so by kindhearted Queen
ie, and she would sit with me superciliously noting, I was
e, my clothes, which if they were a little worn were more

elegant than hers. I thought her somewhat vulgar and if it had
been for her immense fortune I would not have considered
for one moment as a suitable bride for Charles.

Ah, but that fortune! I must set myself out to win it.

'You have never been to England,' I said to her. 'Oh, w
pleasures you have missed.'

'There is not much pleasure to be found there now, Madam

'The green fields are there . . . those little rivers all sparklin
the sun. There is no country quite so beautiful. I confess I long
a glimpse of those white cliffs once more.'

'Let us hope the King is able to keep a hold onto the crown.

'Can anyone doubt it? This is nothing . . . a rebellion c
few wicked men. Rest assured the King will recover all v
shortly.'

'He has been rather long in doing so, dear aunt.'

'Victory is within his grasp.'

She was looking at me cynically. I knew she was thinki
Naseby. Bristol. The King in Scotland feebly trying to win
help of an ancient enemy. The family scattered.

'The Prince is growing up,' I said. 'He will be there to st
with his father.'

'He if fifteen, I believe. I am seventeen.'

'I know it well,' I said. 'But you are much of an age. I hav
feeling that when he comes here you are going to be very g
friends.'

'I do not greatly care for the society of young boys,'
answered slyly.

'Charles is a man. He is older than his years. Why,
Jersey. . . .'

But no. I was being impulsive again. It would be unwise to
her of his philandering with the Governor's daughter.

She went on: 'My aunt died recently, as you know.'

'I still mourn my dear sister,' I said.

'The King of Spain will be looking for a wife, I daresay.
period of mourning will soon be over.'

The minx! I thought. She is teasing me. The King of Spain!
aunt's widower who is now in the marriage market. And he h
crown to offer her . . . not the promise of one.

Those protuberant blue eyes were laughing at me. She v
saying: I see right through you, dear Aunt Henriette. Do

ıgine that I do not know how eager you are to find a rich wife
your son?

'erhaps I had meddled again. Perhaps it would have been
ter to let Charles do his own wooing. If the affair in Jersey was
example he would be able to do that very well indeed.

t was June when my son arrived in Paris. He could not defy his
ıer's orders even for the sake of the Jersey charmer. He arrived
ttle resentful but he was soon on the look-out for fresh con-
·sts.

was delighted to see him and for a few moments we just clung
ether. He had always been a strong boy. He had grown very
and had an air of dignity which pleased me. He looked every
h a King. He still had the swarthy looks he had been born with;
features were too big for good looks and indeed if one studied
face he was really quite ugly; but he was possessed of such
rm – his smile, his voice, his manner – that in any company he
uld be distinguished, and his royal bearing was apparent. I
s proud of him.

Vhen he arrived the Court was at Fontainebleau and kind
een Anne immediately sent an invitation for us to join her
re.

Charles and I rode together and when we were within a few
es of the palace we were met by the Queen in her coach with
e King Louis. She expressed her pleasure to see Charles, and
en we alighted at the palace she gave him her arm to conduct
ı in while I was left to the care of the little King.

: was not long before Charles was engaged in a flirtation with
cousin La Grande Mademoiselle, as she liked to be called, but
vas soon clear to me that she was only amusing herself and
re could be no official ceremony until England was once more
he hands of its King.

ı the meantime the King was in Scotland and I trembled for
at was going on.

ife could not be all sorrow – even mine. What a wonderful day
as when Lady Dalkeith – Lady Morton now that her father-in-
had died – arrived in France with my little Henriette. I could
rcely believe this good fortune, so accustomed was I to bad.
Madame de Motteville brought me the news and I ran down to

find them there. I snatched up my baby. She did not know me
course, for she had been only fifteen days old when I had left
and now she was two years. She could chatter a little and
looked at me gravely. I thought how beautiful she was – the m
beautiful of all my children and the most beloved – and alwa
would be.

It was a wonderful reunion. I could almost believe that
fortunes had changed. From despair I allowed myself to reve
absolute happiness . . . for a short while.

Dear Lady Morton – to whom I had not always been kind, fo
am afraid I had the common fault of blaming others when n
fortune struck me. Who could have been kinder, more loy
more loving than this good woman! Henriette loved her a
would not be separated from her and I welcomed her with all
heart and asked forgiveness for my unjust criticisms of the pa
at which she fell on her knees and said she only wished to se
me and the Princess for the rest of her life.

Ah, I thought, if only we had more faithful servants like t
dear lady!

I settled down to hear of their adventures, because the cle
woman had actually escaped from Oatlands.

'The Commons had decided that the Princess Henriette sho
be placed with her brother and sister at St James's Palace wh
her retinue would be dismissed and that would have meant n
Lady Morton told me. 'I had promised both you, Madam, and
King that I would never leave the Princess except on your ord
so I decided that the only way was to escape to you.'

'Oh, my clever, clever Anne!' I cried.

'We should never have been allowed to leave,' she went on,
I decided on disguise. I had with me a Frenchman, Gaston, w
had been in the household and he posed as a valet and it v
arranged that I should travel as his wife and the Princess wa
be our child – a little boy. I thought that best in case we shoul
suspected. I left letters behind with people whom I could tr
asking them to keep our departure secret for three days, wh
would give us time to get well on our way. And then we left.'

I listened intently. It was the sort of plan I would have wor
out myself.

'I told the Princess that she was not a princess any more.
was a little boy and her name was Pierre, which I thought in

hildish chatter sounded a little like Princess if she should let it be
nown who she really was. She did not like it at all, nor the
agged clothes in which we had to dress her. We had some scares
long the road . . . not the least those resulting from the Princess
erself, who was eager to tell everyone she met that she was not
eally Peter or Pierre but the Princess. I cannot tell you, Madam,
yhat a joy it was to be on that boat.'

'I cannot tell you what joy you have brought me!' I replied.

My little daughter's coming lightened my days considerably. I
ad two of my children with me now: Charles and Henriette, my
ldest and my youngest. It was a comfort to see how those two
oved each other. Charles, whose main interest, I had to admit,
yas in young ladies, still had time to spare for that very small one,
is own sister. He bestowed on her the pet name of Minette; as
or her, her eyes would light up every time they fell on her big
rother.

But naturally we could not be happy for long. How foolish
harles had been to put his hopes on the Scots. I could not
elieve my ears when I heard that they had sold him to the
nglish. The price had been four hundred thousand pounds.

'Oh, the base treachery!' I cried and was mad with grief.

In my heart I knew that this was indeed the end, but I knew too
aat I would go on fighting as soon as I had recovered from the
hock. I would always fight . . . even with death and despair
taring me in the face.

Charles wrote to me: 'I am almost glad of it. I would rather be
yith those who have bought me so dearly than with the faithless
yho have sold me so basely.'

Now the Cavaliers were coming to Paris in large numbers.
hey came to the Louvre and as the royal family was not there
nd I had almost the whole of the vast palace to myself I lodged
aem there. Some of the French criticized me for allowing them to
ave Protestant services in the Louvre and I reminded them that
ing Charles had never denied me the liberty of worshipping in
ay own faith and I could at least do the same for those who came
o me with the object of furthering his cause. Rupert came. He
yas disheartened and somewhat resentful against the King who
ad reviled him after the loss of Bristol and seemed to have
orgotten everything he had done in his service.

I placated him. I begged him to understand the state of mind in

which the King must be . . . a prisoner of his enemies in th
country which he had been chosen by God to rule.

My son went to Holland in the hope of getting help, and ther
his sister Mary, now Princess of Orange on the death of he
husband's father, welcomed him warmly. Poor Charles did no
have a very happy time for almost immediately he contracte
small pox and was laid low for some weeks. I suppose I must b
grateful that he recovered but I did at the time find it difficult to b
grateful for anything, so weighed down was I by my misfortune
My thoughts were all with my husband – a prisoner in the hand
of his enemies!

Looking back, I wonder whether there might have been a hop
even then of saving his crown and his life, for some peopl
seemed to think that he could have come to terms with Cromwel
Now it is clear that he did not understand the people with whor
he had to deal. He had some idea that if he offered them peerage
they would agree to set him back on the throne. He never coul
understand men like Cromwell. I can see the situation mor
clearly now. When it happened I was as blind as he was.

Charles did smuggle out a letter to me in which he stated tha
he was going to win them over and as soon as he gained power h
would hang them all.

Cromwell was too wise a man not to realize this possibility.
had always found it hard to see the enemy's point of view, but
realized that Cromwell's intentions were not entirely to gai
power for himself – although this is what he did. Some though
him a bad man, but few could deny that he was a brave one. H
never spared others, nor did he himself. He was a deepl
religious man. He had said he took up arms for civil and religiou
liberty, but most of us have come to know by now that whe
people talk of giving the people religious liberty they mean libert
to worship as the oppressors think fit. I am sure my dear Charle
did not wish to restrict the religious liberty of his subject
Cromwell referred to himself as 'a mean instrument to do God'
people some good and God service,' but he brought great traged
to many an English family and more to that of his King an
Queen than any other.

I was delighted when my son James escaped to Holland. Tha
was something to enliven the dreary days. He had been placed b
the Parliament with his sister Elizabeth and brother Henry at S

ames's, though they were allowed to visit the King at Caversham
and later at Hampton Court and Zion House, where he was kept
in restraint. I would sit for hours imagining those meetings and
onging to be with them.

James had been playing hide and seek with his sister and
brothers and during the game had managed to elude the guards
and get down to the river where friends were waiting with
clothes – those of a girl – and when he was dressed in them he
must have been a rather attractive sight for James had always
been a pretty chiild. His brother Charles would never have been
able to disguise himself as a girl! They got him across the sea to
Middleburg where his sister was waiting to welcome him.
Charles was already there and I was sorry to hear that they were
soon constantly quarrelling with each other.

I wrote to them reminding them that quarrels within the family
were something we could not afford. We had enemies enough
outside the family. There must be none within.

So that weary year was passing. The King a prisoner, the
Parliament wondering what they would do with him. I longed to
be with him. I wanted to share his fate whatever it was. If I could
join him in his prison and we could spend our last days together, I
would ask nothing more.

I wrote appealingly to the French ambassador, begging him to
put my request before the Parliament. Let them give me permission to be with my husband. I would willingly join him in his
prison. Let them do what they would with me if they would only
let me be with him.

I settled down to await an answer. None came. I learned
afterwards that the French ambassador had presented my letter
to the Parliament and that they would not open it.

Good news at last! Charles had escaped from his gaolers. He
was in the Isle of Wight and had found refuge in Carisbroke
Castle.

It was about this time that war broke out in France. I was so
immersed in my own affairs that I was taken by surprise when it
burst upon us.

Poor Anne, she was distraught and terrified that her son would
lose his crown. The war of the Fronde had started. It was really a
revolt by certain factions against Mazarin to whom, in her infatu-
ation, Anne had handed over the reins of government. Some

people objected to this and it was the same old story: dissatis
faction with the rulers and then war . . . which is no good to
anyone. The nobles were annoyed because there were too many
foreigners in high places – Italians mostly, as Mazarin naturally
favoured his own race. Taxation was oppressive and the Parlia
ment complained that their wishes were overruled by the
arrogant Cardinal.

The people were taking up arms and the name Fronde was
bestowed on the uprising. It was scarcely a war as the name
implied for it was called after a fronde – a kind of catapult used by
the street boys of Paris to fight their mock battles with each other.

When the people put up the barricades I went to see Anne. I felt
I could be of some use to her, my experiences of discontented
subjects being great.

Anne, who had left everything to Mazarin to conduct, was less
worried than she had been.

'It is a slight disturbance,' she said.

'My dear sister,' I replied, 'the rebellion in England began as a
slight disturbance.'

I think she took notice then. She could not ignore that terrible
example across the Channel. The Court fled from Paris and took
up residence first of all in Ruel and afterwards at St Germain.
When the Court left Paris I remained in the Louvre. The in-
surgents had no quarrel with me. But now I knew what it meant
to live in abject poverty. My pension had stopped and because I
had sent the bulk of it to help Charles I had nothing left with
which to buy food and keep us warm.

My little Henriette could not understand what it was all about.
Poor child, she must have thought she had been born into a
hostile world. I wished I could have given her a happy childhood
. . . a royal childhood . . . the sort to which she was entitled. But
we were together . . . I must be thankful for that.

I don't think I have ever been so miserably uncomfortable as I
was that Christmas of 1648. I had suffered much before but now
there was bodily discomfort to add to mental torture. I had
endured illness but never before had I come near to starvation
and, far worse than suffering myself, was to see my child cold and
hungry. Her beautiful dark eyes seemed to grow larger every day.

Paris was in chaos. There was a war and to make life more
uncomfortable the Seine had burst its banks and flooded the

wn. From the windows we could see the roads looking like
nals whipped up by the bitter winds. That wind whistled
rough the windows and there was no way of keeping warm.
I could not see how we could continue in this way. My house-
ld was sadly in need of food. Even Henry Jermyn had lost his
gh spirits. What could we do? Where could we go? This was
pposed to be our refuge.

It was a dark and gloomy morning; the rooms were full of the
ld wintry daylight; outside the clouds scudded by, heavy with
ow. My little Henriette was in my bed. I had gathered every-
ing I could . . . rugs and draperie . . . to put over the bed and
ep her warm. I sat in a chair beside the bed with a counterpane
rapped round me. Henriette watched me with wide eyes. I said:
Vhy don't you try to sleep, my darling?'

Her answer wrung my heart with misery. 'I'm so hungry,
am.'

What could I say to that?

'Perhaps there'll be some soup today,' she went on, her eyes
ightening at the thought.

'Perhaps, my love,' I answered, knowing there was nothing in
e palace with which to make soup.

At that moment Lady Morton came in carrying a piece of a
ooden chest which she put on the fire.

'That's a little better, dear Anne,' I said.

'It's the end of the chest, Your Majesty. Tomorrow we shall
ive to find something else. This will last through the day, and it
iould give a good blaze.'

'Nothing seems to keep out these biting winds.'

Anne looked pale and thin, poor woman. She had come
rough that miraculous escape . . . to this. Was she wishing that
ie were back in England accepting Roundhead rule? At least she
ight not be cold and hungry there.

She went to the bed and felt Henriette's hand.

'It's warm,' she said.

'I keep it hidden away,' Henriette answered. 'When I put it out
freezes. Will there be soup for dinner?'

Anne hesitated. 'We shall have to see.'

It was like a miracle for there was soup for dinner after all. How
trange life was! I was lifted up one moment and cast down the
ext. It must have been about an hour later when we had a visitor

– none other than the Cardinal de Retz, one of the leaders of t
Fronde movement. He had taken it into his head to see how I w
faring at the Louvre and when he entered the room he stared
horror to see me huddled in my chair and my little daught
peeping out from under the mass of rugs which I had throv
over her.

'Your Majesty,' he cried, 'what is the meaning of this?'

He knelt beside me and kissed my hand.

I said: 'You may well ask, my lord Cardinal. We are wonderi
in this place whether we are going to die of cold or starvation.'

'But this is . . . monstrous!'

He was truly shocked. I had always rather liked him. He had
reputation for being somewhat dissolute in his youth and th
seemed to have put a certain kindliness in him, a quick sympat
for other people's troubles which those who have lived vi
tuously sometimes lack. In any case he was horrified.

He stammered: 'That a daughter of our great King should fir
herself thus. My dear lady, I shall not waste time talking to you
am going to have all you need for the time being sent in. I will se
to that myself. Then I shall bring this matter up before Parli
ment. I am sure all noble Frenchmen will be horrified to kno
that you and your daughter are in this state.'

I could have him kissed in my gratitude. He was as good as h
word. Within a few hours logs and food were being delivere
from his own house. it was wonderful to smell food cooking. W
were all very jubilant that day.

The next day he spoke of us in Parliament. A daughter an
granddaughter of our great King Henri IV starving in the Louvr
with her faithful attendants! It must be rectified at once. S
eloquently did he speak that it was; and I was granted the sum
forty thousand livres.

It was useless now to send this to Charles, so it was spent o
bringing comfort to my long-suffering household, and I wa
happy for a while to see my little daughter's eyes sparkle as sh
had her soup and afterwards when she held out her hands to th
logs crackling in the fireplace.

My joy was short-lived. The New Year had come – the mo
bleak and bitter of my life. I had had no letters from Charles bi
news was filtering through. He had been taken from Carisbrok
Castle to Hurst Castle and from there to Windsor. From there h

s brought to St James's Palace to stand trial in Westminster
ll.

Trial!' I cried. 'These villains will *try* the King! One day I
omise you . . . one day . . . we shall see the heads of Cromwell,
sex and Fairfax on London Bridge. The indignity! What is he
nking, my dear Charles, and I am not there at his side.'

I was hysterical with grief and fear. I should never have left
n. I should have stayed by his side. No matter what happened
vould be better for me to be there.

My two chief comforters were Henry Jermyn and Madame de
otteville. Henry assured me that they would not dare condemn
e King. 'The people will never allow it,' he said.

Yes,' I cried, clutching at the smallest hope. 'The people
vays loved him. I was the one they hated. Oh, Henry, do you
ally think the people will stand with him? Will they rally round
m . . . flout those wicked Roundheads?'

They will indeed,' said Henry. 'You will see. Soon he will be
claimed. He will send for you. The family will be united.'

Even if I did not entirely believe him it was good to listen to
m. He was so tall, handsome and commanding that he always
ve an impression of being about to set everything to rights. It
s wonderful to have him with me at such a time. When I told
n so, he kissed my hand and said: 'Do you think I would ever
ve you?'

If you did,' I answered, 'that would be the end of everything
me.'

Madame de Motteville, faithful as she was, could not comfort
in the same way. She was very anxious and it was all for my
ke. She was so gentle and quiet, fearing the most terrible
aster and perhaps trying to prepare me to face it when it came.

February was with us. I could not understand why there was
news.

What was the result of the trial?' I demanded. 'There must
ve been a result. Why don't we hear?'

Henry frowned and looked out of the window. 'It is not always
sy to get news through,' he murmured.

I noticed that some members of the household avoided looking
me.

Something has happened,' I said to Madame de Motteville:
hat is it, I wonder.'

She did not answer.

I was getting frantic. I called Henry and said: 'Henry, you kno[w] something, don't you. For God's sake tell me.'

He was silent for a few moments and then he looked at me a[nd] said: 'Be of good cheer. Yes, he was brought to trial and th[ey] condemned him.'

'Oh . . . God help me . . .'

Henry had his arm about me, supporting me.

'All will be well,' he said. 'Listen . . . listen . . .' His face was [so] distorted he could not speak. It seemed like minutes but it m[ust] have been less than a second. Then the words came rushing o[ut] 'All is well. . . . He was saved . . . at the last moment. . . . Th[ey] were going to behead him. He was taken from St James's [to] Whitehall. . . . He came out of the banqueting hall there to t[he] scaffold. . . .'

'Henry . . . Henry . . . you are killing me. . . .'

He took a deep breath and said firmly: 'As he laid his head [on] the block, the people rose together. They cried, "It shall not b[e]. Charles is our King. Down with the Parliament." '

'Henry. . . .' I was almost fainting with relief.

He said, 'All will be well. . . .' and he kept on repeating tha[t]

I thought his behaviour and his manner of telling very stran[ge] but that was later. At that moment I could think of nothing b[ut] He is safe. The people would not allow it. They were his faith[ful] subjects after all.

'His subjects have a great affection for him,' I said. 'There a[re] many who will sacrifice life and fortune for his sake. I am sure t[he] cruelty of those who persecute him will only make those w[ho] love him the more eager to serve him.'

I talked to Madame de Motteville, to Henry, to all my atten[d]ants, of the miraculous escape the King had had.

'There will be more news soon,' I said. 'Good news. This is t[he] turning point.'

There was no news next day. During the night I had lain in b[ed] listening for the sounds of arrival. None came. Another d[ay] passed and another.

'It is strange,' I said, 'that there is no news.'

Tension was rising. Something very strange was going o[n]. Even Henry seemed different. He had lost his gaiety and I fanc[ied] that Madame de Motteville was avoiding me.

had to do something because the suspense was becoming
olerable.

said to Henry: 'Why do we not hear? The Court will know
at is happening surely? I am going to send one of the gentle-
n to St Germain to find out if they have heard anything.'

I am sure,' said Henry, 'that they would let you know imme-
tely if they had.'

They are concerned with their own troubles. I shall send a man
once with instructions to come back to me with all speed.'

Henry bowed and I sent a man whom I could trust to St
rmain.

We had had dinner. Conversation was stilted. Nobody seemed
vant to talk about what was happening in England, which was
only subject which interested me.

My confessor, Father Cyprien, had said grace when the meal
s over and as he was about to leave Henry went to him, laid a
nd on his shoulder and whispered something.

cried: 'What is wrong? What are you whispering about?'

Henry looked at me, his face stricken and I saw then that Father
prien's hands were shaking.

What is it? Please tell me,' I begged.

Henry came to me, his face a mask of misery. He said: 'I lied to
1. It was not the truth. The people did not come to his aid.'

He led me to a chair and kneeling at my feet lifted his agonized
e to mine.

I could not tell you. I had to lie. . . . It did not happen that
y. They took him out to the scaffold in Whitehall. . . . He died
. like the brave man he was.'

was frozen with grief. I stared ahead of me. I did not see them
round me. I saw only his dear face.

could not move. A stifled sob broke into my consciousness. It
s one of the women. Henry was looking at me, his eyes
ading for forgiveness, for the lies he had told me . . . because
loved me.

There was nothing now. He was gone, my King, my husband,
love. The murderers had taken him from me.

could feel nothing for them. That would come later. At this
ment I could do nothing . . . think of nothing but this over-
elming tragedy.

Charles was dead and I should never see that dear face again.

Despair

I do not know how long I sat there. I was unaware of time, o
those kind people around me who shared my suffering.

It was Madame de Motteville who in due course put her a
about me and helped me to my bed. I lay there and she k
beside it. I could see the tears glistening on her cheeks. I s
none. My grief went too deep for tears. They were for ordir
tragedies, disappointments and frustrations; this was
greatest disaster that could befall me, and I longed above ev
thing else to be lying beside him in his cold grave.

I dare not think of him . . . that beautiful head which I ha
often caressed. . . . No, anything was better than thinkin
that.

'Merciful death,' I prayed, 'take me. Let me be with hin
death as I was in life.'

Madame de Motteville was speaking gently. 'Madame, dea
lady, you must live for your son. There is a new King of Engl
now. God bless Charles the Second.'

She was right, of course. I saw that. I could not selfi
indulge my grief. What would he have said? He believed in
crown, the divine right of kings to rule. The King was dead. N
it was Long Live King Charles the Second. My son was ninet
years old. He was strong; he was royal.

Perhaps there was something yet to be saved.

'Madame,' said Madame de Motteville, 'you will wish to se
message to the Queen of France.'

'Yes, yes,' I answered her. 'Send someone to her, tell her of
state. Tell her that the death of the King, my husband, has m
me the most unhappy woman in the world. Oh, warn her,
dear friend, warn the Queen of France. Tell her never to e:
perate her people unless she is certain she has the powe
subdue them. The people can become as a savage beast. My (

lord the King has proved that. I pray that she will be happier
rance. Now I am desolate. I have lost that which meant more
ne in life than anything else . . . a King, a husband and a
d.'

Madame de Motteville bowed her head and turned away
use, I knew, she could no longer endure looking on my
ble grief.

called on God to help me. I reproached Him for allowing this
g to happen. And then I repented and said that I knew it was
will and I wanted strength to bear it.

Madame de Motteville told me that she would go to Queen
e and tell her what I had said; and as she was about to depart I
d her back.

here is one thing I wish you to say to her. Ask her this for my
. If she does it, there will be a little lightness in the dark gloom
y life. I beg her to acknowledge my son the Prince of Wales as
g of England, King Charles the Second, and my son James,
Duke of York, as his heir presumptive.'

Madame de Motteville left me and I realized that when I
ght of my son I was beginning to live again.

wanted to know all that had led up to that terrible climax in
tehall but it was a long time before I was able to piece together
entire terrible events. Charles's later life had been strewn
misfortune. Even after the escape to Carisbroke, where he
expected to find loyalty, he had been betrayed by Colonel
nmond, the Governor of the island. It was understandable
Charles should have expected Hammond to be his friend for
vas a nephew of his chaplain. What Charles did not know was
he had married a daughter of John Hampden and become an
nt partisan of Oliver Cromwell. At first Hammond had
ted Charles like an honoured guest but even while he was
g this he was informing the Roundheads where Charles was,
my poor husband soon realized that he was a prisoner. How
must have despaired! But he would be calm and more serene
most men would be in his position, and while at the castle he
walked on the ramparts for exercise and played on the
ling green and spent a great deal of time reading.
heard how he had made an attempt to escape when he

discovered the perfidy of Hammond. There was a faithful atte
ant called Firebrace who acted as his page and planned esc
with him. Firebrace's scheme was that he should cut through
bars of the prison window, but Charles had thought this wc
attract attention and he believed he could squeeze his b
through. He tried it with his head. They were ready. A lac
was placed against the window for it was planned that w
Charles was on the ground below Firebrace would get him ac
the main courtyard to the main wall which he could descen
means of a rope. Men were waiting with a spare horse and c
by was a boat which was ready to carry him to France. Everyth
was in order and would have succeeded but for the fact
Charles had miscalculated and although he got his head thro
the bars he was stuck between his breast and shoulders and cc
move neither in nor out.

Alas, poor Charles! Sometimes I think that Heaven itself
against him. If ever I had a chance I would find the good Fireb
and reward him for his attempt to help the King.

After that Charles was taken to Hurst Castle, a dreadful p
which was situated on a kind of promontory off the Isle of Wi;
There could not have been a more uncomfortable place, lashe
it was by the winds and at high tide cut off from the island. I cc
picture him in that grim fortress. He must have thought of sc
of his forebears who had offended their enemies and ended u
places such as Hurst Castle where they were done to hide
death.

Fortunately he was not long in Hurst Castle and from there
brought first to Windsor and then on January the fifteenth
London.

By this time Cromwell was in control and I wondered,
without some satisfaction, how the people liked being ur
the orders of the military. His soldiers took great pleasure
breaking up many of the beautiful churches and homes wh
in their narrow Puritan minds they thought were sinful. T
even desecrated Westminster Abbey. The stupid people! N
they would learn what it was like to be ruled by men who hac
joy in them, who made harsh rules and thought it was a sir
smile.

So they brought my Charles to trial and condemned hin
death. I do not want to recall all the horrendous details. It is

ful even though it is so long ago. He was serene and went to
eath like the brave man he was.

nnot bear to think of the last time when he saw our two little
, Elizabeth and Henry, who were brought from Zion House
ke their last farewell of him.

ave heard it many times from different sources and each time
p.

w could they be so cruel to two innocent children!

hen my daughter Elizabeth saw her father she fell into
onate weeping. She knew what was in store for him and
different he must have looked from the handsome father she
known. He had suffered so much since they had last met. I
red his greying hair, his resigned looks – but he would
ys be handsome, impeccable in dress and manner.

e could not speak to him through her weeping, and little
y seeing his sister cry, joined in.

arles drew them to him and embraced them. Elizabeth was
twelve but immediately afterwards she wrote down exactly
had happened. I have read it many times and each time it
ne with an infinite tender sadness.

m glad you have come,' he told her, 'for there is something I
to say to you which I could not tell to another and the cruelty
I fear, was too great to permit me to write it. . . . But,
theart, you will forget what I tell thee.'

zabeth assured him that she would not. 'For I will write
wn,' she said, 'and it will be with me for as long as I shall

not grieve,' he said. 'Do not torment yourself for me. It will
glorious death which I shall die, it being for the laws of the
and for religion. I have forgiven all my enemies and I hope
will forgive them too. You must forgive them, as must your
ers and sisters. When you see your mother. . . .' And this is
art which I could never read without my tears blinding me
tell her that my thoughts have never strayed from her and
ve for her will be the same until the end. Love her and be
ient to her. Do not grieve for me. I shall die and I doubt not
God will restore the throne to your brother and then you will
happier than you would have been if I had lived.'

en he took little Henry onto his knee. 'Sweetheart,' he said,
they will cut off thy father's head.'

Poor little Henry stared at his father's neck and seemed u'
dismayed and bewildered.

'Heed what I say, my child,' went on the King. 'They wi
off my head and perhaps make thee a King. But mark what
you must not be King as long as your brothers Charles and J
live. Therefore I charge you, do not be made a King by them

Poor little Henry tried hard to understand. Then he dr
deep breath and said: 'I will be torn into pieces first.'

Then they prayed together and Charles commanded
always to fear God and this they promised to do.

One of the bishops came to take the children away; they
weeping bitterly. Charles watched them and when they rea
the door he ran after them and snatched them up that he r
embrace them once more and they clung to him as though
would never let him go.

The hour was fixed. They brought him dinner but he was
mood to eat.

'You should eat, sire,' his Bishop Juxon warned him. 'Yo'
faint for lack of food.'

'Yes,' agreed Charles, 'and it might be misconstrued if
that.' Whereupon he took some wine and food.

When he had eaten he said: 'Let them come. I am ready.'

But they did not come. There was a delay. Two of the mi
commanders who had been chosen to superintend the m'
refused to do so at the last minute. Nothing could shift
decision; they were jeered at and threatened; still they woul
take charge of the grisly task. Their names were Hunks
Phayer. I would remember them, too.

There was a small grain of comfort in knowing that they h
offer one hundred pounds to one who would aid the execut
– and thirty-eight people refused.

In the end they had to threaten one of the sergeants
another regiment to do the deed, and the executioner himsel
tried to hide himself and when he was found he had
threatened, too, and offered thirty pounds to do his work.
insisted on wearing masks as they did not want to be se
executioners of the King.

It must have been a great joy for Charles to receive from ou
Charles a blank sheet of paper with his signature at the bo
Our son had written in a separate note that he would p'

elf to carry out any terms which might be imposed on him in
nge for his father's life.

arles kissed the paper and burned it.

eard that he slept quietly on the night before he went out to
is murderers. Thomas Herbert who, as Groom of the Bed-
ber, was sleeping in the room with him awoke shouting in
eep and he told the King that he had been disturbed by a
mare. He had dreamed that Archbishop Laud had come
the room and knelt before the King while they talked
her.

e King knew why he was shaken. It was because Archbishop
was dead, having been executed four years before.

ey could not sleep after that although it was only five
k.

en Herbert was dressing him he said he wished to be as trim
is day as he had been on the day of his marriage. They said
oice broke a little when he said that and I knew it was
se he was thinking of the sorrow this day would bring to

bade Herbert bring him two shirts.

s cold outside,' he said. 'The wind might cause me to shake
y way to the scaffold and I would have no imputation of fear,
ath is not terrible to me. I am prepared, I thank God. Let the
s come for me when they please.'

not want to think of that scene but I can picture it so clearly
cannot get it out of my mind. I can see the mass of people
would not be allowed to come too close to the scaffold and
kept back by the many soldiers whom Cromwell had com-
ed should be there. How apprehensive he and his friends
have been!

arles stepped out through the banqueting hall for one of the
ows had been removed so that he could do this.

ften wonder what his thoughts were as he went up to the
ld. Of me, I like to think; and yet again I did not want him to
of me then because I knew that to do so would increase his
w.

at does one think of when one faces death? He was a good
a man who had tried to do his duty, and if he had failed to
e his people it was through no lack of effort on his part. He
lways done what he believed to be right; and I knew – and

was proved right in this – that these would be seen to be unh
days for England and those people who had fought – valia
must admit – for Cromwell would soon be longing for the
when people could sing and dance and be joyful; they w
regret those harsh laws of the Puritans ere long. And I was
I hated them. I was not calm and thoughtful like Ch
They were my enemies . . . those men who had put to de
great good man and I fervently wished that they would all b
hell.

So he came out looking beautiful as he always had and wi
showing a tremor of fear.

I could imagine his looks of contempt for the bewigge
masked murderers who had not the courage to do the deed
open but must cower behind disguises.

The executioner knelt and asked forgiveness.

Charles's reply was quiet and dignified. 'I forgive no subj
mine who comes hither to shed my blood.'

When he stepped up to the scaffold there was a terrible hu
the crowd. The executioner in a quiet and respectful voice
him to push his hair under his cap.

This he quietly did.

He said in a clear voice: 'I go from a corruptible to an incor
ible crown.' Then he took off his coat and doublet.

He asked the executioner to make sure that the block was
'Now,' he said, 'I will say a short prayer in silence and wher
my hands I shall be ready for you to strike.'

That was the end.

My Charles, King, husband, lover, friend and martyr
dead.

They told me that a groan was heard through the crov
people and that there was a terrible sense of forebodi
Whitehall that day.

I had to shut myself away for a while. I could not bear to se
attendants, let alone hear them speak to me. There was so
to remind me.

My poor little Henriette, who was not yet five years old
quite bewildered. She would watch me and her eyes wou
with tears.

am doing no good to her and none to myself,' I told Lady
rton. 'She would be better with you alone.'

ady Morton had too much good sense to deny this and so I
ided that for a while I would seek the peace and solace of my
ourite Carmelite convent in the Faubourg St Jacques. I gave
daughter into the care of Lady Morton with instructions that
should look after the child's creature comforts while Father
prien should see to her spiritual welfare. I thought I could not
better than that and I gave myself up to meditation and prayer
I lived a life of seclusion governed by bells. I needed it. I was
;ry with the Almighty for what seemed like indifference to my
fering and for permitting the cruel murder of my husband. I
w I should not complain; it was His will; but I railed against
h treatment and I could not be reconciled until I had wrestled
h myself.

dressed in black, which I swore I would do to the end of my
, I would mourn for Charles as long as I lived. I looked very
one of the nuns of the convent in my long rustling skirts and I
re a cap with a widow's peak which came over my forehead
with a black veil cascading from the back.

Vhen I had been a few weeks in the convent and was begin-
g to accept the fact that I must learn to live without Charles,
her Cyprien came to see me and gave me such a lecture that I
like boxing the man's ears, priest though he was. Then I knew
is becoming myself once more.

What are you doing shutting yourself away from the world?'
nanded Father Cyprien. 'Have you forgotten that you have a
and that he has to regain his throne? Have you forgotten that
are the daughter of the great Henri IV? Is it fitting that you
uld spend your days thus in idleness when there is work to be
ie?'

Have I not done enough . . . and to what avail?' I cried.

Your father did not give up in *his* struggles. When he suffered
porary defeat he fought again and so came to greater glory.'

Murdered,' I reminded him, 'as my husband was . . . but
erently. I'd rather Charles had gone by the knife of a madman
n the action of coldblooded murderers and pilferers of his
one.'

That is more like you. Your household needs you. Have you
;otten your young daughter? She pines for you. And what of

your son? You must bring Charles to Paris. There must be
more delay. He has a throne to fight for.'

Two days later I left the convent.

Father Cyprien was right. I should be planning. It did wond
for me. I was alive again. I was going to live through my childr
I was blessed in them. Charles was a son a mother could be pr
of; James had come to Paris from Holland; he was good look
and his manners were as charming as those of his brot
Charles. I had always insisted on impeccable manners.
was strange but loving my husband as I had I was able to
where he had failed. That aloof manner of his had aliena
people and it may have been one of the causes why so m
turned against him. Rulers must not keep themselves too m
apart from their subjects; it was not easy to keep the bala
between royalty and the necessary bonhomie needed to
people. My father had had it to a great degree; my son Cha
had it; James less so, but it was there and he was yo
yet.

Mary had been a wonderful friend to us and she and the Pri
of Orange, who were so devoted to each other, had showr
comforting hospitality and had done everything to help us. I
my precious Henriette with me now but the two who worried
were little Elizabeth and Henry – both in the hands of the Rou
heads. If I could only have them with me I should be gre
relieved.

What we must do was to get Charles fighting for his throne,
the first thing was for him to come to me here in Paris.

I wrote to him. I had been able to redeem some of my ru
when I first came to France and was hoarding them for the
when I would sell or pawn them to raise money for my son's a
as I used to for my husband's.

Charles must marry and his bride must be someone who c
help him regain his throne.

I was pleased when the Grande Mademoiselle called on m
the Louvre. She was very gracious to me and condoled with
on my loss. I tried not to give way to emotion before her for
was not exactly a comfortable person, very different from wa
hearted Queen Anne who had been so good to me when I nee
help.

I said: 'My son will be coming to me in Paris soon.'

I was under the impression that your son was with you now,
dame,' she said.

You are referring to my son James, the Duke of York. I meant
King.'

Oh yes . . . of course. He will be King now . . . if he can regain
throne.'

There is no doubt that he will do that,' I said sharply.

I am glad to hear it.'

Her eyes were speculative. She could not deceive me, this sly
nde Mademoiselle. She had suffered two disappointments.
King of Spain had married his niece, so poor Mademoiselle
s not to be Queen of Spain. The Emperor of Austria had
sen one of his cousins. Mademoiselle's nose was decidedly
of joint. It might well be that she would not be quite so super-
ous now regarding her cousin Charles. It was true he had yet
egain his throne but having seen those of Spain and Austria
out of her grasp, the ambitious creature might be feeling she
ld not be too selective. Moreover she must be about twenty-
years old – quite mature for a marriageable princess. She had
n considering herself the most delectable marriage prospect
a very long time. Was she beginning to doubt?

When will he be in Paris?' she was clearly trying to keep the
erness out of her voice.

Very soon, I promise you.'

You mean you promise yourself, dear aunt, not me.'

Oh, she was an insolent creature! If it had not been for her
ney I would not have received her, let alone considered her as
aughter-in-law.

Charles did not immediately respond to my summons. First he
de excuses and then he merely said he was not yet ready.

was getting frantic and I suggested to Henry Jermyn that he
roach Mademoiselle and make an offer on Charles's behalf for
hand.

Henry was a little reluctant and wondered if it were wise but I
isted. I had to keep events moving for while something was
ng on, it was balm to my wounds. Only while I was absorbed
ome project could I forget that Charles was dead.

Henry came back in some dismay, and reported what had
pened.

told her that when he had seen her Charles had been so

overcome by admiration that he had become speechle
Mademoiselle has a sharp tongue. She retorted: "Oh, I thou
that was due to his ignorance of the French language. He did
converse at all. In my opinion the inability to converse detra
from a personality more than anything else." '

'She can be a most unpleasant creature.'

'She has always had a high opinion of herself.'

'I thought that she might have been a little more humble a
the snubs she received from Spain and Austria.'

'There had been no commitments for the King of Spain or
Emperor of Austria to enter an alliance with her,' He
reminded me.

'No, but it was an understood possibility. Go on.'

'Then she said that she would prefer to discuss the matter w
Charles himself and could not commit herself to a go-betwe
She added that since Charles was so much in love with her
would doubtless change his religion. If he did that she would
assured of his devotion and then would begin to consider
matter.'

'The minx! She knows that if he changed his religion he wo
have no chance of regaining his throne.'

'Dear Madam, I fear there is nothing we can do but await
arrival of the King.'

It was summer before Charles arrived in Paris. I thought
looked very impressive with his tall figure and ugly go
natured face, his musical voice and his kingly bearing. There
a certain aloofness in his manner towards me. I realized later
it was his way of telling me that he was going to decide his o
affairs for himself. My little Henriette was beside herself with
and it gave me great pleasure to see the affection between th
two. She leaped into his arms and clasped hers about his ne
She was his little Minette and he was more than an ado
brother; in her eyes he was a god.

It was pleasant to watch; but I was impatient to put Ma
moiselle's vast fortune to good use in restoring the crown.

I dismissed everyone so that we were alone and told him
Mademoiselle was more than ready to listen to reason.

'Of course she will try to test you and suggest that you cha
your religion for her sake, but you must not take that
seriously.'

take it very seriously,' retorted Charles. 'And the answer is I have no intention of making it impossible for me to return to [Eng]land as King.'

[I] know. But laugh it off, Charles. Carry her off her feet. She is, [I suppo]se, a somewhat anxious young lady. The King of Spain [and] the Emperor have just chosen elsewhere in spite of her [charm]s and [fam]ine.'

[I] had noticed a young woman in the company who had come [from] Holland with him. She was very handsome in a bold and [brazen] way. I had asked questions about her and had been given [evasi]ve answers, but in view of what I knew of Charles and his [explo]its in Jersey I began to have suspicions.

[I f]elt a twinge of uneasiness when I heard that she had a baby – [a ch]ild of two or three months.

[B]y the way, Charles,' I said, 'who is that handsome young [wom]an who seems to have a place among your attendants?'

[Y]ou must mean Lucy,' he said.

[A]nd who, may I ask, is Lucy?'

[Y]ou may certainly ask, Mam,' said Charles putting on a regal [air,] reminding me that although I was a Dowager Queen he was [the]King. 'Her name is Lucy Walter and she is a special friend of [min]e.'

[A]*special* friend?'

[Y]ou heard aright, Mam. That is what I said.'

[O]h . . . and the child?'

[M]ine, Mam. Mine.'

[C]harles, this is. . . .'

[H]e lifted his shoulders and smiled at me. 'He is a very amiable [chil]d.'

[Y]our father never behaved like this.'

[N]o, Mam. And I must never behave as he did.'

[I f]elt as though he had struck me across the face. He was [peni]tant at once for he had loved his father; but he was right, of [cour]se. Charles's behaviour had been in a great measure respon-[sible] for what had happened to him.

[H]e said gently: 'Lucy is a pleasant girl. She is devoted to me [and]I to her. She is a great diversion.'

[T]here was the Jersey girl.'

[A]lso a charming creature.'

[C]harles, you must be more serious.'

'I assure you, Mam, no one could be more serious than I. I h
one ambition and that is to regain my throne.'

'Mademoiselle must not hear of this Lucy Walter.'

He lifted his shoulders.

'Charles, do you understand this match could be of the grea
use to you. Her fortune. . . .'

'I know her fortune is great.'

'Then Charles, you must woo her. It should not be diffic
She is the most arrogant conceited creature on Earth.'

'And this creature is to be my wife!'

'The money . . . it could make all the difference. Please g
see her. Flatter her. That will be necessary. Queen Anne
arranged that you shall met at Compiègne . . . in the *châ*
there. It is really rather romantic.'

'There is nothing so romantic as a large fortune,' said Cha
cynically.

However he did agree to go to Compiègne.

It was a disaster – as I believe Charles intended it to be.
looked more distinguished than anyone in the company beca
he was so tall that he towered above them all. Queen Anne
there, as eager to help as ever and with her the young Kin
France. I was amused to see that Mademoiselle had dressed v
particular care with her hair specially curled; and her blue pro
nent eyes were taking in every detail of Charles's appearance

He was distantly polite with her and it was rather a diffi
meal. Queen Anne and Mademoiselle were both eager to kr
how everything was going in England but in spite of this bein
paramount importance to him, Charles appeared to know v
little, having been so long in Holland, he explained, and hav
to rely on hearsay. I could see that Mademoiselle was finding I
rather dull and that he was growing more and more indifferer
her opinion of him. His French was not nearly as good as
brother James's and he had to excuse himself more than o
because of his paucity of the language.

When the ortolans were brought in Charles declined and t
instead a piece of mutton, which deeply shocked Mademois
who assumed that his tastes were crude and that he was
husband for a lady of refinement.

When the meal was over Queen Anne, always eager to h
arranged that Charles and Mademoiselle should be alone togeth

Jhat happened during that brief interview – it lasted no more
1 fifteen minutes – I cannot be sure, except of one thing.
irles was determined to choose his own bride and had no
ntion of allowing me to do it for him.

was all very unsatisfactory. Mademoiselle was certainly very
ied; as for Charles he maintained a solemn enigmatical air
I supposed that he who knew so well how to attract women
equally well versed in the art of driving them away.

e told me afterwards that he did not pay her compliments
iuse he could think of none that fitted; but as it appeared to be
ected of him – by both the Queens of England and France – he
made a formal declaration to Mademoiselle by, as he took his
e of her, saying that Henry Jermyn spoke better French than
did and would therefore be better able to explain what he
ied to say to her.

enriette was with her brother whenever she could be. I said to
'You must remember he is the King. You must be very
iectful to him.'

he only laughed and said he was her dear brother Charles and
was his Minette and she did not have to be the least bit
iectful. He loved her dearly and told her so.

aturally I was delighted to see the affection between them.
iriette was a dear child. I kept her close to me and supervised
education myself and with the help of Father Cyprien I was
iging her up in the Catholic Faith.

idy Morton did not altogether approve of this and because I
so fond of her and would never forget how she had brought
iriette out of England to me, I was very anxious for her to have
benefit of the true Faith too. I confided this to Henriette. I
: 'My darling, you love Lady Morton, do you not?'
enriette said she did indeed.

'hen,' I said, 'is it not sad that she should be left in darkness?
should try to bring her into the light with us. . . . It would
me the greatest happiness if our dear Lady Morton would
e to be a Protestant and become a Catholic. We must try to
her. Will you?'

)h I will, Mam,' said my little daughter fervently.

)me days later I asked how she was getting on with the
version and she told me very seriously that she was trying
hard.

'What do you do?' I asked.

'Hug her and kiss her and I say to her, "Dear Madam, do
Catholic. Please be a Catholic. You must be a Catholic to
saved." '

I smiled and I learned that Lady Morton was touched but it
not change her. She implied that she was aware of our little
and she told me with a smile that she believed Father Cyp
was in fact instructing her rather than Henriette.

Henriette soon betrayed her zeal to her brother and this
the beginning of trouble.

One could never be sure what Charles was thinking. He
not a man to lose his temper – he did not take after me in that –
gave the impression of a kind of insouciance, an indifference
times he seemed content to dally on the Continent and I w
dered whether he was making any real efforts to win back
crown. But when he was determined on something he coul
very stubborn. He exasperated me sometimes because it
impossible to quarrel with him. I would rather he had flared u
anger so that I could know what he was thinking.

He said to me: 'Mam, it is unwise for Minette to be brough
as a Catholic.'

'*I* think,' I retorted, 'for the sake of the child's soul it woul
unwise to bring her up in any other way.'

'It was the cause of much of our troubles.'

'One often has to fight for one's Faith. The Faith is strewn w
martyrs.'

'My father one of them.'

He was sorry then because any mention of the late King fi
me with melancholy which persisted for days.

'He had other troubles,' he went on softly, 'God rest his s
But, Mam, if it is known in England that Henriette is be
brought up as a Catholic and I approve of this, it could jeopar
my chances of regaining the crown.'

'I cannot see that.'

'I can,' he said. 'The people will be afraid that I or James m
be the same.'

'I would to God you were! Listen to me, Charles. Wh
married your father there was a clause in the settlement that I
to have charge of my children's religious instruction until
were thirteen years old. That was never carried out.'

'It would have meant that we should all have been Catholics,
what children learn in their early years usually settles them for
. No, Mam, Henriette should not be allowed to talk so con-
ntly of her religion and efforts to convert Lady Morton.'

'She is but a child.'

'It would be better to take her out of the hands of Father
prien.'

'I will not do it,' I said firmly.

Charles sighed. He did not want to hurt me for there was a very
d side to his nature. He hated trouble and when it was there
ed to avoid it by delegating someone else to take care of it. As a
g he could do that. I thought it was a great fault in his nature
t later I began to see that it was an asset. He did not waste his
otions on petty quarrels. He rarely lost that magnificent
enity which later was to give him the reputation of a cynic. So
w he did not insist, but I knew the matter was not at an end,
meone else would be set to persuade me. In fact he gave the
k to Sir Edward Hyde, a man I loathed, but whom I had to
mit had always been loyal to the royalist cause and he was now
arles's constant companion and adviser.

soon despatched him with a few sharp words.

However it did make a coolness between Charles and me and it
owed me clearly that my son had no intention of taking my
vice.

A few weeks later the Emperor lost his young bride and I could
t resist a dig at Mademoiselle.

'Perhaps I should congratulate you on the death of the
npress,' I said slyly. 'For if the affair failed formerly it is sure to
cceed next time.'

She flushed hotly and replied haughtily: 'I had not given
ought to the matter.'

'Some people prefer old men who must be nearly fifty with
ur children to a handsome King of nineteen years old. It is
fficult to understand but must be accepted, I suppose. Do you
e that very handsome young woman over there. My son likes
r very well.'

Charles was standing by at that time and I think he was
noyed to be discussed in his presence; but I, his mother, would
as I pleased.

went on: 'My son is too poor for you, Mademoiselle. All the

same he does not want you to know of his feelings for the you
lady. He is very much afraid that I should mention her to you.

Charles bowed to me and then to Mademoiselle and walk
out of the room, his face inscrutable so that I could not tell h
annoyed he was. But I guessed it was very deeply. He was v
cool to me afterwards though always polite.

I was angry with myself. I had been foolish to say what I k
when all that mattered to me now was my children's affecti
and well being. But I was angry about Mademoiselle and it
seem such a good opportunity missed. And he could h
charmed her had he wished to. Heaven knows he was success
enough with other women.

The French Court was still at St Germain because the Fron
troubles kept starting up and Anne felt it was unsafe to bring
young King back to the Louvre. I was still there but I had notice
growing antagonism towards me. At first they had all been
sorry for me and remembered that I was the daughter of th
beloved Henri IV; now they saw me as royal, closely connect
with Queen Anne and therefore Mazarin; and I was beginning
get hostile looks, and so were members of my household.

Anne was afraid for us and sent messages asking us to come
her and the King at Saint Germain. Charles agreed with me t
we ought to accept the invitation, for the mood of the Parisi
was growing more and more hostile.

So one day we set out; but of course we could not leave in sec
and as we passed through the palace gates an angry crowd w
waiting for us. They jeered at us. It was true that I owed money
many tradesmen and they must have feared that they wou
never get it and that I was leaving in order to escape paying the

I wanted to explain, but how can one talk to a crowd of men
ing people.

I was the one they hated. They crowded round my coach an
had a few horrifying moments when I feared they were going
drag me out and kill me.

Few mobs can be as terrifying as a Paris mob. They seem
more fierce than the English and I feared that they might beco
very violent indeed.

Then just as I was certain that some ruffian was going
wrench open the door of my coach and drag me out, my s
Charles appeared. He looked so tall and dignified in his bl

urning garments that for a few moments he startled the
wd. Those few moments were enough. He laid his hand on
door of the coach and told the coachman to proceed slowly.
walked beside the coach as we went through the crowds, and
as amazed at the manner in which they fell back; and it was all
 to that magnificent presence of his. He was unarmed; he
uld have been unable to defend himself with his sword against
mob; but still they recognized and respected his royalty.
watched him through a haze of tears and I knew that one day
would be a king in very truth.
hat incident moved me deeply and perhaps it did him too, for
r it our relationship began to change. I felt I could not dictate
uch a man; and he seemed to come to a new understanding
 realize that everything I did – however misguided it might
m to him – was meant to be for his benefit and was done out of
xcess of love.

After Worcester

I was glad that the relationship between Charles and myself h
changed and that when he did go we parted as loving parent a
devoted son.

Everything seemed to go wrong for us. We had planned that
should go to Ireland and use it as a stepping stone to England;
no sooner had we agreed that this would be the best plan than
heard that Cromwell had gone to Ireland on a punitive expe
tion, so that put the project out of the question.

Charles decided however that he could not remain in Paris a
set out for Jersey with his retinue, which included his mistr
Lucy Walter and her few months' old son whom they had nan
James. It was very irregular but I had come to the conclusion th
must not try to interfere too much with Charles.

At least in Jersey he could keep an eye on what was happen
in England and be ready to go through Scotland, perhaps
Ireland remained unsuitable.

Just as my hopes were beginning to rise fate struck me anotl
blow. This one I found very hard to bear. It was a long time sin
had seen my two children who were the prisoners of the Rour
heads but I thought of them every day and I was constar
turning over in my mind plans to rescue them.

I worried more about Elizabeth than Henry. She was a li
older and more able to appreciate sorrow, and I knew how dee
affected she had been by her father's death for I had news of I
from time to time and I had written letters to members of
Parliament imploring them to send my daughter and little sor
me. What harm could such children do to any cause?

But those cruel men would not release my children an
continued to fret for them.

I had just had news that Charles had landed in Scotland a
that he was promised help. He had had to buy it dearly and h

eed to the Covenant, to renounce treaties with the Irish rebels
to uproot Popery wherever it should be found once he had
ained his kingdom. For this the Scots would rally to his cause
provide an army with which to invade England and win his
wn for him.

was furious when I heard that. It seemed like a betrayal of his
family. It could only be directed against me. And there was
e Henriette too. She was a Catholic now, even as I was.

fumed with rage and it was Henry Jermyn who reminded me
t my own father had made peace and become King of all
nce because as he had said, when Paris had refused to
render to a Huguenot, 'Paris is worth a Mass.'

o Charles was in Scotland and there was hope. And now . . .
fresh blow. If only I could have been with my child, if I could
e spoken with her, held her in my arms, I should not have felt
itter. What sort of men were these to ruin the lives of little
dren?

My little Elizabeth was only fifteen. What unhappy years they
been for her! She must have been about seven when the
ibles started – a sweet, loving child, my own little daughter
om I had scarcely seen while she was growing up.

he Roundheads had put her and her brother in the care of the
untess of Leicester at Penshurst. I knew Penshurst. A delight-
castle set on a pleasant incline with woods, fields and hop
unds around it. I remembered well the old banqueting hall
ted by its five Gothic windows and I could picture my
dren seated at the oak table there. The Parliament had
ounced that there was no royalty now and that the children
e to be treated as those of an ordinary nobleman. They would
have cared about that, I was sure; what would have broken
ir hearts was the separation from their family. I had heard that
Roundheads suspected the Countess of ignoring orders and
wing the children too much respect; they had even sent some
heir men to Penshurst to make sure their orders were carried
. How I despised them for their persecution of two helpless
dren!

pparently the spies were most dissatisfied by the manner in
ich the Countess treated the children, swearing that she gave
m too much deference. Dear Countess! I had always liked her
it had given me some relief to know that the children were

put into her hands for the reports I had heard at that time fi
me with dread. The talk of apprenticing Henry to a shoema
had horrified me for I knew those wicked men were capabl
doing that. There was a rumour that they were to be sent
charity school and were to be known as Bessy and Harry Stua

Lady Leicester had brought in a tutor for them – a man nam
Richard Lovell, who had instructed her own children; but eve
this brave and noble lady could not go on defying the Parliam
There were frightening rumours at that time. One was that
children were to be poisoned and I was terrified that they wo
disappear as long ago two little Princes had vanished in
Tower of London.

When Charles landed in Scotland the Roundheads must h
been alarmed and perhaps because they thought an attemp
rescue the children might be made they removed them
Carisbroke Castle.

I wondered what my two little ones felt at being sent to
prison where their father had spent some of the last days of
life.

A week after they had arrived at Carisbroke Elizabeth
Henry were playing bowls on that green which had been m
for their father when there was a heavy rain shower and
children were wet through. The next day Elizabeth was in a h
fever and confined to her bed.

She must have been in a low state and very melancholy to b
her father's prison and she must have remembered that
interview with him; she had loved him so dearly and
mourned him ever since. The poor child must have wonde
from day to day what her own fate would be in the hands of
father's murderers.

If only Mayerne could have been with her! But they had
missed him and they were certainly not going to allow
member of the royal family to have the services of the renow
doctor. He was nearly eighty now but still as skilful and it m
have been that he could have saved my child's life.

One of the doctors whom they were obliged to call in –
Bagnall – did send to Mayerne and ask his advice and the g
doctor sent back medicines, but it was too late.

My dear child knew she was dying. I tried to imagine
sorrow and desolation of poor little Henry. Elizabeth gave I

pearl necklace and sent a diamond ornament to the Earl and
ntess of Leicester. It was all she had to leave.

hey were determined that no honour should be paid to her.
was placed in a lead coffin and taken by a borrowed coach to
vport, attended by a few of those who had served her in the
. The coffin was placed in the east part of the chancel in St
mas's Chapel and they put a simple inscription on it

Elizabeth second daughter
of the late King Charles
Deceased September 8th M.D.C.L.

o stone was erected and the letters E.S. were engraved in the
above the spot where the coffin had been laid.

died my daughter, the child I had borne with such joy and
d with such devotion.

was small wonder that I thought Heaven itself was against me.

hildren are both a blessing and an anxiety. I loved mine
ly but we were often in conflict.

here was James. He was growing up very different from his
her; they were unlike in every way except in their impeccably
d manners, which I had insisted be instilled in them. James
fair and Charles had those swarthy looks which must have
e down from an ancestor of Navarre, so they never looked
brothers. James's temperament was difficult and it was the
est thing in the world to quarrel with him whereas it was
ossible to quarrel with Charles, who could be serene, evasive
indifferent, and when one thought he had acquiesced he
ld go away and do exactly what he had planned to do from
first.

now I was not the easiest person to live with. I had been born
a desire to impose my will on others but it was meant to be
heir good, though they so often could not see this.

mes was restive, hating, I suppose, to be cooped up in Paris
le his brother was in Scotland. I think he rather resented
g the younger son and in spite of his undoubted good looks
Charles's far from handsome ones, he was always over-
lowed by his brother.

Well Charles was no longer with us in Paris and James
difficult. I sometimes think he enjoyed quarrelling and loo
round for trouble. Heaven knew life was hard enough for m
bear. What were his troubles compared with mine?

Some trivial matter flared up one day and James too
seriously. He turned on me and said: 'I want to get away.
tired of being here. You tutor me in all things. I am old enoug
think for myself.'

'You are clearly not,' I retorted. 'You talk like a foolish boy
that does not surprise me because you are one.'

In a very short time we were shouting at each other and Ja
was behaving very badly, forgetting entirely the respect du
me, not only as his mother but as Queen of England.

I cried: 'Whatever I do, I do for you children. You are my n
concern.'

Then he turned on me and said something which I four
very hard to forgive. 'Your main concern!' he said aln
sneering. 'I thought your main concern was Henry Jermyn.
are more fond of him than you are of all your children
together.'

I stopped short to stare at him. Then I cried out: 'How
you!' And I struck him hard across his face with the back of
hand.

He turned quite white and for a moment I thought he
going to return the blow. Then he turned away and strode f
the room.

I was very upset. Of course I was fond of Henry Jermyn.
had been beside me, my faithful friend and helper, for m
years. Moreover he was a jolly man, a handsome man who ra
my spirits; and heaven knew I had need of a few like him arou

But what was James suggesting? That he was my lover!

I had never been a sensual woman. What I called 'that sid
marriage' had never greatly appealed to me. It was my dut
produce children and that I had done in full measure. I had lo
my husband completely and still did. But to take a lover now
he was dead . . . I could never do that. It would seem
disloyalty to him.

And yet . . . had I taken a lover? Not in the physical sense,
the truth was that I did love Henry Jermyn and if I lost him my
would be empty indeed.

I was terribly shaken and was expecting James to come to me with apologies, but he did not.

He had left Court.

It was heartbreaking that he should have gone like that before I had had a chance to talk to him. I wondered where he had gone and speculated that he had joined his brother in Scotland. But no. It turned out that he had gone to Brussels where he had been made very welcome.

This was most embarrassing. Not only had James left me after making that devastating statement but in Brussels he was on territory which belonged to Spain and Spain was at war with France.

I made up my mind that I would send him no money and as he could not exist without it he would have to return to me.

Then there was Mary. She had always been a good daughter and the marriage to William of Orange had turned out to be advantageous in the end, although at first we had all thought it was a little degrading for the daughter of the King of England to marry a mere Prince of Orange and we should never have allowed it to happen but for the fact that we had wanted to placate the Parliament by a Protestant match. Yet Holland had been our good friend and it was largely due to Mary and her husband.

I had always thought of Mary as a good daughter. She had extended help to Charles – of whom she was very fond – and her Court had provided a refuge for many of our supporters.

And now for the first time she was pregnant. I was delighted at the thought of a child and I wrote to her telling her that if it were a boy she must name him Charles after her father and brother.

There came sad news. The Prince of Orange had been struck down with small pox and within a few days of contracting the disease had died. The Dowager Princess Amelia who took a great pride in forcing her will on others and whom I had never liked, gave orders that Mary was not to be told of her husband's death until after the confinement.

The news, however, leaked out, but Mary was determined to give birth to a healthy child, and she did. I was delighted when I heard the news. 'Our little Charles,' I called the baby.

My chagrin was great when I heard that the dowager Princess had insisted that the child be named William after his father, and to my disappointment Mary agreed with her.

It was wonderful news that we had the child but his father's death was a tragedy for us all. When I heard it I said it seemed as though God wished to show me that I should detach myself from the world, by taking from me all those who would lead me to think of it. The loss of my son-in-law made me see this very clearly, for my hopes of Charles's restoration to the crown were based largely on William of Orange. And my daughter obeyed the wishes of her mother-in-law rather than those of her own mother!

Wherever I looked for comfort there was none.

The Queen of France however was very good to me. She commiserated with me over the deaths of Elizabeth and my son-in-law.

'Life is very cruel,' she said. 'One can be happy for a time and then it strikes . . . and does not always strike singly but many times as though to stress the fact that we are all at the mercy of our fate.'

I told her then how anxious I was on her behalf.

'Believe me,' I said, 'I have experience of the people. They are like savages when aroused. I shall never forget Charles standing at my coach door when I came out of the Louvre. They were all around me. I am sure it would not have taken them long to tear me to pieces.'

Anne looked a little impatient. She was easy going and I was sure she believed that Mazarin was so shrewd and clever that he could do anything. She did not like me to warn her. My criticism of Anne – and Heaven knew I should not be critical of one who had been so good to me in my need – was that she liked to pretend that what was not pleasant was not there.

After all I had suffered I saw the folly of this. One must be aware all the time. Think the worse . . . and face up to it as a possibility. If only Charles and I had done a little more of that I might not be in the position I found myself in at this time.

But because I felt it was my duty to warn her, her frowns did not stop me, and I went on to give her advice until finally she said in exasperation: 'Sister, do you wish to be the Queen of France as well as the Queen of England?'

I looked at her sadly and did not take offence at the rebuke. I merely said gently: '*I* am nothing. Do *you* be something.'

I think she saw my meaning and at that moment faced the truth

ıd saw herself possibly in my position – a Queen without a
ıngdom. Perhaps she was realizing what an empty title it was
hen one had lost one's throne.

She was immediately sorry for her harsh tone, remembering all
ıad suffered and most of all the recent death of my daughter, for
ıe was a devoted mother, living for her children, so she could
ıderstand the terrible sorrow a child's death could bring.

She put her hands over mine and said: 'Oh, my poor sister, I
ıow your sadness and I know that sometimes you wish to leave
all and go to the Faubourg St Jacques and stay there with the
ıns. Is that what you wish?'

'How well you know me! If I had a choice I would go there and
ıss the rest of my days in peace. But how could I do that? I have
y sons . . . my little Henriette. . . .'

'I know,' said Anne. 'You could not rest there. I have been
inking of you and there is something which I believe could
ing you great cheer.'

'It is difficult to think of what could do that. Only my son's
storation could make me happier and even then there would be
» much sadness to look back on.'

'You are indeed the unhappy Queen, my sister. But I know you
ıve always wished to found an order of your own.'

I looked at her in amazement and she smiled at me.

'I was thinking that to found your own convent would bring
ı eat ease to your mind and spirits. Am I right?'

'To found my own convent! Oh, what a dream! But how could
All the money I have from the sale of my jewels must go to the
ıttle for the throne.'

'I would help you with the convent,' said Anne.

I could not speak. I fell into her arms and hugged her.

At length I said: 'I bless that long ago day, dear sister, when
ey brought you to Paris to be my brother's wife.'

'You did not like me very much at first.'

'True affection is that which grows with the years,' I answered
ıd added, 'I shall never be able to show you my gratitude or to
ıl you what your friendship has meant to me in my adversity.'

'It is in adversity that true friendship is seen,' she answered.
ıow let us plan. First we must find a suitable site. Do you know
ı e country house on the hill at Chaillot?'

'I do,' I cried. 'It is a fine house. The Maréchal de Bassompierre

used to live there. My father gave the house to him. It has be‹
empty since his death.'

'That is why I thought of it. I have asked the price. It is s
thousand pistoles.'

'Dear Anne, would you indeed do this?'

'Guessing that you would like it, I had already decided ‹
it.'

I felt happier than I had for a long time and the Queen an‹
forgot our troubles in planning our convent. We should both u
it as a retreat, and then I looked over the place with her and cho
the apartments we should have when we came to the conver
The windows overlooked the Seine and the Avenue of the Cou
La Reine.

I think Anne was as happy as I was planning it.

It was nearly two years since Charles had left France, and I w
dreadfully worried. Rumours were coming across the Chann‹
Some reported that he was sick; others that he was dead.
refused to believe them. Something within me told me th
Charles would survive. He had had to swear what the Sco
wished him to and this he had done in order to gain their suppo
and for this he had been crowned at Scone but if ever he w
victorious over the Parliamentarians he would be a Presbyteri‹
King on both sides of the border.

Cromwell was marching to Scotland and soon we had news
the Royalist defeat at Dunbar and the capture of Edinburgh by t
Roundheads.

Charles then marched south into England. It was a despera
move but I could see it was the only one to take in the circun
stances. I hoped and prayed that there were some loyal Englis
men left in England to join him. Alas, he was disappointed in th
and few came to augment the ten thousand men who constitut‹
his army. Charles had impressed all with his bravery and ‹
excellence in the field. He was always calm and serene a‹
seemed not in the least perturbed by danger and disaster. It wa‹
wonderful gift to have. I could admire it although it certainly h‹
not come through me.

Battle took place at Worcester and when the news came to us
was the old story. Disaster for the Royalists. Success f

omwell. And what had happened to Charles? He had dis-
peared. It was then that the rumours started to come, thick and
t.

Most people thought he was dead.

My nights were haunted by evil dreams. Where was my son?
nat other and greater evils had Fate in store for me?

was seated in my apartments in the Louvre sunk in the
epest despair when a man burst unceremoniously in. I stared
him, a little alarmed and then incensed by the intrusion. He
s well over six feet tall, gaunt, and his hair was cut in the
nner I loathed – that of the Roundheads.

He cried out: 'Mam. It is I.'

Then I flew to him, tears streaming down my face. 'It *is* you.
1 I dreaming . . . ' I stammered.

No, Mam. I am indeed here . . . and the first thing I did was to
ne to you.'

Oh Charles . . . Charles my son. You are safe then. Oh thanks
to God.'

I come to you defeated, Mam. But it will not always be thus.'

No . . . no. Oh, Charles, I have had such fears . . . such
eams. I will send for your sister. She has been sunk in melan-
oly. First she must know that you are here. Then you can tell
all that happened.'

shouted for attendants and sent them running to the Princess
nriette.

While I waited I took his hands . . . I kissed them. I pressed him
me. He smiled in his rather sardonic way, but there was
iderness in him.

My little seven-year-old daughter ran into the room and into
arms. He picked her up and danced round the room with her.

I knew you would come. I knew you would come,' she kept
inting. 'They couldn't kill *you* . . . not even wicked old
omwell.'

No,' he said, 'not even wicked Old Cromwell. I am indestruct-
e, Minette. You will see.'

And when you have won the crown you will take me to
gland with you. We shall be together for ever and ever. . . .'

When I win the crown miracles will happen.'

I loved to see them together and wished fleetingly that Char
had the same affection for me that he had for his sister. But
course she was a child and children showed only adoration. I h
a duty to perform and that sometimes made one displease tho
whom one loved most.

He must tell us of his adventures, I said. I could not wait
hear.

'You have been away a long time,' Henriette accused him.

'The absence was forced on me. I would rather have been
Paris than in Scotland with those Presbyterians. They are a gr
crowd, dear Minette. *You* would not like them. It is a sin, th
consider, to laugh on a Sunday.'

'Do they save up their jokes for other days?'

'Why, bless you, jokes are sin too. Think of the things you l
doing best and I'll be ready to wager that all would be a sin in t
eyes of the Presbyterians.'

'Then I am glad you are back. Will it be like that in England?

'Not while I am King. For that life is not for a gentleman of t
tastes.'

He talked of his escape after Worcester and the terrible def
his forces had suffered there. He had his faithful friends thou
and chief among them were Derby, Lauderdale, Wilmot a
Buckingham. Yes, the son of that evil genius of my youth was c
of Charles's closest associates. He was about three years ol
than Charles and I hoped he was not going to exert a simi
influence over my son as that which his father had held over t
husband. But I fancied my son was not the sort to be influence
was eager to hear more. Charles had escaped from Worcester
man with a price on his head. He told us how the Earl of Der
had produced a certain gentleman – a Catholic at that – Char
Giffard, to guide him through unknown country to Whitelad
and Boscobel; how he, the King of England, had paused at an i
for food and afraid to stay there and eat it had ridden away w
bread and meat in his hands.

I had never seen Charles so moved as he was when he told us
his first glimpse of Whiteladies, the farmhouse which had on
been a convent. It was the place he had come to for shelter, a
the two brothers who were living there – the Penderels – we
staunch royalists.

'There was I,' said Charles, 'seated in this humble farmhou

rounded by my friends, Derby, Shrewsbury, Cleveland,
mot and Buckingham with Giffard and the Penderels . . .
nning what we should do next. The Penderels sent a message
Boscobel where more Penderels lived. You should have seen
clothes they gave me! A green jerkin and doublet of doeskin
a hat with a steeple crown. I looked like a country yokel. You
uld never have recognized me.'

think I should have recognized you anywhere,' I told him
dly.

Wilmot had sheared my hair to this offensive cut. You know
mot. He made a joke of it – and a bad job, I must say. The
derels trimmed me up afterwards, for as they wisely said, it
st not look like a job that had been hastily done. I had to try to
k as a yokel would, and to talk like one. They were hard
ons, Mam.'

'm glad to hear it,' I told him. 'But you managed well enough I
e no doubt.'

No, indeed not. I made a poor rustic. Wilmot said his lord the
g kept peering out from under my Roundhead haircut. I
ked so far that my feet were bleeding and Joan Penderel, the
e of one of the brothers, washed my feet and put pads of paper
ween my toes where the skin was rubbed. I can tell you I was
sorry state. Then news came that the neighbourhood was full
Roundhead soldiers . . . all bent on one thing. To find me and
me where they had put my father.'

shivered and touched his hand gently.

'm sorry, Mam,' he murmured.

nodded and he went on: 'A very good friend came to Boscobel
varn me. He was Colonel Carlis, a man I greatly trusted. He
me I was most unsafe. The soldiers were searching every
se and could not fail to come to Boscobel. What could we do?
went out of the house and saw near by an enormous oak tree
ull leaf. The Colonel said "That is our only hope." So he and I
bed the tree and hid ourselves among the leaves. The
derels said we were quite invisible and unless the soldiers
ided to climb the tree, they would never see us. And, Mam,
re is my little miracle. From the tree we could see the soliders
rching the wood and the houses . . . and they never thought
ook up into the oak tree.'

o we were back where we were. He was alive and well; he had

had great adventures; and, as I had come to expect, all had en<
in defeat.

He had become very cynical. I sometimes thought he had gi
up all hope of winning the crown and had decided to live wh
he could enjoy life. He liked his friends, good conversation – i
women, of course. I was glad to see that he was rid of that bra
Lucy Walter, who had been blatantly unfaithful to him during
absence. I suppose two years was too long for a woman of t
kind to wait. But she had the boy. What a pity that was! Cha
seemed to have an affection for the child. From what I saw of
infant he was strikingly handsome.

I could not rid myself of the thought of the Grande Ma
moiselle's money lying idle when it might have been equipp
an army. I still hoped for the match.

She was in exile from the Court at this time because she
openly helped the Fronde. Her father, Gaston, was a suppo
of them too, which was disgraceful as he was going against
own family. Always flamboyant, Mademoiselle had on one oc
ion gone into battle and it was significant that she had done thi
the town of Orléans when the Fronde had taken it by storm.

What was she trying to be? Another Jeanne d'Arc!

She did show a certain interest in Charles. He had beco
something of a hero since his adventures after Worcester ar
had never seen him talk as much as he did about them, for usu
he was inclined to silence about his exploits. But these adv
tures seemed to have a fascination for him and he was read
talk of them to any who asked him.

Mademoiselle gave a series of what she called "Assemblié
She was still not able to attend Court but she snapped her fing
at that and made sure that she invited the most interesting pec
and that the food she gave them was far more delicious than t
served at Court.

Charles was always invited to these occasions and I re
believed she was considering him as a husband. She must
getting a little anxious now. She was twenty-five, no young
and the Emperor had married his third wife and again decli
my ambitious niece.

On one of these occasions when I was present she made a p
of talking to me. I think she took a malicious delight in raising
hopes that she might take Charles as a husband.

He has changed since his adventures,' she told me. 'He has
ome more mature . . . more serious . . . more mellowed shall
say? It is wonderful what hiding in an oak tree can do for a
sonality.'

'ou too have changed, niece,' I reminded her. 'You have also
ome more . . . mature. After all it must have been a great
enture to play the Maid of Orléans.'

t was . . . indeed it was. I heard that the King of England is too
d of many women to be faithful to one.'

'ou speak of women . . . not of wives.'

Do you believe then that a man who has been promiscuous in
youth will in marriage become a model husband?'

t is possible.'

t would be something of a miracle. Think of your father, dear
t.'

often do, and he was your grandfather, remember. We
uld both be proud of him. He was the greatest king France has
r known.'

trust my little husband will be as great.'

'our . . . little husband!'

Vell,' she looked at me maliciously, 'there is not much differ-
e in our ages . . . eleven years and a few months. Louis is
ady fourteen.'

He does not seem to be enamoured of the prospect since he
ished you from Court,' I said sharply.

.ittle Louis banish *me*! Oh no, that was old Mazarin and his
nma.'

Nevertheless I doubt. . . .'

he smiled at me sardonically and I dropped the subject for I
afraid my anger would explode.

The Frustrated Mother

Life was not all sorrow. At the end of the year I had word
Cromwell had decided to allow my son Henry to join m
suppose this was because even Roundheads had some feel
and the death of my daughter Elizabeth had caused a cel
amount of dismay throughout the land. She had always t
such a good child – a near saint – and her death had bee
pathetic. Whatever the reason, Henry was given permissio
leave.

Minette was delighted at the prospect of having a new bro
with us. She asked countless questions, which alas I was un
to answer as my little son had been kept away from me for so lo

He arrived in Holland where his sister Mary received him
was so delighted to have him that she wanted to keep him v
her. I had no intention of allowing that because I knew that
would endeavour to bring him up as a Protestant, and it w
secret resolve of mine that he should be, like his sister Henric
Catholic.

He arrived in Paris and was so delighted to be with his
family. He immediately conceived a great admiration for Cha
– whose adventures he had followed whenever he was able
and he and Henriette worshipped him together. There
something about Charles which inspired this fervent devotic
often wondered whether it was partly due to his height or w
his easy-going manner and superficial charm? In any case t
two children adored him.

It was as though when something good happened somet
bad had to follow quickly. We now heard that the countrie
Europe were accepting the new government of England and
Cromwell was making treaties with various countries. Fra
was on the point of making them too, which would mean tha
English government would be having a representative in Par

Charles said to me: 'That would be an intolerable situation as
as I am concerned. You know what would happen. I should be
ked to leave.'

'You should tell them to do no such thing.'

He looked at me in exasperation. 'Dear Mam,' he said, 'if the
ng of France, the Regent or Mazarin ask me to leave, I have no
ernative but to go. There is only one course open to me. I must
ve before they ask me to.'

suppose he was right and in any case he began making
angements.

Henriette was beside herself with grief; so was Henry. I was
ry to see him go but I reminded myself that when he was not
re I could carry out my intentions with regard to Henry's
igious training.

Henry had begged Charles to take him with him. 'I am not a
y any more,' he cried. 'I am nearly fifteen. That is old enough to
ht.'

Charles hesitated. He was very fond of Henry and he liked the
y's spirit. But I was against it.

'He is but a child, Charles,' I said. 'He needs to be educated and
ere better than in Paris? It would be a sin to take him away
m his lessons at his age.'

Charles saw this in time and Henry suffered bitter disappoint-
nt.

Charles said: 'I promise you, brother, that in a few years you
ill be at my side.'

And Henry had to be satisfied with that.

Before Charles left for Cologne where he had decided to stay
a while, he spoke very seriously to me. 'Henry is a Protestant,'
said. 'He is a Prince of a Protestant country. He must remain
You must not try to make him a Catholic, Mam.'

That had been exactly my intention and he knew it.

hesitated and Charles went on: 'If you do not give me your
omise, I cannot leave him with you. I shall either take him with
or send him to my sister Mary who, as you know, was loth to
t with him.'

So I promised and Charles left. But after he had gone I thought
t although I had promised, to bring up my son in the true Faith
uld be such a good thing that it would outweigh anything that
s wrong in breaking a promise.

Henry had brought with him Mr Lovell, the tutor whom
Countess of Leicester had given him when he was at Penshu
The two were devoted to each other and Mr Lovell was a fi
Protestant. Charles favoured Mr Lovell because he had been su
a good tutor and had been in fact responsible in some measure
the release of Henry. The tutor had personally gone to Lond
and seen several of the leading men in Cromwell's governme
and because Mr Lovell was a good Protestant they listened
him, and his advocacy and the death of Elizabeth had be
factors in their decision to release Henry.

Charles said Mr Lovell was a faithful servant, the sort wise m
grapple to them with bands of steel.

Mr Lovell would stand in my way, I knew, and I might have
get rid of him, but I must work carefully and not let him kn
what I planned.

I was feeling more alive now that I had my two youngest w
me and I could plan for them both. Henriette, the best loved
them all, gave me cause for anxiety. She was rather thin a
delicate. I wished that she were more of a conventional beau
although she had great charm and a lovely skin, her back, l
mine, was not quite straight. I watched over her anxiously. I h
great plans for her, which must be kept secret. I did not see w
she should not marry her cousin Louis, in spite of the Grar
Mademoiselle's pretensions. What a glorious prospect! My li
one Queen of France. But why not? They both had the sa
grandfather; she was the daughter of the King of England, a
although the French government was so cruel and misguided
to recognize Cromwell, kings were still kings.

I was beside myself with joy when she was invited to take p
in a ballet in which the King and his brother, Anjou, would ta
part. Henriette danced to perfection and I doubted there w
anyone at Court who was as light on her feet as my chi
And when she danced all that dainty elusive charm w
apparent.

What a delight it was when the curtain rose on that scene
reveal my nephew Louis XIV, who was then about fifte
magnificently attired as Apollo on the throne with the Mu
around him. The piece was the wedding of Peleus and Thetis a
my little Henriette had her part to play in it. I sat watching h
with my eyes filled with tears, sighing and regretting that l

r could not be beside me to applaud our most enchanting
.

hopes were high. She was eminently suitable to be the
of the young King.

d turned my attention to Henry and was finding him rather
born little boy. When I talked to him about the glories of the
lic Church he replied: 'That may be, Mam, but it is not for
promised my father that I would cling to the Faith in which I
aptized and which is the Faith of my country.'
ughed. 'Oh, you are such a dear little boy and it is good to
mber your father, but if only he were here he would under-
. Think what the men of that Faith did to him.'
romised him, Mam,' he said firmly.
ll, he was young and he would be pliable. I would achieve
I wanted in time and that would mean that two of my
ren were saved. In the meantime, to show his independ-
Henry went off every Sunday to the Protestant service
the English residents in Paris had set up.
t if he was determined, so was I. He had a strong supporter
Lovell and I was wondering more and more how I could get
him. To have him dismissed openly – which was what I
d have liked to do – would have caused an outcry. Charles
d hear of it and Charles was the King, whose word had to be
d, even by his mother. My children were not so ready to
ge me as their father had been.
e idea struck me that if I could send Henry away to some
vned tutor, the services of Mr Lovell would no longer be
red. I thought of Walter Montague who was the Abbot of St
n's near Pontoise and also my Grand Almoner. He was a
friend of mine and an ardent Catholic, having been con-
d nearly twenty years before when he had witnessed the
isms of the Ursuline nuns at Loudon. We had been friends
ince he had come to France at the time of my marriage, and
his conversion we had become much closer. He would
rstand at once what I wanted and would be as keen as I was
n my son into a Catholic.
nt word to Charles explaining that Henry was too fond of
ciety of idle boys and that I believed he should be sent to

some quiet place to study. What better than to Pontoise v
our good friend the Abbot could supervise his education.

I could not dismiss Mr Lovell or Charles would have beer
suspicious and he would not believe that Henry had go
Pontoise without his good tutor merely to study quietly.

It must have been disconcerting for Mr Lovell to be the
Protestant – with Henry – in a Catholic community and very
he did not see how he could remain there. It was not diffic
suggest that he take a little trip to Italy as I believed he had a
wanted to see that country.

I was relieved when he went without fuss, not knowing tl
had talked to Henry, explained my motives and those (
Abbot and urged him to stand firm until he could let his bre
the King, know what was happening.

The Abbot wrote to me that he had high hopes that the
version would be soon. He had talked to the boy of the pos
ties which lay before him. As Duke of Gloucester, son of one
and brother to another, he would have special advantages.
a great honour to wear the Cardinal's hat.

But Henry did not see it that way. 'The boy has a strong
wrote Montague. 'He says he cannot attempt to defeat i
argument but he knows what is right and what his br
expects of him and nothing will shake him in his determinat
do his duty. He insists that his father told him to adhere
Faith in which he was baptized and his brother, the King, w
him to do the same. He added: "You can do what you like to
will cling to my Faith as I promised my father before he die

As the weeks passed the Abbot was growing more and
impatient and Henry more stubborn. The boy wrote to me a
for leave to return to Paris, and seeing that it was no use ke
him there, I gave my permission.

When he arrived I noticed the firm set of his lips. I could s
brother Charles in him and it was ironical to realize that the
inherited their determination to have their own way from m
their father.

Henry was clever too and I was incensed when I heard tl
had sent for Bishop Cosin to ask his advice as to how he sl
answer the Abbot when he was cross-examined by him. (
was a staunch Protestant and a real enemy of the Catholic
husband had sent him to Paris to act as chaplain to those (

sehold who belonged to the Church of England and at first he
worked from a private house until that had proved to be
equate when a chapel had been fitted up to accommodate the
nding congregation. Cosin was a man highly respected by
At first I had believed I could convert him. He would certainly
have been accepted in England now because he was almost as
h opposed to the Puritans as he was to the Catholics. He loved
rituals and ceremonies of the Church just as Archbishop Laud
though whereas that had been Laud's undoing, Cosin, who
escaped to France, prospered. Nothing could have been
er from the truth than to imagine he would turn to Catholic-
He was fundamentally against it, and because he was one of
greatest speakers of the day, he was feared while he was
ected.

think that my son Henry had gone to him made me anxious
determined that something must be done at once.

sent Henry back to Pontoise; but this time he had papers
h had been written for him by Cosin and naturally the
port of such a man increased his obstinacy.

determined to act drastically and to send him to the Jesuit
ege of Clermont. When Henry heard what was to happen he
white with rage. Once in a Jesuit college he would be unable
cape. He stormed at me: 'I would rather be the prisoner of the
ndheads at Carisbroke,' he cried. 'At least I was not bullied
to go against my conscience.'

ou are a wicked boy,' I told him. 'You will be grateful one day
n you see the light.'

was on the very morning when he was about to depart that
sengers arrived in haste from the King. There were letters for
nd for Henry. Charles reproached me for having forgotten
promises not only to him but to my husband. There were
rs of rebuke for several of my friends and particularly Henry
yn who, said the King, could have restrained me from my
ponsible actions.

orst of all was the letter to Henry.

ead it myself for Henry could not resist showing it to me. I
incensed because Charles began by saying he was in receipt
enry's letter. So the boy had actually dared write to him!

. . it is the Queen's purpose to do all she can to change your
ion in which if you do hearken to her, you might never see

England or me again. . . . Consider well what it is to be . .
only the cause of ruining a brother who loves you well but
your King and country. . . .

'I am informed that there is a purpose to send you to a Jes
College which I command you, in the same grounds, nev
consent to. . . .'

What could have been more devastating to my plans!

When I read the letter I let it drop to the floor and took H
into my arms.

'Dear child,' I said, 'my thoughts are all for you. I wanted
to push aside these temptations . . . nothing matters so mu
the salvation of your soul.'

'I am determined to save it,' said the young rebel, 'by doin
duty to my King, my country and my religion – and that i
religion into which I was baptized.'

His eyes were blazing. So were mine. How could a son b
disobedient to his mother! I asked angrily.

'I am obedient to my King and my conscience,' said Henry

Where had he learned such things? From Cosin, I suppos

'Go to your apartments,' I said. 'I will send Abbé Montag
you. You must listen to him.'

'I am weary of listening to him. My mind is made up.'

All my calm deserted me. I saw only a disobedient son for w
I had worked and planned. Charles, James, Mary . . . they we
turning against me. And now Henry . . . aided by his brothe

I cried out in fury: 'If you do not embrace the Catholic relig
never want to see you any more.'

Henry looked at me in amazement.

'Yes,' I cried. 'Go! Get out of my sight. You are a wic
ungrateful boy.'

Henry went and I did not see him until a few days later. I
on my way to Chaillot. I needed the peace of the place wh
could contemplate this breach in the family. I could not bea
most of all to see Henriette weeping all over the place. She
been so happy when Henry came; they were always talking a
Charles's adventures and how wonderful it would be whe
regained his throne. And now Henry was in disgrace. She c
not understand it and I could not bear the sight of her
woebegone face. So I would go to my beloved Chaillot for a
days.

I was about to leave the palace Henry ran out and came to

am,' he said quietly, and I knew he was asking that we forget grievances which I should have been so happy to do if he ld only fall in with my wishes; but he was as firm as ever in so I turned my face away from him.

vas smiling grimly on the way to Chaillot. I would show the what it meant to defy me. I was the Queen of England tever those Puritans said. I was also his mother.

heard afterwards that he left me and went straight to the estant service – for it was a Sunday – but when he returned to Palais Royal it was to find that there was no food for him and even the sheets had been taken from his bed to indicate that was no longer a place for him there.

was Henriette who told me what had happened because he come to say goodbye to her before he left. She was heart-en.

ere were Protestants in Paris to rally to his help. Lord Hatton Lord Ormonde both hastily came forward and that very my son Henry left Paris for Cologne. It was what he had ted in the first place. He had gone to join his brother les.

vas very upset by what I called Henry's desertion. Queen e comforted me. She too had hoped that my son would cease a heretic. We were at Chaillot together where we often ussed the difficulties of life. I reminded her that she had little mplain of. She had two fine boys and Louis, now seventeen, ed secure on the throne; he was growing more and more ly every day.

e smiled with pleasure. She doted on her elder son and I d well understand it. He did not bring her the sorrow my ren brought me.

worry a great deal,' I said. 'The months pass and the years and my son is still without his throne and every day the ed rebels of England would seem to grow stronger and use of their strength are accepted by others in a manner h is difficult to understand.'

could not resist reminding her of my resentment that

members of my own family should be ready to make treaties
the roundheaded traitors.

It was not Anne's fault, of course. She was not the
governor of France – merely the Regent – and with Louis gro
up she would not be that much longer. She mentioned
Cromwell now called himself the Lord Protector and tha
people appeared to be accepting him.

'I worry a great deal about my little Henriette. What
become of her? Here she is Princess . . . daughter of the Ki
England . . . living as she does!'

'We must give a ball for her.'

'Oh dear sister, you are so good, but we could not affor
gown . . . and all the necessities. It would be a travesty of w
ball for a Princess of England should be.'

Anne was thoughtful. Then she said: 'I will give some
parties in my apartments. The King and his brother will be
and a few well chosen younger people. Henriette shall com
show us how well she dances.'

I was excited. We could fit her up in a dress which wou
suitable for such an occasion; she was only eleven years old a
and the small party would be ideal.

I was very anxious for her to become good friends wit
cousin. Louis was by no means unkind. He loved to danc
Henriette was the best dancer at Court. I can say that
honestly, setting aside all maternal pride. She was delicate
dainty and she had appeared to enchant people when she
appeared in the *Nuptials of Peleus and Thetis*.

I was thinking: She is only eleven; Louis is seventeen. Th
time. Oh, if only Charles could regain his throne his sister w
be a fitting mate for the King of France.

How I looked forward to that occasion. Little did I realize
mortified I was going to be; and my little Henriette too.

I went back to Henriette and told her that she was going
assembly in the Queen's apartments. 'It will be your party rea
said, 'for I suspect the Queen is giving it for you. She will insis
the King is there. Have you practised your steps? You mus
disgrace us. You will be dancing with the King of France and
my darling, shall be as great an honour for him as it is for you

Henriette said: 'Mam, you say strange things at times.
could that be?'

Never forget you are the daughter of a King of England.'

How wonderful it would be if Charles could win his throne
␣ we could all go back to England. I can think of nothing to
␣sh for which would please me more than to live with Charles
␣ ever.'

␣oolish child's talk! When he regained the throne she should
␣ be here. Queen of France. I wanted nothing less for my
␣ourite child. She was the only one who had not disappointed
␣ – except Elizabeth, who had in a way disappointed me by
␣ing, poor darling.

␣he great day came. How charming my little Henriette looked!
␣r dress might not have been splendid – La Grande Made-
␣iselle would have smiled at its simplicity had she been present
␣ I was thankful that she was not. How I should laugh if my
␣nriette carried off the prize which she – ridiculous old spinster
␣vas hoping to catch. Louis would never agree to marry a
␣man older than himself. It was becoming clear that Louis
␣uld have his way. 'He is young yet,' I had said to Anne. 'But
␣ wait. That one has a will of his own and knows what is due to
␣n.'

␣He always did have,' said Anne proudly; and she recalled the
␣ident when he had been taken to see the Carmelite nuns –
␣ich I had heard at least twenty times – when he had turned his
␣k on them and showed great interest in the latch of the door.
␣ne loved to relate it because of his words. She had ordered him
␣stop playing with the latch and pay attention to the nuns. 'But
␣ a good latch,' he had said, 'and the King likes it.' 'I reproved
␣n,' said Anne, 'for his ill manners towards ladies and holy
␣ns at that. "Come, say a word of greeting to them," I pleaded.
␣uis replied. "I will say nothing. I wish to play with this latch.
␣t one day I shall speak so loudly that I shall make myself
␣rd." ' Whether he actually said that or whether Anne embel-
␣ed it to make it sound prophetic I was not sure. She was really
␣otted with her little King.

␣Vell, he was not so little now and he was going to dance with
␣nriette. He must. Etiquette would demand that he ask first the
␣y of highest rank and as neither I nor his mother would dance,
␣vould have to be Henriette.

␣ was seated beside Anne on a small dais. Henriette was just
␣ow us; the musicians were there but no one could dance until

the King did and he had not yet made his entrance. It woul(
such a pleasure to sit here beside Anne while we watched
beloved children together. She would have her eyes on Loui
the time but I would point out to her the grace of Henriette
what a charming couple they made . . . so graceful . . . so *roy*

Louis had arrived. He really did look quite magnificent. He
growing up. He was very sure of himself, very much the Kir
glanced at Anne whose eyes were glowing with pride.

Everyone stood up as he entered except Anne and myself
he came to the dais and took first his mother's hand, which
kissed, and then mine.

Now that the King had arrived the musicians began to p
Louis looked round the company; he seemed just a little bo
Nobody of course could dance until he did and everyone
eager for him to select a partner – which must be Henriette –
open the dance.

Louis did not seem in any hurry. I was watching him clo
and I saw his eyes alight on Henriette but instead of approach
her he selected some relation of Cardinal Mazarin – a g
looking woman several years his senior.

The Queen was not very easily aroused to anger but she
always been adamant that etiquette should be observed. No
do so was one of the few things which could really upset her.

She could not allow this to pass although it would have b
easier for us all if she had. She rose rather unsteadily; like my
she had got cramped through sitting too long. She was beside
King just as he was offering his arm to the woman.

'Dearest,' she whispered but so that all those around cc
hear, 'you have forgotten that the Princess Henriette is h
Your first dance should be with her.'

'I shall dance with whom I wish,' retorted Louis.

I could bear no more. This was an insult to my daughter. It
to stop at once. I dashed out onto the floor and laid a hand
Anne's arm. I said quickly and so that all could hear:
daughter cannot dance tonight. She has hurt her foot.'

Anne, who rarely lost her temper, did so at that moment.
had, out of the kindness of her heart, arranged this gathering
Henriette. That there should have been a breach of etiquette
such an occasion was more than she could endure and th(
should have been caused by her son, who was the very centr

ife – with his brother, of course – was enough to make her
r break through her usual lethargy.

ad never seen her so angry. She said: 'If the Princess is
le to dance tonight then the King cannot either.'

ith that she called Henriette to her. My poor child, overcome
shame, must of course obey the summons. When she was
enough Queen Anne took her hand and rammed it into that
uis.

ance!' she commanded.

uis looked at the frightened little girl whose hand he held
I think he felt some contrition for he was not naturally unkind
he must suddenly have realized how he had slighted her in
resence of many people.

ey danced – but there was no life in either of them. He gave
daughter a rather wintry smile and said: 'It is not your fault,
riette. It is just that I am in no mood for children tonight.'

e was in a sombre frame of mind for the rest of the evening.
t did that matter? It was spoilt in any case.

e incident had a deep effect on Henriette. More than ever
wanted to get away and join her brother Charles.

e months passed. There was no good news from Charles; he
living that unsatisfactory life of peregrinations to which his
had driven him. Henry was with him and, said Charles, very
py to be there. He was going to make a fine soldier. I did not
t to hear of Henry.

ly children were a disappointment to me . . . except
riette, and if I could get her married to Louis I would snap my
ers at everything else and say that all I had done was worth
le.

leanwhile we went on in this monotonous and most unsatis-
ory manner.

hen my daughter Mary proposed to come to Paris.

was not very pleased with Mary since she had defied me over
ing her son. William! What a dreadful name! It could not
pare with Charles. I knew that the House of Orange was
ttered with Williams but how much more appropriate Charles
ld have been . . . in loving memory of her father and in hope
her brother. But Mary had to be obstinate, as her brothers

were. She had to have her way and was more influenced b
overbearing mother-in-law of hers than by me. So naturally
not feeling very pleased with my daughter.

She had written that she had not been well for some tim
thought a trip to Paris would be beneficial to her. I wrote bac
said that she would probably like to stay at Chaillot whicl
ideal for an invalid who needed to rest.

Mary very soon made it clear that she had not come to P₂
rest. She had brought with her a collection of clothes and j
with which she hoped to impress the French Court. They
have cost a great deal, I commented; I did not add that i
money which might have gone to her brother's cause,
implied it. Of course I had to admit that Mary had done a
deal to help Charles and she had always made her Court a h
for him when he needed it. I was, naturally, a little angry wit
still about being so insistent in getting her own way ove
name of her son.

I had to admit that she was very pretty; she had lovely b
hair with a tinge of red in it and eyes like topaz. Not only di
not wish to stay at Chaillot but expressed only the mildest int
in my beautiful retreat. Her gaiety and good looks made her
popular and the Queen immediately liked her and made sur
was invited to meet all the most interesting people at the Co

I was pleased that she was popular and then I noticed th
her retinue was Edward Hyde's daughter and I thought it
inconsiderate of Mary to have brought the girl to Paris.

'I never liked Edward Hyde,' I said. 'I cannot understand
your brother thinks so highly of him.'

'Because he is clever, Mam,' retorted Mary. 'Charles n
men like Edward Hyde about him. All rulers should have
men to rely on.'

'*I* never liked him,' I said firmly. 'You know this and yet
bring his daughter in your train.'

'*I* quite like the girl.'

'But you know I would rather not see any of the Hyde fam

'I do not feel so and being mistress in my own househo
choose those I like.'

I was hurt. I could not understand why my children wer
inconsiderate towards me.

I was quite amused, however, when the Queen made it kn

she thought it inappropriate for widows to dance, which
nt that Mary had to sit beside the Queen and me to watch.
was not really very old and she did seem to forget that she
a widow. I wondered whether she would marry again and
ther I should be looking round for a suitable husband for her.
ould not surprise me if she told me that was no affair of mine.
ne of the balls given for Mary was that of the Duc d'Anjou.
Duc was there looking what I can only describe as 'pretty'.
had such a flair for clothes and the colours he chose were quite
isite. His jewellery was lovely too. The Queen confided in
:hat young Philippe was not in the least like his brother. Louis
all for manly sports but Philippe liked better to discuss
nes, to design them and choose materials; and he had said
he liked women's clothes better than men's and oddly
ugh sometimes dressed in them. He was a graceful dancer
when he partnered Henriette they looked beautiful dancing
ther. I think they were acknowledged to be the best dancers
ie Court and this made quite a bond between them. But what
sed me most about the ball was that the King was there, and
time, without hesitation, he chose Henriette to open it with
. It showed my little girl was growing up and could no longer
egarded as a child.
prayed fervently that Charles would regain his throne and
Louis and Henriette would marry. Anne had hinted to me
she was very fond of Henriette and that she would welcome
as a daughter-in-law if it were possible for the pair of them to
ry, of course.
it Louis was the King of France and Henriette . . . ? Well she
the daughter of a King who had lost his throne with his head,
the sister of a King who had not yet regained that throne and
wed little sign of doing so.
)h Lord,' I prayed. 'Give Charles his throne . . . soon, and
riette Louis.'
ll the festivities at that time were in honour of Mary. The King
manded that a ballet should be performed for her pleasure;
of course Henriette danced in it. The Queen gave a banquet
Mary, and the Grande Mademoiselle, not to be outdone
ough still in exile from the Court, invited her to the *Château* of
ly where she put on a very grand entertainment. Mary and
lemoiselle got on remarkably well. I couldn't help feeling that

Mary was a little too talkative and that Mademoiselle led he
and I was sure she was going to repeat everything Mary said
hoped my daughter would not be too indiscreet. When I saw
lavish manner in which Mademoiselle entertained I tho
again what a suitable wife she would make for Charles, a
deeply regretted that all that money which was being waste
lavish clothes, jewels, food, wines and spectacle could n
used to raise an army for Charles.

I did get a chance to talk to her. I thought she was looking
and she had never been a beauty. No one would have thoug
marrying her if it were not for her fortune; and after so n
proposed marriages which had come to nothing she mus
wondering whether she was going to get married at all.

I said: 'You must be wondering how Charles is faring.'

'Oh? Must I?'

She was insolent. Foolish woman! If she was not carefu
would remain a spinster all her days.

'He is in love with you, you know,' I said. 'He does not thi
any other woman.'

'I was under the impression that he thought a good deal ab
number of them.'

'I am talking of marriage.'

'Oh, dear little aunt, I cannot believe it is I who am the cau
his single state rather than the fact that he is scarcely in a pos
to keep himself let alone a wife.'

'He has been so upset. When he was here he and I quarr
often. It is because he is unhappy that he is so quarrelsome.
had a wife, I am sure we should be on far better terms.'

'Dear Majesty,' she said lightly, 'if he cannot live happily
you, why should he do so with someone else?'

I could have slapped her simpering face. She was mocking
She knew I only wanted her money for Charles. Indeed what
could I want from her?

She always contrived to spoil any occasion for me. Even
sight of my little Henriette stepping a measure with a hands
nobleman with such grace could not restore my good humo

There was something else which disturbed me very de
although I did not realize then how very significant it w
prove to be. This was the growing attitude of my son Ja
towards Anne Hyde. He was a few years older than she was

e his brother Charles had always had an eye for women. It was
rait in them which they did not get from their father or from
e. But I often wonder whether it actually came through me as it
ɔuld not surprise me in the least if Charles at any rate should
come such another as my father had been as far as women were
ncerned.

I had seen James follow Anne Hyde surreptitiously. Once I
ɛnt after them and my suspicions were confirmed. My son was
ɪbracing the young woman and she was making a great show
reluctance which was an absolute indication of her willingness.
At that time my irritation was simply because I disliked the
ydes. Then it occurred to me that although it was not disastrous
r my sons to have passing love affairs with women like Lucy
alter, who could be cast aside when the matter had run itself
t, it was not quite the same thing with the daughter of a man in
dward Hyde's position.

I decided to tackle James.

I said: 'It has come to my ears that you are indulging in an
ɪour with Anne Hyde.'

'You mean it has come to your eyes, Mam,' retorted James. 'I
ɪs aware of you . . . spying on us.'

I was amazed at the insolence of my children. First Henry, then
ary, now James. At least Charles was always respectful
hough he ignored my advice – and Charles was the King and
ɪght have been forgiven a little assertiveness.

'I consider it my duty. . . .'

He dared to interrupt. 'Oh, Mam, a little amusement is not a
atter of state.'

'I would rather you gave up this woman.'

'I would rather not,' he replied.

'James!'

'Yes, Mam.'

'You are my son.'

'Dear Mam, I know that well, but I am of age, you know. I am
 longer a child and I cannot brook interference with my
rsonal affairs.'

There were dangerous lights in his eyes. He had a temper to
atch mine and was the easiest of my children to quarrel with.
ɪt of sympathy with Mary as I was, I did not want trouble with
nes.

With great restraint I sighed and said: 'I beg of you to take ca
This is the daughter of Edward Hyde of whom your broth
seems to think so highly. She is not a woman like that Lu
Walter who was at the centre of that disgraceful affair with yo
brother, which I am sure did him a great deal of harm and
doubt held him back from his throne.'

'That's ridiculous,' cried James. 'Charles had a very pleasa
time with Lucy. She's a nice creature and you know how Char
dotes on young James . . . when he sees him.'

'I cannot bear to hear such talk. I wish you were like your fath
. . . both of you.'

James looked solemn then as mention of the late King co
always make him. He was going to make some bitter retor
think, but he did not do so. I felt more gentle towards him a
said: 'Take care, James.'

He softened too. The moment when his temper was about
flare up had passed.

'Don't fret, Mam,' he said. 'I can take care of my own affai
You should not concern yourself with them.'

It was tantamount to what Mary had told me. Keep out of
business. It is no affair of yours. Oddly enough both incide
revolved about Anne Hyde. It was foolish to allow such a s
simpering creature to make trouble for me. She was not ve
bright, I gathered, though I had to admit she had a cert
feminine appeal.

It would pass, I promised myself; and I did not want to quar
any more with members of my family.

Soon after that came news from Holland. Little William h
developed measles and very reluctantly Mary tore herself aw
from the delights of Paris to go to him.

The time was passing and nothing seemed to change mu
except that I was growing poorer. I found it so hard to exist on
pension for I felt I owed it to Charles to live as royally as possib
did not want anyone to lose sight of the fact that I was the moth
of the King of England.

I was growing tired of ceremonies – not that so many came
way, but I disliked sitting with Queen Anne watching some ba
or dance. She was not the most exciting of companions, althou

od forbid that I should criticize one who had shown me such
ndness. I often wondered how I could go on without her help,
ad sometimes I thought longingly of the life of some noble lady
ho was not close to Court and did not have to worry constantly
hether she was receiving the respect due to her, who did not
ave to provide certain clothes that she might not appear shabby,
ho did not have to keep a retinue of servants whose wages she
ould not afford.

Yes, it would indeed be pleasant to retire to the country, with
enry Jermyn, of course – that dear faithful man who was getting
o fat now but still retained his healthy complexion and was quite
andsome for his years. I should like to find little Geoffrey again.
often smiled to think how he had stepped out of the pie and
ome to me. What a happy and amusing introduction and what a
ad parting it had been!

Yes, I should like to retire to the country, but I had a daughter
or whom I must find a husband. Henriette was my main concern
the only one of my children to be a Catholic and to live close to
e. I watched her all the time, worrying about her fragile looks –
ae child was so thin and looked so pale often – and marvelling at
er grace when she danced, delighting when she received invita-
ons to assemblies at which the King would be present. But when
ae went to these entertainments I was always anxious as to
hether she would receive her due respect and whether it would
e remembered that she was a princess, a king's daughter, next in
recedence to the Queen and myself.

Nothing ever went smoothly and there were so many upsets.
or one thing Louis was in love and because he was so inexperi-
aced the whole Court knew it. Marie Mancini was one of the
even beautiful nieces whom Mazarin had brought to France
om Italy and no sooner had they arrived than they had become
rominent because of their outstanding good looks. Marie I
ought the least beautiful; her sister Hortense was quite start-
agly so. However it was Marie who caught Louis's attention and
e was quite obsessed by her. Anne told me that he had come to
er and told her that he wished to marry Marie.

'Marry her!' I cried indignantly. 'He must be mad.'

Anne was thoughtful and I was alarmed. 'He says he cannot
ve without her,' she said.

'He is but a child!'

Anne was staring ahead of her and I was suddenly filled wi
horror. What of all those stories I had heard about Anne ar
Mazarin? Some said she had actually married him. Could sh
really be considering a marriage between the King of France ar
the niece of the Cardinal?

She looked at me helplessly. 'He will clearly have to marr
soon.'

'I have great hopes that Charles will recover his crown. I hear
only yesterday that a wise man had prophesied that he would h
back within the next few years.'

'I should like him to marry an Infanta of Spain from my ow
country,' said Anne frankly. 'But if that failed my next choi
would be Henriette, whom you know I love as a daughter. He h
a will of his own.' Her eyes shone with pride. She admired th
quality in her son which I deplored in my children. 'I have spoke
to him.'

'Of Henriette?'

She nodded.

'He loves her I believe,' I almost whispered.

'Yes he loves her . . . as a sister. He says he is sorry for h
because she is so frail and poor and unwell . . . His heart is set c
Marie Mancini.'

'That is quite impossible.'

She hesitated and then said: 'I have spoken to the Cardinal.'

I stared at her in horror. She had spoken to the Cardinal! Sh
must be mad. Of course the Cardinal would do everything h
could to bring about the marriage.

Her next words surprised me. 'The Cardinal says it is impo
sible.'

'His own niece!'

'Yes. He is such a wise man. He said it would go against roy
tradition. The people would never agree to it and would probab
rise against it. And they would blame him. He says unthinkir
people always blame their rulers for anything that goes wror
even when it is in no way connected with them. He said
marriage between Louis and Marie Mancini would be disastrou
for the country . . . and for the Cardinal himself.'

'He is a very wise man.'

'The wisest,' said Anne fondly. 'But Louis is angry. Oh, sister
shall have to find a bride for him soon.'

thought: It must be Henriette. I have set my heart on Louis for
rriette. If I could see Henriette Queen of France I would go
y, live quietly and leave the rest to fate.

here came another irritation and once more it concerned the
nde Mademoiselle. Wherever she was there was trouble. She
no longer banned from Court on account of activities in the
nde and was now to be seen at functions as flamboyant as
r, though perhaps a little faded. Cardinal Mazarin had invited
to a supper party at which the King and the Duc d'Anjou
ıld be present. I was always so delighted to take Henriette
ere the King was, and it was a pleasant evening apart from one
dent. As we were leaving Mademoiselle walked out ahead of
daughter, which was tantamount to saying that she came
ore Henriette in precedence.

had gone out just ahead of them and had expected Henriette
e immediately behind me and was very angry when I dis-
ered what had happened and inwardly railed against
demoiselle, wishing that she could be exiled forever.

hat was not the end of the matter for what had happened
e to the Cardinal's ears. He was a stickler for etiquette and
most annoyed, first because one of the laws of protocol had
n ignored and secondly because Henriette and I had been at
supper party as his guests.

few days later there was a party at his apartments to which
King, the Duc d'Anjou and Mademoiselle had been invited.
tunately neither I nor Henriette were present but there were
nty of people to report to me what had been said.

he Cardinal asked Mademoiselle if it was true that she had
en precedence over the Princess Henriette while the King and
Duc d'Anjou were listening.

: was the Duc d'Anjou who answered. He said very loudly so
t all could hear: 'And what if my cousin did? Why should
ple who rely on us for their food and lodging take precedence
r us? If they do not like the treatment they get here, they
uld go somewhere else.'

was terribly upset. So they regarded us as beggars! And this to
e from the brother of the King – and Louis stood by and did
hing about it. It was more than I could endure.

he horrible realization came to me that they were getting tired
s.

I was so upset that I went to see the Cardinal and I told him
it was humiliating to accept a pension from the Queen. She
bountiful and had been a wonderful friend to me; I could n
repay her for all she had done in my times of need; but I w
like to be independent of her. I thought that as I was the Quee
England who had brought a dowry with her when I marrie
King, I should have some of that dowry back now. It was no
Queen of France who should be paying me a pension, but
English Parliament.

Mazarin shook his head. 'Your Majesty cannot really be
that the English Parliament would give you a pension!'

'I don't know. You have become friendly with this O
Cromwell. You say he is a man of integrity. Let us see somet
of that quality.'

'Such a request could only end in failure.'

'Will you make it?'

'If you insist.'

'I do,' I told him.

The result was more than failure. It was insulting. As I
never been crowned Queen of England the Parliament did
consider me as such.

When I heard those words I was so furious that I lost
temper with the Cardinal.

'Are they suggesting that I was the King's concubine? Is
King of France going to stand aside and hear that said of his a
the daughter of his grandfather. . . .'

Mazarin said quietly: 'They have merely said that as you v
not crowned you lack the rights of a queen. I believe the re
that you were not crowned was your own objection to
ceremony.'

'I can see,' I said, 'that you are ready to accept the logic of y
dear friend Oliver Cromwell.'

Anne asked me to see her. She was a good kind woman a
wished that she did not bore me so much for I should be t
grateful.

She said: 'I know how you long for a place of your own
somewhere not too large . . . somewhere where you could
away from Court and live quietly when you are in the mood t
so.'

'I have Chaillot.'

I did not mean a convent. I meant a little home. I do under-
nd for I often feel I should like to do the same myself. It is
possible for me, of course, though perhaps later when Louis is
arried and has growing children . . . who knows? But I have
en thinking of you, sister. Life is very hard for you.'

You speak truth there. I am poor and dependent, and I and my
ughter are the targets for insults.'

Oh, that affair of the Grande Mademoiselle. I do not take her
ry seriously.'

Her behaviour touches me little. It was the remarks of the Duc
Anjou. . . .'

Philippe sometimes speaks without thinking. I have repri-
anded him strongly for his lack of courtesy. I think he was
ntrite. Let us look round for a suitable place. Do you remember
e pleasure we had over Chaillot?'

Oh, Anne, dear sister, you are so good and kind.'

I understand your feelings so well,' she replied. 'I should like
make life a little easier for you.'

I could never afford to buy such a place if I found it.'

Let us first look for the place and then consider that.'

The dear generous creature was comforting me again.

The outcome was that together we discovered the small *château*
the village of Colombes. It was only seven miles from Paris and
t in the heart of the country. The village was beautiful and
aceful as only such villages can be, brooded over by the church
th its twelfth-century tower. The *château* was small, like a
untry house rather than a castle and I knew that I could be
ppy in it.

I was considerably cheered when Anne and I planned together
at furniture would be put in it and when the place was com-
ted it was indeed a haven.

Perhaps that was the beginning of better days. It was not long
er – a beautiful September day in the year 1658 – when the
essenger came to Colombes where I was staying.

I knew he had some exciting news to tell me for he could
rcely wait.

'A message for the Queen,' he cried. 'Oliver Cromwell is dead!'

So England had a new Lord Protector – Richard Cromwell, son
Oliver.

The Court was buzzing with the news and messages w
coming all the time from England. Richard was not the man
father had been; he lacked authority; he had no desire to gove
he was too soft; some said he was more like the martyred K
than Oliver's son.

What now? everyone was asking.

After the first months the excitement died down and it seem
as though Charles was no nearer winning his rights from Rich.
than he had been from Oliver.

Still, the old ogre was dead and we continued to hear that
new Protector lacked those qualities which had brought victory
his father.

Anne was growing more and more eager to find a bride
Louis and my niece Marguerite, daughter of my sister Christi
was brought to Paris, on trial as it were. She was a very plain
and older than Louis. He took an instant dislike to her and I v
sorry for Marguerite but relieved all the same on account
Henriette.

It was quite clear that Louis had a mind of his own. He was b
the delight and terror of his mother's life. But she was bes
herself with joy when the Cardinal was able to tell her t
his clever diplomacy had not only brought about peace w
Spain but the promise of the Infanta Marie Theresa as bride
Louis.

It was what she had always wanted and she could not hide
joy, although she tried to from me, knowing my aspirations
Henriette.

But I was accustomed to disappointments and I could not h
feeling a twinge of relief that at least my sister Christine's p
daughter had not been chosen. I now had to accept that Henrie
would never be Queen of France.

The French Court had gone to the Spanish border to meet
Spanish Infanta, and Henriette and I remained in Paris. H
glad I was that we did! I had taken Henriette to Colombes w
me. She was rather sad. I do believe that she was a little in l
with Louis and it must have been painful for her to have be
rejected by him, even though she could console herself that
main reason was that she was a dependant on his Court and t

d her brother regained his throne there might have been a
atch between them.

I was seated in my favourite room with some of my friends
hen a visitor was announced and a tall dark man came into the
om.

'Charles!'

It was indeed. Changed after all the years. It must have been six
nce I had seen him and we had parted not such good friends on
count of Henry. In spite of the change in him he had lost none
that charm which was going to smooth his path through life.

He said: 'A fleeting visit, Mam. I do not think it will be long
w. I verily believe they are going to ask me to go back.'

Then he turned and seizing one of my most handsome ladies
ked her up in his arms and kissed her fervently. We were all
tonished – until he called her his dear sister Henriette. Then I
alized that he had mistaken the lady for the Princess. Or had
? I wondered. Or just pretended to? It gave him an opportunity
kissing the pretty girl. I could not be sure. But no matter. He
as here and it was wonderful to see him.

I sent at once for Henriette. She ran to him and they embraced.
e affection between those two had not diminished with his
sence.

My little Henriette was almost in tears to see the brother whom
e adored. There was complete devotion between those two. I
vied it in a way. I should have liked to be on such terms with
arles but I really could not completely forgive him for taking
nry's side and I knew he could not forgive me for my
haviour towards the boy.

But it was too great an occasion for resentments.

He was excited. He was receiving letters from General Monck.
e people were tired of Puritan rule. They looked for the colour
d gaiety of a Court. They yearned for the old days. In fact they
anted the King to come home.

I dismissed all my attendants and sent them to make as grand a
eal as they could for this most honoured arrival; and when I was
one with Charles and Henriette, Charles talked of the state of
airs.

'I do not wish to say too much about this just yet,' he said, 'in
se it fails as so many attempts have before. But this is different.
is is not war. This is peace. It is not a challenge. It is an

invitation. I have a very good friend in General Monck. He wa
supporter of Cromwell at one time, but I don't think he ever to
to the way of life the Roundheads established. Oliver Cromw
did not trust him . . . and rightly so. Monck is a great character
rough soldier perhaps, but with a love for royalty. He shall
rewarded when I am back. He married his washerwoman. .
He gave me an odd look when he said that. 'Ah, that shocks yc
Mam, but I believe the lady had many desirable attributes a
one of these was that she was always an ardent royalist.'

'Do you mean he will help you regain your kingdom . . . tl
General?' I asked.

'He is *the* General, the Head of the Army. He does not like t
Roundheads' rule since Oliver died. He endured it then he s
because Oliver was a *good* ruler and a strong man. Now it
different. I will have to be asked to go back. I have no intentior
making a false start. I promise myself that when I go home it v
be to stay. I have no intention to go wandering again.'

We were too excited to eat. I was glad we were at Colombes
that we could be alone . . . just a family . . . to talk and talk .
and wait.

And so, after all our abortive attempts, all the selling
precious possessions to raise money for arms, all the traged
and defeats and disappointments, it had happened in a tota
unexpected manner.

Charles was invited to go home and on that glorious May d
of the year 1660 he landed at Dover where he was greeted
General Monck, and all the way to London the people assembl
in their crowds to throw flowers at his feet, to cheer him,
welcome him home from his exile.

This was the happiest day I had known since our troub
began.

The Restoration was truly here and I knew that life would
different for us all from now on.

Henriette

Oh yes, life had changed. My dream had come true. My son was now the King of England. I knew it could not be all joy and happiness but the great tragedy was at an end. I had no doubt that Charles would be able to hold the throne. He was not like his father. He lacked the strong moral attitudes; he had shown more than once that he would never cling rigidly to controversial doctrines if by doing so he endangered himself and his throne. He had said he had no intention of wandering again and he meant it. The people adored him already as they never had his father. How strange life was! The good man – moral, religious, virtuous in every way – failed to win them, and yet my son with his ugly looks and excessive charm of manner, his easy-going acceptance of whatever life had to offer, won their hearts in a matter of days. They loved him for his sins – for his love affairs were notorious – as they had never loved his father for his virtues.

It was wonderful for me and for Henriette to hold up our heads again.

Henriette was longing to go to London but I held off for a while as a very interesting situation had arisen.

I had greatly enjoyed the entry into Paris of Louis and his bride Marie Theresa – a rather insipid girl who made me feel how much happier it would have been for everyone if Louis and Anne had not been in such a hurry and had waited until Charles's restoration which would have made my Henriette an acceptable bride.

However, in spite of that disappointment it was a great joy to be no longer a poor supplicant.

Henriette and I sat with the Queen on a balcony of the Hôtel de Beauvais, the canopy of crimson velvet over us – completely royal now. I was proud to be of a similar rank to Anne – mothers, both of us, of reigning sovereigns and nothing to choose between us.

What a magnificent procession it was – magistrates, muske
eers, heralds and the grand equerry holding the royal sword in i
scabbard of blue velvet decorated with the golden fleurs-de-li
And then there was Louis – a King for any country to be proud c
looking magnificently regal seated on his bay horse with
brocaded canopy held over him.

The people cheered him wildly. I felt proud of my nephew ar
I was thinking of course of that other King who had made suc
another entry into his capital city a short time ago. Louis look
like a god in silver lace covered with pearls, the elegant plumes
his hat – which was pinned on by a large diamond brooch – fallir
over his shoulders. Behind him rode Philippe and I could not loc
at him without speculation. He was not the first prize, of cours
but he was a worthy second. He looked very handsome; he w
in fact better looking than his brother though he lacked Loui
manliness. He was also in silver most beautifully embroider￼
with jewels scintillating from his person. I looked sharply
Henriette. She was gazing ahead at Louis. Perhaps a little wis
fully. I was not sure.

The bride came next – not nearly beautiful and elegant enoug
for Louis. And to think it might have been Henriette riding ther
Queen of France! If only they had had the good sense to wait. N
Henriette was not such an undesirable proposition now.

Marie Theresa's coach was covered in gold lace and she herse
was dressed in material which looked like gold. She looked qui
beautiful – and who would not, so attired and in such a setting?
but a little coarse if one looked closely. And how elegant ar
ethereal *my* little one would have looked. I should not hav
dressed her in gold either. It was faintly vulgar and the brid
wore too many jewels of contrasting colours. I should hav
dressed Henriette in silver and her only jewels would have bee
diamonds.

But what was the use? The prize had gone to that little Spanis
Infanta. They would regret it, I knew.

Now I was laughing to myself for behind the bride's coac
came that of the Princesses of France and there sat the Grand
Mademoiselle. She glanced up as she passed so that we were ab
to exchange glances. I smiled at her sardonically and managed
infuse a certain condolence into the smile. She would have inte
preted it and not been very pleased, I knew. I was implying: 'M

r dear niece, so you have missed again. Dear, dear, are we
r going to find a husband for you?'

guessed now that she would have her eyes on Philippe. Oh
That must not be. The daughter of a King is of far greater
nding than the daughter of the brother of a King – particularly
who had disgraced himself by becoming involved with the
nde.

he King was on a level with the balcony now and he paused to
ute us. I noticed that his eyes lingered on Henriette and hers
him. They smiled at each other almost tenderly.

was filled with chagrin.

oo late, I thought angrily. This is another mocking trick which
has played on me.

Queen Anne embraced me warmly. It was the day after Louis's
try with his bride. She was smiling as she did when she had
nething pleasant to convey.

She said: 'I have been made so happy. My son Philippe has
en talking to me. He is in love and wishes to marry.'

My heart started to bounce about in a most uncomfortable way.
nust be Henriette. If it were not she could not look so happy.

tried to steady myself and she went on: 'He wishes to marry
nriette.'

was wildly happy. If it could not be Louis – and that was now
ite out of the question – then Philippe was the next best chance.
little Henriette would be the third lady in France and if Louis
re to die without heirs – but that little Spaniard did look as
ough she might be fertile – my Henriette could still be Queen of
ance.

'I am so delighted,' Anne was saying, 'and he is so much in
ve.'

It was hard to imagine Philippe's being in love with anyone but
mself, although he might spare some affection for that close
end of his, the Comte de Guiche, a young and extremely
ndsome nobleman, who had been married at a very early age
the heiress of the House of Sully though he had never shown
uch interest in his bride, except with regard to her fortune, and
as delighted to be Philippe's close friend.

However he was the brother of the King – next in line to the

throne at the moment, and Henriette had known him for mo
her life. When she married she would not have to go awa
should not lose her. To say the least I was delighted with
prospect.

Anne knew I should be and rejoiced with me.

'Louis has given his consent to the match and the Cardinal
favour of it.'

Of course he would be, the old fox, I thought. Close ties
Spain through Louis' marriage and with England through th
Henriette and Philippe.

It was what I wanted though, what I had angled for, and I
learned most bitterly through the latter part of my life that if
cannot get your heart's desire you must settle for the next
thing.

There was another reason for my pleasure. I knew the Gra
Mademoiselle had wanted Philippe when Louis was out of
reach, so this was a blow for her. I really did believe she was n
going to get a husband and I could not wait to see her face w
she heard that Philippe and Henriette were betrothed.

Henriette was less enthusiastic about the proposed marriag
was often difficult to know what my daughter was thinking.
looked rather sad and said: 'Does Philippe really want to m
. . . and to marry me?'

'Of course he wants to marry. It is his duty. Why, if his bro
died tomorrow he could be King of France.'

'Dear Mam, you should not say such things.'

'So even you are telling me now what I should say and w
should not say. I begin to believe that I have brought a fami
tutors into the world.'

She kissed me and said she knew how I had always loved
cared for my family and if I wished it and Philippe wished i
supposed she must marry him.

'My dear daughter,' I cried, 'you do not sound very app
ative of the second best match in France.'

'I think I would have chosen not to marry for a while. I ha
great fancy to go to England and to be near Charles.'

'Charles is the King and it is right that you should love
admire him, but he is only your brother, remember. You
your own life to lead.'

'But we *are* going to England.'

We are. As soon as I have made sure that the betrothal is firm,
shall visit your brother and then we shall come back for the
edding . . . your wedding, my dear child. I shall see my son on
throne and my best-loved child married. I really begin to see a
eat deal of brightness in the sky. It has been so dark . . . so very
rk . . . for such a long time.'

Enjoyable weeks followed. I revelled in the preparations and
ed not to think of the sea voyage which I always loathed. But it
uld be worthwhile this time. I had had the pleasure of a little
nversation with Mademoiselle who was beside herself with
lousy of Henriette. She called on me and I was sure there was a
rpose in this for in view of the betrothal I should have thought
e would have wanted to keep out of the way.

'You have come to congratulate me,' I said slyly, knowing it
as the last thing she would come to do.

'You must be very pleased that your plans have at last borne
uit,' she said.

'Plans!' I said opening my eyes very wide. 'I had no plans. I can
ll you, niece, I was amazed when the Queen told me that
nilippe had declared his love for Henriette and had stated that
e would have no other for his wife.'

'It must have been a surprise,' she said. 'One would not have
nought Philippe had time to consider such matters, he being so
reoccupied with his dear friend de Guiche.'

'Oh, he has had his eyes on Henriette for a long time. The dear
nild is overjoyed. I wish I could let you know how delightful it is
be loved by such a man.'

There was a slightly strained look on her face. 'I hear you are
lanning to visit London.'

'That is our intention. Then we shall return and the wedding
ill take place.'

'How fares the King of England?'

'Well . . . well indeed.'

'I daresay he remembers his days here in Paris . . . and some of
is old friends. It is a pity to let old friends disappear. I should like
o see the King again.'

I smiled to myself. So that is it, is it? No Louis. No Philippe.
et's try Charles.

Oh no, my dear Mademoiselle. It is too late now. Then he was
n exiled Prince. You declined him. Now he is the King of

England – and the most desirable bachelor in Europe. I
Mademoiselle, you have failed again. Too late. You should h
taken a chance.

She looked so forlorn and so clearly ageing that I felt aln
sorry for her. But she was not for Charles now – in spite of all
money.

A visit to London in the present circumstances should h
been pure delight; but life never worked out quite like that for

As we were on the point of departure news came fom Engl
which completely stunned me. I read the despatch through
could not believe it. I read it again and again. There was
mistake. This terrible thing had happened.

Henriette came in and found me almost dazed by the shocl

She sat beside me and took my hand. I snatched it away.
fury was so great that it would be restrained no longer.

'I cannot believe it,' I cried. 'I simply cannot believe it.'

'Charles . . . ' she murmured turning pale.

'Charles!' I spat out. 'He has given his consent to this folly.
they all mad?'

She begged me to tell her what had happened and I cried
'It is your brother James. He has married that scheming ha
Anne Hyde. That rogue, her father, has planned this, you ca
sure. Without my consent . . . without the King's consent . .
married her in secret.'

'He must love her dearly,' said Henriette a little wistfully.

I could have struck her – yes, even my best-loved child.

'Love!' I cried. 'She has trapped him. I saw it from the f
Mary should never have taken her into her Court. She sho
never have brought her to Paris in the first place. This is disas
My son James . . . married to that woman . . . and just in tin
seems that her bastard may be born in wedlock.'

'James would want his own child to be born in wedlock, Ma

'She wanted it. A child. It has gone as far as that. If only *I*
been there. Charles should have stopped it.'

'But they did it in secret.'

'And your brother Charles is actually receiving the woma
his Court.'

'It is because she is James's wife, Mam.'

ames's harlot! Thank God we shall soon be in England. I may
able to put a stop to all this. We might get the marriage
nulled. And Charles . . . allowing it all, shrugging his
oulders and telling them to go their merry ways. . . . He will
e his crown if he is not careful.'

Henriette was fierce as always when anything derogatory was
d about Charles. 'I think his kindness and good humour will
p him to keep it, Mam.'

could have shaken her. Was she suggesting that her father
t his crown because he was not like her brother? I turned away
m her and she said pleadingly: 'Mam, we must be kind to
es's wife.'

retorted stonily: 'James has no wife as far as I am concerned.'
She was silent for some time and then she said, perhaps think-
to turn me away from my rage, 'And there is Henry.'

stared at her in anger, which she had succeeded in increasing.
He will be there, Mam, and you remember you parted bad
nds.'

I remember what a disobedient boy he was. He defied me and I
wed I would not look on his face again.'

He will be at Court. Charles loves him dearly and has told me
t he has done good service for him. Mam, could you not forget
that? Could you not be friends? It would so please Charles,
d Henry is your son.'

I vowed to the saints that I would never see Henry until he
came a Catholic. He never has done so and until he does I shall
t see him for I would not break my vow.'

For once Henriette became quite fierce. 'You would spurn your
n child, you would hurt your son, the King, for the sake of a
w.'

A vow made to God, child.'

She turned away and did not speak. I could not bear that she,
beloved one, should be on bad terms with me and I said her
me softly. She turned back to me and threw herself into my
ns.

There were tears on her cheeks.

'There, my little one,' I said, 'we must not storm against each
er. I must be able to rely on my little Henriette.'

'Mam, then you will see Henry?'

'No, child, I do not break my vows.'

So this much-looked-forward-to visit was to be marred
James's wicked act and Henry's stubbornness. It was not
Roundheads who were making me unhappy now; it was my ⌐
family.

There was another blow waiting for me.

We had set out for Calais when we received despatches fi
London. An epidemic of small pox had invaded the capital
had claimed a number of victims. One of these was my son Hen

I felt completely numb when I read that. We had been talk
of him so recently and I was preparing myself to refuse
see him. Now I never could. Never again. I remembered w
he had been born, what pleasure his coming had given Cha
and me; and then our bitter quarrel and how he had defied
and how I had turned him away . . . stripped him of his food
lodging, even ordered that the sheets should be taken from
bed to show him that there was no home for him with me.

Poor Henriette, she was stricken with grief. It was a long t
since she had seen Henry, but she had a strong family feeling
she was particularly upset on my account because she felt th
would reproach myself.

It was some time before she could bring herself to talk o
Then she said : 'Dear Mam, you must not blame yourself.'

'Blame myself?' I cried. 'Why should I?'

'Because he died while there was this quarrel between you
because you parted in anger.'

'My dear child, everything I did was for his good. If he
embraced our Faith we should have been as happy togethe
you and I have been. I am not sorry that I kept to my v
Haven't the nuns taught you that vows are sacred when mad
God?'

'Perhaps God would have forgiven you for breaking this or
you had had the chance.'

'I have nothing with which to reproach myself,' I said firr
'Everything I did was for his good.'

But when I was alone I wept for him, wept inconsolably, f
could only remember my little baby whom I had once loved
dearly, and thinking of him – brave boy that he was – I reali
that he believed he had been right too. It was religion which
divided us, and religion had played a major part in all that
happened to me.

he fact remained I had lost a son; I had lost my daughter
zabeth; and both of them had died heretics.

prayed for them that they might be forgiven.

It was not their fault,' I said. 'They were brought up to be
etics.'

hat was what upset me, I tried to tell myself. But it was not
irely true.

ames came to Calais to meet us with a squadron of ships.
es was now becoming renowned for his seamanship.

He embraced me warmly. He looked jaunty and handsome
l said nothing about Anne Hyde. Nor did I. But I had made up
 mind that as soon as I could I would have a private word with
arles. I would put a stop to that little adventure. My son was
: going to marry a nobody; nor was he going to give her child
 name if I could help it.

But at the moment my handsome son James had come to escort
 across the Channel and I gave myself up to the pleasure of
urning to England in the manner which I had always dreamed
doing.

he sea was unusually calm. How different from the face it
ually showed me! So there was no sickness for which I was
remely grateful, but the crossing took two whole days because
 were becalmed. However, in due course those white cliffs
ne into sight and I was filled with emotion thinking of the last
e I had seen them and that brought back poignant memories
ny beloved Charles.

Waiting for us, surrounded by a glittering assembly, was that
er Charles. I was proud of him. He seemed to have grown
er but that was probably because I had not seen him for some
e. He was very gracious and charming to me and his eyes
 one with affection when they rested on Henriette.

Crowds had gathered on the seashore to see the meeting. I
ught the cheers were not quite so spontaneous for me as they
re for the King and James, but it was clear that Henriette
ighted them and the people were pleased to see Charles's
ection for her.

nside the castle a banquet had been prepared for us and I sat
 one side of Charles, Henriette on the other. Charles told us

that Mary was on her way to England and it would make him v◼
happy to have the entire family together.

Later we talked privately and I asked about Henry. Charles h◼
been present at his death, which was rather foolish of him◼
pointed out. Henry had died of small pox which was higl◼
contagious. What if Charles had caught it and succumbed? H◼
he thought what would happen to England without a King?

'James would be waiting to step into my shoes, Mam.'

'The people would never accept him with that woman as ◼
wife. How could you allow that, Charles?'

'Who am I to stand in the way of true love?' He could be ve◼
flippant but there were warning lights in his eyes. Charles h◼
always been very fond of his sisters and brothers and hat◼
family quarrels. But I was not going to be told what I must a◼
must not do by my own son.

I repeated that he should not have risked his life by being wi◼
Henry but as he was there I should like to know if Henry h◼
mentioned me on his death bed.

'Yes,' said Charles coolly, 'he did. He was grieved alwa◼
because of the disagreement between you and how it had bee◼
when you were last together.'

I nodded. 'I thought he would be sorry in time.'

'I told him he should not grieve. I pointed out to him that if ◼
had done what you wanted him to he would have broken h◼
word to his father and gone against his own conscience. I assure◼
him that in God's eyes he had done the right thing.'

'The right thing! He died a heretic. If he had listened ◼
me. . . .'

'Somehow, Mam, I do not think the good Lord will be as ha◼
on him as you have been.'

I protested but there was something about Charles whi◼
warned me that it would be unwise to continue. He could be ve◼
much the King at times.

He looked at me sadly for a moment and then he sai◼
'The years of exile have taught you nothing, Mam. Life is sho◼
Let us enjoy it. Let there be no trouble in the heart of tl◼
family.'

Then he rose and left me. I could never really understar◼
this son of mine. Of all my children he was the most diffic◼
to know and had been ever since he was the serious little b◼

had refused to give up the wooden toy he took to bed with

nriette seemed happier than I had ever known her to be. She
so content to be at her brother's Court and when Charles
ested that she arrange one of the ballets which were so
lar at the Court of Louis XIV, she threw herself whole-
edly into making the arrangements.

e Duke of Buckingham, that dissolute son of a father whom I
lways believed to be evil, fell headlong in love with her. My
child was a little bewildered at first and then appeared to
the attentions of the young man. It was only a light flirta-
Buckingham having a wife and she being betrothed, and in
ase she was a princess and he was only a duke so I did not
pt to reprove her. When I thought of the way she had been
d at the Court of France at one time, I thought it would do
o harm to realize that she was growing into a very attractive
g woman.

ry arrived and it was good to see her and we were for once in
lete agreement for she was incensed when she heard about
s's marriage to Anne Hyde. I could not resist reminding her
she was the one who had allowed this folly to begin by
ng the upstart young woman a member of her household.

w much better it would have been if you had taken my
e then,' I said.

did not exactly agree, but she refused to receive Anne
and the woman would have been very miserable indeed if
es had not gone out of his way to be gracious to her.

e weeks began to fly past – very pleasant weeks. If only I
forget Henry's death and Charles's thinly veiled criticism of
reatment of him, and the fact that James had made this
trous marriage, I could have been happy.

ne Hyde's child was a boy but a weakling and it did not look
ough the child's chances of survival would be great.

nes should have waited awhile,' I said. 'Then the child
t not have been a reason for the marriage.'

as delighted when Sir Charles Berkeley declared that he had
Anne's lover and that he knew of several other gentlemen
had shared her favours and that it was therefore by no

means certain that the father of the child was James.

I wanted to confront James with that evidence, but h
already heard it and was so upset that he became quite i
went down with a fever. We were all afraid that he mig
another victim of small pox.

Anne Hyde was completely ostracized now. Her fathe
upset and even he railed against her, and she had no frie
Court at all. I wanted Charles to dismiss her father – wh
now the Earl of Clarendon – but he would not do so. Clare
was an excellent Chancellor, he said, and was not to be b
for his daughter's affairs.

Christmas was almost upon us. Charles had insisted th
stay for the festivities and I was nothing loth. I was deligh
be on better terms with Mary and it was wonderful t
Henriette blossoming, leading the dancing and amusing h
with the Duke of Buckingham.

Then about five days before Christmas Mary became il
had been feeling unwell for some days and thought this wa
to some minor cause. My distress was great when the d
reported that she was suffering from small pox.

Charles said I was to leave Whitehall at once with Hen
'Take her to St James's,' he said, 'and stay there with her.'

'Henriette shall go to St James's,' I declared, 'but I shal
and nurse Mary.'

'You must not go to the sick room,' Charles retorted firm

'My dear Charles,' I replied, 'King you may be, but yc
my son and this is my daughter. If she is sick I must be
her.'

'Do you realize that you could catch the disease?'

'Of course I know what small pox is. I want to be wit
daughter. She will need me.'

'Mam,' he said slowly, 'this is no time for deathbed co
sions. Mary is ill. She is too sick to be troubled with your vie
what will happen to her soul.'

'I want to nurse her.'

'How could you do that? Go back to Henriette. You v
never forgive yourself if you caught the disease and passe
to her.'

That really did frighten me. The thought of anything ha
ing to my precious child made me waver. On the other

y was my daughter too. Henry had just died, a heretic. Mary
t die one too, if nothing was done.

arles said quietly: 'It would be dangerous. Besides, I forbid it.'

I went to St James's and told Henriette that her sister was
ely ill, and we prayed for her recovery adding that if she were
ined to die let her come to an understanding of the truth that
might not, like her brother Henry, die a heretic.

as our prayers were not answered and on Christmas Eve
y passed away. She was only twenty-nine years old.

arles was with her at the end. He was very shaken. He was
fond of his family, particularly his sisters.

vas in tears. 'It seems as though God has determined to
sh me,' I cried. 'Is there a blight on my family? Elizabeth . . .
Henry . . . now Mary. Why? Why?'

'ho can say?' answered Charles. 'But there is something I
to tell you. When she was dying Mary was very concerned
it one matter.'

urned to him, my eyes shining.

o . . . no . . .' he went on a little impatiently, 'it is nothing to
ith religion. It was Anne Hyde. Mary had a good deal on her
cience.'

know,' I said. 'If she had not taken that woman into her
sehold. . . . I told her she was wrong at the time.'

o, Mam,' said Charles. 'She did not mean that. She was
t because she had maligned Anne. She said she had helped
read the gossip about her when in her heart she did not
ve that it was true. She believed that James loved Anne and
e truly loved James and that James had given her a promise of
iage before she became his mistress.'

he was delirious.'

he was quite clear in her head. She thought that there were
le who had fabricated those stories about Anne because they
v it was an unpopular marriage. Mary blamed herself most
rly. She wanted Anne to come to her that she might beg her
veness. I could not allow Anne, with a new baby, to come to
ick bed.'

hould think not. . . .'

he infectious nature of the disease prevented that,' he went
rmly. 'But I shall go to Anne and tell her that the Princess
y craved her pardon and that I give it on her behalf.'

'I never heard such nonsense.'
He just smiled at me and said no more.

Our next concern was James. He was becoming very ill.
'That woman is a witch,' I said to Henriette. 'First she lured
into marriage and now because he disowns her she is willing
to die.'

Henriette did not answer. I could not understand Henri⟨
The quiet girl who had been so thin – Louis had referred to h⟨
the Bones of the Holy Innocents – now in clothes which v
worthy of her had blossomed into a beauty. Her fragility
become fashionable and ladies of the Court were trying
suppress those protuberances which at one time they had bee
great pains to display. Henriette was at the centre of all
entertainments, with Buckingham in attendance. In fact t⟨
was some scandalous gossip about them. I had to make sure
nothing dangerous could come of that. Charles doted on her
was making as much of her as he did of his favourite mist
Barbara Castlemaine, and knowing his insatiable sexuality, s⟨
even dared hint at the most objectionable slander about
relationship with Henriette.

It was a situation to be watched closely and I told myself tha
soon as we reached France Henriette must be marrie⟨
Philippe, who was now the Duc d'Orléans on the death of
brother Gaston. His death did not affect me greatly beca⟨
although we had been close as children in the nursery, his
volvement in the Fronde had turned me against him.

James's health began to give us cause for alarm. He was ⟨
fortunately, suffering from the small pox, but I really believe⟨
was so upset because he was regretting his marriage to
woman and was now realizing in what an unsavoury invo⟨
ment he had become entangled.

The doctors thought his malady had been brought ab⟨
through emotional stress and Sir Charles Berkeley created qu⟨
furore when he burst into James's bedchamber, threw himsel
his knees, and declared that the accusations he had made aga⟨
Anne Hyde were false. She was a pure woman and had n⟨
had any lover other than James. Berkeley had prevailed u⟨
other men to join with him in accusing her and they had done

ause they thought the Duke of York would be happier if the
rriage were dissolved and he could make another more
able to his position.

he news spread round the Court. Anne Hyde was vindicated.
es quickly recovered, which proved it was the slander about
ne Hyde which had so upset him that he became ill.

harles was pleased about this and said that Anne must come
k to Court and there must be a christening for her son.

Ie then came to tell me what had happened.

So,' I said, 'you are bringing her to Court. Is that what you are
ing me?'

That is so,' he answered, 'and I am very happy at this
come. Anne is a woman of great wit and excellent parts. She
l take advice from her father and be a good influence on James
ho is in need of it.'

When you have finished singing her praises let me tell you that
his woman enters Whitehall by one door, I shall go out by
other.'

Charles was angry. 'I have long known that you cannot exist in
ace,' he said coldly. 'If it is forced on you, you will immediately
out raising storms.'

He left me then.

sighed. What difficult children I had! They either died or
fied me.

Charles was very cool and made no attempt to prevent the
eparations I was making to return to France. Moreover he
isted on bringing Anne Hyde to Court, which meant of course
t I must leave. Henriette was heartbroken. No one would have
ought she was going back to a brilliant marriage. She said she
uld be loth to tear herself away from England and her brother
d she went about with a woebegone face. But I considered I
d been insulted. My son had given preference to a woman of
standing who had brought a child into the world which had
me near to being a bastard – and in any case she was not of the
nk to mate with royalty. And for this woman he was turning his
n mother out of Court!

Henriette explained with exasperating patience that he was not
rning me out. I was going of my own free will.

I said: 'He leaves me no alternative. He forgets that though he
a King I am a Queen . . . and his mother.'

'He does not forget, Mam. He is grieved that you are going
this.'

'A strange way of showing grief! All he has to do is not rec
that woman and I will postpone my departure.'

'He can't do that. She is James's wife.'

'Wife! To how many men has she been what you call a wife

'But they have all confessed to lying about her. I think they
despicable . . . every one of them.'

I turned away. Even Henriette was against me.

A few days before I was to leave a messenger came f
France. News of what had happened had reached the C
there, for scandalous news always travelled faster than
other. The letter was from Mazarin and was very discre
worded, but I read the meaning between the lines and th
could be no mistaking their intent. He clearly implied that
quarrelled with my son I should not be very welcome in Fra
The fact was that Charles had given both me and Henri
handsome pensions and had promised a sizable dowry
Henriette, and Mazarin doubted Charles would pay this if th
was a rift between us. And would Philippe want to m
Henriette without a dowry? It was the return of Charles to
throne which had made Henriette so desirable.

I was in a dilemma. What could I do? Hold up my pride
return to France . . . a beggar almost, for it might well be that
money from England would not be paid. No dowry for Henri
Charles might be pleased for his favourite sister to stay
England and I knew *she* would like that very much. No, I co
not exist again as I had all those years depending on the charit
others, and in my heart I felt I might be in danger of doing so
did not remain on good terms with my son; and I certainly sho
not be if I left England as I was proposing to do.

The only alternative was to accept Anne Hyde. So I agree
receive the woman.

I shall never forget the scene of my humiliation. Charles n
have decided not to spare me. It could have been done n
quietly but Charles pointed out that it must be *seen* to
done.

I was obliged to ask my son James, most formally, to bring
wife to my bedchamber that I might receive her. Natur
because so many knew what had gone before, my bedchan

as crowded with busybodies who had come to witness the conciliation.

I was furious and all the time had to keep reminding myself of e old days of humiliation and that on no account must they cur. It was blackmail. Still I had worked hard for my husband; I uld do the same for my daughter.

When the woman came with James it was less difficult than I d anticipated, for she showed no triumph or aggression and as in fact most humble. I had sent Henriette away as I did not ant her to see me act as I should have to. My excuse was that th the small pox epidemic raging I feared there might be danger r her among so many people.

Anne Hyde knelt to me most deferentially when James esented her and I bent over and kissed her. She was a pleasant- oking young woman with, I had to admit, an open honest face. she had been of nobler birth I could easily have accepted her.

I did feel a twinge of gratitude to her for making my task ghtly easier than it could have been. I led her into the anteroom d with her on one side and James on the other we made our ay through the press of courtiers and sat down and talked a tle.

I asked about the baby whom they were going to call Charles, d James asked if I would be a godmother. I said I would.

Then I had done all that was required of me, I thought. But it peared not quite, for Charles wanted me to receive the Earl of arendon, which I did, although I had always disliked the man d more so since the trouble with his daughter had arisen.

He was very respectful to me and I told him that I was happy to a mother to his daughter. Then I hinted that in return for my pitulation he should do all he could for me. He knew what I eant, for he was a most astute man and as Chancellor had a eat influence in the country. What I was implying was that ere should be no holding back of Henriette's dowry and our nsions.

I felt exhausted after the interview, but I was aware that arendon was very pleased at the outcome and I trusted him to what he had promised for me.

The day after the public reconciliation we prepared to leave for

France and then I had my greatest fright, for I greatly feared th
in spite of my efforts to protect Henriette she too might ha
caught the small pox which had carried off her brother and sist
No sooner had we left Portsmouth and were indeed still in sig
of the harbour than Henriette became violently ill. I was terrifi
because this was not due to the sea. I consulted with the Capta
and persuaded him to take the ship back into port. My daught
was in need of the best possible medical attention.

He did this and I was faintly relieved to be back on shore. I se
a message to the King. He was most distressed and declared th
nothing must be left undone to save Henriette.

To our great joy we discovered that she was suffering fro
measles and not small pox as we had feared and after fourte
anxious days we were ready to sail for France once more.

This time we made a good journey and landed safely at
Havre.

What a welcome was given us! Our journey to Paris was slo
as I did not want to go through Rouen, where I heard that sm
pox was rife. I had preserved my darling so far and had
intention of letting her take more risks.

It was a great joy to see Queen Anne again and to receive h
warm welcome. Philippe seemed very much in love wi
Henriette and very jealous of the Duke of Buckingham, who h
insisted on accompanying us because he could not tear hims
away from Henriette. However we managed to subdu
Philippe's jealousy. Louis was very gracious to us and made
clear that he loved Henriette very much. There were rumours
his interest in various young women at Court, but I had be
right in realizing that after spurning Henriette when they we
children he had come to see that special beauty of hers whi
made her different from the other ladies at Court.

Mazarin died suddenly to the great sorrow of the Queen a
Louis. I guessed that would mean a period of Court mournin
which would postpone the wedding. However, the dispensatio
from the Pope – which had been required because of the clo
relationship of Philippe and Henriette – arrived on the day t
Cardinal died and Louis declared that perhaps preparations f
the wedding should go on, although quietly.

It was at the end of March when the wedding took place. Th
ceremony was performed in a private chapel of the Palais Roy

my own dear Henry Jermyn – I had prevailed on Charles to
te him Earl of St Albans – stood as proxy for Charles.

y dear little Henriette, at seventeen years old, had become
)uchesse d'Orléans. I was very happy. Not the first prize . . .
the second . . . and I could always hope. . . .

.y fortunes must be changing. Charles was on the throne of
land and seemed firmly seated there; and my little girl, the
loved of them all, had come through her delicate childhood,
severe illnesses, and was the second lady in France.

Colombes

The years have now begun to slip by me quickly. I feel that
no longer a participant but a looker-on, living on the fring
affairs, which was strange at first as I had for so long been a
centre of them.

Henriette had no need of me now. She was the star of
Court. The King was in love with her and sometimes, I
pected, she with him. Philippe . . . well, we had always kn
that he would be an indifferent husband, being more attache
his handsome men friends than to any woman. Henri
shrugged that aside; she had become very worldly, quite ur
the quiet little girl who used to cause me so much anxiety.

She seemed indefatigable. She designed and wrote ballet
the King's entertainments; and she was always at the centr
these for she danced exquisitely. The new life she was lea
had beautified her considerably. People said that her comple
was like a mingling of jasmine and roses and that she had po
in her sapphire blue eyes to command the devotion of all
Certainly Louis was her admirer, deferring to her decisions
his little Queen was so jealous that she complained to
mother-in-law. Anne had always hated controversy and
spoke to me about Henriette's friendship with the K
'Henriette must not always be at the King's side,' insisted Ar
'That is the Queen's place.'

I listened and commiserated and all the time was secr
pleased that my daughter was now the most attractive and de
able woman at Court. I told Anne that I would tell Henriette w
she had said, but was it not the King who set the pace and sho
she not speak to him?

But I was very contented and there was nothing I liked to h
more than of Henriette's conquests.

At that time Louis dominated her life and I was sure she

. I would grow furious contemplating what an ideal pair they
uld have made. They were always together and people were
ginning to say: 'Where the King is, there is Madame.'

She was very happy at that time and her happiness was the
eater because of the deprivations of her youth. Her beloved
ther was safe on the throne; and the King of France was in love
th her. She had the deep affection of the two most powerful
en in Europe.

She had a great influence over the King. Through her the Court
came more intellectual. She had always been interested in
riters and musicians and she made Louis so too. She brought
lli the musician to the Court. She patronized Molière.
adeleine de Scudery's works were being widely read. The
urt was not only becoming more elegant but more cultured.
d it was all due to Henriette.

Those were the triumphant days of Henriette's life and what
uld have been the outcome I cannot say if she had not become
egnant. I knew enough of her to believe that the child was
ilippe's and not Louis's. Henriette was like me; she wanted the
mmings of courtship not the culmination. I had never liked *that*
de of marriage, much as I had cared for Charles, and I could
ppily have dispensed with it altogether had it not been my
ity to produce a family. Henriette was the same. When her
ild was born, it must be that of her husband.

But pregnancy was not easy for her. She became ill. I took her
ith me to the Palais Royal. Louis came to see her and to avoid
ssip we arranged that one of Henriette's ladies in waiting
ould be seen with him so that it might seem he had come to visit
er.

This was an insignificant girl who was a little lame and quiet
d unassuming. Her name was Louise de la Vallière; and now
e know what the outcome of that was!

In due course Henriette gave birth to a child – a daughter – and
either Philippe nor Henriette could disguise their disappoint-
ent that she was not a boy.

Henriette was recovering from her confinement but she was a
ttle sad. Rumours about the King and La Vallière were
umerous. Then there was news from England. Charles had
arried Catherine de Braganza and I knew it was time for me to
ay a visit to England.

Henriette accompanied me as far as Beauvais. She was rega
ing her health rapidly and although she still seemed frail was
beautiful as ever. It was a great wrench for us to part and we b
wept bitterly; I think she would have given a great deal to co
with me and she sent many messages for me to give to Charle

I had in my party a young man of about thirteen or fourteen.
was known as James Crofts because when his mother, the not
ious Lucy Walter died, he had been put in the charge of L
Crofts, who passed him off as a kinsman, although everyo
knew he was the King's son.

James himself was well aware of it and if I knew anything
was going to make sure that nobody forgot it. He was extrem
handsome and had a decided look of the Stuarts. If Charles h
wanted to deny paternity – and he certainly did not – he wou
have scarcely been able to.

James Crofts was amusing, bright, and with a manner
audaciously regal and at the same time engaging that I could r
help liking him.

I was looking forward to meeting my new daughter-in-la
Henry Jermyn had been to England recently and had broug
back excellent reports of her, and since she was a Catholic th
delighted me. I hoped she would have some influence on Charle

The crossing was atrocious as it usually was for me. I hat
crossing the sea and was going to England as a duty; I mu
preferred my native land and would never forgive the English f
turning us out and the barbarous treatment of Charles. My s
might forget it; I never could. He seemed to have cast off
resentments and was perfectly happy; and although he had be
forced to travel widely on the Continent, England appeared to
his natural home.

It was a great relief to step onto dry land and we went by stag
to Greenwich where the King and his wife were waiting to gre
us.

It was a wonderful moment to stand face to face with him an
to feel his kiss on my hand and cheek. He always startled n
when I saw him after a lapse of time. It was his imposing height
think, and that dark ugly face which always baffled me because
was so charming.

And there was his Queen! I embraced her warmly. Henry ha
not lied. She was delightful.

said to her: 'I should not have come to England but for the
asure of seeing you. I shall love you as my daughter and serve
 as a Queen.'

'he soft eyes filled with tears and she looked surprised and
eved and I wondered whether her life in England was all that a
 ppy wife's should be.

 he replied that in love and obedience none of my children –
 even the King – should exceed her. Which I thought charming.

 harles smiled at her indulgently and I could see that she was
ove with him as I supposed most women would be. I hoped
t he would make her happy; but I had heard many rumours
 ut the life he led and I knew that he had always been promis-
 us. When he was wandering in Europe perhaps he could be
 given, but it must be different now that he had a Queen and
 s restored to the throne.

 le was absolutely delighted and amused by James Crofts and
 de much of him, which I thought he should not have done
 te so openly before the Queen. I promised myself I would
 nt this out to him when we were alone.

 During his brief stay at Greenwich, Charles asked if I would
 to have Somerset House as a residence while I was in
 land. 'I know you were always fond of the place,' he said; and
 d him I should like that very much.

 n due course Charles and the Queen returned to Hampton
 urt and it was arranged that I should follow later. I would need
 ttle rest, Charles said, after the rigours of the journey, for he
 w how I loathed those sea crossings.

 was not sorry to have a quiet time to myself.

 ames Crofts had gone off with the King's party and just a few
 ny intimates remained so I looked forward to a few peaceful
 s before we moved on. It was pleasant to sit quietly over-
 king the river and talk in a desultory way to Henry, whose
 versation I always found so amusing.

 Henry was a man who always seemed to know what was going
 He could sniff out scandals and rumours and devote himself
 he task of discovering the truth behind them; and it was only
 e expected that he must know of the troubles between the
 g and his new Queen.

 said that I thought Charles was extremely lucky in his Queen
 d how delighted I was that they seemed so happy.

'Ah,' said Henry, 'I am not sure that the Queen is so happy

'What do you mean?' I demanded.

Henry's eyes were sparkling. He loved imparting gos
although as this concerned my son he was quickly looking rat
grave.

'The Queen is hurt and angry.'

'She did not appear to be so.'

'She would not wish you to know of her troubles as soon as
arrived.'

'What troubles are these?'

'The King's mistress. It is Barbara Castlemaine who is at
root of the trouble.'

'I have heard her name.'

'Dearest Majesty, who has not heard of her name? She
completely enslaved the King. She is a most handsome won
. . . the most beautiful in England, some say . . . and a virago
the bargain. It is she who is causing the trouble between the K
and the Queen.'

'She was his mistress . . . was she not? . . . before the Qu
arrived in England?'

'Before and after, dear lady. And now the King wants to m
her one of the women of the bedchamber.'

'No! Surely not.'

'I will tell you what happened. When the list was presente
the Queen, Barbara Castlemaine's name was at the top of it. S
struck it through. Later the King led in the Castlemaine a
presented her to the Queen, who received her graciously a
gave her her hand to be kissed. She was not familiar with Engli
and although she must have heard of the Castlemaine and
place in the King's affections, she did not recognize her na
when it was written down and so behaved in a welcoming w
Then one of her women whispered to her who the lady was, a
the Queen was so shocked and tried so hard to restrain
feelings that the blood gushed from her nose and she fell to
floor in a fit.'

'The poor child! Charles should have known better.'

'Charles was horrified at her behaviour. You see, Madam, h
completely under the spell of the Castlemaine. He said the Que
had behaved badly and incorrectly and should make amend
the lady.'

'Charles said that!'

'I agree that it was most unlike him but when the best of us are
the wrong we seek to make our actions right and perhaps act as
would not in other circumstances. Catherine however refused
receive the lady, and Charles insists that she should.'

'It is monstrous!' I cried.

'Clarendon tried to persuade the King that he was acting
kindly and the King doubtless knew it and it was against his
ture to act so, but as I said he is the slave of my lady Castle-
ine.'

I was very angry because I had taken a great liking to the Queen
sight. I thought she was a gentle woman who would be
enable and want to learn; moreover she was an ardent
tholic and I thought that she would be a good influence on
arles.

What a situation to find as soon as I arrived in England! I sat for
ong time talking it over with Henry.

'Whenever I come to this country there is trouble,' I said. 'Oh,
nry, how I long to be back at Chaillot or Colombes.'

Then I thought of all that was happening in France and of my
ar Henriette, whose life was presenting many problems, and
ddenly I felt old and for the first time in my life indifferent
the actions of my family. They were men and women now –
longer children. I felt a great urge to cut myself off from
uble, to live in that little *château* of Colombes where I could
rround myself with trusted friends. Most of them were as old
I – or almost. We understood each other. There we could live in
ace.

My great desire now was to go back there. I did not want
nflict with Charles for I had a feeling that he would always get
e better of me. I did not want to quarrel with James and I knew
should if I attempted to tell him where he was wrong. And
nriette had shown me that even she would go her own way.
ey were the only ones left to me and I did not want to quarrel
th any of them.

It seemed a wise decision. Charles and Catherine sorted out
eir differences about Lady Castlemaine. He had his way – I
ve come now to think he always did – and Catherine, while

accepting Lady Castlemaine and his other mistresses, did r
seem to love him any less.

Charles had arranged for me to stay at Greenwich ur
Somerset House could be ready. Like many beautiful places
England it had been ravaged by Oliver Cromwell and for a whil
lived between Greenwich Palace and Denmark House. I w
pleased when I could get into Somerset House which was r
until late summer. I found that since I had decided to let them
go their own way and not worry too much about the mistak
they were making, they all seemed to like me so much better.

I was very fond of the Queen and she visited me often. She w
a sad little creature and I am sure felt very much alone. S
longed for a child but although she had miscarriages and so cou
not be barren, she did not seem to be able to produce a healtl
one. It was a great disappointment to Charles but far more so
her. He knew he was not at fault because he had numero
bastards and he never refused to recognize any of them.

I longed to be in my native land. I hated the London winte
which seemed so cold, but most of all I disliked the fogs. Th
affected my chest and I told myself that I must get back to Fran
before long. I was expected to live in England mainly becau
Charles had given me a pension and Clarendon had wanted tl
money spent in England to give employment to English peopl
To have spent it in France would have been tantamount to tl
English crown's paying money to that country. So although the
was no objection to my visiting France now and then, it w
expected of me to make my home in England.

I was a little happier when I was installed in Somerset Hous
The Roundheads had actually occupied it and at first that made
distasteful to me. They had broken up the beautiful rooms but
was to be expected their most devastating work had been in n
chapel; but a great deal of reconstruction had been done and
began to take an interest because I was introducing my ov
designs. I had the ceilings exquisitely painted and chandeliers
gilded brass installed. It was becoming magnificent and I w
able to live there royally. I had crimson silk hung at the windov
and beautiful screens made to keep out the draughts which ble
in from the river. There was one room with a domed roof ove
looking gardens which ran down to the river and from this the
was a private staircase which led to a room where I could take h

cold baths. Gardeners had set to work in the grounds, ing paths down to the river so that I could walk without ing my feet muddy. I wanted to make it as different as it sibly could be from when those men had filled it with their presence.

en I had my household with my dear Henry Jermyn, Lord St ins, as Chancellor, at the head of it; I had my Gentlemen of ic, Master of Games and Buckhounds and Bows. Whenever I t out it was in my Sedan chair or coach and I was accom- ed by my halberdiers in black cassocks with embroidered badges; I had my twelve liveried bargemen to row me when I ded to travel by river. I lived royally. I thought I owed that to elf and to Charles. I wanted to wipe out forever the indigni- I had suffered; and for so long I had lived parsimoniously ng everything I could to bring back the King to England.

ell, now it was done and it was my turn to enjoy luxury, to ind myself that I was no longer a poor relation. I was a royal en and now I would live like one.

was very much in debt when Somerset House was finished that disturbed me a little. Then I saw that it gave me an se to live quietly which I had discovered was what I wanted.

any people came to see me and boats were constantly ing along the river. I gave concerts and in summer evenings strains of sweet music would float along the river. There was iys plenty to see from my windows because there was so h activity on the river. I was finding that I could be much ier if I did not allow myself to be tempted to tell people how should act. I enjoyed my new role – observer rather than icipator. Henry Jermyn agreed with me. When I looked back I zed that he had always been like that. Perhaps that was why vas a happy man. He had become fat and suffered from gout he was the dearest companion and I enjoyed his company er than that of any other person.

arely made a decision now without first consulting him. I oose that was why there were rumours about us. There were y who were absolutely sure that we were married. Some credited me with having had a child by him. We laughed ther at these rumours but we took no heed of them and inued to enjoy our pleasant relationship.

e Duchess of York had a daughter. She was called Mary and

it seemed as though she, unlike her brother who had lived o
few months, would survive. I did hope so. It is so tragic w
children cannot seem to get a grip on life and I had to agree
Charles was right when he had said that Anne was a g
woman. Unfortunately James had tired of her and he had
mistresses just like his brother. Their behaviour really did
the Court a reputation for immorality. But it was none of
business. I had learned to hold myself aloof from it now. I
still wondering how I could get back to Chaillot and Colomb
longed to see Henriette and my good friend Queen Anne.

Because poor Queen Catherine did not seem to be able to g
child, Charles created James Crofts Duke of Monmouth. It w
a way an insult to Catherine, calling attention to the fact tha
fault must be hers as he could get a handsome healthy boy
James Crofts from another woman.

There was a great deal of speculation about Charles's ma
Monmouth his heir. He would have had to legitimize him for
but I supposed he could easily do so.

Nothing came of that. Charles had a habit of shelving cor
versial matters and when I think how he came through I wor
whether that is not the wisest way.

Lady Castlemaine, I was glad to see, was losing her hold
him, which must have been good news for Catherine, but he
obsessed by a new beauty – Frances Stuart. It would alway
like that with Charles and I wished Catherine could accept
fact. But it was difficult for her and I knew full well that had I b
young again and in her place I should never have done s
daresay I would have made his life a misery. He would n
have had that calm resignation from a woman like me.

The winter which began in 1664 and went on into 1665 w
cold one. I became ill and had to take to my bed for a long ti
My doctors told me that I should get out of England if poss
and that was my excuse.

I begged Charles not to close my chapel if I left and he prom
he would not do so and he was most eager for me to take
waters at the Bourbon springs which had been so beneficial to
before.

War with the Dutch had broken out and I was deeply
cerned about that. Charles said that the French might decid
join with the Dutch and he believed that I might do good wor

in France, so I think he was rather glad that I was going.
re was another matter. There had been some cases of plague
London and he feared if the summer was hot they might
ease.

here were several good reasons why I should go besides my
lth.

was due to leave at the end of June but before I left there came
vs of a great sea battle in which my son James had defeated the
tch. James was the hero of the hour but I was afraid for him
begged Charles not to allow him to expose himself too rashly.
re was something very rash about James which his impetuous
rriage had proved.

s I sailed down the Thames I wondered if I should ever come
k.

o there I was – after another dismal sea crossing – back in my
ive country. My spirits rose as soon as I set foot in it, but there
bad news awaiting me. Henriette was very ill. She had heard
lse rumour that her brother James had been killed in battle and
shock had brought about the premature birth of the child she
carrying. She was delighted to see me and I do believe that
arrival helped to pull her through. She was far from happy
I began to wonder whether great titles were worth all one had
pay for them. I had found a crown and a happy marriage
ough it had ended in tragedy, but all through that marriage
arles and I had meant everything to each other.

thought of Charles and his poor little Queen who had to
ept his mistresses and could not get the child she longed for. I
ught of James and Anne Hyde who had married so roman-
lly and were now no longer in love; I thought most of all of
nriette who had married Philippe, Duc d'Orléans, brother of
King of France, and who was the most wretched of them all.

he confided to me that Philippe flew into jealous rages which
re incomprehensible as he was not interested in her himself;
he simply could not bear her to enjoy the society of other
n. Moreover he had brought his lover, the Chevalier of
raine, into the house and they conducted their amour openly
all to see and laugh at.

here was sad news from London. Two of my priests had died
the plague. The Court was no longer there and red crosses
re put on the houses of the plague-stricken to warn people to

keep away. Throughout the night the dismal knell of the de⟨
cart was heard in the deserted streets with the cry: 'Bring out y⟨
dead.'

I went to see my old friend Queen Anne. She was in a desp⟨
ate state and suffering excruciating pain for she had a malign⟨
growth in her breast which she knew would kill her.

Early the next year she died and I could not be sorry becau⟨
poor soul, she who had done so many kindnesses had suffe⟨
greatly. I could only be relieved that she had found peace at la⟨

To my dismay France declared war on England in suppor⟨
the Dutch. Louis had no wish for it, I knew; and although ⟨
people of France hated the English and the people of Engl⟨
hated the French, both Charles and Louis were trying to com⟨
some agreement. It was during this time that the Dutch fl⟨
smarting under the humiliation of the English victory at s⟨
sailed up the Medway and burned several men-of-war includ⟨
the *Royal Charles*, which was lying at Chatham.

That was a year of disaster and the biggest of all was the g⟨
fire of London when two-thirds of the city were burned to ⟨
ground. Eighty-nine churches including St Paul's Cathe⟨
were destroyed, with more than thirteen thousand dwell⟨
houses. I was so pained when I heard that the Catholics had b⟨
accused of starting the fire and for the first time in years felt ⟨
old fighting spirit rising in me. I wanted to go to England to ⟨
them how false that accusation was. I wanted to tell them h⟨
wicked and cruel they were to suggest it.

England was in a sorry state. The terrible plague had brou⟨
trade almost to a standstill; the war had crippled its finances e⟨
more. My pension was reduced and I was indignant and wrot⟨
Charles to tell him so. I was trying so hard to live within ⟨
means and my greatest pleasure was to give to the poor ⟨
needy and at the same time bring those who had strayed fro⟨
back to the Catholic Faith.

I went to Colombes and lived as quietly as I could there. I ⟨
my friends about me – chief of all dear Henry without who⟨
should have been desolate indeed.

I had my music; my reading; my chapel. I prayed constar⟨
and thought a good deal about the past.

I began to grow introspective, reliving those long-ago sce⟨
and asking myself what might have happened if I had done⟨

ot done, this and that. Such thoughts intruded and I found eep difficult. My cough was worrying me and sometimes I felt ery ill indeed.

Henriette came to see me and she expressed her horror at the ght of me. She said she was going to call in the doctors in whom he had great faith.

I said: 'There is nothing wrong with me. When I feel a little etter I will go to Bourbon for the waters. Please do not make such fuss, Henriette.'

'But, Mam,' she cried anxiously, 'I can see you are not well. ou might as well admit it because it is obvious.'

'I do not want to be like those women who cry for a little pain in he head or a cut finger,' I retorted.

'Dear Mam, I am not going to ask your permission. I am going o call in the best doctors we have in France.'

I had to give way; and I certainly was feeling ill. 'If only I could eep soundly,' I said. 'But I simply cannot. As soon as my head is own, I am going over the past and I am blaming myself so much, enriette.'

'They will give you something to make you sleep.'

'And I shall not take it. Old Mayerne said I was never to take nything like that.'

'We will hear what the doctors have to say,' Henriette insisted rmly.

They were the leading doctors in France. M. Valot was one and e was the first physician to Louis. M. Espoit was first physician o Philippe and M. Juelin to Henriette. They came to Colombes to onsult with M. d'Aquin, my own doctor.

I submitted to their examination and lay back listening while hey talked to Henriette in a far corner where they had gone so hat I should not hear too much of what they said.

I felt rather indifferent and impatient with them. I was old; had had a long and arduous life; I must die soon and I was eady.

M. Valot was saying: 'By the grace of God the Queen has no atal malady. Inconvenient . . . but not dangerous. She would be o much better if she slept and put whatever it is on her mind out of her thoughts. Now I am going to add three grains to the prescription you are giving her, M. d'Aquin. That will ensure leep and when she is rested we shall find her disorder clearing.'

Grains! I thought. That means opium. I had never taken opiu
and I was not going to now.

They came to my bedside and I said: 'I am not taking yo
grains.'

'Your Majesty,' said M. Valot, 'they will do you no harm, on
great good. They will bring you sleep.'

'Sir Theodore Mayerne said I was never to take any su
things.'

'He was old and out of date, Your Majesty. Medicine h
improved since then.'

They were all talking to me, including Henriette.

'Dear Mam, you will take it. You will feel so much better. . .

'I do not promise,' I said. 'I shall try to sleep without it.'

It has been a good day. I have worked a little, prayed a goo
deal and conversed with my friends.

At supper we were quite merry and Henry amused us all wit
some scandalous stories he had gleaned about people at Court.

I had had a good meal and could not help laughing at him. I a
so tired. If I could only sleep, but however tired I am when I am i
bed thoughts come between me and sleep.

I was prepared for bed as usual and the nearer the time came
say goodnight to my friends the more wide awake I became.

I am very thoughtful tonight. More than ever the past come
back – haunting me, robbing me of peace. I can see everything i
especial clarity tonight – my coming to England, my quarrels wit
Charles. Oh what a foolish girl I was then! And then our great jo
in each other . . . but the troubles came too quickly. I am ver
uneasy tonight. Something is telling me that everything migh
have been so different and I cannot stop myself wondering wha
would have happened to Charles if he had had a different Queen
How much had I contributed to that murder in Whitehall?

What has happened to me in the last years? I have becom
more myself than I ever was before. Had I in the past been livin
other people's lives? I had constantly told them what they shoul
do. I had been estranged from my son Henry and he had die
without a reconciliation. Mary and I had not been good friends.
had quarrelled with James and should have done so with Charle
if he had been of a nature to quarrel.

I cannot endure this feeling of doubt which envelops me. I had always felt before that I knew, that I was right in everything I did.

Now I am haunted by fears. Perhaps I was not right. Perhaps I was tragically wrong.

These thoughts are tormenting me. They have completely chased away sleep. I am frightened. In the last years I have seen events more clearly than I did when they were happening and a fearful sense of guilt is settling on me. I had been so sure of my place in Heaven. I had loved my husband deeply; I had loved my children. But what had I done to them?

I must sleep. I will call in one of my attendants and tell her that I give in. I will take M. Valot's grains for I must sleep. I cannot endure this burden of guilt. I will take the grains . . . and sleep.

Now I will lay down my pen and call the attendant.

Epilogue

On that August night of the year 1669 Henriette Maria sent one of
her ladies to M. d'Aquin to tell him that as she could not sleep she
would take the medicine which the doctors had prescribed and it
was brought to her in the white of an egg.

After she had drunk it she was soon fast asleep.

When her lady in waiting came to her bedside the next morning
to ask how she had slept, there was no answer.

Henriette Maria was dead.

Bibliography

brey, William Hickman Smith, *The National and Domestic History of England*

ch, Thomas, *The Court and Times of Charles I*

ne, Quentin, *Henrietta Maria*

rnet, Gilbert (Bishop of Salisbury), *Bishop Burnet's History of his Own Time*

rtwright, Julia, *Madame: Memoirs of Henrietta Duchess of Orleans*

rendon, Edward Earl of (edited by W. Dunn Macray), *The History of the Rebellion and Civil Wars in England*

vies, Godfrey, *England under the Early Stuarts*

ry of John Evelyn (edited by William Bray, Prefatory Notes by George W. E. Russell)

th, C. H., *Oliver Cromwell and the Rule of the Puritans in England*

ser, Antonia, *Cromwell, Our Chief of Men*

rdiner, Samuel Rawson, *History of England from the Accession of James I to the Outbreak of the Civil War*

een, Mary Anne Everett, *Letters of Royal and Illustrious Ladies*

een, Mary Anne Everett, *Lives of the Princesses of England*

izot, M. (edited by Robert Black), *History of France*

xter, J. H., *King Pym*

me, David, *History of England*

kson, Lady Catherine Charlotte, *Old Paris: Its Court and Literary Salons*

nyon, J. P., *The Stuarts*

tters of Charles I to Henrietta Maria (edited by John Bruce)

acaulay, Lord, *History of England*

nn, Heinrich, *The Last Days of Henri Quatre*

e Trial of Charles I Memoirs of Sir Thomas Herbert and John Rushworth (edited by Roger Lockyer, with Introduction by C. V. Wedgwood)

tmore, Katherine Alexandra, *The Court of Louis XIII*

Pepys, Samuel, Diary and Correspondence of

Quennell, Marjorie and Peter, *A History of Everyday Things: England 1500–1799*

Roots, Ivan, *The Great Rebellion*

Sir Leslie Stevens and Sir Sydney Lee (editors), *The Dictionary National Biography*

Timbs, John and Gunn, Alexander, *Abbeys, Castles and Ancient Halls of England and Wales*

Trevelyan, George Macaulay, *England under the Stuarts*

Wade, John, *British History*

Wedgwood, C.V., *The King's Peace*

Wedgwood, C.V., *The King's War*

Wingfield-Stratford, Esmé, *King Charles and the Conspirators*

JEAN PLAIDY HAS ALSO WRITTEN